# Eagles Rising
## The Augustus Caesar Saga Books 1 & 2

## RICHARD FOREMAN

# TABLE OF CONTENTS

Augustus: Son of Rome

The house was situated just outside of Apollonia, a Macedonian coastal town. But the architecture and character of the building were deliberately Roman. The expansive rectangular villa was of a single storey with few windows. The exterior was austere, but upon entering the house one would have been impressed by a picturesque atrium. Sunlight wafted down upon the feathery breeze illuminating much of the courtyard and the ornate mosaics which adorned the interior.

The famous owner of the house, who had still to visit his new property, had given a swift nod of assent to the blueprints and cost of the estate during a brief pause from which his intelligent eyes perused the map of some distant, supposedly barbaric land.

An unforgiving saffron sun, thankfully tempered by merciful coastal winds, bleached the coral-white walls of the house and baked the grasslands which encircled the property like an emerald moat. Upon a patch of this lawn sat two adolescents, conversing and playing with the brittle grass in their fingers.

The dusky skinned youths were similarly aged, but of dramatically differing builds.

The first boy, as lean as the poplar trunks in the background, was Rufus Salvidienus - the son of the quaestor for the region. His father, who considered himself as shrewd as he was ambitious, had encouraged his son to make friends with their auspicious new neighbours as soon as the family moved to the province. At first the aristocratic Rufus baulked at the idea of forcing a friendship. He believed that he might have to act subserviently to the youth with his great uncle's name, but little noble blood himself. But what at first was set as a politic task soon became an effortlessly enjoyable one.

With his sharp jaw and beak nose Rufus was often nicknamed 'the hawk' - a colourful title which at various times the boy and later man would be proud, teased and ashamed of. The youth's long glossy black hair, which he frequently fingered as if he were a courtesan, was also a source of ridicule and vanity to the patrician.

The second youth, broad shouldered - and broadly smiling - was one Marcus Vipsanius Agrippa.

Gusts of laughter could occasionally be heard from the two youngsters upon the lawn as they waited for their friend. The reason for his delay was due to yet another disagreement between son, mother and step-father. Again the adolescent, after trying to be reasonable, was near to throwing a tantrum about him not wanting to be accompanied by a personal bodyguard. The young master of the house eventually got his way and the family sat down to breakfast as if the argument had not taken place. The meandering conversation between the two waiting companions was eventually manipulated by Rufus towards the subject of politics - a subject that the youth was hopeful of making a career in one day. The innate Republican knew exactly what to say to stimulate and rile the ardent Caesarian and would-be centurion. It amused Salvidienus to antagonise the passionate Agrippa who, albeit being his friend, he duly considered to be his intellectual and social inferior.

"The Senate is Rome," Rufus pronounced, not without a modicum of conceit and self-appointed authority.

"What has the Senate ever done for the glory of Rome?" Marcus Agrippa replied, expressing a certain derision and even bewilderment in his tone.

"The Senate has tried to maintain that which is the glory of Rome - the Law."

"The Law is but a means to a senator's true end, self-interested profit and power. As he said the other day," Marcus Agrippa remarked as he motioned his head towards the house ("he" being their tardy friend), "justice goes to the highest bidder in Rome. He who can afford the most expensive advocate invariably wins the case. Truth has become tautologous."

"But too much has changed," exclaimed the son of the zealous optimate - quoting his father. At the same time a solemn looking Rufus Salvidienus also shook his head, in objection and pity, as if to stress the sincerity of his argument. The would-be senator had seen the technique used by an advocate during a visit to Rome a few years back.

"I would argue too little."

"Now you are just being contrary."

"No, I'm not."

And with that the two teenagers smiled and simultaneously launched what blades of grass they held in their hands at each other in playfulness. A short burst of laughter from them then echoed its way up the contoured slope and reached the ears of their companion, Gaius Octavius. For most of his teens Octavius had been a slight and sickly child, but the boy had owned the motivation to toughen himself up after spending some time on campaign with his great-uncle around a year ago. His face was tanned, but his skin and hair were still fairer than that of the two other Roman youths. His expression was sometimes broody, sometimes tranquil, and sometimes ironic - but as with now his usually serious mien could dramatically transform itself and his features could become amiable, engaging and not a little handsome.

His face was screwed up from squinting in the sunlight and from biting upon, and visibly enjoying, a crust of bread smeared in honey. Rufus and Marcus Agrippa shielded their eyes from the late morning sun as their companion descended upon them.

"Late again," issued Agrippa, sighing and comically rolling his eyes to his best friend.

"Up all night again? Were you reading, or just thinking about Briseis?" Salvidienus chipped in with a lewd expression plastered on his face. Briseis was a Greek servant girl within the household who Octavius had seduced and bedded a week before. Or rather one could argue that the alluring, experienced Briseis had seduced the lusty young Roman master of the house. The enamoured seducer had told his friends about the episode just to tell them, for they were his close companions, but perhaps more so he had recounted the experience in order to boast and make his friends feel jealous of him.

"Reading," Octavius replied with a wry smile, as well as a blush - lying slightly. For the most part however the conscientious student had been up all night - to the point where the dawn had eclipsed his lamp as a reading light - annotating notes from the texts that his part-time tutor, Cleanthes, had lent to his pupil from his private library. His ivory coloured tunic was clean, but plain and devoid of any ostentation or accessory, which marked out his family's status and wealth. There was a self-confidence, but not swagger, to his easy gait.

"Well I hope you also got some rest. Our Master said we are having a special lesson today," Marcus Agrippa said with relish in his eyes, excited as he was by the prospect of what their fencing teacher, an ex-legionary, had in store for their class this afternoon.

Salvidienus briefly smiled, trying but unable to share his pugilistic friend's attitude. He then got up, adjusting his tunic and smoothing his hair, to follow his classmate down the slope and out of the gates of the estate.

Octavius' initial reaction to the prospective lesson was one of feigned disinterest. He shrugged his shoulders and raised his eyebrow at his friend to affect being bored by, or above, such news. But when Agrippa's back was turned the wry smile disintegrated into an apprehensive frown. He realised the importance of the lessons, and there were times when Octavius tried to apply himself to the old legionary's instruction, but the thought regularly clouded the young Roman's mood that he was just not born to be a soldier. "You cannot put in what the Gods have left out," his step-father had once remarked. As a thing in itself this might not have worried the would-be philosopher, but the sense of failure troubled him because he imagined that it gave credence to the whispered arguments that Gaius Octavius was not a true Caesar.

2.

A line of shrubbery, dotted with poisonous berries, fenced off the property from the neighbouring villas. Where the flanking estates housed gardens or pens for various livestock outside their villas though, there resided, at the front of Tiro Casca's modest property, a large circle - or "arena" as he called it - of sand and gravel. Rumour had it - rumours which the laconic proprietor neither confirmed nor denied - that the old Roman soldier had campaigned with both Pompey in Spain and Caesar in Long-Haired Gaul - and that he had killed more men than cholera. Some even reported that, before joining the army, Casca had been a famous gladiator who had won his freedom. Or rather, Crassus had bought it. His "war was now over" however. The ex-legionary, despite often pining for his beloved Rome, had retired to the Macedonian province, establishing a school for combat and athletics for the area's privileged Roman and Greek youth.

A receding crop of dusty brown hair, flecked with grey, crowned an ageing but still strong-jawed face. The grizzled soldier's skin was as leathery as the bloodied, cracked breastplate which Casca had proudly mounted upon his bedroom wall. His build was still stocky, with his arms, shoulders and legs as muscular and supple as a man half his fifty-five years of age. His ever expanding waistline however, forcing his belt to cut into his hips sometimes, betrayed the old soldier's fondness for red meat, washed down with undiluted red wine - which was as strong as it was sour. Like its vintner.

Having lost one of his front teeth in a battle some years ago, and chipping the other in a tavern brawl, there was a strange, almost comical sibilance to his voice - although people were fearful enough of the gnarled veteran not to comment about the minor affliction. Casca was an unapologetic disciplinarian, as well as an excellent teacher, and his students duly felt a mixture of fear and respect when in his presence. The fencing master was not without a sense of humour though, and his raucous cackle was unmistakable. But for the most part his demeanour was stern, as though Casca thought ill of everyone he encountered until they could prove him wrong. The scowling, former legionary breathed heavily through his nostrils, bushy with nose hair, almost snorting. He then addressed his class again for the day.

"So far I have taught you ladies basic swordsmanship. Today I'm going to teach you how to fight. If nothing else you'll learn how the two things are somewhat different animals."

Octavius had just recovered his breath. For the first half an hour of the session Casca had instructed Agrippa, who was a kind of prefect for the class, to have the pupils warm up. Stretching exercises were succeeded by a run. The scorching heat had sapped Octavius' body as much as the exertion. An all too brief interlude had followed in which the perpetually unimpressed tutor allowed his students to drink a ladle of warm water, each from the stone trough which was situated next to the house.

The twenty youths stood to attention in two rows of ten, wooden practise swords (tipped with padded leather) in their hands. Sweat trickled down Octavius' face, his temples seeming to be a magical font for the stuff, and his heart began to beat that much faster as he stood in the front rank. For a fleeting second after Casca had spoken, Octavius caught his intimidating tutor's eye - an act which usually presaged him picking out the student to take part in one of his training exercises. During which the pupil might suffer a bloodied nose or bruised ribs for the greater good of a martial education.

Casca noted the sheepish look on the pupil's face and, inwardly, he sighed. The ex-legionary, who had fought under his great-uncle, genuinely liked the boy. His affection for the intelligent youth however only accentuated his sense of disappointment. Casca could not fault the youth for his effort - and his intelligence made up for deficiencies in his lack of natural strength and skill - but Octavius would never make a good soldier or be a match for someone like Agrippa. It was with a heavy heart that he had to report upon Octavius' progress every month, if he could call it that, to Lucius Oppius. Oppius was a high-ranking centurion in the legion posted just outside of Apollonia. He was a veteran of Caesar's campaigns and was presently charged with the protection of the dictator's nephew. Lucius in turn reported on the youth to Cornelius Balbus, Caesar's private secretary.

Octavius couldn't help but observe Agrippa out of the corner of his eye. Marcus' hand gripped his practise sword and his brow was corrugated in determination. His muscular body, which already was no different from a fully-fledged soldier's, was taut in readiness. He was like a young lion about to pounce.

Agrippa gave off a slight grunt however, whilst Octavius quietly breathed a sigh of relief, as Casca proceeded to choose another five students to take part in his demonstration. The group was assorted, consisting of Romans and Greeks of varying abilities. Some, perhaps rightly so, were scared. Others wiped sweaty palms across their tunics to grip their weapons more tightly in preparation. They would do their best. The old soldier respected that.

"Now, using all that I have taught you and anything you ladies have taught yourselves, I want you to come at me at full speed." Casca used three training modes, slow, half, and full speed, depending upon his mood and the safety levels of the exercise. "Give no quarter, because I can assure you I won't be going easy on you," Tiro remarked and grinned, to the point where one could see the black hole of his mouth through the crooked gap in his teeth. For a second or two the students' attention was distracted by a brace of crows who cawed loudly and perched themselves on top of the tiled roof of the house, watching over the scene as if they had come to enjoy a show. Or pick over the entrails of any victims.

Even from around ten yards away, Octavius could hear the ex-legionary's scarred knuckles crack as he clasped the practise gladius. Cnaeus Tiberius, perhaps the only student in the class who could match Agrippa for strength and skill, took charge of his other four assailants. This was allowed; indeed Casca encouraged the use of teamwork and leadership. The son of one of the wealthiest merchants in the province, Cnaeus Tiberius directed, with a nod of his head and wave of his sword, for the other four to encircle their teacher as if they were hunters about to bring down a boar with their spears. He was certainly ready to give no quarter - he just hoped that his fellow students had the guts to do so too.

"Good, good," Casca remarked through narrowing eyes, impressed either with Tiberius' authority or the other four's willingness to work together. "But remember ladies, this is combat. Not swordplay."

Cnaeus subtly nodded to his two Greek classmates who were stationed behind their tutor to attack, conveying that he would try to simultaneously assail their target from the front. Casca smiled, anticipating the simple and obvious tactic. He swiftly turned to face the charging Greeks. Such was the huge arc of the Greek's swing, and the ex-soldier's strength, that he knocked the sword clean out of his first opponent's hand. Not having time to bring his weapon back in place to thrust at the second Greek, Casca merely made a fist and punched the youth square in the chest, flooring him. Sensing his attack, the fencing master swivelled to parry the efficient stroke from Tiberius. Sword clacked upon sword again as Cnaeus followed up his first attack with another well-balanced lunge. The student then took a couple of steps back from his tutor, as if he wanted to stop and admire his technique and have his master praise him also. Casca rightly did no such thing, not only because he was disappointed in Tiberius' predictable attack, but more so because his attention was directed towards the two students who were approaching him from both flanks. The first stupidly emitted an embarrassing battle-cry and held his sword aloft for too long. Before the spindly boy could bring his weapon bearing down on his opponent, Casca merely grabbed him by the wrist, to the hand which carried the imitation gladius; he then threw the youth around, as if he were a rag-doll, onto his fellow assailant who was charging at him from the opposite direction. The two students duly collided and collapsed into a heap on top of each other. One of them spluttered as he swallowed a mouthful of sand. It all happened quickly, yet Agrippa absorbed and admired the teacher's movements and control. Increasingly Marcus had come to believe that combat and warfare were sciences; one had to be deliberate, efficient. Methodical conditioning and foresight were as essential as numbers and the choice of terrain.

Cnaeus cursed his ineffectual unit underneath his breath. They reflected badly on him. Casca laughed, gleefully, sadistically, surveying the field of combat. The lad who had been punched in the stomach still groaned, prostrate, on the ground. His fellow Greek nursed a wooden gladius with a debilitating crack running through it. Tangled limbs, and bare behinds from hitched up skirts, sprang up from the ground where the final two assailants rested.

Octavius heard the crows on top of the roof caw again, as if either laughing at the pathetic display or applauding the wily teacher.

Only Cnaeus Tiberius remained on his feet with a sword in his hand.

"C'mon. Don't fence, fight," the gruff master commanded.

The tutor was tested a little by his accomplished pupil's agility. His footwork was excellent. He was also pleased to witness the pluck of the lad who got up and fought on after being knocked down a couple of times, from the result of the old soldier fighting dirty and tripping his opponent. Casca was pleased to observe that Tiberius was not just a cliché-ridden bully and spoiled brat. He had some steel, as well as skill. At the end though, for all of Tiberius' ability with a gladius in his hand, he had not quite grasped the point of the lesson. Casca, soon after, closed the sparring session by disarming the lad, kicking the back of his legs and holding the point of the splintered sword to Tiberius' throat.

"Good, good Tiberius. But I am still looking for more. You're still fencing, not fighting. Who wants to try and surprise me then? Anyone? None of you other ladies want to dance?"

"Agrippa. I might've known you'd be up for some punishment. No sooner have the bruises disappeared from our last bout than you want me to paint some more on your body. You're either brave or stupid lad."

Agrippa merely raised a corner of his mouth in a half-smile as a reply. He then swung his sword around in his hand to loosen up his wrist whilst walking towards an opponent who he - and every other pupil in the class - had still to best. Rufus smirked and shook his head in bafflement that Agrippa would volunteer to face the sadistic veteran.

At first, pupil and teacher sized each other up and moved around in a circle together, but then they simultaneously locked horns. Agrippa rarely lunged or lost his composure in this initial exchange however, preferring to keep his distance, parrying Casca with energy saving wristy flicks of his birch wood gladius. Conscious of retaining a good defence, Agrippa also easily evaded the ex-soldier's sweeping leg, which had twice caught out Tiberius.

Octavius noted how the fencing master, for once, was breaking sweat also. He had watched Marcus observing the footwork and potential weaknesses in the tutor's technique. Agrippa had once remarked to his friend that Casca's tactic was always to counter-attack and let his opponent make a mistake.

"Again class, we have someone who can fence but can't fight. Your blood would be browning the sand if this was a battle right now," the goading teacher issued, wiping the perspiration away from his forehead. Whilst Casca was distracted with this little speech however, Agrippa subtly dug one of his open-toed sandals into the blanket of fine sand which covered the ground. In a further bid to distract and disorientate his opponent, the fresh faced student winked at the cantankerous veteran. And with that Agrippa flicked up the mound of sand he carried in his sandal into the eyes of the unsuspecting fencing master. Without hesitating, he thrust his sword and body in one movement towards the half-blinded Casca. The experienced combatant put his sword up however, and successfully blocked the incoming blow, with sword upon sword momentarily resting on each other like a hammer upon an anvil. But Agrippa was not finished fighting yet. Deploying the plan of attack that he had formulated beforehand, Agrippa made a fist with his spare hand and swiftly crouched and punched his half-blinded opponent in the groin. Casca roared in pain and stepped backwards, doubled up in acute torture. Before he even knew what was happening, the old soldier felt the rough edge of a wooden gladius upon his leathery neck.

Neither Agrippa, nor the rest of the class, knew what was coming next however, as they had yet to see their master bested. His opponent more than anyone was fearful - more scared now than at the beginning of the bout even - of what the egotistical teacher might do in response to being defeated. Breathless - and still somewhat in that certain agony and discomfort peculiar to man - Casca gazed up at his pupil and spoke.

"So you do know how to fight, as well as fence," he exclaimed, with a child-like expression on his face that Agrippa had not seen before. And with this remark and brief, private look between teacher and student, Agrippa too smiled and the tension went out of his still combat-ready body.

"I must teach you one final lesson now Agrippa," the tutor announced to the class in general, "After the heat of battle, one must learn to cool off." The doubled-over old soldier suddenly mustered all the speed and strength inside of him and picked his unprepared student up. Casca then carried Agrippa over his shoulder and dropped him into the trough of water by the house. Laughter trumpeted out from every student within the watching class, bar the envious and resentful Tiberius. Agrippa took the joke in good spirit. A glow of pride also filled his heart as Casca offered him his hand in order to help him out of the trough. As he did so the teacher quietly remarked to his favourite pupil, "You will not just be fighting with legions one day lad - you will be leading them."

3.

After instructing Agrippa to go inside and ask a servant to attend to him, Casca reverted back to his severe self and gave a lecture to the attentive class. "Viciousness, allied to intelligence, triumphs on the battlefield". He proceeded to run through various tactics - such as eye gouging, stamping and hamstringing - that would come in handy in a melee.

"If you have a helmet and your opponent doesn't, butt him...your shield should not just be used for defensive means. The umbo here protrudes for a reason - to ram into the pate of your opponent."

After the lecture the teacher arranged for a number of demonstrations, at half speed without actual contact, to illustrate the practicalities and effectiveness of fighting - as opposed to fencing. He closed the demonstration by dressing up one of the class in a Roman legionary's armour and discussing its weak points - and when and where to use the edge and point of the gladius upon such targets as the groin and neck. Upon asking if there were any questions a young Roman, he must have been no older than fifteen, wondered why they were being shown the weak spots in Roman armour, as opposed to those of their enemies?

"Romans shouldn't fight Romans," a corpulent and over privileged youth, one Ulpius Gabinus, remarked sententiously.

"They shouldn't, but unfortunately they do. And if you spent as much time learning your history, as you do eating Gabinus, you'd know that also," the veteran said with a practiced sneer, formed from half a lifetime of having to take orders from equally ignorant and pompous legates.

In the final hour or so of the lesson, Casca organised a small tournament, consisting of sword and shield bouts between classmates. Octavius won two but lost three of his contests, which was a disappointing but not unprecedented result for the diffident swordsman. Even Rufus bested him. The smug grin across the aristocrat's face smarted more than the bruise on his shoulder, which was also a reminder of his defeat. More so it preyed upon Octavius' mind that the result of the contest might find its way back to Oppius, who in return might report the poor display back to Caesar. A cloud of potent shame hung over the sensitive youth, imagining his uncle's disappointment. "Always be the best," Caesar had asserted to his nephew. He so desperately wanted for his great-uncle to be proud of him. He wanted to repay his faith in him - be worthy of the name.

Bored by the petering out of the action the crows eventually departed, cawing now in criticism at the lack of bloodshed. Shortly afterwards, peppered in dust and sweat-strewn, the students also scattered in various directions after their teacher called time on their demanding but rewarding lesson.

*

After class the three companions took shelter from the glaring afternoon sun. Passing through Rufus' father's estate the three youths rested their aching frames and sunburnt faces on a cool quilt of lush grass. A glade of willow trees, which Rufus' father cultivated in order that his slaves could produce baskets from them, provided a healthy measure of shade for their desired repose. The rippling sound of a dimpled rivulet trickled in the background and the faint but distinctive fragrance of lemon trees, from a neighbouring orchard, sang in the air to clothe the scene in further meditative pleasure.

Agrippa reclined on the verdure, practising his reflexes. With his eyes alert and the adrenaline still pumping, he regularly shot his hands up in the air in the attempt to catch the flies which dared to buzz over his head. He duly caught more than he missed, carefully keeping track of the score to see if he could beat his record, but eventually the young man grew tired of the game.

Salvidienus, with his fingers laced behind his head in order to protect his hair from the grass and soil, idly dreamed of a life in the Senate. He again listed, and charted, the 'course of honours' - the order and offices in which an ambitious politician might make his name in the capital. *Quaestor*: a junior rank, in which one could serve as a financial officer with the treasury or a clerk with the army responsible for the administration of supplies and plunder. *Aedile*: an officer charged with administration in Rome itself, the maintenance of its public buildings, streets and aqueducts. Rufus was suitably aware though that his time as an aedile would equally be concerned with staging the ludi Romani, the public games in the city. People today still talked about the games that Caesar put on during his tenure as an aedile. He too would win over the electorate through the spectacles he would arrange. Rufus selfishly hoped that his father will have passed away by then so he could afford the gladiatorial contests and parade of exotic animals from his inheritance. After Aedile comes *Praetor* - one of the oldest and most revered offices in the state. As praetor Rufus could be elected to govern an entire army or province. He could sit as a magistrate in various criminal cases, possessing the power to either condemn or pardon. The sun shone through the leafy arbour as Rufus basked in the warm glow of the idea of *Consul* - and then *Pro Consul*. He would be the first Salvidienus to win the honour. Clients would lobby him with petitions. He would make his money, like Crassus, from property - not that Salvidienus would brook at accepting the odd bribe also to finance his honourable course. He would hold court at dinner parties, which would run on till late and turn into private orgies that he indulged. In his mind's eye a procession of beautiful girls and wives were paraded before him and he picked them out, as if plucking fruits from the bough, to be his lovers. And such would be his success, good reputation and popularity that he would have the pick of commands when proconsul - he would push back the frontiers of the Empire like Pompey the Great and write his name in the annals of Rome.

His eyelids felt as heavy as his limbs, but still Octavius squinted through them and lazily gazed up through a gap in the trees to take in the shimmering blue sky. He was momentarily distracted by a pair of pink finches darting about above him, the female teasingly evading the male in an aerial courtship dance. Eventually she would let herself be caught. Tufts of drifting white cloud parted and came together like giant lumps of wool. As if divinely inspired by Apollo, Octavius suddenly realised why he enjoyed nature so, and found himself at peace in the secluded bower. Nature did not have any opinion of him, or expect anything from him. He closed his eyes in an effort to remember the pleasant vista and reposeful feeling, so as to one day retrieve the memory when aggravated by less concordant scenes. Even this revelation, and the will to record it, became hazy however as the cusp of sleep wafted over him like a precious dream. But just as Octavius was about to pass over into the blissful realm, he was disturbed by a conversation which sprouted up and demanded his attention.

"Has your father said anything about you wanting to become a legionary?" Rufus, seemingly out of the blue, asked Agrippa.

"No, but I've still yet to tell him. He knows that I'm no farmer, though. Besides, I'll tell him that someone needs to keep Octavius out of trouble."

"I'd be more worried about you leading him into it. I have visions of you stepping out of the ranks, like you did today, and volunteering to take on the entire Parthian army. But your mind is made up; you definitely want to be a soldier?"

"Yes. Unlike you two, my family has yet to make a name for itself. I want the house of Agrippa to come out from underneath the shade of anonymity."

"Anonymity can sometimes be a blessing, as well as a curse, Marcus. And, like your virginity, once sacrificed you can never get it back again," Octavius mused, as much to himself perhaps as his companion.

"That's far from the best of your conceits. I'm convinced that most people would happily lose both sooner rather than later," Rufus replied.

"So when and where are you hoping to lose your anonymity, Rufus?"

"In the Senate, as an advocate. Sooner rather than later as well."

"You sound determined, Rufus. Why do you want to be an advocate, if you don't mind me asking?" Octavius inquired, mildly curious.

"I'm going to study to be an advocate so I never lose an argument with my friends. But seriously, look at our history. Advocates, senators, are the ones who are all powerful in Rome. What laws we don't make up, we can always interpret to our own devices. I'm joking, or at least half-joking. But the pen is mightier than the sword."

"So does that mean you'll be bringing a pen along to Casca's next sparring session then?" Agrippa posited, grinning at both his own witticism and also Rufus' self-important air.

Out of the corner of his eye Rufus saw Octavius smile also, and he felt that infrequent but familiar twinge of jealousy again that he wasn't as close to Octavius as Agrippa was. No matter what he did or said they would always have a special, closer relationship. To silence these envious, sullen murmurings however, Rufus spoke and tried to continue the conversation.

"So what do you want to be, Octavius?"

Agrippa here propped himself up and turned to where his best friend lay. Surprisingly he had never asked Octavius such a question. And so too, Octavius had never confided in him as to what might be the answer, if indeed he had one. Being Caesar's nephew Gaius could surely have the pick of any career he wished, whether he chose to work his way up the political ladder, be given a foreign posting or commission in the army. Or he could afford to carry on with his studies, which he seemed to enjoy.

"I want to be…left in peace for an hour or two so I can take a nap," the evasive student answered, wryly smiling. Octavius enjoyed keeping people guessing, as though the whole of life was but a game in which he who could keep people guessing most, won. Or it was a cynical play, in which one acted out various parts to garner applause. "It is where you are placed at the end of the race that counts," his great-uncle had said with a boyish wink to him one time.

*

The sun arched overhead and lost some of its sting, to be replaced by a stodgy humidity. Octavius glanced at the sky, increasingly fomented and furrowing his brow. It would rain before he made it home. Three became two. Octavius and Agrippa had bid Rufus a farewell and the two remaining companions made their way home. Agrippa did not need to tell his friend to keep it between them when he spoke to Octavius about what Casca had said.

"And he should know. You should be rightly proud. I'd certainly want you on my side in a fight, Marcus." Octavius would later be gladdened by the realisation that he felt better, happier, for hearing this praise for his friend - as compared to the shallow vanity he felt at boasting about his bedding of Briseis.

"And I will be, against the Parthians. I meant what I said Gaius about wanting to come with you. Has your uncle said when he intends to join the army and disembark?"

Gaius, partly to impress Agrippa and partly to signify how much he trusted his friend, had confided in him earlier in the year. Caesar had written to Octavius and sketched out to his nephew the scope and intention of his newest - and most ambitious - campaign. After conquering the Parthians, and winning back the eagles that Crassus had lost, Caesar planned to march around the Black Sea and then onto the Caucasus. From there he would invade and subdue Scythia. The lands bordering Germany - and eventually Germany itself - would then be added to Caesar's conquests. He would write his name in the annals of Roman History again. Finally Caesar would return to Italy via Gaul, thus completing the circuit of his Empire, which would be bounded on all sides by the ocean. Pompey would finally live in Caesar's shadow. Perhaps more than the dictator even, Marcus Agrippa was champing at the bit to take part in the historic campaign.

Octavius' brow began to further crease as warm droplets of rain began to pelt down. A dreary shade of grey poured across the sky, like smoke. After a pause he finally answered his friend as to when they would depart.

"Soon, after the Ides."

4.

When Octavius returned to the house the young master was handed a towel by one of the servants to dry himself off from the rain. There was a frantic and industrious atmosphere around the estate as slaves and a small retinue of soldiers busied themselves for the departure the next day. The axles to baggage carts were being greased with tallow. Food and presents were being packed. Clothes were folded. Rose petals were being scattered in order to perfume the carriage for the long journey. Atia and Octavius' step-father, Lucius Marcus Phillipus, were travelling back to Rome for business - and pleasure - in the morning. So as not to disturb his studies and military training Octavius had been asked to remain at home, a situation which the youth understood and complied with.

Octavius passed into the atrium and heard voices emanate from the triclinium. He tensed slightly as he heard Lucius Oppius' terse voice. A second later a brace of soldiers marched out of the room and brushed past him.

As if he had sensed his presence, Oppius stuck his head around the curtained door and glared at Octavius. The youth always felt a little intimidated under the stern centurion's gaze - as though he felt that he should be impressing the soldier, but wasn't. His compressed jaw was covered with stubble that was as abrasive as sandpaper. The careerist soldier, who might have been aged anywhere between thirty-five and forty-five, towered over most in terms of his height and build. Oppius was a keen rider and swimmer; furthermore, when not attending to the drilling and administration of the legion, the consummate centurion would spend his time in frequent fencing and combat practise. "The harder I practise, the luckier I get," Octavius had once overheard him drily state. His blue eyes were striking but ultimately cold, like two sapphires set within a marble statue. The only time when Octavius had witnessed the centurion enjoy himself was when he was in the company of his great-uncle or Mark Antony. Caesar was the only man who Oppius truly respected. Octavius could still recall the scene when his great-uncle asked one of his most trusted lieutenants why he wasn't married.

"Because I already have been - twice. The first nagged me that I always seemed distant. The second because I wasn't distant enough,"

Oppius replied - his tone being funnier for seeming all the more sincere.

Octavius ventured into the triclinium. Oppius had not said a word, nor did he communicate the request with his eyes, but somehow Octavius felt compelled to assent to the centurion's unspoken order to join them. It appeared that the soldier had been conversing with his mother and step-father, not that the taciturn officer ever uttered a word more than necessary. Even his step-father was intimidated, or confounded, by the manner of Oppius at times.

"Make sure you dry yourself off properly," Atia immediately remarked to her son. Her tone was cosseting, as if she wished to impress upon Lucius Oppius, and herself, how much she cared for her child - Caesar's nephew. Atia was the daughter of the First Man of Rome's sister, Julia. The elegant woman was approaching middle age but her former beauty and spirit could still very much be traced in her figure and bearing. Atia, confident, intelligent, and proud - in short, a Caesar, had first been married to Marcus Atius Balbus, a former praetor and governor of Macedonia. Due to his senatorial commitments and foreign postings, Octavius saw very little of his father as a young child. Balbus passed away before his son's fifth birthday. Octavius sadly could not claim to have truly known his father, but he was conscious of his achievements and reputation. He was a good man by all accounts, who had gleaned praise from Cicero no less. His mother also never spoke ill of his father, which was a further testament to his character, and for a time it had been a source of frustration and regret to Gaius that he had never got to know him. In his own eyes it did not bother Octavius that his father had not been born into true noble family. But a certain anxiety and irritation had crept into his thoughts of late in that it might prejudice him in other people's eyes. But a man should be judged on his merit, the idealistic youth believed.

"Leave him be, Atia," Phillipus announced, partly amused and partly critical of his wife's mollycoddling. His hair was now grey and his face a little wrinkled but there was still a healthy vigour in the senator's eyes. His expression was thoughtful, kind and trustworthy. It was an expression, unlike many a politician's, which mirrored his character. Atia's marriage to Phillipus had of course been politically motivated. Phillipus, the son of a former consul, was both an amiable and influential senator. As well as being intimate with Caesar and Pompey, Phillipus could also be seen to have had a foot in the opposing political camp - due to the fact that Cato had married

Phillipus' daughter from a previous marriage. Indeed some argued that Caesar had ultimately chosen Phillipus over the rest of Atia's suitors because he felt, with his influence and relationship to Cato, that Atia and the boy would be safe if ever his own position became endangered. Marcus Phillipus' suit was not just the one favoured by Caesar however, for Atia too would have chosen the quietly virtuous older man as her husband. And a mutual fondness soon matured into something deeper, stronger. Love.

Octavius was fond of his step-father also. Marcus Phillipus embodied most of what was good about being Roman, Gaius believed. His step-father was brave, intelligent, superior, just.

"Now as you know Octavius, Marcus and I are leaving for Rome tomorrow. What you do not know however is that I received a letter from your great-uncle today," Atia announced and then paused.

The boy's heart skipped a beat and yet pounded a moment later. News from Rome. Would Caesar be here soon? Did he have some new honour to confer on him? Were there any words of praise for his great-nephew in the letter? Was he even in Caesar's thoughts?

"He has asked us that you be left in the care of Lucius Oppius while we are away," Marcus Phillipus remarked, finishing his wife's sentence. Caesar had 'asked' but the request was tantamount to an order. "I'm sure Caesar knows that you can look after yourself, Octavius. So too your mother and I will sleep easier, knowing that Lucius will be keeping an eye on you. I dare say though that you won't notice that he is even there."

"As long as he doesn't mind," Octavius replied, shrugging. The adolescent masked his feelings well. He was slightly hurt and resentful thinking that it was considered that he couldn't be trusted. It naturally nettled the youth to think that Caesar still thought of him as a child who needed looking after. But still his face did not, would not, betray his disappointment, a disappointment which was exacerbated by the fact that he wouldn't now be able to spend as many nights with Briseis, with Oppius keeping a hawkish eye upon him. He acted indifferently to the news. Yet later that evening, when Octavius reflected upon the situation, he realised that he was, or could be, genuinely indifferent to the minor change in events. There were far worse fates to endure than being in possession of a bodyguard. His existence was not an unhappy one he pondered, philosophically.

Bored by his mother's gossip as to who was marrying who in Rome, what spices were in fashion and what she should wear for her entry back into the city, Octavius excused himself. He bathed himself, declining the offer of a pug-faced serving woman to assist him, and then retreated into his room to catch up on his re-reading of Polybius and Catullus.

*

It was now late. Gaius yawned and put his book down. A breeze whistled through the gap beneath the door and wafted over the candle next to his bed. For half a minute or so the contemplative youth just sat transfixed, gazing at the wriggling flame. Buffeted. Straining. He admired how, no matter how much the breeze desired to extinguish the torch, the flame remained alight and always returned to its calm, beautiful form when the attacks subsided. The would-be stoic fancied, promised, that he too would be akin to the candlelight no matter how much fortune attempted to bend or break him. Octavius gently smiled at his own conceit and drifted off to sleep.

Maybe the dream was provoked by the drumming of the rain on the roof outside, but Octavius was plunged back into the sublime scene of the storm from a year ago. The ship was bound for Spain. A large wave arched over the creaking trireme as if it was a claw about to swat a gad-fly from the ocean's skin. Or as if they were caught in the jaws of an aquatic monster, which was foaming at the mouth. Oars littered the ocean like twigs within a brook. Octavius bumped and cut his head as he tried to negotiate his way onto the deck. Spotting the blood trickling from the youth's temple, Oppius immediately ceased reining in an untamed sail. Without warning, or a word said, he rushed up to the boy and checked the extent of his injury - and then resumed his task of fastening down the flapping sail. The wind ululated like a wolf, baying for blood. If it wasn't for the inky night the Spanish coast would have been in sight, but the mortal craft, at the mercy of Neptune, was a world away from safety. Timber bent and then splintered. Twice the land-legged young Gaius slipped upon the slick deck, but fell not. Water slapped Octavius across the face as a wave crashed into the side of the vessel. The sensation both enlivened and disorientated him to his peril. Voices also jabbed into his ears. Half were arguing to abandon ship, half were ordering to ride the storm out. Before Octavius even began to assess his best course of action, his mind was made up for him. Roscius, a hulking legionary - whom Octavius recognised as being part of Oppius' cohort - bellowed in his ears above the roaring storm to follow him.

The steely centurion but nodded his head to indicate to Octavius that he wished for the adolescent to clamber down the rope ladder into the lifeboat, which bobbed up and down on the churning ocean and continually knocked against the larger vessel. The commanding Oppius wore neither a look of worry on his face, nor did he try to give his young charge a comforting glance, as if to convey that everything would be alright. Octavius descended slowly into the small boat. Half a dozen sailors challenged Oppius and Roscius above him - complaining about commandeering the lifeboat. Either through violence, or the threat of it, the two soldiers soon out-argued the protesting mob.

On board the ship, and on land, Roscius had been a rock. His hard, weathered face was a paradigm of fearlessness and authority. Octavius almost gasped one time when the giant of a man made a couple of fists - likening the sight to seeing two boulders on the ends of his brawny arms. An expression of doubt and fright immediately overcame the stout legionary as soon as he placed a foot upon the puny lifeboat. The craft moved beneath his feet and Roscius nearly fell overboard. A serendipitous clap and rumble of thunder drowned out the curses which shot from the seasoned soldier's mouth. Oppius briefly smiled, witnessing the panic on his loyal friend's face. It was perhaps the first time Octavius had observed the professional, emotionless centurion do so. At the time of the crossing Oppius had been assigned to the protection of Octavius - upon the personal commission of Caesar himself - for less than a month. At first Gaius had been in awe of the Roman officer, admiring his physique and the air of authority which surrounded him. He was intrigued by the enigmatic officer. "Men want to be him and women want to be with him," his step-father had remarked. He soon grew even more intimidated and frightened by the centurion, however. After suffering monosyllabic replies, or having the soldier just walk away from him as if he wasn't there, Octavius stopped trying to engage his bodyguard. Phillipus also revealed to Octavius that Oppius had the ear of his great-uncle, and that he would doubtlessly be reporting his behaviour and progress back to Caesar. As a result the youth was conscious of what he had said and done in the presence of the centurion. In some ways he played the obedient child in front of the soldier, yet at other opportunities Octavius would do or say something to prove how much of a good Roman he was. But, after suffering the demoralising indifference of the soldier towards him on one too many occasion, Octavius eventually experienced fits of resentment where admiration once resided.

The centurion's smirk was fleeting however, and Oppius soon handed an oar to Roscius.

"Are you a strong swimmer, boy?" the officer then shouted at Octavius over the snarling wind. Such was the threatening tone of his voice that the pallid youth would have nodded in assertion even if the answer was no. Oppius ordered Roscius to abandon his greaves and breastplate, as he too dropped half of his uniform overboard. Sooner or later they would have to make a swim for it. It would be sooner rather than later as, not twenty yards from the ship, the lifeboat began to fill with water. Oppius instructed Octavius to try and bail out the pool of sea water forming at their feet using Roscius' large helmet.

The two powerful soldiers began to find some rhythm and Gaius even began to win the war against the incoming water.

"She's lying low in the water," Roscius huskily remarked to his officer, referring to their storm battered ship - his brow wrinkled in concern.

"It'll be lying even lower within the hour," Oppius replied matter-of-factly, seemingly unperturbed and resigned to the situation of losing both the craft and his men. Over the next few evenings though, a self-consciously sensitive and noble Octavius would recall the loss of life and try to honour the dead with generous and solemn thoughts. Caesar's great-nephew felt guilty because he reasoned that, if not for him, the men would not have even been out in the storm.

Before Octavius had a chance, however, to glance around to see how low the trireme was in the water, a hurtling wave, spurred on by a gust of wind, shunted into the side of the lifeboat. The three figures within the craft were tossed into the water like coins into a well. Disorientated. Frightened. At first Octavius was dragged deeper below as the water soaked and weighed down his tunic. His eyes and mind were a blur. It was as if someone had tied an anchor around his waist. But the adrenaline rush from his panic soon aided the strength Gaius needed to pull himself back up to the surface.

As his face broke through the skin of the sea and he gasped for air, Octavius woke up from his realistic nightmare, feeling now the same mixture of fear and exhilaration as he felt then, or rather just after the ordeal. Where the dream left off, his memory took over. Oppius had to perhaps worry more about Roscius than Octavius in terms of getting them to shore. He constantly swam back and forth between the two - with and against the tide - to encourage and watch over them as they made their way onto the secluded beach.

Heavy-limbed, shivering with cold and his muscles quivering with exhaustion, Octavius gulped in the air as he lay across the powdery sand. He had been delivered. Rain coughed upon his face. Darkness was legion. He sought but found not the silhouette of the doomed ship within the oily night. The lap of the incoming waves, which sometimes kissed his feet, made a shushing noise as if to demand silence. But all Gaius could hear was Roscius, short of breath too, lying beside him. Either he slept, or passed out, but the next thing Octavius recalled was Oppius - as if by magic - starting a fire. Not only did the small fire serve to dry them all off, but more importantly it acted as a beacon for those soldiers and slaves who had also bested the squall to make it to shore. The storm eventually abated. But they were still in danger. Having memorised the map during the crossing Gaius overheard Oppius confide in Roscius that they had landed upon a beach in enemy territory.

Octavius here decided however to switch off his memory, as if he were blowing out a candle. Not only did he want to be fresh for when his mother and Phillipus left the next morning, but he also wanted to be rested for his afternoon lesson with Cleanthes.

5.

Morning. Spring again augured summer. It had been an unnaturally hot early March. Octavius sat out in the garden, eating a pomegranate, waiting for the moment when his mother and step-father would finally depart and he would say his farewells. He sat in the cooling shade close to the house, but the rising sun began to bathe more and more of the garden in its pristine light. The buxom flower beds, which bordered a large square carpet of grass, were erupting with colour - crisp red roses, glassy lilies, trumpeting bluebells. The fish pond, in which Marcus Phillipus vainly attempted to breed his beloved koi carp, seemed to sparkle with petals of golden light - appearing and vanishing on the surface of the turquoise water with hypnotic charm. The sound of a babbling fountain, in the shape of a curvaceous nereid with the water dribbling from out of her mouth, could irritate or placate the listener depending on their mood. Octavius smiled, remembering how when he first arrived at the house, he had practised his kissing technique in secret on the fountain, employing the excuse for himself and any potential watcher that he was merely quenching his thirst. Fortunately he had Briseis now for such things, Octavius reflected - grinning now to himself in a different way.

The pomegranate sweetened and freshened up his mouth, displacing the furry taste of sleep which had hung at the back of his tongue. The moreish smell of fresh bread also made its way around from the kitchen and enlivened the air. Perhaps because Cleanthes too baked his own bread, Octavius suddenly thought of his tutor and, as if now in the philosopher's company, a pensive expression shaped his features. Octavius suddenly appeared ten years older and troubled by things. It was at this ill-timed moment that Atia came out to speak to her son.

"What's wrong?" Atia remarked, crouching down beside her seated son and laying her fingers on his shoulder. Octavius loved his mother, and appreciated her consideration, but at this particular moment he would've preferred not to have been disturbed by her.

"I am fine, mother," Octavius replied and pursed his lips - preventing himself from uttering anything more.

"I never know these days whether you are looking sad, or just serious. But you never seem as happy as you once were," Atia posed. She knew by the tone of his voice and body language that he didn't want to be disturbed or confronted. Atia's maternal concern, and curiosity, made her want to force the issue. She was worried that her child was becoming too withdrawn. Perhaps it was this Cleanthes' influence. When he did speak to anyone nowadays he would often be glib or sarcastic, or quote philosophy to her to win an argument. She had increasingly grown frustrated and sad over the past year, feeling that Octavius was becoming too self-reliant and melancholy. Sometimes Atia melodramatically thought to herself that she didn't know her son anymore. She was becoming redundant in his life. He no longer got sick. She missed taking care of him. Intellectually and emotionally he had grown independent, superior even. As much as Phillipus had argued that it was a good thing that the youth had matured and changed, a doting Atia was not quite ready to say goodbye to her special boy yet.

"I am content, mother. Truly, you have no need to worry about me."

"You can always come to me, you know that? A problem shared is a problem halved," Atia remarked and smiled, as if Octavius were twelve years old again.

Still my sorrows would be double the next man's Octavius fancied, but he kept the conceit to himself. He also bit his tongue in response to the scorn he felt for his mother's sententiousness and unconsidered way of looking at life.

"No man is an island," Atia then added, briefly stroking her child's fair hair, gazing at him fondly, conveying that she understood whatever he was going through and that he could confide in her.

Octavius didn't say a word in reply, although he was tempted to argue the contrary. He thought how Cleanthes was independent, craving no man's flattery or counsel; he served no master, nor wanted for a servant. He inwardly smiled, recollecting the story Cleanthes told him about Diogenes. When Alexander the Great asked if he could do anything for the philosopher, Diogenes merely requested for the king to get out of his light.

"I know, mother," Octavius finally replied, sighing a little as he said so.

As only a woman can, Atia here changed the subject and mood as if nothing had come before.

"Now, how does your mother look?" she gaily announced, beaming and twirling before her son. Her dress was crisp and white, patterned and bordered in a shade of purple which had become associated with Caesar. The cut highlighted rather than revealed Atia's envied figure. Her hair was blonde, which had grown even fairer of late in the Greek sun, and was stylishly pinned on her head. Her slender, bronzed forearms were decorated by a couple of elegant gold bangles. Rouge reddened her cheeks and Egyptian kohl lined her fine blue eyes, but the make-up was in no way garishly employed by the naturally attractive woman.

"You look lovely mother, so much so that I'm worried your friends in Rome will begin to resent you out of jealousy."

"Friends are worth sacrificing for looking so beautiful," Marcus Phillipus similarly satirically expressed, entering the garden and smiling broadly. The elderly but red-blooded senator was still as attracted to his wife today as he had been on their wedding night. Phillipus was also happily not immune to the feelings of pride and satisfaction he felt by having such a sophisticated and admired wife by his side.

"Now you are teasing and confusing me as to whether you're being serious or not," Atia replied, radiating from the compliment and from having her family around her. Only Octavia, her daughter, was missing from the pretty and familial scene. But she hoped to soon see her also, and her husband, during their visit to Rome.

Atia cuddled up to her husband whilst still caressing her son's hair. Having so seldom been apart from her child over the years, it was an emotional enough occasion for the devoted mother to bring a tear to her eye. Partly because her playing with his hair had irritated him, Octavius got up to hug his mother.

"Now, you promise to write?" Atia half demanded, rather than requested.

"Only if you promise not to cry, mother. If nothing else it will ruin your make-up," Octavius replied, touched by his mother's love and silliness. Atia's response was to let out a laugh cum sob. She clasped her son close, as if he were still a baby, and wetly kissed him upon his cheek. Unseen by Atia, Octavius rolled his eyes and raised his eyebrows to his step-father, partly from embarrassment, and also to display how he was himself above such womanly sentiment as his daffy mother. Marcus Phillipus knowingly grinned and nodded his head at his step-son, pleased and approving of Octavius for indulging his mother so.

Octavius indulged his mother also by waving and remaining in sight of the litter until the Rome-bound party disappeared over the hilly horizon. He returned to the house and checked the rusting sundial in the courtyard. He still had a few hours to kill before his afternoon lesson with Cleanthes. As Octavius here thought of Briseis he felt a little ashamed and dejected as he remembered how Cleanthes had warned of such consuming passions and unbecoming behaviour. But nevertheless the philosophical youth was compelled to venture into the staff quarters of the house to seek out the pleasure-loving girl. Frustration and indignation heated his blood however, after being told that the mistress of the house had allowed Briseis some time off to visit her mother. Atia had suspected that something might be going on between the servant girl and her son, so out of precaution (telling herself that she was protecting both the girl and her son) she had sent the temptation away.

For the next hour or so Octavius lay on his bed, unable to read. Simmering. He was furious at his mother for ruining his fun, interfering. He was also troubled by the fact that her sending Briseis away meant that she had most likely discovered the extent of their relations, and he dreaded the scene of having to discuss the matter with her. But more so Octavius was annoyed with himself - that the servant girl's absence had made him burn with such emotion and affect his mood. It did not help that every time he closed his eyes he thought of her. Although she probably had little choice in the matter, Octavius now turned against the object of his ardency for leaving him. Why had she gone? She hadn't even tried to say goodbye to him. She was just a whore and he should treat her that way. His frustration was intensified by the fact that there were no other girls like Briseis in the household. Not only did Octavius duly want to relieve himself of his disappointment and stress - and forget about Briseis - but in the act of taking another girl he would also be getting his revenge on her, not to mention his overly possessive mother. Octavius slyly smiled at the prospect of turning defeat into a victory. But his dejection soon returned, restlessly bubbling his blood and thoughts alike.

The sullen young noble unfairly and irrationally snapped at a couple of slaves when getting ready to depart for his afternoon lesson. Partly because he wanted to be alone, Octavius decided to ignore the instructions of his mother and venture over to Cleanthes' house without an escort. He ordered one of the staff to tell Oppius that he would be making his own way to the tutor's house. The centurion would not be happy - and the slave might even suffer a beating for being somehow remiss, but such was the saturnine mood that Octavius was enmeshed in that he didn't much care for the consequences of his actions.

6.

A wide-brimmed straw hat shaded his face in the midday sun. Octavius moistened his lips and as he did so, tasted the salt in the air. The journey would take a little longer, but he had decided to take the coastal path to his tutor's villa. As the solitary walker wended his way around a secluded bay, he couldn't help but be reminded of that similar, crescent shaped beach which he had landed upon that stormy evening.

The first thing Octavius remembered about the morning after was Roscius defending and deflecting jibes in relation to his aquatic prowess, or rather lack of.

"I come from Umbria. We have no need to be strong swimmers. When we do drown ourselves, it's in drink."

Perhaps it was from this morning onwards that Octavius noticed and liked the infantryman more. Roscius had been a soldier for most of his life, to the point where he knew nothing different. One campaign had blurred into another. The legionary held a vague dream of settling down one day on some land outside of Rome, but he was realistic enough to know that the idea was but a dream. The standard bearer was obedient in taking orders, yet could be left to think for himself in carrying them out. He was good-humoured yet disciplined; Octavius noted how the men respected, or feared, the giant of a soldier also. In battle he became a bear of a man. Yet Roscius was generous and patient with the inquisitive youth when Octavius near pestered him as to the life and details of soldiering. And also stories about Caesar. In return the illiterate legionary avidly listened to Octavius when he reported the feats of Odysseus, Achilles and Aeneas to him - sometimes quoting Homer from memory, word for word. So too Roscius was never far away from the boy when there was a hint of danger. Oppius had observed how the youth had taken to his friend - and so ordered Roscius to watch over the boy until they reached Caesar's camp.

For his own part, Oppius had little time for the privileged adolescent. He would do his duty by him - or rather Caesar - but that was all. Indeed a splinter of resentment towards the boy couldn't help but lodge in the centurion's heart as Oppius' task of babysitting had kept him from Caesar's side - and the rewards of a true campaign. He feared that, absent from the great dictator's side, he might miss out on worthwhile spoils and advancement. Campaigns, or deaths rather, provided promotions. There is always someone willing to stab you in the back and take your place, Lucius judged from experience. For a brief moment however, during the previous night, Oppius had been pleasantly surprised by the youth with his calm and courage under pressure; the boy had kept his head in the confusion and terror of the storm - and he had displayed hidden stamina in his swim to shore. But the sickly and over-studious boy would, at best, grow to be but the shadow of the man Caesar was. Although granting Octavius a modicum of respect for his display the night before, Oppius couldn't help but recall and compare the scene in Alexandria with his general. Whilst leading a sortie on a bridge in the city, Caesar and his cohort were suddenly counter-attacked. To save himself from capture Caesar daringly jumped off the bridge and into a boat. His men soon followed. Realising how the wounded needed space, he quickly ordered himself and his officers out of the small vessel. Oppius smiled, remembering the majestic sight of Caesar swimming two hundred yards to reach his fleet, holding his left hand out of the water to preserve some documents he was carrying, and clenching his purple cloak in his teeth to prevent his enemy from recovering it as a trophy.

There were around thirty survivors on the beach come morning. After the small reconnaissance and foraging party returned, Oppius took command of the bedraggled group (consisting of another centurion, a dozen legionaries and various other members of the cohort's retinue). Small cliques were forming, with the sound of the tide accompanied by murmurings of discontent. Some wanted to remain on the beach in the hope that a friendly vessel would sail by. Others wished to take their chances on their own, as a large group would attract attention and more likely be captured. But the focused centurion ordered that they break camp immediately. They would all make their way to Caesar's stronghold, which Oppius calculated was a three day march away.

"If we stay here, we die. What ships we spot will be enemy or pirate vessels. Storms on land I can steer us through. We have given our oaths to Caesar that we would deliver his nephew to him. Anyone that forsakes that oath will forsake their life."

"But how will we cross enemy territory?" a dissenting soldier, who was not a member of Oppius' own cohort, protested, taking it upon himself to speak what he thought was the majority opinion of the group.

"By not crossing me. I have time to *fight* anyone over this, but not argue," the centurion pronounced, with even the men who little knew of Oppius' reputation believing that he would make good his word - both in terms of leading them through the next few days and punishing anyone who opposed him. No one said a word later that afternoon when the dissenting soldier returned from a toilet break with a bruised eye and broken rib. Roscius came back with a sore hand.

"Be ready to leave by the time I've sharpened my sword. Anyone who lags behind will get left behind," the stone-faced soldier closed his brief address by stating.

Oppius' fellow centurion was no doubt disgruntled that he had assumed sole command, and a portion of the party were far from optimistic in regards to their fate, but nevertheless they broke camp and, much like now (as he stood and appreciated the Apollonian shore), Octavius gazed back down along the Spanish sands and thought to himself how beautiful nature was, as if created by the gods for our enjoyment and praise.

Not wishing to appear lacking, Octavius steeled and drove himself on whilst marching on that first day. Scouts were sent ahead and occasionally the group had to retreat into the woodland which flanked the dusty road on both sides, but for the most part the first day's march proved uneventful. From the bloodied and broken state of the soldiers, they observed it was clear to Oppius that the war was almost over in favour of Rome. Caesar had done it again.

Partly due to Octavius pushing himself to his physical limit, and having developed a slight chill from his swim, he grew weak and began to suffer shortness of breath as evening closed in. Without conveying the fact to the boy however, Roscius and Oppius had a pre-prepared signal, which Roscius would initiate, when he considered that Octavius needed to rest. At that point Oppius would allow the entire party to take a water break or catch their breath. He rolled his eyes or grunted slightly at having to organise his plans around the over-indulged youth, but nevertheless Oppius faltered not in doing his duty to the boy, or rather Caesar. Although it had been his intention to march throughout most of the evening, a brief word from Roscius made up his mind that the group should cessate their progress and sleep for an hour or so. With Oppius not permitting the group to light fires, arguing that it was "better to wake up shivering, than dead", Roscius sacrificed his cloak for the good-natured youth and used it as an extra blanket to keep the boy warm while he slept.

Later that evening, in the grey light of a swollen moon, Oppius and Roscius spoke about the day's events and the plan for the morrow.

"Will he be able to keep pace?" Oppius asked, fearing that he already knew the answer.

"Our pace? No. But the lad has done well. You should be pleased with him, impressed even," Roscius dared to say, in hope more than expectation of receiving a positive reaction from the hard-hearted centurion.

"You more than most of my friends know that I'm not easily impressed. I dare say necessity has also become the mother of invention for the boy to exert himself, rather than his mother exerting her need to be a necessity."

"You're too hard on the lad."

"He should thank me for it. Everyone else is far too easy on him. And he is nearly a man, not a boy. By the time I was his age I had killed - and more than once."

"And you're now old enough to know that's nothing to be proud of," Roscius replied, his expression momentarily pained as the veteran's heart recalled some of the best forgotten experiences of his own youth. Roscius fleetingly placed his hand on his brow, as if he felt a headache coming on, but then took a healthy swig from his fast emptying cup and regained his good humour.

"Would you want him standing by your side in a shield wall? That should be the question," Oppius asked.

"Not yet. But I'd certainly sit around and share a drink with him."

"But you'd drink with anyone."

"I know. Cheers." And with an affable smile upon Roscius' face, the two friends clinked cups and finished the last of the wine they had saved.

Despite nursing a hangover, Oppius made the aching-limbed party rouse with the dawn. They still had a lot of ground to cover. Again, scouts were sent ahead to reconnoitre the roads they intended to take. Oppius was now certain that Caesar had bested the enemy - the rebellious, Republican forces of Pompey's sons, Sextus and Gnaeus.

Perhaps even more so than yesterday, the day seemed uneventful to Octavius. It was now a matter of routine to stealthily retreat into the woods whenever a scout warned of a group of soldiers or natives approaching. At times Octavius even forgot his situation and his mind wandered. He noted how similar the landscape was to that of his family's estate in Velitrae, a small town just outside of Rome. The dry but fragrant air was the same. The wind rustled through the cypress trees in a familiar way. The crickets and thrushes spoke the same language. Even considering his bouts of illness and the loss of his father, Octavius' childhood in Velitrae had not been an unhappy one. In some ways his name had been a burden, but equally so the studious youth looked upon it as being something he should live up to. From as early as Octavius could remember it had been his heart's desire to please his great-uncle. And from his infrequent visits over the years and inspirational letters, Caesar was proud of his nephew. The gratification spurred the youth on the more to better himself, to study harder and be a good Roman. Octavius often couldn't help but fondly smile, remembering his privileged and fulfilling upbringing. But then a knowing and cautious expression would shape his features. Octavius was wise and pragmatic enough to focus on the future rather than dwell in the past.

The day was long. Dusk was short however. A deep mauve, which soon darkened to a bluish-black, combed itself across the sky. The firmament then grew hazier as a brash storm exploded in the air above them.

Octavius' feet grew even more leaden as the rain mulched the dirt road into mud. He might have even been pleased when one of the scouts returned and reported to Oppius that there was potential danger up ahead. They could now hide and find shelter. Rest.

A thin wisp of smoke spiralled upwards from a small house on the side of the road. Coarse laughter, as well as the smell of roasted venison, emanated from the dwelling. The second scout, who had remained with the house (and who had smeared himself in mud, camouflaged himself in branches, climbed a tree and assessed the enemy from close quarters), reported to Oppius that the enemy soldiers in the house numbered a dozen. He had also yet to notice a picket stationed up the road.

"I think we deserve that shelter and a hot meal more than they do men, eh?" Oppius said, wolfishly grinning to the soldiers who nodded in agreement, their eyes alert with the happy anticipation of both the fight and food. Oppius drew a quick sketch with a stick on some soft ground of the target. Four men, armed with javelins, would first attack in pairs through the two windows of the house. As soon as they struck however, Oppius, along with six other men from his legion, would come through the entrance to the cottage.

"Lose anything from your belt that isn't necessary. You'll need to be free to manoeuvre and react quickly once we're inside the house. Surprise is on our side and will do half the job. Immobilise rather than kill to begin with. Make every hit, cut, count. Roscius, I want you to remain here with Octavius. Regardless of what happens, I want you both to keep out of sight."

No word or movement was wasted. Octavius was frightened and excited as he watched Oppius and his band of brothers stealthily move through the woodland and approach the cottage. His chest swelled with the pride that he was in the presence of the best soldiers in the world, Roman legionaries. Out of the corner of his eye he noticed an anxious looking Roscius nervously biting his lip. He well knew that Oppius would succeed - and he understood how he needed to take care of Caesar's nephew - but it still felt strange being absent from his centurion's side in a fight. The water annoyingly collected and then heavily dripped down on his face from the leaves above, but Octavius, still wide-eyed, sucked in the scene.

The sound of the hissing shower was broken by the grunt of a legionary throwing his first javelin. The noise was quickly succeeded by a cacophony of confusing roars and agonising screams. Roscius grabbed the youth's shoulder, as if to hold him back, whilst in reality the action was taken to remind him why he had to remain back from the fight.

Oppius soon returned however, his face spotted with blood and crumbs of flesh - which were soon washed away in the drizzle. His arm however, up to his elbow, was dark crimson - and his sword was streaked with gore. He offered his standard bearer a brief nod to convey that everything and everyone was fine. Octavius heard the desperate protests and pleadings of an enemy prisoner in the background, but they were soon silenced. The brief blood-curdling scream which sliced through the night and into Octavius' ears turned his stomach, but still the youth was eager to witness the sight of the carnage in the house. Oppius frustrated this desire though and ordered that Roscius and he remain where they were until sentries were posted and the house was cleaned up.

Fed and warmed by the room's crackling fire, Octavius still found it difficult to sleep. His feverish imagination played tricks on his mind. The owl's hoot was amplified to a howl. The scuttling of a spider became a rat, with teeth as big as a hare's. The sound of the sentry's patrol outside was turned into the enemy approaching the house. As the Romans had ambushed the Spanish, Octavius imagined how they too could be assailed at any moment. He feared waking suddenly in the night to see a swarthy barbarian over him, with a blade at his throat, and thus was prevented from swiftly drifting off to sleep. Eventually however exhaustion got the better of his febrile thoughts and Octavius finally slipped into a quilted slumber.

7.

A gassy stench, similar to that of the refuse which sometimes built up when neglected from outside his own house, wafted up Octavius' nostrils as he went inland in the direction of his tutor's villa.

"Far more than my rumoured misanthropy, the inhospitable smell of the marshes keeps prospective visitors away," Cleanthes had once wryly remarked to his pupil. "I also can't help but have affection for the marshes, as their location and aesthetic saved me a welcome sum of money when purchasing the land."

Octavius scrunched up his features in disgust at the foul smell, and swept his hand in front of his face to brush away the cluster of flying insects swirling around him. He quickly ventured forward, however, along the squelching path, knowing full-well that he would soon come out into a quite different setting.

As the nauseating odour of the marshes had suddenly descended on Octavius like a noxious rain cloud, so too did the kaleidoscope of fragrances and colour strike his senses as he entered his tutor's garden through a half-concealed entrance. The menthol crispness of fresh mint and rosemary, as well as various other herbs, cleared out his nose immediately.

The faint sound of rustling, accompanied by the frequent metallic snap of a pair of garden shears, reverberated in the air. Octavius gazed, admiringly and amusedly, at his teacher whilst his back was turned to him. He was wearing a belted careworn cream gown made of a coarse material over an equally shabby tunic. His figure and movements were robust and senses alert though as, either through hearing or even smelling his pupil, Cleanthes ceased pruning his clematis and turned to Octavius.

Although he had been tutoring now for half of his adult life, Cleanthes considered himself to be an eternal student, rather than a teacher. His green eyes sparkled at seeing his accomplished pupil. There was an air of philosophical calm about the wistful gardener yet at the same time one sensed a restless mind at work: observing, collating, concluding, disregarding. His jade eyes shone brightly, but his skin was sallow and marked - both through pox scars and also insect bites. His dark brown hair and beard were also as unkempt as his clothes, shining with a film of grease.

Cleanthes was born in Athens. His father had been stable master to a series of Roman administrators. Such was his service to one of the ruling governors during his tenure upon the estate that the quaestor granted the stable master his freedom. Cleanthes' father, taking out a loan, quickly prospered as a horse trader, providing cavalry horses to the Roman army during its conflict with Mithridates. Wanting to give his son the kind of education that had been denied to him, Cleanthes' father enrolled his son in the finest academies and hired the most expensive tutors to teach his only child. And initially his investment paid off. Cleanthes proved to be a gifted pupil, proficient in logic, rhetoric and the practical sciences. When the feted student completed his studies he was courted by a number of wealthy patrons who offered the tutor various sums of money and gifts to join their particular household in a bid to out-do their neighbours. Initially Cleanthes declined. The attraction of spurning these incentives - and affecting an air of incorruptibility and intellectual independence - soon waned however, especially when his policy of rejection caused patrons to increase their offers.

Although it did not happen overnight, a certain dissoluteness and rebellious streak eventually instilled itself in the young sophist's life. Drink and women displaced his scholarly interests. Having tasted the pleasures of Athens, the moneyed young man even ventured to visit Rome to satiate his circadian appetites. The conceited academic told himself that his new way of life, centred among the taverns and brothels, was a philosophical experiment - for how can one know true virtue unless one has experienced vice? His dissolute reputation soon preceded him however, and his employment dried up.

Despondency and impoverishment followed hard. His father all but disowned him. An aged gardener, who worked outside of Athens, took him on. Cleanthes learned a trade and eventually freed himself from those vices which had eaten away at so much of the rest of his life - partly because he just couldn't afford his former lifestyle anymore. A year or so later his father died. He left his only son with a modest inheritance. Desiring a fresh start, Cleanthes moved to Apollonia and purchased the client list and equipment of a gardener there. He worked hard and supplemented his income, in order to buy some land and build a house, by privately tutoring a few select pupils. Within five years Cleanthes had earned enough money to settle into semi-retirement. He produced most of the food he needed himself and sold off any surplus at the market. He studied horticulture and occasionally still tutored the odd pupil who he believed had potential.

On the recommendation of Atticus, Cicero's trusted and learned friend, to Marcus Phillipus, Octavius was interviewed one day by the reclusive, but respected, tutor. Cleanthes was impressed by the youth and his willingness to learn - and it was a source of pleasure more than a task when Octavius visited him every week now. Such was the youth's progress that, in certain areas of epistemology and ethics, he had little left to learn. Cleanthes was impressed, yet a little saddened, by the young man's nihilistic thinking. Octavius had argued how there was no sovereign rationale for any course of action. "Meaning can be negated, or made to seem relative." It was one's will, or emotions - one's personality - which ultimately stimulated action. "Ideals are frippery, or afterthoughts that seemingly justify one's purpose. We put them on and take them off again like garments, according to the weather or whims. All is vanity." Octavius here briefly uncoupled his chain of thought. He half-smiled and shrugged, and then remarked, "Philosophers can and do argue themselves to death. Is it not soldiers, men of action - Alexanders, Sullas, Caesars - who rule and shape the world?" Upon another occasion recently, Cleanthes was struck by how much further reading his student must have been doing, unprompted by the tutor. Debating the theory of knowledge Octavius suddenly quoted Timons, "That honey is sweet I refuse to assert; that it appears sweet, I fully grant ... And how do we know what is sweet? What is sweetness? - We can infer, but we can never know ... Philosophy is but the sum of meaningless words ... Words, words, words." As superior as Octavius could feel in arguing such things, these conclusions would often dissatisfy the once idealistic student. Life should not be so annulled. Occasionally however such conclusions and theses would liberate the young nihilist: "If nothing is for certain, then everything is possible."

"You're late Octavius, again. The opening and closing of my tulips keeps better time."

"Fortunately or not, they do not have half of Polybius to read before they rise."

"You are beginning to have an answer for everything."

"I have had a good teacher."

"Or maybe your lateness furnished you with plenty of time to prepare an excuse. Whether you consider it a reward or punishment, I'd have you read the other half of Polybius to make up for your tardiness."

Octavius smiled and nodded his head slightly, assenting to his teacher's instruction, acknowledging his wit and apologising for his misdemeanour all in one gesture.

*

By now there were very few formal aspects to Octavius' lessons. For the most part Cleanthes just talked to his pupil and answered his questions, as one might converse with a familiar, older acquaintance. Whilst doing so Cleanthes often tended to his garden, infecting his student with an interest in horticulture and botany. Towards the end of the afternoon, as was his custom, Octavius turned the conversation towards Rome. He enjoyed his tutor's insights and witticisms in regards to the city's history, as well as its current statesmen and policies.

"When Caesar crossed the Rubicon, that now bloody river, Rome, as well as Caesar, crossed a point of no return. Or perhaps it was Gracchus who brought us here, or Sulla even. But Rome is fated to be seen as a prize that's won, rather than a master which must be served," Cleanthes remarked, his tone neither critical nor lauding Caesar, as he tied back some wayward vines on his plants with twine. "One can mourn the idea of the Republic, but not the reality. There were too many personalities, but not enough characters. Money spoke in the Forum, rather than principles. Vetoes were issued for petty reasons, such as who was sleeping with whose wife. Tribunes became demagogues or thugs, serving themselves rather than the electorate. People went hungry whilst others glutted themselves during extravagant feasts. The social and economic divides between rich and poor grew too pronounced - and everything tumbled into the chasm which was created by the divide. Soldiers were given broken promises. The Republic, Senate, was only consistent in its themes of greed and hypocrisy. Marians fought Sullans and vice versa, long after both men were dead. There were too many parasites bleeding Rome dry. 'Tis an unweeded garden," Cleanthes wryly posited, as he stretched down and plucked a couple of weeds out of the black soil of his vegetable patch.

"Men's ambitions and their desire to make a profit are among the most frequent causes of deliberate acts of injustice. People who lay out sums of money to secure office get into the habit, not unnaturally, of looking for something in return," Octavius enjoined, with a tinge of both sadness and anger in his tone, making reference perhaps to the corruption of the ability to collect taxes for Rome going to the highest bidder. Cleanthes nodded in agreement, and also in appreciation, of his student quoting Aristotle in his argument.

"But yet whilst terminally ill, the Republic is not quite dead yet. The Senate might have been won with the sword, but your great uncle's victory must be maintained by him unsheathing his wits and knowing when to compromise. Caesar will not be able to cut off the heads of all his enemies, for he will unleash a hydra by doing so. Should he unfairly vanquish an enemy, then two will stand in his place," Cleanthes warned, briefly pausing to watch a spider spin his web across his blackberry bush - smiling in anticipation and revenge, in that the web would catch some of the irksome insects which plagued him of an evening whilst he slept.

"Why do you not go to Rome? You could make a name for yourself. I could write to my uncle," the student asked his teacher, after a short pause.

"Thank you for the offer Octavius, but success would be the ruin of me," the tutor replied, his green eyes glimmering with a private joke as if he were quoting someone else.

"You could be the new Cicero."

"I'm not sure whether Marcus Tullius would be flattered by that or not. I reckon the ex-consul feels that he has some life in him yet, before he's replaced."

"Did you ever meet Cicero when you went to Rome?"

"Our meeting was brief, but memorable on my part. We met at a party thrown by a friend of mine. Cicero was the guest of honour, a position which he felt quite happy and comfortable with I dare say. He dressed smartly, but not ostentatiously - much like you, Gaius. He was neither old nor young when I encountered him, though there was definitely more vigour in his intellect than in his body. For a while I but observed the famous ex-consul. He was a great conversationalist, enjoying listening as well as speaking, albeit I dare say his favourite pastime was to act modestly when listening to people praise him. He could be vain, but self-effacing; critical, but forgiving. I couldn't help but be impressed by his naturally good, or assiduously trained, memory. He seemed to know everyone's name and business at the gathering, charming each guest equally with the attention he bestowed upon them. I finally drank enough wine to summon up the courage to approach him. He put me at ease immediately. We talked briefly about philosophy, with Cicero picking holes in his own writings. He also described a Cynic as being "but an ill-dressed and impoverished Stoic". He was openly satirical about his fellow senators, and the more powerful the patrician, the crueller the barb. He also instructed me a little about the art of oratory, principally by advising me of what not to do. "Just as lame men ride on horseback because they cannot walk, so too our new crops of orators shout because they cannot speak," he posited. My true claim to fame however, in regards to Cicero, is that I had the honour of witnessing him compose an original epigram in my presence. I commented upon how fine the port was. He paused briefly, with a good-humoured smile upon his face, and remarked, or rather I should say composed the following:

*'There is nothing more to this life*
*Than some cheap port and a good wife.*
*But a cheap wife and some good port*
*Is a life too I cannot fault.'*

I smiled as much at the witticism as upon seeing the great Cicero a little drunk. In some ways he is still the First Man of Rome and I know Cicero would be flattered to hear you say that. But even Caesar remarked that he should have won greater laurels than that of Rome's Generals, for rather than expand its territories, Cicero has expanded Rome's genius. Many men have tried to be the voice of Rome over the years, but Cicero has I warrant more of a claim now than most, for in his speeches and writings he has revolutionised its vocabulary and articulated its ideals. It's still important to let the old consul be heard, but of equal importance is not to listen sometimes," Cleanthes said in a hushed, confidential voice, as though someone else might be listening.

"What about Cato? Did you ever encounter him?"

"No. Unfortunately, or fortunately, I didn't ever have the opportunity to meet Cato. I still quite haven't worked him out. But not even the greatest philosopher in the world - which the Senator might have once argued was himself - could rightly discern when Cato was displaying virtue, or vanity."

"And Pompey the Great?"

"He spent half his life making his name - and the other half failing to live up to it. But now I am giving you witticisms rather than answers, Gaius. And that is no laughing matter," the whimsical teacher remarked, amusing himself rather than his pupil now.

8.

Octavius ventured back home. It was now late afternoon but dusk was resting on the horizon to take the sting out of the vermillion sun. The baked dirt track meandered, as too did the young man's thoughts idly wander - sifting and remembering his recent conversations with Cleanthes. The subject of Cicero (the "Greek-Roman" as his tutor described him) in particular coloured his thoughts. He half-smiled again, recalling his tutor's judgement of him.

"Cicero is fond of saying that he is dedicated to truth, which is why he has admitted in the past that he is nothing but an actor."

Yet, for all of the satire and barbed comments surrounding the ex-consul, both Cleanthes and Caesar had spoken well of Cicero. Octavius remembered how Caesar had even given his copy of '*On The Nature Of The Gods*' to him - and for a month or so he immersed himself in Cicero's dialogues and philosophy. The adolescent couldn't help but admire and be inspired by some of his teachings, and equally so his elegant writing style, which impressed upon the intellect and heart alike. Octavius had read his works avidly and repeatedly. Night time had been illuminated by his polished prose and enlightening instruction. Many a time had he hoped to be in Rome with Caesar and introduced to the legendary statesman. Yet always Cicero had been away, or Caesar had been busy.

*"I am one of those people who can more easily see why something is false than why it is true ... If conscience goes, then everything collapses around it ... Philosophy is a physician for souls, taking away the burden of empty troubles, setting us free from desires, vanquishing fears ... There is nothing so absurd but some philosopher has said it."*

As much as his step-father, or Caesar even, Cicero had influenced his education and character Octavius suddenly thought, surprising himself a little by the realisation.

The student was wrenched from his reveries however, on hearing the increasing tamp of horse hooves upon the road ahead. His heart began to canter also in ominous trepidation. Even when young Octavius couldn't help but be conscious of the potential dangers and enemies he might incur in being Caesar's nephew. As either a target for ransoming, or a source of bloody revenge, he was fair game for the many opponents of Caesar. And Octavius was still young; he still became unnerved by the introduction of a furtive looking stranger, lively footsteps across the gravel pathway in the dead of night, and the sound of a potential raiding party of horsemen or pirates. Childhood nightmares, consisting of him waking up and having his throat slit, or being hunted down by a band of bloodthirsty cavalry, had not receded completely.

The sound of the four horses, sixteen hooves, drummed upon the ground to create one continuous, violent roar. The ox bow curve of the trail meant that Octavius was blind to the approaching group of horsemen. Surrounded by a cloud of dust the snorting horses careered around the corner. Octavius recognised the Roman uniform and the man leading the quartet immediately. His tense body justly uncoiled itself when he spied Roscius. The legionary, slightly ungainly on top of his chestnut mare, shouted out an order to stop to his men. Octavius remained where he stood upon the side of the road, affecting a state of calm insouciance in marked contrast to the breathless horsemen. The imposing legionary, cursing his charge (and also himself), clumsily wheeled his horse around and trotted back towards the wayward youth.

Roscius' bristled face conveyed relief and then stern authority. He was thankful of locating the boy quickly.

"You shouldn't be travelling alone, Octavius. More importantly, you shouldn't be upsetting Oppius," Roscius remarked, torn between wishing to rebuke the young master of the house, and finding his daring and defiance amusing. For all of the years he had known his centurion, through winning over his men and campaigning on four corners of the map, it was a teenager who now proved to be his most challenging antagonist.

Octavius but half heard the advice and warnings of Roscius, partly distracted as he was by the memory of a similar scene. Fear had also been happily and swiftly succeeded by relief back then as a group of ominous sounding horsemen approached their shipwrecked party in Spain. It had been the morning after the attack on the cottage. The woodlands had thinned out and the group marched through dusty plains and farmland. A couple of distant plumes of smoke animated the pale skies from where Pompeians, or Caesar, had instigated a scorched earth policy. The party was weary with each member, bar the tireless lead centurion, harbouring a suspicion that they were perhaps lost. Oppius heard the doom-laden noise first, fearing that his scouts up ahead had been lost to the prospective enemy horsemen. With an absence of forest cover to retreat into, Oppius quickly, but far from desperately, ordered the party to form square - the cohort's defensive formation to combat a cavalry attack. A square was efficiently formed, betraying years of practise and drilling. Shields were interlocked. Spears then protruded out from the fence of large, curved scutums like the spines on the hide of a porcupine - upon which not even the most daring, or stupid, horse would ride onto. A half a dozen men - including Oppius, Roscius and Octavius - occupied the centre of the square. Oppius was thankful - and praised Fortuna under his breath - that he had a trio of archers next to him. Roman confidence, with a shard of a threat, imbued his tone as the centurion advised the party that if they held their defensive positions and made their arrows and javelins count, they had nothing to fear.

"We will be fighting an already defeated army. They won't even need an excuse to flee, but I'd like to give them one all the same," Oppius exclaimed in order to ease some of the tension etched in the faces around him.

Octavius stood close behind the battle-ready Roscius. His mouth was dry, with both thirst and fright. His legs, which not five minutes before had felt stiff from marching, now felt loose - to the point where he thought that they would give way if he ran. A natural sense of dread sent a shudder down his spine, to a degree where the youth felt that an actual serpent could be slithering up and down his back. He shivered, yet sweated in the heat.

The thunderous tumult of hooves grew closer, louder. Octavius darted a quick look at Oppius and even he wiped the perspiration from his brow and gripped his javelin with apprehension. Out of the corner of his other eye Octavius was briefly distracted by the sight of an archer's bicep bulge as he nocked an arrow and drew the drawstring back on his bow in readiness.

The bright scarlet plume on the Roman cavalry officer's helmet shone all the more starkly in the sepia-tinged landscape. The collective sigh of relief, or deliverance even, from the shipwrecked party was palpable as the decurion and his patrol saluted their fellow Caesarians. Believers and non-believers alike gave praise to Victoria, Jove, or some other indistinct deity.

The decurion, having encountered Oppius' scout, had galloped towards the party upon hearing that Caesar's nephew was with the group. After the battle Caesar had been looking forward to seeing the boy - yet over the last day or so he had grown anxious as to the reason why he hadn't reached them already. Knowing how much Caesar favoured the youth, the decurion was keen to treat the boy well. He made sure to warmly, yet deferentially, greet the dictator's nephew.

Octavius was all too aware of the cavalry officer's flattery also upon saying how brave and tough he was to have survived the shipwreck and marched so far, so quickly. Although Octavius replied that everyone was to be praised for equalling the feat he duly separated himself from the hardship of the group by accepting the decurion's offer to ride with him as they escorted everyone back to the camp.

Octavius' privileged position also afforded him the opportunity to catch-up on the latest news as the cavalry officer reported upon the success of the campaign to Oppius. Gnaeus Pompeius was dead, killed whilst fleeing. Sextus was still believed to be commanding his troops in Cordoba, but he could well now be retreating and heading for the coast. The key battle had been at Munda, on a slope outside of the hill town. Caesar had tried to draw the enemy down from the higher ground but Gnaeus Pompey, learning from his father's mistake at Pharsalus, refused to give up his advantage and remained resolute. Caesar would have to come to him.

And so Caesar's legions, outnumbered yet more experienced than their opponents, moved up the slope towards Pompey's forces. They wavered yet broke not under a shower of javelins. Many of his men were already fatigued from the long march to reach the enemy. Perhaps this was one battle too many for even the indomitable Tenth Legion, Caesar's loyal favourite which had followed him across Gaul, Germania, Britannia and to Pharsalus and Egypt. His army wasn't retreating, but the momentum of his advance had faltered. At best the battle hung in the balance. Caesar acted. He suddenly dismounted and charged through his own battle lines, grabbing a shield from a mesmerised legionary. The General then imperiously stood out in front of his army, his scarlet cloak billowing in the wind. To attract the attention of his men - and enforce the fact that it was indeed Caesar who stood before them - he removed his burnished helmet.

At the very least the front ranks were distracted from their burgeoning fears and the gruesome sight of so many of their fallen comrades bloodily strewn around them.

"Aren't you ashamed to let your general be beaten by mere boys?" Caesar opened with, waving a dismissive hand towards an enemy army filled with raw, teenage recruits. A storm of anger and defiance was worn in the imperator's usually gregarious and handsome brow.

"Only victory will bring peace to Rome and these lands. Defeat will bring more than dishonour. If we win that hill then we shall not only win the spoils of war, but also our freedom and the right to return home. But if we fail here, this will be the end of my life - and the end of more than just your careers."

Pride, fury and resolution began to transform the visages of the officers and legionaries around Caesar. Centurions ordered men to form ranks again. The familiar, rousing sound of swords and spears drumming upon shields began to reverberate down the line. The ever-alert general also heard the sound however of orders and movement behind him, from the enemy, as a section of their front rank released a volley of javelins - aimed at the commander. The deadly missiles spewed into the air, clouding out the blue sky, screaming with violence. Agile for his age - and fearless from so many victorious campaigns - Caesar (or 'Fortune's son', as some of his friends and enemies had called him over the years) evaded some of the whistling darts, whilst angling his shield to deflect the others. Still the hordes of spears arched over the hillside and stabbed down upon the general to the point where the sight of Caesar disappeared in the rainstorm of missiles. Both sides knew - cut off the head, the body will fall. Even the veterans of the Tenth held their breath in anticipatory fear - and so too the rest of the legions instinctively realised that if Caesar fell their cause, livelihoods, were lost. His fate was inexplicably, yet tangibly, linked to theirs. They were one. A collective sigh of relief succeeded the baited quiet. Caesar, his splintered shield resembling a pin cushion, lived. Perhaps the gods truly did favour their undefeated general. Perhaps Caesar was even a god himself. A cheer, part triumphal, part goading towards their enemy, went up.

"It looks like their aim is as steady as their hearts. Well, what are you waiting for?!" And, to the thunderous roar of the stirred-up ranks, Caesar drew his sword and proceeded to stride up the slope towards Pompey's formations, as if he were prepared to fight the enemy on his own. But Caesar would be far from alone. Even before a riled centurion bellowed and punctured the air with a rousing "Onward!" many of the men had already commenced to surge forward, a rippling tide of steel and nerve. The ground rumbled. Men flocked around their valorous general, forming a protective wall of shields around him. The thought that they had nearly just lost him redoubled their efforts to protect their commander in chief - and fight for him. Yet Caesar had no intention to remain behind a shield wall and survey the battle from a distance. He would stay at the vanguard of his beloved Tenth Legion, spurring them on. His sword was as bloodied as any man's in the ensuing fight. Rear ranks on both sides pushed the forward ranks on, the roars of the former often drowning out the wails of the latter. For a time the battle remained at a stalemate, with Death alone reigning supreme. Charon, the ferryman, would be busy by nightfall. Bloodily, steadily, Caesar and his Tenth Legion began to inch their way forward up the hill, diminishing Pompey's left wing. Pompey, realising the danger - and fearing that history was about to repeat itself (it had been Caesar's veteran Tenth Legion which had broken his father's left flank at Pharsalus) ordered his cavalry over from his own right wing to bolster his wavering left. Caesar, upon being informed of the opposing general's move, promptly told one of his staff officers to seek out his own cavalry commander, Nonius Asprenas. The order relayed was for Asprenas to attack the enemy's left wing, preying upon the withdrawal and weakening of Pompey's forces there. The young, inexperienced recruits however, which populated Gnaeus Pompey's centre, mistook their general's troop movement for a retreat. Confusion fed upon itself. Like men jumping from a sinking ship the resolve of the virginal soldiers dissolved. Men fled - in their thousands - dropping weapons, either running towards Munda or out into the expansive Spanish plains behind them. The retreat was soon transformed into a rout. Caesar's cavalry cut down hundreds, like farmhands scything down wheat. A few of Pompey's men fought on, like Pompey the Great's veteran Fourteenth Legion - fighting to the death rather than surrendering. But Caesar had remained undefeated in his final battle. The civil war, after five long years, was all but over.

After the decurion's summary of the battle, Oppius questioned the cavalry officer as to who had survived, or who had been lost, in the engagement - concerned as he was for old comrades and his chances of advancement. Octavius, however, lost interest in the exchange and became occupied with his own thoughts. As gripped as the youth had been by the account, he also felt awe-struck by Caesar's dramatic heroism - and anxious that he was now about to be confronted by him again. As egotistical as the accomplished teenager had become over the last couple of years, he naturally felt small, inadequate, as he placed himself before Caesar. A wave of admiration, other-worldliness and intimidation, ran through him even upon just whispering the name. Caesar was dictator, pontifex maximus, the conqueror of Gaul, Germania and Pompey. He had won more battles - and pushed back the frontiers of the Empire - more than any other Roman. Writer. Great orator. Winner of the corona civica. Indeed Octavius realised that he perhaps had a deeper and firmer relationship with the idea of Caesar, rather than with the actual man. As well as being quite daunted by the prospect of being summoned by Caesar,

Octavius felt a certain privilege in that, whereas kings and other great men would bow and call him Caesar, he could call him his great-uncle. At the same time though, Octavius could be acutely aware that, rather than being his own person, his existence only inherited any value through being Caesar's nephew. But why had he been now summoned by his great-uncle, Caesar? Had the last five years changed him? Octavius smiled when recalling the affection and generosity his uncle had once bestowed on him after the twelve year old boy had composed the oration at Caesar's mother's funeral. Caesar had wept at his words. The following morning Octavius woke to the gift of being presented with half a dozen books that his uncle had recommended him to read the evening before, as the two of them, alone, had spoken about literature and "being a Caesar" on the balcony of his villa. "Always be the best," his uncle had stated. Those words had been a spur, and burden, to the sickly boy ever since. Octavius' fond, reflective expression soon returned to a more serious, anxious form. Years of campaigning, a war which had torn the world in two, must have taken its toll. Stories of executions had replaced stories remarking upon Caesar's clemency. He had heard the gossip of how Caesar had been seduced by a young Egyptian queen. The dictator had even erected a statue made from gold, dedicated to his decadent mistress, inside the Temple Of Venus. It was sacrilege. What the young, stoical Roman first considered untrue eventually became unjustifiable, un-Roman.

*

Whilst in Munda the weary teenager had accepted the offer to ride on the back of a horse towards the army camp, Octavius politely here declined Roscius' invitation to ride on the back of his mount in order to reach home sooner - and placate Oppius. He would walk. Despite his fatigue and eagerness to return home Octavius, to flaunt the fact that he considered himself free from the authority of the domineering centurion, occasionally slowed himself down and stopped altogether on his way back to the house, whether to take in a view or examine a specimen of plant life. But it wasn't the flint-faced, reproving figure of Oppius who greeted Gaius Octavius when he returned home. It was someone rather different, in every way.

9.

Briseis. The lone demure figure of the eighteen year old servant girl standing outside of the front of the house captured Octavius' attention immediately, like thunder or sunshine. Roscius, and the small group of horsemen flanking him, took their leave of the young master of the house after they had passed through the gates of the estate. She cocked her head a little, slyly smiling as he approached - as though she knew and appreciated what the lusty youth was thinking. Her almond eyes narrowed and smiled, as sultry as the heat. Octavius tried to conceal his pleasure at seeing the girl, but for once his marble expression was fractured and his feelings, desires, poured through the cracks. They walked towards each other, a certain humorous (giggly, flirtatious) expression lining their semblances. Octavius removed his sun hat and ran his hand through his golden hair to straighten it out. Her honey skin glowed in the blush of dusk; she prettily tucked a couple of strands of her long, sable hair out of her eyes and behind her ears. Her dress was cream-coloured, made from Egyptian cotton; the perspiration from her previous labours caused the material to cling to her alluring figure (her round, pert breasts, contoured waist and strong, supple thighs). In order to make herself pretty for her young master, and to stress how the servant considered herself above a slave, Briseis adorned herself with jewellery - a necklace strung together with some semi-precious amethyst stones, which shimmered with the azure of the ocean. Bright copper bangles decorated her wrists. The serving girl had also borrowed a delicate gold chain, which she had stolen from her mother's room at home, which she wore as an anklet to help direct attention to her feet and shapely calves. Briseis' mother had herself used the trinket, a gift from a lover, many years before. Before, when Briseis had tried to wear jewellery, Atia had chastised the serving girl, ordering her to remove "every last cheap bauble" and to not get ideas above her station again. But the jealous old woman wasn't here anymore. Briseis would have Octavius to herself for once. Briseis' mother, Helena, was at first both a little confused and upset in response to her daughter's request to return to her duties having been given time off - but her daughter's performance of displaying a sense of duty and a work ethic eclipsed any suspicions or doubts she owned in regards to her motives.

Helena had herself been a slave who had obtained her freedom. Or rather the master of the house had conveniently bestowed it upon her out of precaution from his wife finding out about his affair with the kitchen girl. Once free, Briseis' mother sold herself as a prostitute. At first Helena resented the arrival of the unwanted Briseis, but she duly brought the girl up on her own. Her father could have been any number of men, none of which she could dare compromise. She found time to earn a good living as mistress to various Roman officers and bureaucrats. As her beauty waned - and her trade dried up - Helena increasingly sacrificed her own time and energies for her daughter. She saved some money in order that her daughter would not have to lead the life that she had. She would try and give Briseis the right education - so she could marry and become a lady. But Helena was not an alchemist - and one cannot fashion gold from brass. The first tutor she had, the teenage girl seduced. The second attempted to seduce her. The next couple of tutors – women - gave up on the wilful, ignorant girl. And so, to teach her a lesson so to speak, Helena had sent her daughter off to work as a servant - in hope that in discovering how desultory the work was she would prefer to return to her studies and embrace her mother's ambitions for her. Yet Briseis cultivated ambition more than her mother could have fancied. She would be a Caesar's concubine - was that not better than a life of being a wife to any other man?

The fatigue that Octavius had experienced - and the anxiety he felt at having to encounter a rankled Oppius - evaporated as soon as he entered the gates to the estate. The centurion wasn't even a memory anymore. Desire now consumed his heart...as well as other organs. Briseis had returned for no other reason but him. Octavius had hoped that he'd performed well as a lover, but did this not prove it? Yet, in quieter moments, Octavius also hoped that he was stimulating the girl not just through the act of sex, but rather he desired to touch her heart and instil in the girl the kind of finer feelings that he felt for her. He could not remember who had made the first advance between them. Initially they shared but clandestine glances. More than anyone else it was Briseis who Octavius would request to perform an errand for him. She laughed at his jokes. Her Latin was poor and so he used Greek, improving it as he did so. Indeed Octavius began to ask Cleanthes how he could improve his vocabulary - and what did Greek girls like? The former amorous tutor duly advised his pupil, half amused by the smitten student and half concerned for him. Love can be a sickness, as well as a salve he warned. Coy glances over the dinner table soon became more open and coquettish on the girl's part. She often brushed past him; her dress would be unbuttoned a little to reveal the promise of her perspiring bosom as she leaned over and re-filled his water jug. He tried to engage her intellectually. He would quote Euripides. He mentioned how beautiful her name was - and was she named after the Briseis of the Iliad, the woman who captured the heart of Achilles? Her reply was to shrug disinterestedly, cutting off Octavius' intended speech about Homer and the power of poetry before he even began. Yet he happily dropped the subject, captivated by the enticing smile upon her moist, pink lips.

He soon veritably lived for her laugh, and Octavius was but a shadow of himself when out of her company. They got into the routine of Briseis bringing the young master some light supper to his room of an early evening. She gazed at him with wonder and seduction as Octavius recounted some of the deeds and sayings of his great-uncle. Briseis, for her part, would tell him how other servants mistreated her, or confess how she worried for her future and that she did not want to marry someone she didn't love. Or the girl would ask him how she should wear her hair, or if a new piece of jewellery looked nice. One evening, when Atia and Marcus Phillipus were staying the weekend on a neighbouring estate, the serving girl stole a jug of wine to bring it to Octavius with his meal. They drank it together. His aspect glowed with drunkenness and desire. After a bout of giggling about nothing in particular, Briseis suddenly got up from the bed which they were sitting upon and twirled in front of the virginal youth.

"Oh, I forgot. Do you like? I just bought it?" the girl said excitedly, showing off both her new dress and the sweet-smelling figure inside of it. Briseis tantalisingly hitched up the skirt of the russet coloured garment to reveal a sun-kissed leg.

Octavius was too dumbstruck, awed, shy, possessed to reply. Before he had a chance however to give in to the temptation to reach out and touch the dress, or rather drunkenly paw its wearer, Briseis twirled once more, lost her balance and fell upon the Roman. He caught her by her hips as she fell towards him upon the bed, yet also he clutched her towards him - and Briseis fell willingly into his arms. Her soft thigh nestled itself into his groin. Her hands were pressed either side of his head, her scented hair falling around his flushed face. For a brief moment there was a pause, but then their lips mutually met. They kissed tentatively at first, then seductively - and then hungrily. The bed creaked a little. The flame upon the candle wriggled. The aromatic smell of the girl's hands, from where she had been working in the kitchen with spices, filled the air. For half a minute or so an aroused, awakened Octavius groped and felt every part of the girl's lithe body, which he had yearned to touch for so long. Briseis soon took control however - she grabbed his hands, entwining her spidery fingers in his. She kissed him softly and slowly, briefly sucking on his bottom lip as she withdrew. By now, without him noticing it - but yet Octavius appreciated it all the same - Briseis had straddled herself over her young master. The nubile but experienced woman pulled her skirt up so it was bunched around her waist, her thighs bare and bronze in the candlelight. With one hand she undid the buttons of her dress, provocatively slipping each side off her smooth shoulders to let the dress fall and reveal her round, hardening breasts. Octavius gazed up at her, adoringly, absorbing and admiring Briseis as if she were a goddess who had sparked a fire within him. His erotic dreams of her were coming true. On another night he might've even wept with happiness at the scene.

They made love when possible after that revelatory evening, although no matter how many times Octavius took Briseis, or vice versa, it was never enough for the youth. Satisfaction only fed his appetite. Sometimes the servant girl almost had to fight her young lover off as she refused to allow stolen kisses to transform themselves into something more time and energy consuming. And partly she denied Octavius to tease him - and increase his anticipation, as well as her power over him.

10.

Rome.

The moon slipped behind a brown-grey cloud but still his lean, bony face shone pale in the glossy night. On more than one occasion his senatorial companion for the evening thought that Cassius Longinus looked like a ghost, such was his bloodless pallor. The milky radiance of the moonlight was displaced by the orange glow of torches as a quartet of former lictors, who had served two optimate consuls, illuminated the meeting between the two conspiratorial statesmen.

It was the dead of night, even the stars appeared sleepy. The two men stood atop Capitoline Hill, under the adamantine gaze of Lucius Iunius Brutus. The sword was unsheathed in the hand of the statue, symbolic of the legendary figure's duty to forever defend the Republic. He had even executed his own two sons for conspiring against the state. Marcus Brutus thought it was a cheap, transparent trick for Cassius to arrange for them to meet before his ancestor's statue, but more than once of late he had himself traversed up the hill and stood before the famed Roman who had vanquished Tarquin the Proud - a despotic King - and established the Republic. Neither of the two men mentioned the graffiti that had been inscribed upon part of the plinth. '*O that we had you now, Brutus.*' '*Would that Brutus was alive.*' The descendant of the first consul did not need to read the phrases again, for it seemed now they were carved, or branded, upon his conscience. Cassius however did not need to scan and mention the graffiti because he had been the author behind the inscriptions; so too Cassius had been behind the anonymous letters sent to the praetor's house, calling on him to defend the Republic. '*Brutus, are you asleep?*' '*You are no true Brutus.*' In the past the spiteful practical joker had employed the use of similar anonymous letters to cause mischief. Cassius had revealed to fellow senators that their wives were having affairs, or alternatively he had blackmailed and extorted money out of his victims to help him pay off his debts. Or sometimes he composed various missives just to amuse his black humour. Yet now Cassius could tell himself that his deceptions were ultimately honourable, to the extent even that he could and should be forgiven for all his previous misdemeanours.

An acrid smell filled Brutus' nostrils as Cassius' breath misted up in front of him in the gelid air. For a moment Brutus fleetingly fancied that the smell came directly from the source of the man's bitter heart. More than from any Republican principle Brutus knew only too well that Cassius' motives were borne from ambition and a personal sense of vengeance against Caesar. It still rankled Cassius that Caesar had confiscated his pride of lions which he had intended to display during Rome's Public Games. So too Brutus himself had been involved in provoking Cassius, yet was not Caesar also responsible for that episode? Both men had been competing for the Praetorship of Rome. The dictator finally summoned both candidates to stand before him, his judgement being thus, "Cassius has the stronger case, but we must give Brutus the first Praetorship." It was not a love of Republicanism which had eventually prompted Cassius to heal his rift with Brutus, but rather it was his hatred for Caesar and his need to recruit Brutus to his cause. Whilst Brutus resented the idea of dictatorship, Cassius resented the dictator.

"Soon Caesar will join his army; or rather I should call them hired mercenaries, for they serve him rather than Rome. Once ensconced with his legions he will prove untouchable. We must strike at the heart of his despotism in the Forum, the home of the Republic. And we must act soon. After the Ides I warrant that it is his intention to leave for Apollonia to collect his precious whelp of a nephew and march on to subdue the Parthians."

Brutus here briefly thought of Octavius. He had met him on a couple of occasions and was justly impressed with the youth. At first he seemed shy, or rather observant, as he positioned himself in a corner of the room. When Caesar introduced his nephew to Brutus though he found the teenager to be confident, well-read and witty. Brutus hoped however that Octavius was not susceptible to certain other, darker, Caesarian traits.

"Agreed. The Forum it is," Brutus replied, with perhaps as much resignation as resolution entwined in his voice.

Marcus Brutus was a man of few words but yet when he spoke people listened. And whatever he said, he meant. The loose folds of his woollen toga could not disguise his muscular build. His face was squarish, strong and handsome - if a little humourless. Pompey once joked that Brutus had even come out of the womb with the demeanour and seriousness of a forty-three-year-old. Yet Brutus was not without a sense of humour, contrary to what some of his detractors might have sniped - but the need to laugh, smile and flatter were of secondary importance to the judicious Roman.

Cassius smiled - his white teeth momentarily flashing in the darkness - and clasped a fraternal hand upon his fellow conspirator's shoulder. As much as Cassius was central to the plot, he knew that he needed Brutus, his reputation and name, as a figurehead. Finally Cassius dared to call the priggish but influential senator a "libertore", a freedom fighter.

"You represent both the old and hopefully new Rome my friend. The people look to other praetors for public doles, spectacles and gladiatorial shows but they look to you to deliver them from tyranny."

"Should we include Cicero?" Brutus asked, all but ignoring Cassius' rehearsed flattery.

"No. The new man is now an old man. Even if I thought he could keep his mouth shut before the deed, I dare say he would be unbearable should we succeed. He would doubtless try to propagate the argument that he was the saviour of Rome again - and that we should honour him with a triumph for delivering the Republic. No, Cicero has become weak, foolish. He's become as garrulous as Nestor. He either lives in the past or dreams of fantastical futures that only he can orchestrate. Did you also catch the story of how he cried like a baby after hearing about his daughter's death?"

Brutus declined to respond, but he judged that it was not weakness which had made Cicero weep so for the estimable Tullia, but love. And love bred strength. He briefly thought of the strength he gained from Porcia and fondly smiled to himself (albeit Cassius believed his companion was smirking at his jibes). But no, Cicero could not wholly be trusted, Brutus concluded. Despite being opposed to the idea of dictatorship, there was a strange bond between Caesar and Cicero - and the personal could affect the political. Brutus respected the ex-consul, perhaps as much as his former mentor Cato, but Cicero would want to seek a compromise. For Brutus there could be none. His reasoning, or rather logical syllogism was thus: Monarchy is bad. Caesar desires to be King. Therefore, Caesar is bad.

"My concern is rather with Antony," Cassius issued.

"No. Our cause is to kill a man who would make himself a King, not murder one of his subjects who could redeem himself and become a good citizen and servant of Rome. Mark Antony may have proved himself to be corrupt, incompetent and a bully - but he isn't a tyrant. The purity of our cause would be tainted with his blood on our hands. History must judge us as liberators, not murderers," Brutus replied.

"You underestimate how much trouble he could cause."

"And you overestimate him, Cassius. He's little more than a drunk and a letch. Once we have done the deed, as you say, we will send him off to some distant battlefield, where he belongs. I would stake my honour on posterity not remembering Mark Antony."

"But he is Caesar's right arm."

"And he can do no more than Caesar's arm, when Caesar's head is off. Our cause is justice Cassius, not revenge or ire," Brutus calmly, but firmly, charged.

The wind suddenly howled, congealing the air even more. Cassius drew his toga tighter to his lean body - trapping the warm air between his skin and the silk laden material. He stamped his feet to quicken his ice-ridden blood. He glanced at his companion to see him register the cold also, but Brutus remained unperturbed by the sudden drop in temperature. Cassius believed that his fellow conspirator was equally chilled however - but that he was either too proud or affected to admit it.

"Lepidus too will serve Rome rather than Caesar when he is removed. He is a soldier, and soldiers follow orders," Brutus confidently remarked in reference to Rome's Master of the Horse, whose troops were posted just outside the city.

"And what about the people? His reforms have purchased their love. They could riot," Cassius warned.

"You say the people love Caesar. But the people also loved Gracchus and Marius and Clodius and Pompey. They love anyone who puts on a show for them and doles out corn. They are as constant, yet changeable, as the weather," Brutus issued; his tone imbued with a certain amount of disdain for 'the people', who he was intending to liberate and, as a praetor, had vowed to serve. "I will address the people afterwards. You saw their reaction at Lupercalia. For all of their wishes to put their demagogue up on a pedestal, they will be grateful for us toppling Caesar when they are told the truth."

Cassius nodded in agreement, but shared not his friend's confidence.

\*

Brutus, along with his torch bearers, descended the hill alone. Cassius walked off in the opposite direction, deflecting the question as to where he was heading. Brutus marched, as if still on campaign with a legion, and every now and then the former lictors trotted a couple of steps to keep up with their master.

Even from half-way down the hill the senator could still see a fair amount of the city below him, white and grey in the moonlight. From left to right he scanned the Campus Martius and the phalanx of tents, ordered like its own city. The meandering Tiber, like liquid jade, flowed and glistened in the background. Brutus briefly remembered how Caesar, when he had been his mother's lover, had taught him to swim in the river one summer. Always his thoughts turned back to Julius. Compelled. Condemned.

The gardens of Lucullus possessed an air of colour and vitality even in the distance, in the dark. Maybe the pleasure-loving ex-consul had been right to retire from the political circus of Rome and the Senate. But this idle fancy of the Roman praetor was ultimately rootless. Duty was the highest pleasure.

The Forum, Senate House and Sacred Way remained bold and divine even in silhouette for the devout Republican as they stood before him. Yet, whereas he once strode up the Sacrae Via filled with the pride of achieving his ambition of becoming a Senator, Brutus of late felt repulsed and righteously indignant during his time spent, wasted, in the Forum. It was a farce to think that the Republic was still just that. It was fast becoming a royal court, filled with cronies and profligates.

A patternless group of dimly burning oil lamps littered a large part of the landscape, where the masses resided. A fire from a house, which thankfully seemed to be under control, illuminated the less scenic and less celebrated quarter of the city, the Subura. Caesar had once lived there. Was that why he could sympathise with the people so? The flames flickered out into the void like a serpent's tongue tasting the air, and lit up the wooden and red clay roofs of the surrounding jerry-built tenement blocks which stood, or rather leant, like a blot upon the landscape. Each room would be crammed with more than one family, often immigrants, with little or no access to running water or other basic amenities. Sooner or later the building would collapse or be consumed in a fire, if disease did not kill off the tenants first. When would Rome finally have its own official fire brigade and all-encompassing sewer and aqueduct system? The Senate would not pay for it and the people couldn't. As much concern and compassion as Brutus felt for some of his fellow citizens - indigent, trapped - the Roman aristocrat could also feel a strain of contempt and snobbery towards "the great unwashed", as Cicero called them, slavish to demagogues like Caesar and parasitic by nature.

It was so late that Brutus barely encountered a soul during his walk home. Even the nocturnal thugs and low-lives had drunk themselves into a stupor by now, or were in the arms of some poxed harlot within one of the city's sordid brothels. Despite pondering Rome's splendour, depravity, history and various odours (of stale wine, exotic spices, sweat, ordure, musty perfumes, damp and smoke) Brutus returned to looking inwards and was again absorbed by his thoughts.

His footsteps across the stone streets sounded like a sculptor chipping away at a block of marble, as Brutus chipped away again at why his personal feelings should not influence his sense of duty. Personal feelings, and self-serving motives, were certainly influencing many of his co-conspirators. Some were former Caesarians who felt resentful towards the dictator for overlooking them and advancing their rivals. Some craved revenge for fallen comrades and family members that Julius had vanquished in the Civil War. Others were offended and rebellious due to Caesar's undemocratic reforms, which favoured the people over the plutocrats; the once all powerful oligarchs were now being taxed on their extravagant lifestyles and their wealth distributed to the poor. Their dignitas was being insulted, their authoritas undermined.

Brutus smiled, thinking about Caesar's brio when announcing his reforms and remembering the confounded looks upon certain faces as they heard the revolutionary proclamations. Yet whereas personal feelings and self-serving motives spurred Cassius on, if Brutus considered his personal feelings towards Caesar then perhaps he would be dying for him now rather than plotting to kill his friend and sometime surrogate father. More than any other enemy soldier it had been Brutus who Caesar had sought out in order to spare his life after the Battle of Pharsalus. Caesar trusted him. Brutus experienced the shame again, as if he were in the room once more, when Caesar, not two weeks ago, dismissed the suggestion that there was a conspiracy against him - and that Brutus had somehow been implicated in the plot. Julius merely smiled confidently, paternally, at his adviser. He remarked, whilst laying a hand on his body, that "Brutus will wait for this skin of mine," - not only implying that Brutus was worthy to take his place, but that if he did so he would act honourably. In many ways Julius was worth a thousand squabbling, corrupt senators. And that same day hadn't he himself renounced any monarchical ambitions, replying to a supplicant who called him a king that "he was Caesar, not king?"

Thunder growled in the background, seemingly undecided as to whether it should unleash itself or not. Rain began to spot his toga but Brutus reached his house before the downpour commenced in earnest. He entered quietly, not wishing to disturb his wife. He had been an inconsiderate enough husband of late. With a brief nod of his head Marcus Brutus dismissed his man-servants and thanked them for their service for the evening. He retained one of their torches however and, retreating into the triclinium, lit a brazier and sat with his head in his hands before it. Tired. Tortured.

Brutus momentarily lifted a corner of his mouth, straining it upwards as if a weight dangled from his face, as he caught the pleasant fragrance in the air. Porcia had scented the coals with his favourite aromatic oil. The praetor again thought how he would be lost without her.

The flames flickered - dancing in the air to the rhythmic drumming of the swirling rain upon the tiled roof - and created hypnotic shadows along the plaster wall behind. Brutus scrunched up his crop of black hair in his hands. He suddenly got up, strode over to a low pine table next to the end of the couch and poured himself a large measure of wine. The sediment was heavy at the bottom of the jug from where he usually didn't touch the intoxicating vintage. He winced slightly at the taste of the first mouthful but then adjusted himself to the flavour. It was impossible to discern whether the troubled figure was drinking to find his resolve, or lose himself.

After a couple more cups Brutus, with a wistful drowsiness in his expression, half-smiled as he recalled how much the present scene resembled that of when Caesar crossed the Rubicon, and he had to choose between his friend and Pompey. Reason had overruled his personal feelings then; despite his attachment to Caesar - and his resentment of Pompey for being involved in his father's death. But yet, like now, Brutus served the Republic, not any one man. The debt he owed Caesar for sparing his life should not overrule his debt, duty, to Rome. He again mournfully, angrily, weighed up the case against Caesar in his mind.

Although there had once been three hundred senators - and now there were over eight hundred - power had increasingly become conferred upon one man. He had even dared to proclaim himself Dictator for Life. Caesar was a King in all but name. Officials were no longer elected, but personally chosen by Caesar - he bestowed offices like favours - and in return his supplicants would support his radical reforms. Statues had been commissioned - and placed in the company of images of the gods. Brutus sneered in contempt at the egoist as he remembered his near blasphemous comments, attacking the state and constitution that his heroic ancestor had helped establish.

Caesar had dismissively called the Republic "a mere name without a substance" in front of everyone.

And then there was the would-be coronation at Lupercalia. Mid-February. Ironically the festival was in part a celebration of the renewal of civic order, but Brutus' sense of irony was eventually replaced with indignation. The day owned a religious and ritual significance. Young noblemen would dress up in animal skins. Carrying small leather thongs they would proceed to chase women around the city who were childless - and then gently whip them across the hand, or more indecorous areas. Many desired to be caught, believing in the superstition that the touch of the whip would increase fertility. Caesar presided over the rite, sitting on top of a gilded throne. He wore a lavish purple toga and red boots, similar to those worn by the legendary monarchs of the past. Mark Antony was also there. Although a little too old for such sport - and it was a blight on the honour of the Consulship which he held - he also dressed himself up in the ceremonial goat-skin loin cloth and joined in the ritual, half-drunk and debauched from the night before. Brutus thought he looked ridiculous and was at first as contemptuous as he was confused as to why Mark Antony was taking part in the far from august festivities. One couldn't help but notice also how Antony gave certain girls a kiss on the hand that he had first struck, intending no doubt to increase their fertility through less superstitious means in the near future. As well as a whip however, the consul produced a diadem and a wreath when he approached the rostra on which Caesar surveyed the crowds before him. It was here that Cassius gave Brutus his first knowing, conspiratorial look.

"The people offer this to you through me," Antony grandly announced whilst lifting the golden wreath aloft. A small section of the crowd cheered enthusiastically, as if on cue. Their enthusiasm however proved to be far from infectious. Yet Antony was but one of the actors performing in the regal drama. If not for the sacrilege and malign ambition involved, Brutus might have deemed the display a mere pantomime act.

"Jupiter alone is King of the Romans," Caesar replied, refusing the wreath in a grandiose manner. A genuine wave of applause and love here erupted, drowning out those who called for the people's hero to accept the crown. Facing away from him, Marcus found it hard to discern Julius' expression - but for a moment or two he thought he saw him wryly smile. Perhaps he knew that it was the people's love - and power - which were important to him, not the ornaments of a crown and title. And Brutus truly believed that Julius loved the people in return. He had done so much for them - and not just from the cynical motives of ambition and the vanity of a legacy. His clemency was sincere, his reforms were progressive and his generosity was not a smokescreen.

Mark Antony, either desiring the spotlight or merely obeying pre-arranged stage direction, attempted however to bestow the crown on Caesar again. Boos and jeers though accompanied the mock coronation - and this time it was Brutus who permitted himself a discreet smile in favour of the people. Rome did not want a King, but yet Caesar here perhaps mistook their displeasure as a rejection of him. Mark Antony, either too drunk or obtuse, misjudged his performance - and his audience. He insisted on playing his part. Although seemingly not part of the script Caesar wrestled the wreath from his clownish lieutenant and tossed it aside. A few cheers here punctured the boos, but the damage was done.

The official record stored in the archive for the Lupercalia read *'Caesar offered the kingship: Caesar was unwilling.'*

Rome must not become a monarchy Brutus again told himself, his face ploughed with determination. There was an almost religious fervour in his aspect. The removal of Caesar would be tantamount to a ritual killing, a purge. He could not compromise his ideals. If he sacrificed his idealism, that which sets Man apart from the beasts, then Man, Rome, was not worth saving. Marcus Brutus would rather die than live ignobly. "I love the name honour more than fear death," he had once proudly exclaimed to Cassius, unwittingly plagiarising the line from a play that he had seen over a year ago.

Brutus' eyelids soon weighed as heavy upon him as his mood. Drowsiness swiftly succeeded his fervent resolution, dovetailing almost within the blink of an eye. His brow throbbed from the wine and the heat, which pounded out from the roaring brazier. His head swayed and drooped as if set upon a pivot, as if sleep were about to draw a veil over his evening. A gust of cold air feathered his flushed cheek however. The door creaked open.

Porcia entered. She walked a little gingerly at first but then, realising that her husband was aware of her presence, regained her natural poise and graceful gait. Despite his fatigue Brutus awoke to his wife immediately, revitalised. Her black hair cascaded down her elegant shoulders and back like liquid ebony. Her eyes were dark, but warm - and a little red and puffy from sleeplessness. Her face was feminine without being coquettish. She wore a sky-blue linen gown which stretched down to her ankles but revealed her slender arms and fine, ivory hands and fingers. Her features were aristocratic and intelligent, an inheritance from her father Cato, but yet as soon as she gazed at her husband her countenance softened and expressed devotion. Only after moving out of the half-light did Brutus notice the pale, almost translucent hue, to her skin. He felt an immediate mixture of both pity towards his wife and anger directed at himself for being so distant over the past month. But yet he could not burden her with his own anxieties. He loved her too much. And if she was party to the plot then she would be in mortal peril. Porcia smiled a little falteringly. She then wordlessly cuddled up to her husband, slotting her contoured body into his; his tautness lessened as she stroked his hair and kissed him upon the cheek. Either from the strain, or his love for his wife, Brutus was close to tears. She nestled her head against his muscular shoulder. Torrents of rain still splintered the air in the background. They both simultaneously looked up and furrowed their brows in slight apprehension at the storm growing stronger. Out of the corner of his sight Brutus observed his wife briefly close her eyes - either in sorrow or wincing in actual pain - before resting her head on his shoulder. Caesar was not to blame for this anguish. He was. Brutus burned with impotence and guilt, his feelings unleashed like Cerberus, yet muzzled.

"Are you not coming to bed? What's wrong?" Porcia asked. Although she had ached to ask this question before, she had not relented until now.

"Nothing."

"Nothing can come from nothing Marcus," she replied, both wittily and ruefully.

"Telling you would only make me worry for you my love, and thus increase my worries still. I will take care of things. I promise that everything will be alright," Brutus remarked with unconvincing reassurance.

"For better or for worse, remember? I would share your worries, as well as your love Marcus," she expressed whilst removing her head from his side and raising herself to look her husband in the eye.

He loved her. She was beautiful. Porcia was much younger than her husband but her good sense and wit belied the maturity of a woman twice her age. She first cupped his sorrowful face in her satin hands and then tenderly, almost maternally, stroked his cheek. He strangely never noticed it himself but others remarked how much Porcia resembled her aunt, Brutus' mother. Yet his wife had loved him more unconditionally than his mother. Whilst growing up Servilia had been more concerned with playing mistress to Crassus and Caesar, than she had been with being a mother to her son. Only when she finally lost her looks and the patronage of certain men of power dried up (Crassus had died in battle and Caesar now had his Egyptian consort) had Servilia turned her attention to her son and her ambitions for him.

"You have not been yourself lately," Porcia said, concerned. Probing.

"Aye, I have been more subject than citizen," Brutus replied, ruefully and wittily.

The thoughtful young woman paused before speaking, as if either mustering the courage for what needed to be said or pausing to remember her lines like an actress.

"Marcus, I am Cato's daughter, and I gave myself to you not just to share your bed and board, but to be a true partner in your joys and suffering. I have no reproach to make, but what proof can I give you of my love, if you forbid me to share the kind of trouble that demands a loyal friend to confide, and keep your suffering to yourself? I know that men think women's nature too weak to be entrusted with secrets, but surely a good upbringing and the company of honourable men can do much to strengthen us, and at least Porcia can claim that she is the daughter of Cato and the wife of Brutus. I did not know before how either of these blessings could help me, but now I have put myself to the test and find that I can conquer pain."

As her father had suffered from a surfeit of conceit, Porcia too was not immune to a strain of Cato's pride and self-consciousness. Thankfully however the daughter did not inherit from her father his frigidity and haughtiness. Indeed more so than conceit one may have argued that Porcia suffered rather from an excess of sensibility, which was heightened all the more by the trappings of youth and her bookish education.

For a moment Brutus was confused as to the content - and portent - of his wife's remarks. He merely looked quizzically into her mahogany eyes. Confusion blurred into apprehension however as Porcia's lace-like features unbound themselves. The wild fervour of her looks then possessed the rest of her delicate figure as she dramatically scrunched up the skirt to her gown in two small fists and ripped the garment open to reveal her right thigh, stained with both dry and fresh blood. With a trembling hand the stoical woman peeled back the scarlet bandage and displayed her glistening, gory wound. Porcia had sliced into a major vein in her leg with a small knife that she used to cut her nails earlier in the evening. She wanted to prove to herself, and her husband, that she was strong - and could conceal a secret. Cherry-red blood still oozed out of the cut.

Brutus - shocked, cherishing - hastily pressed the blood-strewn gauze back onto the unsightly wound and with his other clasped his wife's head to his.

"I'm so sorry. I should have trusted you. I love you so much. I don't deserve you," Brutus half whispered, half moaned, whilst tears streamed from his eyes - tears of sorrow, devotion and rage. His marble heart crumbled. He kissed her on her snow-white cheek, slaked lips and brackish eyelids. Porcia, drained, barely heard what Marcus said. She just felt that a weight had been lifted from her heart and dreamily smiled whilst leaning into her virtuous husband.

He picked her up like a child and carried her into their room. All through the night Brutus attended to his wife. He redressed the wound and sent for a physician. Not once did he let go of her limp, but responsive hand. After the surgeon departed, and Porcia had regained some of her strength, Brutus poured out his dilemma to his wife. As tempted as the young woman was to influence her husband - for although she kept it from Brutus she had never forgiven Caesar for her father's suicide - Porcia for the most part just listened. She knew how much Marcus admired and loved Julius as a friend, or father figure even. Porcia felt more concern for Brutus' torment than vengeance towards Caesar. The morning sun eventually poured through the window like honey. Porcia drew her husband close, tenderly kissed him on the temple and whispered, "I know that you will do what you believe is right, my love."

11.

Octavius opened his eyes, squinting in the half-light. His stiff limbs ached and his head felt like an anvil after a day's work at the blacksmiths. Briseis was no longer lying beside him, having crept out before dawn to avoid being caught in the young master's bedroom by a loose-lipped slave or soldier. The room still reeked of wine and body odours, as well as the girl's cheap perfume, but Octavius smirked when recalling the scenes of the night before.

After their encounter outside of the house, Briseis, wordlessly, suggestively, led him by the hand into the bath house of the estate. The love-struck youth followed her. She immediately placed a finger over his lips when Octavius tried to say something, and then kissed him teasingly, with the unspoken promise of more kisses to come. Water sizzled across the red hot stones, producing even more steam. The comely serving girl gently ran the back of her hand down her master's arm, following and stroking in the droplets of perspiration which formed upon his skin. She then sat him down on the large wicker chair which occupied the centre of the room. His eyes only diverted themselves from hers when he glanced and admired the rest of her provocative curves. Again he tried to speak but Briseis grinned and shook her head as she crouched down and placed her hands into a bowl filled with warm water and a sponge. Her skin and eyes glowed in the mellow light of the torches which adorned the chamber. First she removed his sandals, dusty from the bouts of walking during the day. For a moment the water tickled as it trickled down his foot, but then the sensation grew more sensuous as she freshened his skin. Her eyes slinkily gazed up at his servile aspect as she knelt before him. Once his feet and calves were washed, scraped and dried, Octavius, unable to contain himself, reached out to touch the girl but Briseis deftly moved away, denying and arousing her master with a playful, chiding look. He grinned, lasciviously. She smiled, deliciously, as she knelt before him again and, dipping her hand into a small bowl beneath the chair, rubbed olive oil into his feet. Slowly, deliberately, alluringly, Briseis moved around to the back of her lover. With neither master nor mistress issuing a word she began to loosen his tunic. Octavius drew in the scent of her breath, skin and damp hair as if it were the finest of fragrances. Briseis, hardly able to contain her own self now, leaned over Gaius and, before he had time to fully respond, kissed him hungrily upon the mouth. He tried to turn his head and return her amorous sortie but once more the girl tantalisingly retreated and shook her head, indicating that he was breaking the rules or not playing to her script. The pace again grew slower, sultrier, as Briseis returned to her position close behind Octavius. Her left hand stroked his ear and cheek as her right, soaked in oil, massaged his chest - delving down to his stomach and beyond. Octavius soaked up the warm sensations - the seduction. Yet he could not totally tame his excitement; his heart pumped blood into a somewhat different but equally ardent organ and he tapped his foot impatiently. Anticipant.

Gaius closed his eyes and cocked his head back, emitting a sound of pleasure - which somehow eased his troubled soul as well. Briseis couldn't help but sigh with gratification, half-lost in the eroticism, too. But then the handmaiden suddenly ceased her caresses. All was silent, apart from the noise of Octavius breathing - and the slight rustling sound of the seductress disrobing. Octavius remained speechless as Briseis appeared before him, naked - her ripened flesh glistening with perspiration and oil. She licked her lips, moistening their splendour even more. The look the lovers shared conveyed a million words - playful, carnal, and intimate. For a brief second or two a shy teenage girl was also to be seen in the sexually powerful woman as Briseis coyly bit her bottom lip and smiled a little nervously - but then her prowess returned as she grasped the two wooden arms of the chair and inserted her slender legs each side of her master, to perch herself upon his lap. Octavius clasped his hands around her waist and brought the girl towards him, her firm yet soft breasts pressing against his chest. Despite the fervour of their passion the maturing lovers kissed each other tenderly. He then kissed her neck as Briseis pulled her head back in response to Octavius stroking his fingertips up and down her back.

They made love.

A cold bath succeeded their exertions in the steam room. The blazing torch of the sun had also extinguished its orange embers. By the time Octavius returned to his room the moon shone supreme in a cloudless sky. His face buried itself in his pillow. Although exhausted his thoughts were still enlivened by the sensations and memories of his lovemaking. Gaius soon missed her - and desired her again. And Briseis soon duly re-appeared, carrying a jug of wine and bowl of figs, under the cover of nightfall. Waiting until her jealous sorority of servants were asleep she had changed into one of her mother's old dresses - which left little to the imagination (but fired it just the same)

- she slipped in and out of the shadows towards the young Caesar's room.

Octavius creased his brow, trying to remember how much wine he had consumed the night before, and how many times they had made love. Dehydrated, Gaius turned to the table beside his bed to see if Briseis had left him a jug of water. She hadn't. It was perhaps the only thing she hadn't thought of yesterday he speculated, grinning.

The groggy youth tried to get back to sleep but his thirst finally conquered his desire to rest and so he arose from his bed. The sundial in the atrium confirmed his internal clock. It was late morning, approaching midday. He would have to miss his afternoon lesson with Cleanthes. The tutor would be disappointed, but forgiving. Octavius would feel guilty later but at present he was too tired to feel anything too keenly. Where Octavius more often than not had been outside the house during this part of the day he was suddenly struck by the sight of the redolent rays of the sun striking one of the mosaic-filled walls decorating the atrium. The mural was a replica to that which adorned Caesar's family home; Venus and Aeneas populated both Caesar's wall and ancestry. Senators struck poses and soldiers won victories within the mosaic, lineage, with the triumphs of Caesar himself dominating the lavish and awe-inspiring picture. His great-uncle had once stood before a statue of Alexander and wept. "I have something worth being sorry about, when I reflect that at my age Alexander was already king over so many peoples, while I have yet to achieve anything remarkable." So too Gaius felt hollow, shame again, in comparing his life to Caesar's. His life did not merit even a solitary tile upon the mural.

\*

Spain.

The site of the camp, especially reconnaissanced by an experienced centurion, was set on a vast undulating plain. A sedate and crystal clear river flowed along its left side. The ground was hard, crisped by the Iberian sun, but still workable. It had not taken the legions an undue amount of time to dig the deep trenches and build the ramparts which encircled the camp. A nearby forest had provided the timber which had been used to construct the four watchtowers which stood at each corner of the rectangular encampment. The commander-in-chief's tent, topped with a gloriously bright and rippling vexillion, dominated the skyline as Octavius, still seated behind the decurion, approached the camp. He was immediately and intensely awe-struck by the scale and order of the sight before him, inspiring in him a feeling that was particular to being Roman he imagined - a martial pride. A couple of large tents flanked Caesar's own. Octavius would later find out that they housed an engineering workshop and quartermaster's store. Two main 'streets' ran down from Caesar's tents - which were marked out by rows of spears - called the Principalis and Via Praetoria.

To prevent attacks from flaming enemy arrows and artillery fire, a gap was set between the palisades and the vast grid of tents which housed the army. The area was then filled with the army's livestock (mules, draft oxen, pack horses), as well as prisoners of war and various plunder.

Broiled beef, sour wine, ordure and the smell of leather assailed Octavius' nostrils as he slowly made his way through the gates of the camp and up the Principalis. Such was the spectacle and sensory influx of the scenes before him that Octavius was even distracted from his thoughts concerning his imminent meeting with Caesar. Men sat around hunched over bowls of steaming hot porridge or glugged down water or something stronger from their skeins. Choruses of laughter, occasionally counter-pointed with the odd curse or scuffle, also coloured the air. Half of the men seemed to bustle with industry and discipline (or just habit) whilst the other half, off duty, relaxed in various ways - yet all remained fit for service should the trumpets sound. Most ignored the ragged party accompanying the returning cavalry patrol. Others couldn't help but stare at the fair-haired and studious-looking youth, hazarding a guess as to who he might be.

Caesar.

His dark brown eyes were warm and lively, but the strains and privations of the constant campaigning over the years had weathered his complexion a little in the time since Octavius had last seen his great-uncle. He was as close shaved as ever and his hair was trim and carefully spread over his receding crown. Caesar wore a leather breastplate with matching greaves - the armour inwrought with a golden eagle on each impressive piece. A gladius hung from his left hip.

Julius looked his nephew up and down. His features softened with relief and pride; a charming smile also enlivened an already engaging countenance as Caesar noticed how a poppy-seed stubble had replaced the down upon his cheeks from when he had last seen Octavius.

"I hear you have bested both Neptune and the Pompeans to reach us. It bodes well, for if they link up through Sextus recruiting an army of pirates then Caesar might have to call on his nephew to defeat them."

The men, those from the shipwrecked party and the general's staff, grinned and laughed a little at their commander's joke. Octavius blushed, partly because he did not know how to accept the comment.

"But I should not let my manners be enveloped by my happiness. You must all be both famished and tired. Decimus, please see to all of the men's needs. Spare no luxury. I thank you all for delivering my nephew to me. This will neither be forgotten nor go unrewarded," Caesar gregariously declared. Decimus, an adjutant upon Caesar's personal staff, immediately carried out his orders, instructing others to lead the shipwrecked party off and provision them. Sprits were lifted. The result of their commander's commending words produced an almost metaphysical alchemy in the souls of the party. They now suddenly looked back at the experience of the last few days with pride rather than bitterness.

"Lucius, Roscius, I would detain you a little longer. Please, join me for some wine. I dare say you must all be thirsty."

Octavius dismounted - with the decurion and his patrol taking their leave - and tentatively approached the dictator. Caesar, who observed and was a little saddened by his nephew's wariness of him, pretended not to notice Octavius' nerves. He first addressed the loyal centurion and legionary who stood to attention before him.

"Relax, my friends. You are not on the parade ground now. How are you Roscius, are you still keeping your officer out of trouble?"

Not for the last time over the next few weeks, Octavius would be struck by his great-uncle's familiarity and affection for various soldiers, from all ranks, under his command.

"I'm trying Caesar," Roscius replied, smiling.

"Nay, it rather seems you are succeeding. And I thank you for your service to him, and me."

Octavius would think to himself that evening that for all of the criticism Caesar received for him acting like a king, or deity even, few senators deigned to ever lower themselves to talk with such courtesy and sympathy to the lowliest soldier or citizen. He admired Caesar's graciousness. Gaius promised himself that he would always try to emulate his great-uncle's virtues - albeit his tiredness and deep slumber that night temporarily relieved him of the ardour of his new vow.

Caesar turned to Oppius. The general heartily clapped his hand upon his officer's shoulder and embraced him. Octavius also observed the brief, solemn nod of gratitude he offered his centurion after their embrace. To Oppius the gesture and expression meant more to him than any flattering speech or token honour.

"Before the battle at Munda Lucius, I wished you by my side. But such is the service you have done me in bringing my nephew to me, I am glad that you were with him rather than me. You have my gratitude once again, my friend. Caesar will not forget this."

There was a history and mutual admiration between the two men that one couldn't help but be conscious of and intrigued by. A day or so later Octavius discovered how Oppius had been the famed anonymous standard bearer of the Tenth Legion, who had inspired the army to capture the beach against the Britons. Octavius had perhaps been no older than ten when he had first read about the deciding moment in the campaign. The attack was faltering. The Britons still held the beach. The water was deep, the currents strong. A torrent of rain - and missiles - lashed down upon the legions; they steadfastly remained in the relative safety of their transports, furrowing their brows and shaking their heads at the prospect of trying to take the beach. Either from a sense of madness, or ambition, a nameless standard bearer acted - and offered up the legionary's prayer.

"Jupiter Greatest and Best, protect this legion, soldiers every one. May my act bring good fortune to us all."

To the amazement and condemnation of his comrades, Oppius leapt over the rail of the vessel and plunged into the murky ocean. The gleaming head of the legion's standard first appeared out of the foaming water. The eagle was the pride of every soldier. When in camp the standard was kept at an altar, surrounded by lamps which burned all through the night; both the eagle and the ground it stood upon were deemed to be sacred. The protection of the standard was every legionary's duty - and its loss would blight every soldier's honour. Roscius followed his aquilifer into the surf out of friendship, yet the rest of the Tenth Legion bravely, absurdly, followed the silver eagle - to protect and fight for it. And the eagle seemed to come to life itself as it soared upwards and into the chest of the first enemy cavalryman who opposed the seemingly suicidal standard bearer. The fizzing spray of the ocean blurred his vision so Oppius did not see the second cavalryman attack his flank, yet he heard the sound of him shriek and fall as Roscius' pilum skewered his stomach. Support was soon mustered around the precious standard though. Witnessing the Tenth's courage - and success - the Seventh Legion also abandoned their transports and advanced towards the shore. Caesar swiftly ordered reinforcements. By the time the sun lowered on the horizon the sea seemed to be weeping blood, but a beachhead was finally secured. "You captured my respect and loyalty today Oppius, as well as that beach. You have earned my gratitude - and a promotion," the enigmatic General remarked to his new officer in a private meeting that evening. Reciprocated respect, loyalty and gratitude would be further earned from that day hence.

Both men had aged since that night, but Oppius had been a young man at the time. Octavius couldn't help but notice however the lines and wrinkles in his great-uncle's visage as Caesar approached and surveyed his nephew. A touching paternity could be seen in Caesar's fond expression, which was all the more marked due to the seriousness which had been carved into his demeanour of late. Tears glistened in his eyes, but fell not. For once he could be Julius again, not "Caesar". He beamed - cherishingly, happily, memorably. Octavius smiled back and his apprehension and aching limbs vanished into the ether. Although he was conscious of wanting to appear manly, Roman, he couldn't help but feel the urge to run to his uncle and bury his head in his chest. As Caesar proposed to speak to Octavius and opened his arms to fulfil this desire, a figure and voice intruded upon their familial reunion.

"I came as soon as I heard. It seems you have a Caesar's determination and luck, Octavius," the voice, alien to Octavius yet over-familiar, expressed. The soldier's warmth and flattery were intended more for his general's ears than the boy's however.

"Octavius, this is Mark Antony," Caesar cordially remarked. Although irked a little by his lieutenant's intrusion upon his private moment with his nephew, Julius was a practiced enough actor to be able not to show his displeasure.

The celebrated soldier's forehead was smooth and broad. The lines of a strong and square jaw were softened by a well-kept beard. A short-sleeved tunic showed off his muscular biceps, seemingly hewn from bronze. Not without some credence Antony claimed descent from Anton, a son of Hercules - and from his build and soldierly virtues few people found cause to argue the point against his supposed bloodline. His chestnut brown eyes sparkled with masculine charm and good humour, or wine. His glossy black hair was artfully brushed upon his head in a perfectly formed centre parting. A large spatha (cavalry sword) hung down from his left side, its gold-plated guard and pommel encrusted with semi-precious stones.

Antony had not fought at Munda. He had been in Rome. After hearing of Caesar's decisive victory though he had sped like winged Mercury to the dictator's side to congratulate him and share in the jubilant mood of the army. The Civil War was finally over. The soldier had been all too pleased to vacate Rome, tired and harassed as he was by the constant petitions and the business of office that Caesar had asked him to attend to in his absence. More so though Antony had attended to his mistresses, cronies and vintner.

"Julius has told me much about you, Gaius," Mark Antony cheerfully expressed whilst placing a hand on Caesar's shoulder, as well as Octavius'. It was Antony's custom to treat Caesar with such familiarity and affection - but on this occasion the lieutenant did so to mark out to the nephew how close he was to his great-uncle. Whether he was conscious of it or not Mark Antony was jealous of the unique bond between Caesar and the youth. His jealousy would grow more pronounced over the next couple of months as the dictator spent more and more time with his nephew.

"And all of it was good, I can assure you," Mark Antony added, clapping the slender built adolescent on the back. Caesar's lieutenant was affable, without ever being as naturally witty or charming as his mentor.

Octavius raised a corner of his mouth in a gesture towards a smile, but he reciprocated not the soldier's familiarity and warmth. Indeed if anything Antony's behaviour reinforced the young stoic's pre-disposed dislike of the renowned soldier and bacchant. Octavius was familiar with some of Antony's history. In his youth the pleasure-loving aristocrat had attached himself to Clodius - a self-serving demagogue who had courted the mob and reduced politics to little more than criminality. Antony's capacity for drinking and womanising was notorious. When he did attend to his duties in the Senate he would often arrive hung-over, or debauched. Vomit rather than words would issue from his mouth when he was due to speak, although Octavius fancied that his oratory would be scarce more eloquent than vomit should it ever be given voice. His retinue was filled with low-born prostitutes and actors - and often at least one wife of a fellow senator. Octavius also disparaged his uncle's lieutenant, however because he was partly envious of the popular, powerful soldier.

"And Lucius, it's good to see you again," Antony remarked at seeing the centurion, walking up to his old friend and embracing him. "I've already arranged some wine and women for you, although you might want to take them in the opposite order," the carouser added, laughing at his own joke.

As he looked at him then - and as Octavius thought about Mark Antony now in Apollonia - an expression of suspicion and disdain laced his features. Octavius smiled at recalling Cleanthes' comment about Antony.

"I don't know much about him. But what little I know makes me want to know him even less."

\*

Whilst Caesar made preparations to return to Rome - and formulated his tactics to deal with the guerrilla war which would ensue with Sextus Pompey's remaining forces - the general instructed Roscius to introduce his nephew to military life during their remaining weeks in Spain.

Firstly the legionary issued the new recruit with a uniform. He was given a linen military tunic, which was longer than his civilian one and reached down past Gaius' knees. As to the style of the day though Roscius taught the youth how to bunch some of the material up over his military belt - and leave the bottom of the tunic curved as he did so. He was at the same time issued with caligae - the tough, leather hob-nailed boot of the Roman legionary.

Although he seldom wore it over the succeeding weeks (the scorching heat and sheer weight of the garment suppressed the inclination) Octavius was given a mail cuirass formed from hundreds of tiny iron rings. The armour was both strong and flexible and Roscius assured Octavius that the shirt would one day save his life - for it had his own on many occasions, the standard bearer was pleased to confess.

To top off his uniform Octavius was given a standard legionary's helmet. The bronze bowl owned a peak at the back to protect the neck and also large protective cheek pieces, designed to leave the ear uncovered so as one could still hear orders. Such was its size - and the youth's slender head - that, to almost comic effect, Octavius found himself having to continually adjust the helmet, either tilting it backwards to prevent the rim from slanting over his eyes or pushing it forward to stop the bowl from slipping off the back of his head.

A gladius - with a blade around twenty inches long - and scabbard were next handed to the youth in the quartermaster's area. The sword felt heavy and unfamiliar in Octavius' hand, yet the sensation was still prized (and he suitably swished the weapon about that night in his tent, cutting down and slaying invisible foes). Roscius also handed the new recruit a pilum - the lethal javelin of the legions. Octavius felt a tinge of pride as Roscius described how Marius (the legendary consul and general who had also been Caesar's uncle) had re-designed the weapon. Marius changed the manufacture of the pilum so that the metal between the shaft and point was soft and pliable. Once the pilum was thrown - and lodged into a target - the shaft sagged down and the weapon was rendered useless should the enemy wish to throw it back. So too, should the pilum strike an enemy shield, it was awkward to remove.

"This, as much as this, has carved out Rome's progress," Roscius then somewhat sagely announced as he held up a shovel, as well as his own razor sharp gladius. A dolobra (a military pick-axe), saw and bill-hook were also exhibited to Octavius as being the tools of the Roman legionary.

Finally the veteran produced a scutum - decorated with the Bull emblem of Caesar's famed Tenth Legion - and presented it to the youth. The shield stood four feet high and was as thick as a man's palm. Rectangular and semi-cylindrical in shape, the shield was made from plywood and covered with a layer of canvas and calfskin - and was reinforced with a bronze central boss. The scutum was strong and flexible - and such was its weight that it had to be supported by both the hand and forearm through leather straps across the reverse. Within just a minute of holding the legionary's shield Octavius' arm ached and he felt again a wave of doubt that he would be able to live up to Roscius' - and more importantly Caesar's - expectations.

During that first day Roscius took Octavius on a whirlwind tour of the camp and he immediately began to appreciate the scope and specialist nature to the make-up of the army. Caesar's nephew was introduced to engineers, craftsmen, clerks, cooks, surveyors, farriers, artillerymen, surgeons and drill masters alike. Partly as an attempt to echo the virtues and manner of Caesar, Octavius was attentive and friendly towards everyone he met. He made a conscious effort to ask and remember everyone's name - and was genuinely interested in certain facets of various tasks and trades.

That evening Octavius listened avidly as Roscius told him more stories of their general's exploits and achievements. He reported an anecdote of when Caesar was once invited to a meal by a friend, one Valerius Leo - and the asparagus somehow got accidentally dressed with myrrh instead of olive oil. Caesar however ate the dish, courteously ignoring the mistake. Others in his party though complained and composed snide comments. Before long however

Caesar reprimanded the ungrateful - and ungracious - group. "If you didn't like it there was no need to have eaten it. But if one reflects on one's host's lack of breeding it merely shows that one is ill-bred oneself," Roscius reported Caesar as saying.

Roscius had also been there in person when the army had been forced to stop marching one storm-filled night. The only real shelter that was available was a farmer's hut. When offered to Caesar however he refused the accommodation, arguing that "honours should go to the strongest, but necessities should go to the weakest.' He subsequently slept in the roofed doorway of the building, allowing the injured to take refuge inside the dwelling.

"Soldiers respect Caesar, because Caesar respects us. Whether it be because of his ability, or his luck, we know that he will do his best by us. We are loyal to Caesar, rather than the Senate, because if and when we ever get discharged we know to look to our general, rather than some politician back in Rome, to look after us - and maybe provide us with a plot of land somewhere that we can call our own. Caesar rewards loyalty. The Senate, filled with over-weaned aristocrats who live off their family name - and who look down on the soldier class - would happily wash its hands of the legions after their service to the state though. And why do soldiers love Caesar? He doubled our pay to two hundred and twenty-five silver denarii per year," Roscius finally said with a grin on his face, whilst raising a wine-filled cup to his absent commander.

Realising how late the hour must have been though Roscius suddenly brought a close to their evening, for the legionary was all too aware of how long the following day (and following two weeks or so) would prove for the youth. For the remainder of Octavius' stay within the bounds of the camp he received regular rudimentary weapons training and drill instruction. Moreover Roscius was conscious of developing Octavius' physical condition - and although the youth could not justly claim to have attained the standards of fellow new recruits, Octavius brimmed with a sense of achievement in relation to the change in his constitution and abilities.

12.

Marcus Vipsanius Agrippa had woken early that morning - yet his father was still up and dressed before him, impatiently waiting to give his son his chores for the day. Summer was coming, if not with them already, and Domitius Agrippa wanted his eldest son to service the series of mini-aqueducts - that Marcus Vipsanius had himself designed - which helped irrigate some of his farmlands. Although the youth had plans for the day, Agrippa duly complied with his father's request. Rather than completing the task by himself however, he quickly trained up half a dozen slaves to clean and service the matrix of stone and oak channels that provided water to a particularly arid corner of his family's estate.

And so by noon Marcus was racing across the olive groves of neighbouring properties in a shortcut to reach the Roman fort, situated just outside of the main town of Apollonia. The camp was a hive of activity and preparation in lieu of Caesar's imminent arrival. The historic campaign could then begin in earnest. The talk was of glory, eastern riches, the retrieval of the standards that Crassus had lost - and the tits and virtues of Parthian women.

Sweat dripped down his plain-looking and honest face and a smile seemed to brighten Agrippa's features because, and not in spite of, his arduous run. The guards had now grown used to the tough but good natured youth turning up at the camp. His introduction to the fort had first come via Octavius. Yet while he had increasingly devoted less time to his martial education over the months - choosing to spend his time reading and in the company of Cleanthes - Agrippa received the training and conditioning that Octavius could and should have benefited from.

When his schedule allowed him the time Oppius himself took the enthusiastic and fast-learning Agrippa under his wing, teaching him about basic tactics, swordsmanship and survival techniques. The centurion had first noticed the youth through overhearing a bunch of legionaries chattering during their evening meal of fish stew. Agrippa was among the group. They were discussing which god they'd offer up thanks to before entering a sea battle - Mars, Jove or Neptune?

"I wouldn't want to impress Neptune too much with my devotion, in case he took me down into the deep with him," one legionary jokingly piped up.

"And too many legionaries offer up prayers to Mars, so I'd worry if he could hear mine over the rest," his comrade countered. "So who would you give thanks to, young'un?" the man, idly whittling away a piece of wood into nothingness, added.

"I'd offer up thanks to the man who invented the corvus," Agrippa drily posited.

Oppius, hearing the unfamiliar voice and unconventional answer, abruptly turned his head. The centurion was amused and impressed to hear such a thing come from such a young recruit. The next day Oppius asked Casca about the would-be soldier. After hearing the old legionary's report, the centurion invited the youth to train with his own cohort. With an air of confidence, rather than arrogance, Agrippa fought and bested many of his own men during combat practice. Before long Oppius was tutoring the recruit personally, imparting his knowledge and sharing his experiences with the lad. Agrippa's rapid progress even infused in the stern and insular centurion a feeling which was something akin to paternal pride.

\*

An open, contented expression could be found on Octavius' face as if his sister were actually in the garden with him, rather than just a name upon the top of a letter.

*Dearest Octavia,*

*I have missed you, and not just because you helped share the burden of mother's dotage.*

*Thank you for your last letter. I am well. I am sometimes afflicted with the ague of boredom, but thankfully I am keeping myself busy and, although one cannot perhaps totally remedy the mutating disease, prevention is as good as a permanent cure.*

*Please pass on my thanks also to Athenobus for the copy of Plato's Laws. You may wish to add that I said to you that he is a superior tutor to Cleanthes - and that I have remained a devotee of his Plato, rather than an adherent of Cleanthes' Aristotle. I can forgive myself the lie, if you can - for the sun will be shining that much brighter for the old librarian when you tell him.*

*However, I cannot lie to you sister. You asked how I was progressing in my military training. My progress marches on like myself, slowly and out of step. I try, but I often also fail. I am perhaps still more versed in the conquests of Catullus than I am in the campaigns of Scipio. But I do not fear the rigours of military life as I once did, albeit I warrant that I'll be about as useful in a battle to the army as a knife and fork would be to Tantalus.*

*Marcus is also fine. I can't help but admire him. I often think that I should perhaps envy or resent him, such are his virtues and accomplishments, but he possesses such a noble nature - and I love him so much - that I would rather part with all that I own than lose his friendship. Marcus is twice the soldier I am Octavia, but I would be perhaps half the soldier I am, if it were not for his instruction and encouragement. In return I have helped him with his other studies. Together we could perhaps take on the world. As I often write about him to you - and speak of you to him - I am very much looking forward to a time when I can introduce you. If nothing else it will save me both time and energy in acting as a go-between.*

*Salvidienus is also doing well. He will make a marvellous advocate. He has perhaps been rehearsing for the role all his life, such are the lies he tells himself and others. I shall miss him when I depart for Parthia though. He has been a good friend. We are at present planning a day together and fishing trip so we can say our farewells properly.*

*Should you receive this letter in time you might want to request to return with mother. I would dearly love us to spend some time together before I embark upon the campaign. You could also mediate between mother and me when we argue - it'll be just like old times!*

Octavius loved his sister - and admired her. Her virtues were as plentiful as the summer harvest. She was patient, generous, loyal, kind and forgiving. He occasionally found himself having to invent flaws for his sister when describing her to people, for fear of his true opinion and portrait appearing too biased or unbelievable. She was perhaps as equally intelligent as him, yet Octavius himself could not be sure, as Octavia had spent half her life concealing the education she had given herself in private. For fear of earning people's prejudice, or envy, she never flaunted her intellect or engaged men on their own level, except when conversing privately with her brother. Yet she was content, or seemed so. Octavia was far from beautiful in a classical sense - she was no Clodia or young Servilia - but yet she was pretty. Her hair was fair, straight and just shy of shoulder length. Her features were round and soft, her light brown eyes gentle and charming.

Octavius had been sincere in his wish to want to see his sister again; if anything he had understated his desire. He hoped however that his brother-in-law, Marcus Marcellus, would be too busy to accompany his wife. Partly Octavius disliked and distrusted the eminent senator because of his initial siding with Pompey during the Civil War, as he had even been the one to hand Pompey the ceremonial sword to defend the Republic against the outlaw Caesar, but perhaps more so Octavius was jealous of his brother-in-law. Octavia - who he had shared so much with and loved more deeply than anyone else in the world - had to be now a wife first and sister second.

For a minute or so Octavius chewed the end of his stylus and pondered whether to tell his sister about Briseis - and how and what he should say - but then he desisted. He did not want to come across as a lovesick poet, worthy of the satires they had both read when younger. So too Octavius was worried that his sister - who appreciated modesty and duty - might think less of him for bedding a servant girl.

Despite his fondness and affection for Octavia though - and his intention to finish the letter quickly in order to dispatch it - the comely figure of the serving girl danced before his mind's eye again and distracted the youth from his correspondence. Did he love her? He would never be allowed to marry her. Yet he would not ask permission. Octavius briefly imagined the scenario of what would happen should he declare his love for the serving girl to his family - and society. He would be ridiculed and shunned. Caesar perhaps might even turn his back on him. Yet the young romantic felt that he would sacrifice the entire world to spend just one more night with the girl, who had touched him in a way like no other. His heart beat faster just thinking of her. Pictures, both carnal and poetic, were painted in his mind's eye. The afternoon sun baptised his face in apricot light and Gaius surrendered to his daydream. His was an affair to rival that of Paris and Helen, Catullus and Lesbia.

*Let's live and love, my love,*
*Ignore the snide talk*
*Of all these crabbed old men.*

*The sun sets, and rises:*
*Once our candle's snuffed*
*We're out for a long night.*

*A thousand kisses, then,*
*A hundred thousand thousand,*
*Till we will lose count.*

*Don't keep score, for no*
*Evil eye can blight us*
*If our love seems infinite.*

The glowing expression across Octavius' face suddenly altered however - and he wryly, or even scornfully, smiled to himself. Cynicism succeeded idealism, love. Cynicism should act as life's strigil, scraping away unwanted and dead or dying material. The selfishness of Paris and Helen doomed Troy. Clodia was unfaithful - Catullus, conceited. Gaius was a victim of lust, not love - yet he would still surrender to it, he indulgently mused. Rather than Catullus, he now recalled Cleanthes. The brief cautionary tale that the tutor told to his hormonal student was originally composed by a satirical Jewish playwright who Cleanthes had once encountered in a brothel in Capua.

*"If Man was put on this earth to serve the Gods, then was not Woman created to serve the god in Man? Originally there was only one sex, Adam. Gloriously endowed was he, the personification of the gods. And, in the beginning, the gods were proud of their son. But when Man began to stand on his own two feet, not only did the gods start to envy his mortal magnificence, they also began to fear this spark that Adam burned autonomously of his origin. The gods did not want an heir. Adam was created for their amusement. But nevertheless the subject of Man became no laughing matter, for they feared that one day this zealous son might strike out at his father. So the High Council of the gods called a secret meeting to address what was to be done about this issue. Ere the hammer could crack upon the block to open the meeting the flame-haired Mars barged in and declared that "The gods should lift up the clouds and squash Man like the louse that he is!" But not only did the brash Mars underestimate the resilient pest of Man, more importantly he was not thinking that secret thought of the even prouder gods. If the deities compelled Man by force it would mean that they would be treating him as a worthy opponent, or equal; Cronos battling Neptune is a fair contest, but noble Achilles is in a no win situation if he defeats a lowly helot. Then Venus, lisping like an asp, spoke. She announced that she could concoct a potion to induce Man to fall vainly in love with himself, "he will do nothing but look in the mirror all day". But Zeus objected and ruled that even perfect Apollo would get bored with such a fate after a time. "No", proclaimed that god whose name I dare not mention, "we must subdue Man in such a way so he knows not he is being subdued; and even if*

*he should discover that he is under the spell of such a force then its sweets will compel him anyway. This force must be weaker than Man, yet stronger. This diversion I shall create and call Eve," He sagely ordered to much approval, obsequious or otherwise. "But what if Eve falls in love with Adam - and confesses the ruse?" an impish Pan called out from the back benches. "I have thought of that comrades. I will make Eve innocent of her attractions; her modesty will prove all the more alluring to Man. He will be possessed in possessing her - and in their contract he will be a slave to being her master." "But if Man serves Woman he serves not the gods" Seth posited, his brow wrinkled in either worry or scepticism. "Then we cannot make Eve's love as faithful as ours is," He stolidly replied, "We must also drug Man with the tonic of boredom once in a while. He will adore Woman - and he will praise us for creating her for him - but Man cannot make an idol out of just one of the creatures. He cannot live for her solely, else it will lead to bad faith and other blasphemies. We should prick him as such so that as soon as he has eaten of her fruit he'll look to pick another. If he doesn't, then either he is mad or then one of our Angels has escaped again." Only when the gavel was struck to seal the motion did Tiresias know that there would be sufficient quiet for him to be heard. "But what if Eve should dare eat from the Tree of Knowledge?" But by then it was too late - and the rest is History.*

Octavius was duly amused by the story but also conscious of the lessons it tried to impart. Rather than a Helen he wanted to find his Penelope. Conscious of how much time and energy he was devoting to the self-serving girl, Octavius shifted the tone of his thoughts towards her, in order to denigrate and dismiss Briseis' significance. His affair would not be, could not be, akin to some plot by Plautus - where obstacles are overcome and love conquers all. Reality always plays chaperone. She would not enchant him like Circe - and have him behave like some mere animal or lovesick slave. He was a Roman, a Caesar. As such Octavius turned again to his sister's letter and read over the news concerning the city and its dictator.

*"The Games were as grand a spectacle as ever, with Caesar competing with himself - and winning. An artificial lake was created on the site of the Campus Martius and scaled down fleets of ships acted out battles, as well as gladiators and teams of Roman cavalry defeating British chariots ... Jaws dusted the ground and eyes were rubbed into the back of heads when a creature called a 'giraffe' was*

*exhibited, which Caesar had imported from Africa. As you can see from the sketch I've done for you its neck is as long as Cato's face - and the animal can run faster from danger than mother can to a shoe sale."*

## 13.

Rome.

The meandering Tiber, glassy in the moonlight, attracted his attention through its serenity and nocturnal beauty. Caesar stood on the balcony of his Janiculum villa - the 'Mons Aureas' (the golden hill of sand). Situated west of Rome, Caesar had given the extensive and luxurious property to his mistress, Cleopatra.

Cleopatra. He still recalled their first meeting, as if it was burned within his memory. The smell of Egyptian oil of roses still lingered in his nostrils. A similar balcony adjoined a similar reception room, but the eastern sky was ruby red, oozing heat. Various official papers, like now, littered the chamber. Confusion and faction-fighting reigned supreme in Egypt back then. Caesar was close to returning to Rome. He was fatigued, bored perhaps of the east - and he had his own civil war to attend to. His epilepsy had also returned. Balbus, ever loyal and quick-witted, had explained away a fainting fit as heat exhaustion.

An exotic looking slave, Apollodorus, appeared before him. Oil or sweat glistened across his bare, muscular torso. Over his shoulder the Nubian carried a finely decorated carpet, a gift no doubt.

"Yes?" Caesar rudely demanded, unusually curt from tiredness or tedium, after a pregnant pause between the two men.

Without a word said the slave bowed to Caesar, smiling slightly and awkwardly like one unpractised in the art - and then rolled out the carpet.

Cleopatra. Caesar could not remember the last time that he had been so astonished, or aroused - perhaps the one fed off the other. The Conqueror of the World was rendered temporarily speechless.

Her eyes, oriental-like, were rimmed with ash - and would prove both engaging and unreadable, shaped either in perpetual satisfaction or desire. A satin tyrian purple skirt, worn low upon her hips to display a bejeweled navel, clung to her thighs and reached down to her feet - where pretty toes, painted gold, peeped out. A V-shaped split ran down the satin skirt, revealing tantalising glimpses of silken thighs. A low-necked sable cloak adorned her shoulders and breasts, leaving most of her arms bare - and shone as glossily in the candle light as her long jet hair.

"I come to you both as a queen and supplicant," the girl issued, her voice strong yet feminine. She bowed before him, yet her eyes - equal in pride, ambition and charm to the Roman's - met his. An alluring face, more Greek than Egyptian, gazed up at him. Her full, sensual lips, which would prove as amorous as they could be eloquent, were slightly parted. The tawny skin of the nubile girl, barely out of her teens, glowed like the burnished gold decorating her ears and long-nailed, tapering fingers. Her perfume was as intoxicating as her singular beauty. Only mistresses could entice and enthral Caesar so - never wives.

Apollodorus silently excused himself, his task completed.

Cleopatra, Queen and the Goddess Isis incarnate, rose and unclasped the scarab brooch which fastened her cloak. The garment slid from her shoulders and onto the floor, revealing her young, succulent flesh and breasts.

"I am your slave," she issued playfully, ardently.

Caesar was tempted to reply "No, I am yours", but refrained from doing so. He merely drew the beautiful, sensuous girl towards him and kissed her.

"My father was known as Ptolemy the Flute-Player. I too will show you how I can use my mouth and fingers."

The evening was memorable, to say the least, Caesar judged, half-smiling.

Pillow talk was of politics, the grain supply and the strength and tactics of armies. He was impressed by her intellect and ambition. The woman batted not an eyelid when plotting the usurpation of her brother-husband's throne. She was both a goddess and a whore - and as manipulative as both Caesar fancied. Yet she had seduced him. He remembered again making love to the exotic queen on her imperial barge, soaring up and down upon the rhythmic waves - the eastern sun kissing and massaging his skin, along with the woman he was with. She complained not when he took another mistress (which he rarely did for once, satisfied and excited as he was by his semi-divine lover) yet Cleopatra was wise enough to remain faithful to Caesar. The dictator told himself that he had still not been swayed by the woman into doing anything that Caesar didn't want to do - but then Julius smiled, knowing it to be untrue. He had fought and won half a country for her. Mark Antony had joked that, in terms of the young queen, Caesar could also declare, "I came, I saw, I conquered" - but rather could not the Egyptian say that in reference to the Roman?

Was it their advice, or the veiled threat of his legions to abandon him, which convinced Caesar to finally free himself from the seductions of the east and return to Rome - to attend to his own civil war, rather than those of his paramour? Caesar had returned though, bringing his trophy mistress with him and establishing her in his Janiculum villa. And she had given him that which he most craved, a son.

The dictator yawned and rubbed his brow - being careful not to disturb the laurel wreath which rested on his head and half-disguised his balding pate - as he gazed out over the undulating, turquoise river. A voice, doused in wine and amours, breezed out from the bedroom.

"Come back to bed."

Her appetites could rival Mark Antony's, Caesar mused.

"Give me a moment or so," he replied.

After this evening he would return and stay with Calpurnia, his wife, for a while. He missed her uncomplicated devotion and friendship. Her love had become unconditional, like his mother's and Julia's had once been. He still missed his daughter. For a while Cleopatra had filled the void, but not anymore. Caesar recalled the incident, argument, of yester night between him and his mistress.

"But Caesarion is your son!" she had posited, her eyes ablaze with the heat of a passion far removed from love.

"But he is not my heir. Octavius is," Caesar had firmly replied.

The young queen and mother responded with a tantrum. Curses, in a language Caesar was unfamiliar with, emanated from the woman, as well as cat-like hisses and wild protestations. Her arguments seemed scripted though to Caesar - and he had already made his judgement. He intended to adopt Octavius. Eventually he silenced the politic queen, either through his rhetoric or the threats implicit behind his words.

"Julius," she called from inside, now demanding, yearning.

An increasingly familiar mournfulness, or atrophy, overcame the dictator again - darkening his mood and eyes, as if a veil had been placed over him. Even Caesar could not conquer time, old age. He tried to muster his spirits. The Parthian campaign would be his last, but greatest, triumph. He looked forward to seeing Octavius again, imparting his memories and wisdom to him. More than his mistress, his nephew made him feel enthused and purposeful again.

"Julius," she exclaimed once more, her musical voice a little less harmonious - harder and flatter. The queen was not used to being ignored, or defied.

Would he even return from the campaign? He honestly didn't know he conceded - and occasionally of late a world-weary Caesar thought to himself how he didn't care.

*

Spain.

Ribbons of cloud, like deft white brush strokes across a light blue canvas, striped the sky. Lowing cattle could be heard in the background, perhaps moaning about the oppressive heat. Caesar fanned himself with some papers that he had just finished reading and signing. He sat with his nephew in a carriage, cantering along - but still tarrying too much for the dictator. Finally they were on their way home.

Caesar closed his eyes in a vain effort to suppress an oncoming migraine. Finally he had earned a moment or two of peace - and private time with his beloved nephew. Since dawn, since their party had set off, Caesar had been hard at work - replying to urgent matters of state that Antony had ignored and re-writing chapters of his book with Hirtius, which would recount the history of the recent civil war. Julius also caught up with his personal correspondence. Among which Cassius Longinus had composed a servile and long-winded petition to be considered for the Praetorship of Rome. Cleopatra had written to him, stressing how she loved and desired Caesar - and that she had remained chaste in his absence. Aemilius Lepidus was memorably forgettable in a routine, fawning letter. Atticus still wouldn't sell his life-size bronze statue of Aeneas, yet Caesar perhaps admired the art-collector more for prizing beauty over money. Added to a clear and insightful review of the mood in the Senate, Brutus had also written a critical but fair appraisal of "*The Journey*", a poem that Caesar had recently composed.

Whilst Caesar closed his eyes Octavius, sitting opposite and half-reading a play by Terence, surveyed his uncle. Although the youth had been impressed by his general's infectious energy and dynamism in front of his legions and staff, Octavius had spent many evenings of late with the dictator - and Caesar could not sustain his public face in private. His tanned skin could not quite conceal the small clusters of liver spots dotting his head, which would have been discernible to all if not for the civic crown or bronze helmet which the dictator wore. Wrinkles increasingly carved themselves, as deep as scars, around his neck and brow. Caesar joked to his nephew that they were just 'laughter lines'. He slept more, often dozing off in the middle of reading, or during his evening meal. Octavius would often take the book or plate away from his uncle on such occasions, not wishing for anyone else to see him so vulnerable looking. When he would wake, Julius would smile to himself, appreciating his nephew's consideration. His head seemed to weigh heavier in his hands when deep in thought. His joints ached during cold nights. So too Caesar secretly asked his quartermaster to forge a new, lighter cavalry sword. He could no longer leap up and mount his horse from behind, yet the keen rider derived the utmost pleasure one afternoon from teaching his surrogate son to perform the trick. "Not even Caesar can conquer old age," Julius confessed to Octavius one evening, his wistful smile eventually faltering. He confessed to bouts of falling sickness also to his nephew. Although saddened by his slight demise Octavius felt privileged that his great uncle should allow him to see him at his most human and fallible.

The wheels of the carriage, along with four hundred hooves and numberless hob-nailed infantry boots, spewed up dust along the corrugated track, enveloping the entire army almost in a sandy mist. The curtains were closed over the windows of the regal carriage, but still gusts of dust infiltrated the compartment and made the two passengers cough.

A scroll and a pair of ewers upon a tray, containing the dregs of some watered-down Falernian, fell to the floor as the carriage suddenly jolted, having passed over another large rut in the track. Caesar scrunched his face up in frustration and condemnation. The dictator thought to himself how he could have worked through his correspondence in half the time if they had been travelling along a Roman road. Roman roads were valuable as things in themselves - as arteries for both trade and the military - but equally so they embodied Roman superiority and progressiveness. Their flagstones marked out and extended the Empire.

After a pause - during which Caesar gazed through a crack in the window and up at the sapphire sky as if he were an augur searching for or receiving inspiration - he spoke in confidence to his nephew in an attempt to justify himself to the boy, or perhaps himself.

"People will doubtless scoff and claim that I fought this war for myself. I would be lying Octavius if I said that that was not partly true. But know that I have sacrificed part of myself for this triumph. I have been cruel as well as clement. I have lost many friends and comrades. But I fought for them - and for peace. I freely admit to you that I, in part, acted in pride in defying the Senate. Caesar could not have those self-serving parasites and honourless politicians sit in judgement on him. But didn't Caesar merit such pride? But if I was proud, they were envious. Aye, their envy condemned me. They dusted off ancient laws for convenience - but remember that they served not their own precious laws and traditions when they overturned the rightful petitions of the tribunes and proclaimed me an enemy of the state - a state which I had enriched and served for over a decade.

I honestly believed that my rightful cause would not instigate such a terrible war. I was not the only one to be prompted by pride. I did not force Pompey to abandon Rome. He was flattered and manipulated into challenging me. If we could have only talked face to face, imbued in each other that same spirit of trust and equanimity that we shared when Julia was alive; we could have ruled and bettered Rome together, perhaps.

But the past is dead. Pompey is dead - and I have mourned him enough. More than perhaps his conceited and ambitious sons did.

If they could not see that the old order was dying, how could they have possibly imagined anything different, more enlightened? - A Rome re-born. The Senate is but a cartel run by a few ancient clans, who have become so in-bred as to be retarded. Merchants lobby the Senate and direct Rome. The people are taxed to fund the Empire but their interests are not represented or respected. Only their taxes, not their rights, reach the Senate House.

But I will change things when I return Octavius - that I can promise you. Caesar has to be Caesar," the eloquent and forceful dictator expressed, yet this final statement was conveyed with perhaps a tinge of sadness - as if "Caesar" was its own animal, too powerful and proud for even its own creator to control.

The carriage bumped over another rut in the track, causing Octavius' book to fall to the floor.

"And I promise you also that this Spanish road, or poor excuse for such a thing, will become a Roman one by the end of the year."

*

The surface of the Tiber shimmered, like the jade-coloured silk gown Cleopatra was wearing over her soft tawny skin - if she had not already disrobed by now. The wind soughed through the stone vents of the balcony. The sky grew leaden, dampening out the stars. Caesar continued to glare down upon the hypnotic swirls and currents of the mournful river. *"The Tiber was full of citizens' corpses, the public sewers were choked with them and the blood that streamed from the Forum had to be mopped up with sponges,"* Cicero had written, in response to the violence and civil disorder during the years when Clodius and Milo fought for political supremacy on the streets of Rome. Caesar recalled the lines again, briefly and morbidly imagining a corpse-strewn Tiber - but then the dictator permitted himself a self-satisfied smile, for no longer would his beloved capital suffer such scenes. Caesar had brought peace, reconciliation to Rome. His life - and the sometimes compromising means he had adopted to achieve his ends - proved justified. He had fulfilled his self-appointed destiny.

"Julius," the voice issued again, this time purring - sultrily rather than sulking. Caesar finally ventured back inside.

"I'm tired," the dictator exclaimed, before even entering the chamber. Before seeing her Caesar encountered her scent. The queen's musky perfume reached almost as far as her voice, albeit the Roman turned his nose up at the overly potent fragrance. His villa smelt like a brothel, Caesar disdainfully thought to himself.

"I have enough love for the both of us." The purring was now somewhat slurred. She had been drinking again.

"I haven't any for either of us," Caesar was tempted to reply, but refrained from doing so.

14.

Time passes.

The wind seemed to shush itself as the skeletal branches of the willow trees, swaying in the breeze, swiped over the three youths like giant hands. On more than one occasion Octavius nearly had his sun hat knocked off and Agrippa had to nimbly dodge left and right to avoid the top of his bow - which was slung over his shoulder - from being caught up in the trees. The scent of pine and salt mingled in the air.

The three adolescents finally came to the end of the disused woodland trail. They stood on top of a cliff looking out across an ocean glowing purple beneath the embers of dusk. Beneath them was 'Monster Bay', named as such because of the steep jagged cliff walls and semi-circular shape to the bay, as if a titan had reared up from the ocean and taken a bite out of the coastline. Winged clouds scudded the crimson horizon. Agrippa rubbed his face - routinely checking to see if his stubble was duly transforming itself into a beard - and grinned, appreciating the sumptuous view. Salvidienus however, surveying the same seascape, still wore a look of disgruntlement on his haughty countenance. The Roman aristocrat was still cursing the fact, beneath his breath, that he had to carry his own provisions and fishing equipment, having been out-voted by his two friends on the subject of whether they wanted slaves to accompany them on their expedition or not.

The companions had spent the afternoon fishing. Agrippa had won the unspoken competition between the three as to who had caught the most fish. They had then cooked and eaten their catch, washed down by some Arvisium wine which Salvidienus had borrowed from his father's cellar. The friends had laughed, argued, and then slept on the riverbank. Realising that the light was falling they decided to venture to the coast. Their plan was to shoot fire arrows out into the ocean - again in unspoken competition with each other to see who could shoot the furthest.

Octavius took in the memorable seascape, but yet he was still absorbed by the contents of Octavia's most recent letter. Rome was thriving again. Caesar's reforms were working. By enfranchising a number of colonies in Gaul and Spain - and investing in the regions - Caesar had encouraged emigration from Rome. Overcrowding and crime were also down due to the dictator having cut the number of recipients of the free corn dole - thus those who had once over-relied on the state had to emigrate or find employment. Public amenities were again being built and maintained. To pay for these state projects Caesar had confiscated the estates of eminent Pompeians who had refused to surrender after Pharsalus. So too he had levied fines and taxes upon the Spanish and African towns who had opposed him during the Civil War.

Yet, although inwardly proud of Caesar's regeneration of the capital, Octavius still brooded over the contents of his sister's correspondence.

*"Whilst in the market yesterday, concealed in my litter, I heard a water vender call our uncle the new Gracchus."* Octavius, conscious of his history, briefly and darkly wondered if Caesar would meet the other legendary reformer's fate.

Success breeds as many enemies as failure.

\*

The prow of the sleek vessel cut through the water like a freshly-sharpened plough moving through virgin soil. The trireme had been built for speed, its crew bred for violence. The wind fed the sails, giving the ship's oarsmen a well-earned rest. Many of the crew whetted blades, in preparation for the raid. Dice tumbled upon the slick deck. Lucky talismans were kissed - and prayers offered up to Neptune - out of superstitious routine. The spray from the ocean freckled piratical faces.

The breeze hissed. The signet ring on the hand of Sextus Pompey tapped upon the figurehead of a lion, painted gold, which gazed out from the bow of the ship. The commander's gaze was as adamantine as the vessel's totem. Internally he was uncharacteristically anxious for once though, for his crew were a long way from the waters in which they usually operated. Yet the ambitious commander wanted to expand the frontiers of his marine empire and influence. Rome shuddered at his name, or so the young man believed; soon Greece would suffer for Caesar's sins as well.

A sun-polished complexion gifted an already attractive countenance a healthy glow. His build was that of a soldier's but his features, mannerisms and dress were those of an aristocrat. His hair was blond, as golden as his lion's mane, and was styled and fixed into a distinctive quiff at the front, to help pronounce and remind people that he was his father's son. An air of brooding melancholy made the famous, or infamous commander, even more handsome and enigmatic - but the

Roman corsair finally permitted himself a slight smile, for the bay seemed perfect. Perhaps the gods were smiling on this new campaign after all.

"Do you want to disembark now, or head further down the coast?" his loyal lieutenant, Menodorus, asked.

"Here will be fine. We will be in danger of being seen if we venture too close to a settlement. We are far from home my friend. Surprise must be our ally."

"I will get the men to ready the anchor and launch the boats. Hmm, it seems we have a small audience," Menodorus then remarked, squinting up at the cliff face, rippling the vicious scar which ran from his temple down his right cheek.

The commander's piercing blue eyes scrutinised the three figures approaching from above - assessing their age, social status and the potential threat they posed.

"Give the nod to Alexander and Pollux, just in case," Sextus Pompeius finally ordered.

"That's neither a merchant nor military vessel," Agrippa said gravely.

"But these waters are supposed to be free of pirates," Salvidienus argued, unconvincingly. "What shall we do? Surely we should run back and warn someone?"

"We have the higher ground. We also have fire arrows, which will not react too kindly to their timbers or sails," Agrippa wryly announced, grinning.

"Are you saying we should fight, rather than flee?" Octavius asked.

"Perhaps we should do both. One of us should run back and sound the alarm. We have warships in port that can set sail immediately and hunt them down," Agrippa replied.

The pirate vessel continued to skim closer towards them, borne upon the incoming tide. There is such a thing as animal cowardice, as well as animal courage. The former - whilst gripping Octavius' heart like a bear trap - dictated that he should run as fast as his legs could carry him. Although Octavius did not want to volunteer to be the one to sound the alarm, hope swam through his veins like adrenaline that Marcus might suggest that he be the one to escape any perilous confrontation. Yet so too a voice sounded within Caesar's nephew, that he could not leave his companions. "Nobility has its responsibilities," Caesar had remarked.

Whilst unhooking his bow from his shoulder and unsheathing the quiver of arrows which were specially coated so as to set them on fire

Agrippa spoke, or rather commanded: "Rufus, you're the fastest runner over a long distance, so you must head back to town. Octavius and I will do our best to stop their raid from here."

A short silence ensued, as though the reality and risk of the situation fully dawned upon the three adolescents. They might never ever see each other again. Their laughter and reminiscences beside the riverbank not two hours ago now seemed a world away, unreal. Octavius nodded, as if trying to convince himself, as well as Rufus, that it was a good plan and everything would turn out well. The pirates appeared to be without horses. Should a group of the raiders land and make their way up the steep track, which was located over the other side of the bay, then Octavius and Agrippa could still make their escape without their pursuers even knowing in which direction they had fled.

A nervy Salvidienus nodded back and smiled encouragingly at his two friends. He would repay the relief he felt at being picked to sound the alarm by running as if his life depended on it. As the wiry youth dropped his provisions and bow to the ground, Octavius advised him to:

"Make haste slowly. Pace yourself. We'll be okay, so don't you burn yourself out with the burden of our safety on your shoulders, Rufus. Even Oppius couldn't hit us with an arrow from down there - but even you couldn't miss in terms of us shooting down upon their ship," Octavius reassured his companion.

"I'll be back before you know," Salvidienus replied.

"Aye, and bring a bottle of Falernian with you this time, to toast our victory," Agrippa exclaimed, attempting to lighten the mood.

Salvidienus nodded, filled his lungs twice with the sea air, and sped off.

*

"And now there are just two it seems," Sextus remarked to his second-in-command.

"If they have any sense they'd all be off. We should not suffer the young fools gladly. But rather we should gladly see the young fools suffer," Menodorus drily replied, whilst polishing the decorous ball of amber on his sword.

"Unhoist the sails. Bring us to a stop. Put down the anchor. We are close enough I think," Sextus quietly informed his lieutenant - who then bellowed out his commander's orders - all the while not taking his eyes off the two youths on the cliff top.

"You're not worried about those two cubs are you?" Menodorus asked, observing the slight disquiet in his friend's expression.

"More curious than worried I'd say. Why haven't they all fled? Are they ignorant of our intent? Or just curious themselves?"

"Either way, they'll pay for their ignorance or curiosity - and they'll either be dead, slaves or hostages worth ransoming by sun down," the pirate replied in his raspy, Spanish accent.

Menodorus now removed his gladius and, with a sharpening stone that he wore like a lucky pendant, he began to whet an already well kept edge. The blade gleamed, mirroring the cold glint in the sadist's eye. He licked his lips in anticipation of the youths' imminent deaths, for deaths presaged plunder, good food and women. Indeed Menodorus couldn't remember the last instance when so much time had passed without him having killed someone; such had been the length of their voyage. Sextus had sensed the men's disquiet too - Alexander and Pollux were only too pleased to be let off the leash - which is partly why he had finally decided to launch his first raid. So too he had sailed in these waters many years ago, with his father, and recalled the relative seclusion and affluence of the region.

*

The claret firmament faded to a dull brown. The timbers of the pirate ship turned black, the sea charcoal grey. The first flaming arrow shot across the sky like a comet, roaring and then thudding into the deck of the ship. For a second or two mouths were agape - and hearts stood still - as if the fiery bolt had been sent by the gods. But petrification but lasted a moment before half a dozen men frantically ran to the shaft and stamped out every cinder of the unexpected, abominable missile.

Fire stokes the nightmares of every sailor. Ships seldom sink, but they often burn. People drown in silence, but the death rattles curdle the blood of men being burned alive. Even the imperious air of the self-titled 'Son of Neptune' was shattered. Menodorus bared a set of small, sharp yellow teeth and spat out a curse.

"We have more arrows than you have feet to stamp them out. You would do well to leave these shores," a youthful but purposeful voice issued from above. Sextus could but make out the build of the figure above, as Octavius too failed to pick up the facial features of the person he addressed.

Sextus allowed himself a brief, begrudging smile at the audacity of the youths.

"What's your name, boy?" the commander then bellowed up, in an attempt to buy some time.

"You can call me Teucer," Gaius replied, naming himself after the famed Greek archer in the Illiad. Agrippa had no need to warn Octavius about not using his real name. Either the pirates would not believe him, or they would target him as a hostage worth ransoming.

"Well then young Teucer, how would you like to cut a deal?"

"I would much rather cut your throat," Agrippa replied, his voice echoing through the air and scaring off a brace of gulls who were loitering on the cliff top.

"And who might you be?" an amused, rather than threatened, Sextus Pompey replied.

"Ajax," Marcus Agrippa immediately retorted, taking the name of Teucer's brother. "What's yours?"

"Odysseus," the wily commander answered, smirking. Sextus did not want to reveal his presence in the region quite yet. So too the youths might just have figured that he was lying - trying to scare them - should the Son of Neptune have announced himself. "I'm actually beginning to like these two scoundrels. It's somewhat apt though that they've named themselves after a couple of dead heroes," Pompey remarked to his lieutenant. Menodorus barely registered the comment however, watching as he was the two figures of Alexander and Pollux nimbly scaling the cliff face.

"Your first shot could have but been guided by fortune. Prove to me that you're a threat, rather than just lucky - and we'll be on our way."

Octavius this time allowed Agrippa to nock his arrow, set the tip alight via the uncovered lamp that rested on the ground, and fire the shaft down at the stationary vessel.

An arrow once more thudded into the deck of the trireme - with pirates and buckets of water this time extinguishing the dangerous bolt with less drama. Sextus raised his eyebrow in appreciation of the keen eye and strong arm behind the missile. He grinned to himself however as well, for the adolescents had risen to his bait - and arrows would now be absent from their bows for when Pollux and Alexander surprised them.

Their limbs ached but the two cutthroats gave no indication of their fatigue as they suddenly and terrifyingly emerged from climbing the cliff face. The first, Pollux, had been a gladiator, freed by Spartacus. He had escaped over the Alps years ago and made his way to the Spanish coast, turning pirate there. A harelip gave the muscular Athenian a permanent mocking expression, which now chilled the blood of Octavius. The second assassin, Alexander, was as wiry as his comrade was brawny. His dark eyes glittered with prospective sadism, his villainous grin revealing a brace of dog teeth in his radish coloured gums. Both men removed their swords from the backs of their belts, seemingly in unison. Sextus would reward them well for a job well done - and they would relish the easy kills.

Octavius and Agrippa edged back immediately, out of range of retrieving their arrows. Octavius gulped and was perhaps on the brink of running - and abandoning his friend - or begging for mercy.

First there was the faint sound of the knife scraping against its sheath. Then there came the whisper of the weapon darting through the air. Then there came the abrupt thud, as Agrippa's hunting knife found its target of the pirate's barrel chest. The freshly sharpened blade managed to puncture the former gladiator's heart and lungs. Although his twisted mouth was agape in agony, silence but issued forth from the Athenian.

Agrippa no sooner observed his hunting knife buried up to its hilt in the large cutthroat's chest, than he quickly turned to Octavius and grabbed the fishing knife from his friend's belt. He deftly threw it at the second assassin. Disbelief first lined Alexander's expression after observing his friend Pollux felled by the adolescent, but shock was quickly displaced by rage. Not only was Agrippa's second throw less accurate than his first, but the slender fishing blade lacked the power and potency of his own knife.

The dog-toothed pirate seethed in pain as the knife lodged into his left shoulder. The air was filled with curses and spittle. Rather than wait for the pirate to attack him however Marcus suddenly launched himself at the assassin. As Alexander was half-way through swinging his gladius at his target, his shoulder - and seemingly his entire left side - flared up in fiery pain as Agrippa's bow, carved from yew and horn, smacked into his upper left arm. Steel jagged into bone and sinew. Taking advantage of his enemy's brief disorientation Agrippa proceeded to grab the hilt of the knife, twisting it in unison with the sneer which appeared on his face. With his other hand Marcus grabbed Alexander by the throat. Within half a second he pushed the weakened pirate back, throwing him off the cliff. His scream curdled the air. Sextus and his crew were gripped by the sight of the flailing figure fall to his death in the shallow waters below, yet none could discern in the falling light whether the victim was friend or foe.

Pollux lay upon his back, semi-conscious. Blood trickled out from his mouth, accompanying the shallow breathing of the giant, but vulnerable, man. The large hunting knife was still lodged in his sternum, the ribs acting like teeth, chomping down on the blade. Agrippa's hand slipped off the handle of the weapon at first, such was the amount of slick blood covering it, but once he had wrestled the blade free the remorseless youth immediately cut the assassin's throat, terminating the gurgling noise of his shallow breathing completely.

Despite his exertions Agrippa's demeanour still appeared calmer than Octavius'. Octavius had remained rooted to the spot during the entire fight and now gazed at his friend - who peered over the edge of the cliff for further assailants - as if he was a stranger. There had been both a sense of method and instinct in the actions of Agrippa during the fight. One would have scarcely believed that the youth hadn't killed before. Later that night Marcus would replay the encounter - and he would suffer fearful nightmares based upon how the violence could have unfolded; yet more so he felt a sense of purpose and pride in regards to what had happened. Finally he'd had an opportunity to test his skills and mettle. He had killed an enemy of Rome. And he had protected Octavius, as if it had been his duty to do so.

Agrippa collected his thoughts for a few moments and, briefly, an expression of pensiveness and something else overcame him - borne from the overwhelming experience and emotion which besieged his nerves. But then he reined himself, took two deep breaths and picked up his bow.

The scarlet sun finally sunk over the horizon, darkening further the young lion's glowering countenance.

Sextus Pompey nervously bit his bottom lip and glanced up at the cliff top. He stood at the prow of the ship so his men could not observe the burgeoning worry and frustration in his features. Surely Pollux and Alexander had dispatched the two irksome youths without any trouble? Or had the boys not been alone? Perhaps they had been with their girlfriends - and they'd been trying to impress them by challenging the pirate ship? The two brutish assassins had enjoyed themselves with women before – 'spoils' they had called them. But just as Pompey sensed that something was somehow wrong, he was duly proved right.

The bow creaked, almost wincing in pain, as Agrippa drew the string back more than perhaps he had ever done in his life. Anger fed his strength. The following morning the youth would offer up a prayer of thanks to Mars for inspiring him the night before - but equally his heart pumped oxygen and adrenaline through his body to power his bulging forearms. The bow sang, twanged, and the flaming arrow roared through the raven-black air, akin to the sound of the air whooshing inside a seashell. The bolt rained down like a fist of molten lava from a volcano.

Missile after missile was unleashed, pimpling the deck and rigging in flames. Octavius would hand the arrow to Agrippa. Agrippa would set the bolt into place and draw the bow. Octavius would then hold the lamp up and, as soon as the arrow-head caught alight, Agrippa would fire. Before the shaft even found its target, Octavius would have another shaft ready.

"Back! Back! Retreat you dogs!" Menodorus snarled at his company of oarsman, whilst the rest of the crew scrambled around the vessel, attempting to stamp and douse out the growing epidemic of small fires.

Smoke, instead of the familiar smell of sea air, filled the nostrils of the Son of Neptune. If he wanted to land and raid now - and take his revenge on those sons of fortune above - then he would be in danger of losing his ship and means of escape. Sextus Pompey appreciated the value of living to fight another day however, and had ordered Menodoros to sound a tactical retreat.

The rhythm of the drum, which set the pace of the company of oarsman, skipped a beat as one of the accursed missiles landed at the stroke-master's feet. He further comically lost time by trying to stamp out the potential blaze, whilst simultaneously attempting to keep stroke. An oarsman was even gruesomely struck in the neck by an arrow, his eyes bulging out of his head - but his comrades either side of him principally regarded the dying man as motivation to row quicker.

The pirate ship finally began to crease the sea around it and move away from the shore. Menodorus marshalled the bucket teams and oarsman. Before long Agrippa had to fire up into the air to reach the vessel, instead of just down upon them - and eventfully, despite pulling a muscle in his shoulder, the trireme was out of range. Finally his efforts caught up with him and Agrippa, his arms feeling like jelly, dropped his bow and gasped for air. Octavius put a fraternal hand on his back and retrieved his canteen of water for his fatigued friend.

Sextus Pompey saw the last arrow sizzle into the ocean behind him. Ribbons of foam littered the sea, but for the most part the sea was as black as the pirate commander's mood.

"Perhaps they are worthy of their nicknames. If only those two nobodies realised who they had just encountered Menodoros," the Son of Neptune posed, allowing himself a brief philosophical smile amidst his ire and frustration.

"It's a shame we don't know who they are," his lieutenant replied bitterly, "as I'd cut their throats without you even having to ask."

15.

Under a gibbous moon the two friends sat down and toasted their victory. Their drunkenness provided a welcome release for the pair's frayed nerves and erratic hearts. Exhilaration had succeeded terror within the space of ten minutes. Octavius especially was edgy, shifting between nervous laughter and energy - and then sinking into moments of chilling gloom. After one such bout of silence between the two youths, Octavius suddenly retrieved his good humour and asked, "How did you learn to throw a knife like that?"

"The harder I practise, the luckier I get," a grinning Agrippa replied.

Octavius raised a corner of his mouth in a knowing smile, yet later that night when contemplating Oppius' tutelage of Marcus he felt a stabbing sense of jealousy, that his friend had somehow eclipsed him and was favoured by the centurion, who was supposed to be attending to him.

Envy again would hiss in his ear like a snake a few days later. Agrippa revealed how Oppius and Roscius had taken him into town. They had spent the night in the tavern - and then brothel - as a reward for the youth's first kill. "He has lost his virginity as a soldier, now he has to as a man," Lucius had drunkenly proposed to Roscius. The two men then pooled their funds and paid for a clean whore who specialised in first-timers. Her make-up papered over the cracks of her fading beauty, but she was coaxing and patient with the handsome youth. By the morning Agrippa had lost his shyness without losing his courteousness and the woman said that he should come again, which he did.

Yet more than envy, Octavius experienced an overwhelming sense of gratitude and love in regards to his friend. They shared an uncommon and unspoken sense of trust and respect. They would share in each other's successes - and be a pillar of support for the misfortunes. If they argued, they could forgive as well. Their interests differed, but not their values or sense of humour. "To have a friend is to be one," Cleanthes had once expressed, and Octavius was now fortunate enough to understand what he meant by it.

Oppius headed up the group of cavalry, which arrived a couple of hours after the pirate ship had long since been swallowed into the night. He first questioned the two youths as to the size of the vessel and its crew complement. The officer then sent orders back for a couple of warships to disembark and patrol the waters in the direction to where the vessel was heading.

16.

The Ides were a public holiday, to mark the end of winter. Hydra-headed Rome was rousing itself early this morning, in preparation for the day's festivities. Wine had been uncorked before even the dawn had un-bottled its honey-coloured light. Best tunics had been washed and were drying on the line. Picnics were being packed for those who were visiting the delights and quietude of the countryside. Even the horses and bullocks seemed ebullient, chomping on dewy hay and best, crunchy oats. The paint was still moist and glistening upon gaudy and garish banners, competing for attention in wishing Caesar well for his forthcoming campaign. It was as if the city was a creature coming out of hibernation and he now craved sustenance, society and merriment.

Drovers, dyers, farriers, furriers, tanners, tonsors, waggoners, wharfmen, carpenters, cobblers, blacksmiths, boatmen, surgeons, shipwrights, merchants, mid-wives, perfumers, pastry-chefs, rope makers, ribbon-sellers, quaestors, quacks, actors, aediles, augurs, jewellers, jugglers, vintners, vendors, haberdashers, herbalists, upholsterers, urchins, kitchen-hands and knife-sharpeners all buzzed around the streets, as industrious and content as a colony of bees.

*

Caesar woke and was briefly startled to see, hazing in and out of focus in his sleep-filled eyes, various attendants positioned around his bed, smiling obsequiously or gawping. Fury briefly knitted his brow before the statesman realised that he had instructed many of his staff to be ready to attend him as soon as he arose.

Dimpled serving girls held strigils, oils, soaps and sponges in their hands, ready should Caesar wish to take a bath. An over-worked but ever-ready secretary stood poised with a wax tablet and stylus, should Caesar suddenly decide to write a letter. Two dressers, brothers, held a woollen, circular-shaped piece of material aloft which - after meticulous draping, folding and pleating - would be transformed into Caesar's magisterial toga.

For a telling moment the pontifex maximus, and dictator perpetuus, closed his eyes again after waking, perhaps wishing that the bothersome retinue could vanish and he could continue to bury his head in the swan down of his pillow. But the purple, gold-bordered garment loomed large in the tired fifty-five year old's eyes, reminding the consul of the significance of the day ahead. It was to be the last gathering of the Senate before Caesar departed for Apollonia - and then onto Parthia.

He yawned and stretched simultaneously - the yawn dovetailing into a small roar. Caesar duly put the clicking of his joints down to the frigid morning air, rather than his age. Julius smiled winsomely at his retinue.

"Would you like some breakfast Caesar?" Joseph, one of the dictator's oldest servants, asked. 'Joseph the Jew' as he was called, to mark him out from 'Joseph the Carpenter' (who was also a Jew), had been with the Jullii household for as long as Julius could recall, to the point where the duteous and sometimes over fussy manservant had asked his master's father the same question once as a serving boy.

"A cup of water will suffice Joseph, thank you."

"Is that all Caesar?" Joseph replied, with a hint of disappointment and criticism in his voice. The servant was forever trying to encourage his master to eat more.

"If you're worried it's not enough Joseph, I'll have two cups," Julius replied, his features bright with fondness and charm. The good-humoured smile ebbed from Caesar's expression however as he noticed his wife's absence from the other side of the bed - and the uncommonly ruffled state she had left it in. Was something wrong?

*

The early dawn had been snuffed out by leaden skies. Slowly but surely though the overcast clouds, slate by slate, had been lifted and fine sunshine sprinkled itself over Rome as if nature wished to give the city a climate deserving of its jubilant mood.

Brutus stood, where others leaned, next to a pillar in the large portico before Pompey's Theatre. Cassius had once satirically commented that the praetor's posture was "as upright as his morals". Sometimes his ashen expression seemed watchful, sometimes pre-occupied. He bit his nails again. The rings around his eyes marked out a sleepless night. Brutus had tried to read to take his mind off things but familiar friends - such as Cato the Elder, Carneades and Hesiod - brought little or no consolation for once. The words seemed empty, or loose on the page, as if a gust of wind could blow them all away. And the bookish praetor would have noticed not, or cared little, should they have done so. Books could not help him now. Where once a copy of Plato's Symposium rested in the inside fold of his toga, there now resided a dagger.

Usually the stoical statesman dressed himself in the morning, having been taught by Cato how to don his toga without assistance, but this morning Porcia had helped him. His hands had been shaking too much. She had also calmly placed the ceremonial dagger, used for religious sacrifices, into the large inside pleat of the garment. Again, the conspirator covertly touched his midriff to check if the weapon was still there.

"He who many fear must go in fear of many."

At first the words but sounded as loud as an echo in his ears - and they emanated from a man who appeared and disappeared in front of his person in a blur. But then reality, oppressive reality, took hold. The quote was from a play by Liberius - and Cassius had adopted the phrase as code for the conspirators, to indicate that a member would be in his designated position. Brutus but caught the back of the libertore but he recognised the figure as Servius Galba, a former general of Caesar's in Gaul. Was his cause the Republic? - Or was Galba rather acting out of envy or revenge, for being passed over for promotion in Caesar's new campaign? Brutus sadly already knew the answer to the question.

The ill-at-ease senator seemed strangely out of place in the gay, bustling square. The mood seemed especially fraternal. Citizens had even been considerate enough to avoid dumping their toilet buckets on passers-by beneath their windows this morning, the praetor had noticed. Banter and laughter were freely exchanged, between friends and strangers alike. Gossips twittered like crickets. People were either purposeful in the act of shopping, or setting up shop. Brutus overheard the latest epigram doing the rounds and, for the first time that morning, his dour countenance fleetingly broke out into a smile.

*"I have heard that Fulvia cries*
*Ev'rytime her husband returns home late.*
*Either Mark Antony must change his ways*
*Or his wife will dehydrate."*

The ardent Republican surveyed the scene however and his expression became pained. Was this really a tyranny? Was Caesar really a tyrant? More than the people and Caesar even, had it not been resentful patricians and the taxed merchant class who had propagated the idea of the consul acting like a king? Brutus even posed that some had perhaps feted and honoured Julius - commissioning statues and awarding him further bombastic titles - in order to build him up and inspire jealousy, breeding reasons to knock him down.

"He who many fear must go in fear of many."

The words sent a chill down the conspirator's spine. Instead of a sense of duty the call to arms began to stir feelings of doubt, guilt. The line this time had been uttered by Decimus Brutus, a distant relation and a man Marcus had perhaps admired more before the instigation of the conspiracy. Where once he had thought Decimus intelligent, he now thought him politic; ambition whispered in his ear as much as a sense of justice. Cassius had called Decimus "a good man" but he meant it in the treacherous rather than true sense of the term, Brutus despondently judged.

Taking charge somewhat of the libetores' final gathering it had been Brutus himself who had recommended that Decimus be the one to make sure Caesar attended the Senate meeting on the Ides. And so Marcus now watched his fellow conspirator walk off in the direction of Julius' house. His voice and resolution were too weak to call him back.

The die was cast.

*

Caesar was torn. The duty of office, rather than a desire to do so, suggested that he should attend to the Senate. Yet Calpurnia had asked him to remain at home for the day. First she had said that she was unwell, which from her abnormal pallor and strange manner Caesar could well discern himself - and then she had argued that they did not have that much time left before he departed on his new campaign. She wanted to spend some time with him. It was uncharacteristic of her to plead and make a demand on her husband's day in such a way, which is why Caesar wanted to oblige her. Unlike Cleopatra, Calpurnia seldom asked anything of Caesar.

Rather than answer yes or no, then and there, the consummate politician had told his wife that he would think about it - and make his decision after his morning shave. As to their daily routine Caesar took his chair and Joseph stropped the razor. The dictator liked to be clean-shaven to the point of it seeming an obsession. He once joked to his servant that he liked to remain so because it gave the impression of him having more hair upon his head.

"I'm a dog caught between the call of two masters Joseph, the Senate and my wife. What would you do?" Caesar posed, half-jokingly, as he sat down.

"I would pray to my God for direction."

"And what do you think He would say?"

"For an easy life He will say whatever my wife tells him to," Joseph said after a short mock-philosophical pause, the barest flicker of a smile upon his face. Julius smirked, enjoying the dry wit of his old friend. Behind closed doors Caesar gave licence to Joseph to say anything he wished to his master.

"You have a wise God, Joseph."

"Or a frightening wife," the old Jew wryly replied.

*

Brutus nervously fingered the dagger beneath his toga, repositioning the weapon once more. A small volcano of terror suddenly erupted within his stomach, thinking how if Caesar should embrace him he would notice the knife press against him. His breath quivered. The logician reined himself in however by arguing that Caesar only embraced him after an absence of seeing him - and had he not last seen his former mentor only yester night? There had been a dinner party at Lepidus' house. Brutus' stomach had tightened and the blood drained from, and then flooded his face in succession as the topic of conversation turned to "a good death". A pregnant silence filled the room just before their dictator spoke.

"Let it come quickly and unexpectedly," Caesar had expressed. Brutus darted an anxious glance towards Cassius, but his co-conspirator merely popped a grape into his mouth and nodded in agreement with the dictator, briefly raising a corner of his thin cruel mouth in an amused smirk.

"One cannot spend one's life constantly worrying about and trying to prevent one's inevitable demise. The sands of time will always slip through our fingers. Cowards die many times before their deaths; the valiant never taste of death but once."

"Wise words, Caesar," Lepidus ingratiatingly pronounced in reply, raising his cup of second-rate Chianti and toasting his consul. The Master of Horse's most pronounced feature, in Brutus' eyes, was his mediocrity. He was as bald as Caesar, as uneducated as Mark Antony and as self-serving as Cassius. His virtues as a general were that of being a good administrator and following the orders of his superiors. Cassius, who had served with Lepidus in Spain, thought little of him - but Cassius thought little of everybody, Brutus mused.

It was an act of courage, bravado and hubris for Caesar to dismiss his bodyguard like he did. "There is no worse fate than to be continuously protected, for that means you are in constant fear," Julius had remarked to Brutus in private. Cassius had exclaimed that it was fitting that it should be Caesar's pride and arrogance, those traits that had made him First Man of Rome, which should also be the authors of his downfall.

Out of the corner of his eye Brutus saw now his sharp-faced co-conspirator, leading his own personal bodyguard of a dozen gladiators. The plan was for them to be stationed outside of the Senate meeting, just in case Caesar's supporters should come to his aid. Cassius had not informed them of the plot, only that he might call on them to restore order. Trebonius, Pompey's former fleet-commander, also stood in place. His task was to detain Mark Antony, so he would not be present when the deed was done. Everyone was now in their place, like actors waiting for their cues upon the stage, except for the villain. For so long Julius had been Marcus' hero. He owed Caesar gratitude and respect. As well as a gift of a necklace or silks for Servilia, his mother's lover would always bring the budding scholar a copy of the latest translation of Plato or Euripides. So too it had been Julius who had financed the opportunity for Brutus to further his education and visit Athens all those years ago. He was still the greatest man Marcus had ever known, eclipsing even Pompey, Cato and Cicero in his range of virtues and accomplishments.

Punctuality was never one of the dictator's most prevalent virtues, however. Or had the conspiracy been uncovered? It surprised Brutus how much this last thought did not alarm him. Perhaps he just wanted for the day to be over.

"Either this dagger will end Caesar's or my own life by the end of today," he had flatly stated to his wife that morning.

*

"You have not usually suffered from such superstitions before my dear."

"I have not suffered such a dream before," Calpurnia replied. The couple sat ensconced in a small arbour within the villa's garden. Lilies bloomed at their feet. Ivy hung down like the auburn ringlets framing Calpurnia's once elegant, now grief-stricken, features. A tardy lark warbled its dawn chorus. Dark rings still circled her teary aspect - and the image of Caesar, bloody and dying in her arms, still plagued her inward eye. She had at first lied, pleaded and then raged to keep her husband at home for the day. The violent nightmare scarred her waking reality. Caesar had been loving and patient towards his wife all throughout her pained histrionics - all the while rehearsing his arguments as to why he still needed to attend the Senate meeting that morning.

"I dreamed you were murdered."

"Even if death is calling, duty is also calling my love."

"Are you not worried about the auspices? It might be written in the stars."

"Then I shall change the calendar again if need be," Caesar replied, tenderly cupping her distraught face in his strong hand - and smiled that smile which had conquered more hearts than just his wife's. "Let it not be said that Caesar does not know how to compromise. I will be as quick as I can in dealing with the Senate - and then I will return home and we can spend the day together. Indeed I promise to spend so much time with you my love that you'll be veritably sick of me by the time I leave."

Calpurnia let out a laugh cum sob at her husband's sardonic wit. More than anyone, Julius knew how to judge his wife's mood and make her feel good. It had not always been the case. Their marriage had originally been one of political convenience. So too Caesar nearly divorced his high-born wife, offering her to Pompey in order to maintain strong relations with his fellow triumvir. Yet fondness, respect and love eventually fostered themselves into the union. Calpurnia's cold patrician humour melted under the light of Caesar's charm; duty turned into devotion. Caesar appreciated his wife's faithfulness - and forgiving nature; she tolerated his indiscretions, moods and vanity. She nursed him like his mother and Cornelia - and kept it secret when he suffered from his increasing bouts of falling sickness. Julius in return enjoyed lavishing her with gifts of jewellery and clothes (although Calpurnia would rather have had her husband spend time, than money, on her). He even made love to her outside of her cycle, when she was least fertile. It had frustrated and saddened Caesar that Calpurnia had not been able to furnish him with an heir, but after being informed that his wife might be barren Caesar dismissed the idea of re-marrying. Julius had of late appreciated his wife's Roman virtues in light of his mistress' recent behaviour and demands. When Cleopatra had witnessed an attack of his epilepsy Caesar somehow felt ashamed or vulnerable in the politic queen's eyes; when it similarly occurred under the gaze of his wife, he absorbed love and compassion in her maternal aspect. Calpurnia was, as much as Mark Antony and Marcus Brutus, a friend and confidante. He had enjoyed the dinner last night, partly because he could see how much Calpurnia had enjoyed it, basking in the attention and honour of being Caesar's wife. When they had returned home Calpurnia had read to her husband (which, as much of a pleasure as it was, it had of late became a practicality - as Caesar's eyesight seemed to be receding as quickly as his hairline).

Caesar paced up and down in the courtyard of his villa, his sandals clacking over the veined marble floor. He ruminated still upon his wife's unnerved - and unnerving - state of mind. She had said how she had never ever asked anything of Caesar, except to stay at home with her for this one day - and she was right. Guilt prodded at him, like a blunt bodkin into his ribcage.

"Morning Caesar," a bleary-eyed Mark Antony tiredly but amiably announced when entering the courtyard. Caesar smiled, thinking how, even hung over, his lieutenant was strikingly handsome and good humoured.

"Late night?"

"Let's just say I spent half the evening drinking with Lepidus - and the other half eating with his niece," Mark Antony replied, lazily raising a corner of his mouth in a boyish smirk.

"You seem to be systematically working your way through our Master of Horse's stable. I would ask you to refrain from riding his wife though Mark Antony," Caesar expressed, with the hint of a warning.

"Fear not, she's a nag. So are we off to the Senate today?" the soldier asked - and then yawned. He hoped that Caesar wouldn't have any official business or role for him to perform at the session. Sleep was beckoning him like a mistress to bed.

"No, you are off to the Senate today my old friend, alone. Announce that I have urgent business to attend to. Calpurnia is unwell. I promised to spend the day with her."

"Nothing too serious I hope. Would you like me to summon a physician before I attend to the rabble?" Mark Antony asked with genuine concern in his voice for his friend and his wife. His disdain for the Senate was equally sincere.

"No, I have a feeling it will just be a twenty-four hour fever, but thank you. How is your wife by the way? I didn't get the chance to speak with Fulvia last night."

"Lucky you. Two of her slaves died this week. She says she has nothing to wear. Her brassiere keeps pinching. And she's putting on too much weight. I've never heard her complain so much. In short, Fulvia's as happy as she's ever been and back to her old self. Never mind wedding feasts, the party should come when people divorce."

Caesar laughed, happily and unaffectedly. It would be the last time that he would do so.

"I am going to miss you my friend when I leave for Parthia. I can't quite decide whether you have been a son or brother to me Antony, but Caesar would not be now Caesar without you."

A sense of gratitude and love permeated the heart of the sybarite and wastrel. Caesar was the only man who Antony could, or would, serve as a lieutenant to. The two men shared a brief, wordless moment. Mark Antony approached his surrogate father and older brother - and hugged him as such. Tears glistened in soldierly aspects.

*

Mark Antony formally nodded to Decimus Brutus as he exited the courtyard. The two men tolerated rather than liked each other. Mark Antony couldn't help but notice the disdain and disapproval which Decimus cultivated in regard to the dissolute soldier. In return Mark Antony was suspicious of the patrician's sobriety and ambition.

Decimus Brutus had served under Caesar in Gaul and, although from a prominent optimate family, he had sided with Julius in the civil war. His military successes had been many - and many of them had been key. Yet his victories had always been under Caesar's banner. Decimus believed that he deserved to share some of the pages of history that had been written by Caesar, Pompey and Lucullus - rather than just serve as a footnote to their triumphs. Like so many of his fellow libertores he trumpeted the cause of the Republic, but more so it rankled with the patrician that scoundrels like Mark Antony had been promoted to consul ahead of him. He seethed with resentment as well, believing that Caesar intended to announce his nephew as a successor. Caesar wanted to establish a dynasty, as well as a monarchy. His dagger would plunge deep into such transgressions Decimus had promised himself and the others, baring his teeth as he did so. "Let us see how immortal the self-proclaimed son of Venus is," he had sardonically added in a private chamber of Servilia's house, where the conspirators had hatched their plan. Trebonius had called it a coup, yet Decimus argued that, rather than a coup or revolution, they were merely re-establishing the rightful government of Rome.

The middle-aged senator straightened out a pleat in his toga and smoothed his oiled hair. Baring his teeth, this time in the form of an oleaginous smile, Decimus approached Caesar.

"To what do I owe this unexpected pleasure, Decimus?" Caesar exclaimed upon seeing his former General, clasping and scrunching his shoulder in fraternal affection.

"I was just passing, Julius, and I thought you might like some company in walking to the Senate meeting."

"I'm afraid you've had a wasted journey, Decimus. I will not be attending the session today. Mark Antony has just left to send word of the fact. Would you like some refreshment?" Caesar said, distracted somewhat as he took in the new pastoral landscape which Calpurnia had purchased to decorate a wall of the atrium. As such the dictator did not notice his friend blanch, or almost choke on his words before he replied.

"May I ask why?"

"Calpurnia is unwell, or rather she had a bad dream last night and she remains unsettled." Julius pursed his lips, pouting almost, and gently nodded his approval at the picture. The landscape was a little too symmetrical, artificial, but the colours and style of the painting were striking. The deep blue sky briefly reminded Julius of the woad-dyed faces of the barbaric Britons. Caesar smiled, remembering his triumph over the distant isle, but then his smile faltered as he remembered the cost of his victory.

"Permission to speak freely Caesar?" Decimus asked, as if he were back upon the battlefields of Gaul.

"Granted," Caesar replied, curious and concerned by his friend's tone.

"It might be interpreted that you are somehow dishonouring the Senate, should you listen to your wife's dreams rather than the dictates of your duty."

"The Senate has been dishonouring itself for years Decimus. Another day will not make much difference I warrant."

"But more than criticise you Julius, they will laugh at you. The Senate can abide the judgement of Caesar directing the governance of Rome, but I fear they will not be able to stomach the dreams of your wife dictating policy and state business. The paint of the graffiti artists will have dried upon the cartoons before the close of day."

Creases found their way into his brow at Decimus' frank words. Caesar pursed his lips, in deliberation. Calpurnia was asleep. He would be home before she woke, he argued. Caesar did not wish to leave for Parthia with a chorus of laughter or satirical comments echoing up from the city. More than his love for his wife Caesar ultimately cared for his own pride and auctoritas - and Decimus knew the dictator well enough to play upon Caesar's weakness, and strength.

"You're a persuasive fellow Decimus - and a good friend. I feel that not even Massilia was besieged as much by you as I am now. To Pompey's theatre then. 'Tis time for a final performance before I leave this stage for good," Julius exclaimed, clapping his lieutenant affectionately on the back and leading him out.

*

Marcus Brutus heard the procession before he saw it. The praetor was standing outside Pompey's Theatre.

Caesar's litter was unmistakable and unrivalled. Disgust, despondency and envy fought for pre-eminence in the Republican's heart as he witnessed various people, from the Sabura and Palatine districts alike, throng around their consul, behaving like beggars more than citizens.

The procession and adoration was akin to that of an official Triumph, at which a Roman general would celebrate a historic victory over the city's enemies. Rather than a chariot however Caesar rode in an ornate litter - the polished gold of which radiated in the sunlight, giving its occupant a further divine aura. Yet, unlike a Triumph, Brutus judged, no voice would be now whispering in Julius' ear, "Remember you are mortal, remember you are mortal". Would Julius even hear such sage advice though at present, over the chants of "Caesar? Caesar!" which rose up like puffs of smoke and choked out all other sounds?

People continued to flock towards Caesar, like iron filings to a magnet. A young couple finished kissing, people gave up their places in the queues for various food stalls and augurs lost their audiences. And the litter continued to make its way through the undulating sea of people. Heads bobbed upon necks, as if they were pigeons about to be fed, as the adoring crowd attempted to sneak a peek at the dictator. Maybe Cleopatra was with him? "She can turn more heads than a garrotte" a cartoon had once commented on a wall next to the Forum.

Faces beamed with religious adulation. A few children were crushed in the chaos. Drunken cheers were thrown up for no apparent reason. Rome had forgotten its sober spirit, Brutus lamented.

Even through the frenetic and knotted forest of limbs Brutus could still discern the calf-length red leather boots of Julius as he stepped out from his carriage. The roar from the various supplicants eclipsed even that of what had come before, as if the people were attempting to send man-made thunder from earth up into the heavens. Brutus was not the only one to close his eyes and shake his head in derision at the raucous din.

Across the portico Cassius sneered at the ignoble exhibition. His eyes became two slits as he tried to focus on the swirling and slavish congregation and pick out Caesar; the sight of Julius' self-satisfied and pompous air would feed his blood-lust. The senator's knuckles turned white as he viciously clasped the hilt of his dagger beneath his toga.

The brawny litter bearers formed a protective cordon around their master, albeit even they found themselves buffeted by the force of the eddying mob. Caesar, in the eye of the hurricane, was a picture of imperious calm however. He gratefully collected scrolls and petitions which were thrust over and through the arms of his entourage. He smiled and waved, sparking a sense of devotion and satisfaction in every soul he interacted with.

Brutus was suddenly checked in his derision by the sight of a friend of his, Artemidoros, a Greek teacher of public speaking, fighting his way through the tightly-knit horde in order to contact Caesar. Brutus squinted in an attempt to better observe the exchange. Artemidoros seemed to be trying to articulate something to the Consul - and hand him a scroll. Caesar cupped a hand to his ear yet still couldn't understand the strange petitioner above the applause of the crowd. Brutus wasn't aware that Artemidoros was on familiar terms with Julius. The Greek orator had even stayed over at his house a week ago - Brutus gave his friend permission to use his library and study - and he hadn't mentioned having any business in regards to Caesar.

The scroll contained details of the conspiracy. Julius was momentarily tempted to peruse the document then and there such was the singular manner of the fellow who had made such an effort to give it to him, as if his life depended on it. But he merely passed the document over to his clerk and continued to make his way towards the surrogate Forum for the day.

Pompey's Theatre. It was rare, if far from unprecedented, that the Senate would gather here. The grand building, constructed to celebrate Pompey's equally grand victories, was the first stone theatre to be permanently housed in the capital. The stone seating, preferably softened by a cushion, could accommodate close to ten thousand people. The monument was a testament to the great man's achievements as well as his (then) unparalleled wealth and unrivalled status. The semi-circular theatre was situated on the edge of the Campus Martius, next to - and towering over - various other temples and buildings dedicated to Rome's triumphs and heroes over the centuries.

A boisterous sun reflected off the luna marble as Caesar gazed up at the row of elaborate statues built into the monument. Venus Victrix (Venus the Victorious) was the most prominent and beautiful sculpture. Julius allowed himself a brief smile, thinking how he had stolen her as his mistress from Pompey, as well as the title of First Man of Rome.

At seeing Brutus, Caesar waved off his entourage and walked towards his old friend. The dictator nodded his head backwards at the commotion behind him and rolled his eyes to express how he felt suitably divorced from the scenes in the square, and a little embarrassed by them.

"Morning Brutus."

"Morning Julius."

"You look a little pale my friend."

"It's nothing. I think I was just close to being bored to death by Lepidus last night, that's all. I spent all this morning remembering to forget his insights into the merits of satin compared to silk - and how his augur is exceptional at reading the entrails of seagulls and quails, but not blackbirds."

"In other words, he was talking shit. I tell Aemilius that the reason why I keep him busy so much is that I trust and value him as an administrator, which I confess I do - but more so I am just trying to save other people from suffering his company for too long."

Brutus smiled. Julius was one of the few people who could make him laugh.

A group of senators walked past the two men. Out of sight of Caesar, a couple eyed Brutus anxiously. Sweaty palms clutched their stylus cases. Rather than writing implements though, the cases carried their daggers.

"Right, let's get this over with. Are you coming in now?"

"I will be with you in a moment," Brutus replied. Whether Brutus knew it or not, the cancer of guilt had already lodged itself into his soul.

"If I don't see you afterwards, please try and call on me before I leave. Calpurnia and I would dearly love to have yourself and Porcia over for dinner. Just the four of us. Have a good day, my friend."

Marcus could not quite look his friend in the eye as Caesar said this, and clasped his forearm in a Roman handshake. He quickly turned away, sheepish, pained - and observed that, as to plan, Trebonius was detaining Mark Antony in the portico outside the theatre. As instructed the libertore was advising the consul on how he could consolidate his debts and decrease his interest payments.

*

Julius strode into the meeting and sat down on the gilded throne, which resided next to, but above, Antony's curule chair. The murmuring gathering quietened. Sleepers were nudged and woken up. Some still gazed down at the speeches they had prepared. Caesar apologised for his lateness and then immediately asked if there were any urgent petitions which needed to be addressed.

A few statesmen duly approached the dictator, some clutching scrolls or pieces of papyrus. Julius was far from impressed at seeing Tillius Cimber step forward however. This was now the third time that he would try and persuade Caesar to permit his brother to return from exile.

"You are wasting your time. Hannibal has more chance of returning to Rome than your brother. And my patience is now growing short with you," Caesar exclaimed, responding to Tillius' petition - shaping his features so as to leave Cimber in no doubt as to his displeasure at having to address the issue again.

Pretending to be desperate and unhinged the libertore suddenly rushed up to Caesar and grabbed him by the arms, pulling the dictator's toga tight. "Once Cimber has grabbed his toga, we strike, all of us," Cassius had coldly ordered at the final gathering of the conspirators. Caesar was at first shocked and disgusted at the supplicant's unbecoming display, but then Julius saw the glint of the first blade.

Servilius Casca was the first assassin to strike. He aimed for the dictator's bare neck but, with reflexes and strength hewn from years of campaigning, Caesar managed to free himself from Cimber and avoid the intended blow. Instead of stabbing his neck Casca merely sliced his chest.

"This is violence!" the dictator roared, calling out to his friends. But only his enemies sped towards him. Caesar wounded Casca in the arm with his stylus, but as he did so Julius felt the point of a dagger skewer into his side. The pain brought Caesar down onto one knee, but he gritted his teeth and rose again, punching one assassin in the throat and throwing another off. Such was the confusion and unwieldy strategy with which the attackers each attempted to get their blow in that many ended up stabbing or cutting each other. Blood flowed and stained like wine. Already a number of senators ran for the door, believing themselves to be fleeing for their lives.

Such was Cassius' determination to deliver the fatal blow that he actually pulled off one of his fellow conspirators to get to Caesar, who was still fending off many of his attackers. The blade arced over the shoulder of a blood strewn libertore. Cassius screwed up his face in bitterness and fury, exorcising all his jealousy and hatred in a paroxysm of violence. The dagger was just about to stab at Caesar's once imperious - but now crimson and contorted - countenance when it suddenly failed to reach its target. To Cassius' astonishment he witnessed Caesar standing there, his forearm bulging, his hand dripping blood from where he had hold of the blade up to its hilt. For a second, not even that, the two men glowered at each other - Caesar with contempt, Cassius with venom - before the dictator finally floored the wiry assassin by knocking him to the floor.

Julius fought on, leonine. A knife cut into the back of his right leg, slicing his hamstring. Again he fell to one knee. The old soldier found a dagger on the floor and returned to his feet. A wounded, cornered animal. Yet blood increasingly seeped out of him, sapping his strength.

For a time Brutus had but watched on, mournfully transfixed. He had believed that by the time he delivered his obligatory blow Julius would have already perished - and he would not have to look his friend, the man who had spared his life, in the eye. Marcus finally got to his feet and approached his enemy.

Julius stumbled once more, his right leg giving way, but he rose again, his visage still showing signs of life and fight. It was not just his blood now which splattered the marble floor. Such was their wariness of Caesar that, to re-group and check the extent of their wounds and losses, there was a lull in the attack as they circled their victim.

The groans of injured assassins and the sight and sounds of panicking senators fell into the background as Brutus entered the cordon of assassins, which surrounded their prey. For a second or so Caesar believed that Brutus had come to save him, but then the praetor plunged his dagger into the dictator's stomach.

"You too, my son?"

"I'm sorry," his killer immediately whispered, unsure as to whether his victim had heard.

Caesar slumped to the floor for the third and final time. His mind was becoming, like his sight, a blur. Tears cut streaks into his bloodied face. Twenty-three stab wounds punctured his body, which lay beneath the cold gaze of Pompey's statue. He would not allow them to hear or see him suffer though. Caesar would die as he lived - with dignitas. Julius' final act was to cover his toga over his head.

Terror and confusion reigned in the Senate, rather than a sense of justice and liberty. Brutus finally woke from his trance-like stupor and realised the ensuing state of anarchy.

"Cicero, Cicero. Rome needs you again," the praetor suddenly shouted, noticing his former mentor fleeing the scene as well.

But the elder statesman, after hearing his name being called out, merely turned around to the assassin and shook his head - either in condemnation of the deed, or to convey his inability to bring order to the pandemonium the conspirators had unleashed.

Dapple-grey clouds flocked together over the city and cast Rome in darkness.

17.

*Dear Atticus,*

*You will forgive me if this letter lacks niceties and pleasantries, but know that your friendship is one of the few things which I still have faith in.*

*The thunder-clap has no doubt reached you by now. I will recount however what transpired after the deed. I'll attempt to be brief - to save both your time and mine - and so too you may already have received news of the assassination and aftermath from other sources, albeit that news might contain more garnish that Gaulish stew.*

*Where rumour is married to truth is that, immediately after the killing, my name was called out, either as a cry for help or to lend my authority to the bloody act. Suffice to say the 'libertores' should have applied for my help and to lend authority to the deed earlier. We would not now be in the state we're in, so to speak, if they had. So the tyranny survives, though the tyrant is dead.*

*The theatre emptied, faster than if a troupe of lepers should have taken to the stage. Fear and panic were legion. Mark Antony was perhaps as frightened and confused as anyone - and it was only after when he realised that everyone was terrified that he emerged from his hiding-place.*

*Three loyal servants returned for the body and took it back to Caesar's house.*

*Come late afternoon I ventured out and appealed for peace. I also appealed for Brutus to take a lead as praetor, who along with others had taken refuge in the Capitol. But instead Antony took the lead, as consul. We overestimated our authority, but more so we underestimated him. During the dead of night he seized control of the treasury and also Caesar's papers and will. He also secured the support of Lepidus - and therefore the soldiers under his command which are posted just outside of Rome. Where were we? Sleeping, or biting our nails.*

*The morning appeared to bring a certain amount of hope and conciliation. A Senate meeting was called, albeit, claiming to fear for his life, Antony was notable by his absence. Neither the optimates nor Caesarians wanted to inflame the situation too much, partly because neither knew the strength of the other I suspect. The sole exception to this was Cornelius Cinna, who denounced Caesar as a tyrant and that not only should his legislation be decreed null and void, but his murderers should be declared heroes and rewarded.*

*Brutus and Cassius appeared before us. The murder, Brutus argued, had been an act in the name of peace, not war. He would refuse any money or honour offered to him for deposing Caesar. Rome had been their cause, not personal ambition (I think we are both raising our eyebrows to that one my friend). Cassius then moved centre-stage and was fulsome of his praise of his fellow libertore. Brutus, he exclaimed, had "fulfilled his destiny". As his noble ancestor had delivered Rome from the tyranny of Tarquin the Proud, "our Brutus" had once again saved Rome from despotism. Once again "Rome would be a republic, not a monarchy".*

*A bout of cheering here issued forth from their supporters, but although they won over many they did not win over a majority.*

*Deputations from Antony then addressed the Senate. It was and would be the consul's duty to maintain order. "Peace and order" would be sovereign. Despite the danger to his own personal safety his representatives announced that the consul would address the Senate the following day.*

*That afternoon Brutus appeared before the people. He was eloquent and persuasive, although far from inspirational. He listed Caesar's crimes or 'illegalities' as he pedantically called them and argued that the dictator was in fact a tyrant. Corruption was rife (but, unlike the beard Marcus has taken to growing, hasn't it always been in fashion?). Caesar had employed the law arbitrarily. I sensed that people left the Capitol feeling partly satisfied with Brutus' arguments, though more so they were still just in shock and worried that civil war could again break out.*

*The following day saw Antony appear before the Senate - with Brutus and Cassius now absent, fearing for their lives. Although he had sworn an oath to protect Caesar and avenge his death - Rome, public order, peace, took precedence over one man's honour. I must confess I even begrudgingly admired his performance in certain respects. Yet it was "because of the dictates of peace and order that we should not regard Caesar as a tyrant and ratify his legislation" he exclaimed. For stability's sake Dolabella should succeed Caesar as consul. Moreover the various positions and promotions that Caesar had planned should be honoured. As you can well imagine a large number of senators nodded sagely in agreement with this proposition, being beneficiaries of the policy. "Peace is what we are all trying for," Antony reiterated, before positing that "If we nullify one act of Caesar's, must we not do so for all? And who will tell Caesar's veterans, entitled to their land settlements, that they now own nothing?" Fear swept over many of the neutrals now, if indeed one could have still considered them neutrals.*

*Can you imagine how shocked and suspicious I was to then not only hear Antony amiably call my name, but also agree with me in that we should establish an amnesty for the assassins? "We should pardon both Caesar and his murderers," he generously proclaimed, to the approval of the majority. The motion was speedily passed. To cement a bond of trust and good faith Antony then motioned to abolish the office of Dictator, a motion which was also duly ratified. The dramatic session ended with the announcement that Caesar's will would be opened and read the next day.*

*The will was read by Piso, as self-important and insignificant a fellow as one could hope to avoid, at Antony's house. I attended, despite the tasteless decor. In a predictably self-glorifying gesture Caesar bequeathed his gardens upon the Tiber to the people to enjoy at their leisure, for free. Added to which he bequeathed to each citizen 300 sesterces, a sum so generous as to be ridiculous, and they'll surely never even receive three sesterces of the entitlement.*

*The most dramatic revelation however, which was unbeknown even to Calpurnia, involved the news that Caesar had apportioned three-quarters of his estate to his great-nephew, Octavius. Yet can we now not rightly call the boy his son? For Caesar also stated in the will that he had legally adopted the child. Even Antony's solemn countenance displayed flickers of distress and amazement.*

*The news filtered through to the great unwashed and people perhaps now loved Caesar more in death than they did in life. Their love and sympathy increased for Caesar as markedly as their shame and disdain for Decimus Brutus, who was named in the will as a legatee. Even in death Julius is still out-manoeuvring us all.*

*A few days passed without major incident. Cleopatra thankfully left Rome, taking her child of dubious parentage with her. Decimus made a tactical retreat back to his province in Gaul. Antony, Brutus and Cassius met for dinner. I was absent but I was informed that the mood was conciliatory. I dared to hope.*

*I have dared not commit to such folly since the funeral however. For once, I believe that Mark Antony was sober. We should perhaps be thankful that he is usually drunk, for in his oratory and stratagems that day he reminded me of his esteemed grand-father. I sensed that it was not just his hand behind the speech and spectacle which followed though. Suffice to say I spotted phrases and techniques borrowed from Hortensius, Caesar and even myself. Antony has a new lieutenant, one Enobarbus, who has come to my attention. My sources tell me he is both an accomplished soldier and orator. Unfortunately my agents also tell me that he is unswervingly loyal to Antony. Or maybe Fulvia is sticking her oar in and stirring up trouble. She was not one to rule a household when she could rule a consul instead.*

*The pyre was a work of art in itself my friend, indeed such was its impossible height that you might have even witnessed its peak from Greece. The duteous consul and mournful friend took up his position in the forum next to Caesar's bier, facing an already captivated and emotional audience.*

*The colourful panegyric came first, listing Caesar's titles and achievements. After praising Caesar's accomplishments as a general and statesman he then artfully listed his virtues as a friend and mentor. The men nodded in fraternal appreciation, the women batted their eyelids at the handsome - but sensitive - consul to such extent as to create a draught. Antony recounted the oath that he had taken to protect his general and avenge his death. The collective gasp here sucked in the draught before Antony assured everyone again that peace meant more to him than his own oath. Cue applause.*

*Tears came next, from Antony. I was somewhat underwhelmed in regards to Antony being overwhelmed. But the pliable crowd drunk down his lies like a bottle of cheap Massic. Such was his seeming loss of self-control that eventually Antony began to speak as if he were Caesar himself, trying to make sense of the heinous crime, apologising for being misunderstood - and them damning his murderers. "Did I save these men that they might murder me?" he finally, dramatically, expressed as a wax figure of Caesar, replete with painted wounds, was brought into view. Women - and men - wailed. The pyre was lit - and the flames of people's passions fanned. Mourners fuelled the flames as all manner of junk (jewels, wreaths, and robes) was tossed onto the pyre. Stools, benches and curtains followed. Antony created the spark, but the conflagration of hate and lawlessness fed itself. Rioting ensued. The Senate House was set alight. Enraged mobs marched through the streets, torches and weapons in hand, seeking vengeance upon the assassins who had felled the "people's champion".*

*For more than a few days Brutus and Cassius became prisoners in their own homes, such was the appetite for destruction and revenge from the mob. Order was eventually restored, although one suspects*

*Antony could have restored it sooner. Concerned for their safety - and to get rid of his rivals - Antony proposed that Brutus and Cassius take over the governance of the corn supply in Asia and Crete respectively. Without either accepting or refusing the offer, both conspirators abandoned Rome. I too followed them, fearing that Mark Antony might get around to considering me an enemy or, worse still, a potential ally.*

*And so a number of the noble but daft libertores - and myself - met at Antium yesterday. I advised Brutus that he should accept Antony's way out and re-group in Asia. Antony has not been as clever as he thinks I argued, for rather than raise taxes and crops, Brutus will hopefully raise an army. My intention is for Cassius to do the same in Crete. I also have faith in Decimus Brutus to defy Mark Antony when it comes to him handing over his province in Gaul, later on in the year. This triumvirate will cut Mark Antony down to size. Brutus is the key however in unlocking the gates of the Republic again. We must protect, laud and fund him. Both the patricians and the people trust him. Once I cited how he should not only venture to Asia for his own safety, but for Porcia's, he saw reason. I fear I will have to rely on Brutus to persuade Cassius though. Looking most valorous I assure you, the picture of a warrior, Cassius announced that he had no intention of going to Crete, "Should I take an insult as though it were given as a favour," he protested. His fate is linked to Brutus' though. And he's astute enough to know that the capital is controlled now by Antony. He has the support of enough of the people and enough of the soldiers who are camped just north of the city - like the Sword of Damocles hanging over our head.*

*I should just mention that Servilia was present at the meeting also and got on her high horse about my involvement, especially when I lectured the group on failing to deal with Mark Antony originally, "A pity you didn't invite me to dinner on the Ides of March. Let me tell you, there would have been no leftovers," I remarked. Suffice to say that Servilia has grown too old and dry for anyone to look up her skirt whenever she gets on her high horse, though. I warrant that old age is making me cantankerous my friend. Everything irritates me.*

*Gaius Matius lamented, before I left for Antium, that "If Caesar, for all of his genius, could not find a way out, who is going to find one now?" Perhaps I agree with him. War seems inevitable. Sullans, Marians, Populares, Optimates, Caesarians, Republicans - Rome is perhaps fated to be divided. I used to ask "Who will bring harmony to the classes?" Now I think to myself, 'Who can?'*

*I have just received news from Salvidienus in Apollonia that Octavius intends to come to Rome in order to claim his inheritance. Salvidienus also insists that he is at my and the Republic's disposal. Not two months ago he was making similar ingratiating noises to Caesar.*

*I understand that the boy has a tutor, which you recommended the family to. Are you still in contact with this tutor? Can we trust him? Does he have any influence over the boy? - And can we influence him?*

*If I can get to the boy - before some assassin's knife - then we might be able to use him. Antony will never freely hand over his inheritance. With his new name - and the fact that he can afford, unlike Antony, to win over the ardent Caesarians by promising to avenge his great-uncle's murder - Octavius may be able to create a schism in the Caesarian camp.*

*Balbus has no doubt been informed of the news or it might even be the case that he influenced the boy's decision. The old Spaniard has been suspiciously quiet. I have received but one letter from him, in which he expresses a desire to maintain the peace at all costs and, for the moment, make friends with Antony. In short, as much as I enjoy his company I don't trust him a yard. One letter is perhaps as stingy as Crassus also, for such is the proximity of our estates that the secretary could deliver it himself.*

*Take care my friend. My apologies for this abrupt ending.*

*Cicero.*

18.

Octavius gazed back at the Apollonian coastline, conscious of the fact that he might never see its shores again. The ocean appeared as black as Styx. Aye, was he now sailing to his death? Had Caesar taken charge in Hades by now? The lights from the harbour blinked but they were soon enveloped by the kohl-black night.

Oppius, once he had dried his own tears, had given the boy the news. Octavius betrayed a flicker of resentment and additional shock after hearing that Marcus Brutus had been part of the treacherous act, but otherwise he remained stone-faced. Only when alone did he break down and weep for his great-uncle. A pit, or grave, opened up inside of him – grief was like a vacuum, consuming all. All the sadness in the world could not fill the black hole. Only hate and revenge could help clot the void, he darkly surmised. Octavius asked Oppius for the names of all the murderers, he refused to call them libertores. He etched them into his mind; only their deaths could erase them from the list, branded upon his thoughts as the names were.

His step-father had entreated Octavius to remain in the care of Oppius and the loyal legion at Apollonia. Cleanthes too had warned his student about acting rashly. "Let the light of reason guide you", the philosopher had advised. But the light of a funeral pyre, made up of the bodies of his enemies, held a more powerful sway in his mind's eye.

Octavius still wore the inky cloak of his black funeral toga. He felt frustrated that he was so far from Rome – and his enemies. The youth had composed an oration for his great-uncle - or rather now father - which no one would ever hear.

*"Caesar was not just a father to me but rather he was a father to Rome – a protector and provider ... Caesar was loyal to his friends, compassionate towards his enemies ... He believed that Rome should provide prosperity for the many, not the few ... the self-interested Senate judged Caesar a tyrant, but rather, upon opening his will did we not discover that he was Rome's benefactor? Will Brutus bequeath his library to Rome, as Caesar opened up his gardens? How many sesterces will Cassius give to each citizen in his will? Hopefully enough for us to purchase a dagger and plant it in his grave before any floral wreath ... And how can we trust Decimus Brutus to honour*

*the land agreement for the legionaries when he dishonourably murdered the man who made that promise? ... It is not just I who has lost a father. We have all lost a father."*

Agrippa slept peacefully in the corner of their cabin. Tiro Casca, Roscius, Cleanthes and Oppius sat around the table, a half-eaten meal of salted squid and olives before them.

"Can we trust Antony?" Casca asked.

"No," Cleanthes replied.

"Yes," Oppius argued, defending his friend and Caesarian comrade. "Antony will want to avenge Julius as much as any man – more so even, as he has the means to do so."

"The means coming from Octavius' inheritance," Cleanthes drily stated.

"Antony is not our enemy. We should trust him, partly for fear of earning his distrust."

Roscius kept his own counsel but sensed that Oppius was trying to convince himself of Antony's loyalty as much as he was the group.

"Antony holds the reins of power within Rome as consul – and through Lepidus and his own relations with those legions loyal to Caesar he controls enough of the army," Oppius went on to say. "In some ways Antony is Caesar's heir."

"Are you suggesting that we get into bed with Antony?" Casca asked, believing that it would not be such a bad move to ally themselves with the consul. With Caesar gone Antony could lay claim to being Rome's greatest general, too.

"Antony has enough bodies in his bed already I warrant," Cleanthes remarked. "Gaius should be his own man."

"But he's just a boy," Oppius replied, shaking his head. "I appreciate your loyalty and affection for the lad, Cleanthes, but I must ask why you think we should share your faith in him?"

"I'm not asking you to share my faith in him, I'm asking you to share the faith that Caesar had in him."

A short pause ensued. "So the plan is still the plan? We are to venture to Puteoli, to Marcus Phillipis, Atia and Balbus," Casca determined.

"And Cicero," Cleanthes added.

"It looks like Gaius may have found another pro-consul who wants to adopt him," Oppius wryly asserted.

\*

Agrippa slept on in the corner. Tiro Casca could be heard snoring and – due to his missing teeth – hissing in the adjacent cabin. Oppius had decided to take some air. Roscius and Cleanthes worked their way through the remaining wine.

"It seems that you can hold your drink Cleanthes, but can you hold your own in a fight too?"

"I can unsheathe my wit, if you think that'll help."

"Just stay close to me if we get into a scrape, or run."

"To live to run away another day. I can drink to that."

The two men grinned and clinked cups.

"You know Oppius as well as any man it seems, Roscius. One can see how much he was devoted to Caesar. To what extent is he devoted to Octavius though? How deep is his loyalty to Antony? I fear sooner or later that Caesar's heirs will have to fight for their inheritance. Upon whose side do you think Oppius will stand?"

"Lucius gave his word to Caesar that he would protect Octavius."

"But Caesar's death may have relinquished Oppius of that duty."

"Not in his eyes. Lucius is a soldier Cleanthes, not a politician. He will keep his word. I will confess to you that Lucius was far from enamoured with his task of protecting Gaius. Should Caesar had lived Oppius may well have asked his General to free him from his duty. But rest assured both Lucius and I will stand between Antony and Octavius should it come to it. I dare say we will be but his second line of defence, though."

"And his first?" Cleanthes asked, whilst pouring the dregs of the wine.

"He's sleeping over there in the corner."

\*

Octavius stood at the bow of the ship, his aspect as foreboding as the mushrooming clouds upon the horizon. The sea was still relatively calm though, unfurling itself before the vessel like a blank scroll. His future was similarly blank, or black, Gaius reflected.

"This is a bad decision," Cleanthes judged after hearing of his student's intention to travel to Rome to claim his inheritance.

"Nothing is good or bad but thinking makes it so," Gaius replied, quoting from a text that the tutor had recently instructed him to read.

"Rome is like an un-weeded garden at present."

"It's why I'll need a gardener to accompany me."

"And how are you going to pay me?"

"In compliments."

"Ah, the currency of Cicero."

Although Cleanthes had disagreed with Octavius he nevertheless supported his student and chose to join his party. Oppius had asked Casca if he could commit to one last campaign for Julius. He said no, but he could commit to his first campaign under the banner of Octavius. "Roscius, I've spoken for you," Lucius had told his comrade. "Just so long as you don't drink or whore for me on the way," the legionary replied.

Agrippa had been the first to offer his unconditional support for his friend however. The two youths sat in the garden under a night sky more lustrous than their hearts. Six months previous the adolescents, working their way through one of Marcus Phillipus' vintages, would have told each other lewd jokes or discussed Herodotus.

"You have my sword, Gaius."

"I'd rather you kept it, I'm useless with the thing. You are the brother I never had and the friend I always wished for Marcus. Caesar's work in Rome is but half finished. I cannot do what I mean to do alone, but together we can be greater than the sum of our parts and complete Caesar's vision. We will find a Rome built with brick, but found one clothed in marble."

"There's a storm on the horizon," Oppius remarked, raising his voice above the swirling wind.

"Do you mean here, or in Rome?" Octavius replied, staring out into the churning ocean.

"Both."

"Tell me about Balbus."

"First Pompey - and then Caesar - found Balbus indispensible as a secretary. He will whisper in your ear but that does not mean that you have to listen to him. Be aware that there will be self-interest as well as wisdom in some of the things that he counsels – not that those two things are mutually exclusive. But for the most part he can be trusted. Partly through envying his wealth, partly through looking down on him as a foreigner, the Senate has little love for Balbus. He has no great personal loyalty to Antony but Balbus was devoted to Julius. He will support your cause. Rumour has it that he instructed Lepidus to use the troops outside of Rome to avenge Caesar's death immediately after the Ides. But as much as Balbus loved Caesar know that Cornelius is a politician – he loves himself more."

Oppius gazed at the steely-eyed youth. Thunder rumbled ahead.

"No more will I wear this funeral toga. This son should avenge his father, not mourn him," Octavius expressed, as much to himself as the centurion.

"I will not lie to you Gaius, this could well be a suicide mission that we're on," Oppius issued whilst placing a hand on the youth's shoulder.

Octavius appreciated the centurion's candour and, with a wry smile lining his features, replied, "Julius would've liked those odds."

19.

Late morning. Although approaching midday a violet gloom still entombed Rome, dulling its lustre and stone walls. Grey showers gushed down, fuelling rather than washing away the filth and funereal air of the city.

Mark Antony, his toga awry, slouched across Caesar's old throne in Pompey's old villa. Bleary-eyed carousers made their way out of the opulent chamber, either trying to remember - or forget - the depraved events of the night before. A few of the revellers - be they senators, soldiers, actresses, usurers - were still draped over sofas or slumped over cold tiles. The bouquet of yester night's wine had grown as stale as the atmosphere. Insects and rodents devoured half-eaten delicacies - sugared cucumbers in cream, spiced asparagus, lamprey in cranberry sauce, duck stuffed with truffles, Damascus plums and oysters, which either raised one's sex drive or turned one's stomach. Stolas, togas, goblets, olives, figs and the like also littered the room. A young, exotic Jewish prostitute retched in the corner, next to one of the Numidian marble statues of Hercules which populated the hall. For a brief moment one could have imagined the Nemean lion coming to life and attacking the whore, for spoiling his mane so. Wine - and a less seemly fluid - ran down her leg.

Upon the floor, by the Consul's feet, rested his cavalry sword and heavy red cloak, which the former lieutenant wore in imitation of his former general. His cloak however had been sequestered as a blanket by his new mistress, Tertia, an actress and former lover of Cassius. Her uncovered breasts were still stained red from the wine that Antony had poured over them and drunk off during the bacchanalian festivities.

The evening had not just proved a success because Antony had secured a new mistress; as well as feeling that he had won over a number of moderate Caesarians and the more pragmatic (corrupt) Republicans, Antony had also secured the loyalty of his co-consul, Dolabella, through paying off his considerable debts. Dolabella would now support any of his legislation; he would be Antony's subordinate, as much as Bibulus had been a consul in name only during Caesar's first tenure in the office. It was known as the consulship of 'Julius and Caesar'. Antony here drowsily smiled to himself, thinking that he might inspire similar comments and be compared to Julius. His smile faltered however at recalling just how much money it had cost him to clear his co-consul's debts. In a small way Antony even admired his profligacy. But it would be worth it. Dolabella was now indebted to him. And who was Antony indebted to? The boy - seeing as it had been part of his inheritance that Antony had used to buy Dolabella's loyalty. But Caesar's bastard had more chance of fencing with lightning than receiving a single coin out of his war chest, Antony vowed.

The sound of the giant oak doors closing juddered through the room and Antony, or rather his headache, cringed at the noise. He was just about to berate and dismiss the unwelcome attendant when he noticed that it was his capable lieutenant.

Domitius Enobarbus stood at six feet tall. His build was trim, his features pleasing. He briskly, efficiently walked towards Antony. The lieutenant raised his eyebrows in wry amusement at the scene of the party's debris around him. His eyebrows were raised in a questioning fashion, as well as in amusement, as he reached his friend and glanced down at the girl sleeping at the consul's feet.

"Her name's Tertia," Antony said, answering his lieutenant's unspoken question, whilst rubbing his brow in a vain attempt to massage away his throbbing headache.

"I take it then that Chrythis has left for Greece?" Domitius replied, asking after Antony's actress mistress. One of her patrons had requested that her company perform in Athens. Antony, looking upon her prospective absence as an opportunity to taste more forbidden fruit, magnanimously allowed his mistress to further her career.

"She sailed yesterday evening."

"So did Octavius Caesar, if the intelligence reports are true. I fear his destination is Rome, rather than Athens, though. In anticipation of this move I posted a couple of men to Brundisium a week ago," Enobarbus conveyed, lowering his voice.

"Assassins?"

"No, just a couple of my agents. I've ordered them to just shadow the boy."

"I received a letter from Salvidienus Rufus, the father of one of the boy's friends in Apollonia, confirming your report. Rufus pledges his support to our cause. I'd rather he put his money where his mouth was and pledged sesterces. So do you think the whelp will come to Rome?" Antony asked, sadly confident that he already knew the answer to his question.

"If he's smart, or even if he isn't, he will at some point seek the advice of Cicero or Balbus, or both - if they haven't already contacted the boy themselves. I can imagine that both will counsel the heir to come to Rome, if only to stir up trouble and undermine your support with the army and ardent Caesarians. Yet there is a chance that Octavius might listen to his step-father also. I believe that Phillipus will advise the boy to refrain from coming to Rome and claiming his inheritance. But you've met the boy. What are your thoughts?"

"He'd be nothing without his uncle's name," Antony remarked with a sneer, remembering the slight youth with the studious manner who had somehow wormed his way into the affections of Caesar and supplanted him as his designated successor.

"But with his name, what is he capable of?"

Antony paused before answering, as if during that pause he was deciding the youth's fate, rather than thinking about the question.

"His own downfall. We can't let him get to Rome or obtain the support of any of Caesar's legions. I already have enough to contend with here, juggling more balls than a Cretan acrobat. Are Gravius and his cohort still encamped on the Campus Martius?"

Enobarbus nodded, both to confirm that they were and also to convey that he understood Antony's unspoken order.

"The road to Rome is rife with bandits is it not?" Antony remarked with a murderous twinkle in his eye.

"If it's not, it soon will be."

The consul smiled. Caesar would have approved of the swiftness and expediency of the decision - if not the victim of it – Antony mused.

*

His belt used to hang below his waist in the name of style, but now it had become fixed there due to his burgeoning pot-belly, Antony thought to himself. He was beginning to cultivate the figure and lifestyle of a politician rather than a soldier. Sulla, Lucullus, Pompey - all had grown to seed to an extent when they had swapped their general's cloak for the toga of office. Only Caesar had worn both well.

Antony's self-castigation was perhaps prompted due to comparing his physique with that of his lieutenant's, as he invited Enobarbus into his study. Unopened scrolls and unanswered correspondence littered the desk, along with goblets filled with the dregs of various beverages.

"Any other news to report?"

"Cicero is ensconced in his villa in Puteoli. All important correspondence is being handled through Tiro - and the man is as slippery as he is incorruptible," Domitius expressed, privately admiring the former slave who Cicero had freed, educated and employed as his personal secretary.

"The old man can cause us little trouble now. As much as Brutus might still heed his out-dated ideals Cassius is far too proud to be led by our former self-titled saviour of Rome. Soldiers matter now, not scribblers," Antony judged, disdainful of the elder statesman.

"I can devote fewer agents to him if you wish," Domitius replied, secretly believing that Antony might be letting his contempt for Cicero blind him from his influence and potential threat.

"Feel free to do so. What else?"

"I believe that Balbus is starting to court the favour - and whisper into the ears - of Hirtius and Pansa."

Antony here stopped cutting himself a slice of venison from the joint of meat which rested on the table. Having served with Caesar for so long Antony had experienced first-hand the cunning and sway of the Spaniard. As Antony had been Julius' lieutenant on the battlefield, Balbus had been Caesar's principle agent and strategist in his political campaigns. It was even rumoured that Balbus had been the author and facilitator of the triumvirate between Caesar, Pompey and Crassus.

"Do you think it's possible to court and whisper into the ear of Balbus? He was sympathetic to us after the assassination."

"That was when he believed that you would avenge Caesar's death."

"I still might. Can he not be persuaded, or bought off?"

"The wily old Spaniard has riches enough - and Balbus has devoted his life to the art of persuasion, rather than being persuaded."

Antony compressed his lips in either deliberation, or frustration, but then his rugged countenance regained its natural amiability and confidence.

"Well, my friend, we fought on two fronts at Alesia and triumphed. History will just have to repeat itself again," Antony posed, with an assurance which convinced its author more than audience.

*

The Campus Martius began to crackle with the numerous camp fires which sprouted up in the gelid darkness. A crescent moon shone but half-heartedly over the city, as if sympathising with the mournful mood of the soldiers who had so recently lost their general. Talk and rumour were rife - and varied. Some whispered that they would not serve their Master of Horse. Some would serve under Antony, but only if he avenged Caesar's death. Yet most soldiers ironically craved peace over all else, having experienced the bloodshed and privations of the previous civil war.

Domitius Enobarbus made his way through the rows of tents. Ribald jokes (one involving an Egyptian eunuch and a boar's tusk), drinking songs and hushed discussions swirled about in the air like the smoke around his ears, but he appeared oblivious to it all.

Enobarbus was from patrician stock, but his father - through bad investments and living beyond his means - had squandered away most of the family's estate. Refusing to allow his son to become a soldier - both because of his wife's protestations and the shame that would befall the family name to have a son toil in such a profession - Enobarbus joined the staff of a legate and commenced to go on campaign that way. The educated and diligent Enobarbus was proficient in his duties as secretary to the legate, to the point where he performed most of the legate's responsibilities himself. But he always aspired to be a soldier, rather than administer to them. After his father's death the young man proceeded to gain a commission to realise his ambition.

Enobarbus originally encountered Antony during his posting as a junior officer in Syria. He admired the courageous and charismatic Roman from afar however, as he observed Antony being the first man to scale the fortifications of an enemy town. Though outnumbered, he outfought the defenders upon the ramparts and led the army to victory.

He continued to idolise the famous son of Rome, desiring to join Antony's feted company of cavalry and emulate his gallantry. Enobarbus admired Antony for being a great tactician and popular leader, as well as esteeming him for his personal bravery. A young and idealistic Enobarbus would write back home positing how Antony was a "man of honour", humane to the soldiers under his command and gracious in victory. After defeating Archelaus, an Egyptian Prince, Antony sought out his body and arranged a funeral with full royal honours.

People often criticised Caesar's lieutenant for his vices and profligacy but his debts were due to his generosity, Enobarbus could argue. He smiled, relieving the tension in his habitually serious-looking countenance, as he recalled the incident with the steward. Antony had ordered that a sum of two hundred and fifty thousand drachmas, or a decies, be presented to a centurion to accompany his promotion. His steward was astonished at his master's liberality, believing that Antony was underestimating the size of the gift. In order to subtly inform his master of the extent of the sum the steward decided to place the amount upon the table before him. Aware of the steward's ploy, Antony decided to further shock his servant and reward his centurion. "I thought a decies amounted to more than that. This is just a trifle: you had better double it!"

Antony was generous with his time and energy though, as well as with his money. He often exercised with his men or sat with them at the mess table, happily sharing a joke or amphora of wine with them. So too the arch-seducer would often play Cupid, rather than Dionysus, and devote himself to the affairs of his friends. Enobarbus had lost his own virginity thanks to the advice and encouragement of his commanding officer.

Yet more than the delights of love Enobarbus was conscious of being indebted to Antony for his very life. Alesia. Enobarbus and his cohort were fighting on the outer rim of the ramparts, repelling the relief force which had arrived to support Vercingetorix's besieged army. The fighting was as ferocious as it was unrelenting. An arrow pierced Enobarbus' left shoulder, knocking him to the ground. Before he could recover a giant, flame-haired Gaul stood over him, his axe strewn with Roman gore. His blood-curdling scream, emitted as he raised the terrifying weapon above his head in preparation to bury it into the Roman, was suddenly drowned out by the tamp of a cavalry horse. At full gallop Antony propelled himself off his grey gelding and floored Enobarbus' assailant. With little use or desire to emit a similar barbaric howl, Antony first plunged his cavalry sword into his enemy's stomach - and then, with swiftness matching ruthlessness, chopped off his head with a single blow. The timely arrival of Antony proved not to just save Enobarbus' life but it inspired the legionaries fighting around him as well as diminishing the ardour of any Gaul who witnessed the fall of their formerly head-strong champion.

With the arrowhead still lodged in his shoulder Enobarbus fought on that day. Antony noted the young man's bravery and transferred him onto his staff. Such was the industry of his new officer, in military and clerical matters alike, that Antony suppressed the urge to praise the youth in Caesar's presence, for fear that his general might poach him for his own staff. Enobarbus eventually became aware of this situation and was content to remain in Antony's employment and subdue any ambitious urge he might have in relation to being promoted to Caesar's inner circle. He owed a debt of gratitude and loyalty towards Antony. Moreover Enobarbus rightly reasoned that both he and Caesar's lieutenant had time on their side and would be well placed when someone would succeed their general.

As much as Enobarbus admired Antony - and as deep as the bonds of friendship reached - Enobarbus wasn't so partisan as to be blind to the consul's faults. Pleasure too often took precedent over duty, he was too easily swayed by women and he could be at the very least lazy - and at worst inept - when it came to the details and demands of political office.

Yet in the same way that the loyal lieutenant could forgive Antony's faults in light of his virtues, so too he now buried his feelings of unease in the name of duty - in regards to Caesar's nephew. Enobarbus had not known Caesar personally, but he had admired his courage and progressive reforms in relation to Rome and its army. Enobarbus had served Caesar well, serving under Antony, towards the end of his campaign in Gaul and throughout the civil war. It seemed now strange at best - at worst dishonourable - that he should be ordering the murder of Caesar's innocent nephew and lawful heir.

Four legs of salted pork glowed and turned above the campfire. Gravius - and his chosen men - always ate well. Enshrouded in semi-darkness Enobarbus intruded upon half a dozen or so legionaries who sat with their famous, or infamous, centurion. With a brief and subtle nod of his head he instructed Gravius to dismiss his men.

"Leave us," the officer, who was awarded his rank despite not being able to read, barked. Although their stomachs grumbled at the order the legionaries protested not and vacated the campfire.

Gravius would boast that he was the first man into battle, the first man over the wall and the first man into bed. He joked that he had raped more women than Zeus and Apollo combined. Both his boasts and jokes though were often true. Enobarbus had encountered soldiers before who enjoyed fighting (partly because it was the only thing that they felt that they were any good at in life) but Gravius seemed to take things one step further - he seemed to enjoy killing, to the point of it being an addiction. Gravius and his cohort of chosen men were often frowned upon by other soldiers in the camp, yet at heart they recognised their value. They were the first to volunteer to stand in the shield wall, they fought with a savagery that had even made the barbarian Britons turn and run - and Gravius and his cohort never needed to be ordered twice in regards to executing prisoners or hostages, women and children included. War breeds necessary evils.

Gravius, ignoring the formalities of address and rank, remained seated upon his makeshift throne as Enobarbus stood before him. His visage had won more fights than fair hearts Enobarbus judged, albeit he kept the judgement to himself. His powerful arms and torso were tattooed with various scars, collected from all four corners of Rome's dominions. Enobarbus liked to think that he was afeared of no man, but could Gravius be described as human? Those that did not regard him as a wild animal superstitiously believed him to be the son of Mars, sent by the gods to wreak vengeance on Rome's enemies. The only thing that could kill Gravius was Gravius, the legion judged.

"I hope your purse is fuller than this moon, should you want something," the Sicilian centurion expressed, his voice as rough as gravel, smugly grinning to himself at Antony having to lower himself and employ his cohort for more mercenary work. Yet Gravius had no qualms about getting his hands dirty in order for the consul to keep his clean.

"You'll be well paid, double the going rate."

Gravius grunted with satisfaction, or indifference. In truth one man's life, or death rather, was worth as much as another's, he had long since considered.

"Why so much?" the centurion replied, curious rather than suspicious.

"There will be twice the number of people to kill."

Gravius smirked, salivating as much at the prospect of the fight as he was at the fatty joints of pork spitting and roasting before his psychotic aspect.

Enobarbus went on to list some of the requirements of the mission. The centurion would need to enlist at least thirty of his most trusted and capable men for the job. They would also need to be ready to march in the next day or so - and equip themselves with non-military issue weapons and clothing.

"Where are we heading?" Gravius finally asked, after emptying his throat of phlegm - his eyes, one jaundiced, one bloodshot, unnaturally glinting in the camp fire.

"Puteoli," Enobarbus replied, repulsed by the nefarious soldier - but at the same time reassured that he had the right man for the job. As mixed as his feelings might be towards the fact, Enobarbus knew that Caesar's nephew was now as good as dead.

20.

The night sky appeared encrusted with diamonds and the ruby red lights of Brundisium's harbour pulsed in the distance. After spying the port on the horizon Oppius instructed the captain of the vessel to alter course. So as not to advertise their arrival on the mainland they would make their landing along the coast, at a quiet beach that he knew of near Lupiae. Money - and the implied threat of repercussions should they speak of their passengers - purchased the silence of the captain and crew.

The crossing had passed without incident, save for the minor storm as evening descended. In a rare fit of superstition, recalling the nightmarish squall during his voyage to Spain, Octavius retreated below deck. He locked himself in his cabin and prayed to Neptune and Venus to spare the ship.

With the merchant vessel unable to venture any closer, for fear of encountering shallow waters, the party clambered into the ship's two lifeboats and rowed to shore. The foaming water slurped as the crafts kissed the shingled beach. Roscius was the first to leap out of one of the boats, relieved to regain the familiarity of land. The sturdy legionary even stamped his feet, in reassurance or even happiness, at the sensation.

Octavius pulled his cloak around him in the blustering wind. His eyes shone in the moonlight and scanned the cliff-top for witnesses to the suspicious party coming ashore.

Oppius, Agrippa, Casca and Cleanthes immediately commenced unloading their baggage and provisions. Weapons were distributed and worn, but concealed. Oppius reminded the group that they should now consider themselves wine merchants - and act accordingly. Suspecting that Brundisium would be populated by various agents - and perhaps even assassins - Oppius would call upon an ex-legionary comrade, who had once served in his cohort, to provide shelter for the evening.

Come the morning, Roscius and Cleanthes would journey into town and purchase a couple of horses and a wagon, as well as a few casks of wine, to authenticate their disguise. By tomorrow afternoon they would safely and anonymously be on their way to Puteoli, where they would call on Balbus and plan their next move.

21.

Puteoli.

The buttery rays of the sun spread themselves over the villa and well attended gardens. Mayflowers speckled and scented the air. Wood-finches hopped from branch to branch on the various birch and fruit trees which seemed to be unfolding their limbs in the increasingly vernal climate.

Yet, rather than mining pleasure from the scene outside his window, Marcus Tullius Cicero sat with his head in his hands at his rosewood desk. His fingers stained with ink, his skin sallow with age, he read over his latest letter to his life-long confidante.

*"Dear Atticus,*

*What we want is a leader, someone to lend moral weight. Some of the people might well suggest me, but I am too old. I can mentor, but not lead. My agents have reported on potential support for Sextus Pompey. He is starting to make a name for himself, aside from the one he inherited. But we need an army of men, rather than ships, to reinstate the Republic. And I'd rather not swap a tyrant for a pirate.*

*No, our energies and capital must be directed towards Brutus. He will venture to Greece, raising both funds and an army (Cassius will do the same elsewhere). I fear that Antony's pockets are deeper and his forces greater however. Again, we have too easily surrendered Rome to the enemy. History teaches us that history repeats itself.*

*Civil war is certain, as sure as the changing season. I suspect that the first blood will be spilled in Gaul. Decimus will not hand over his troops or governance to Antony, out of pride as much as principle. I am confident that I can persuade Hirtius and Pansa, once they have obtained office, to side with the Senate over Antony. The consuls-elect have little love for Antony. But will our combined forces be strong enough? I'm hoping that Gaul will prove to be the beginning and the end of the bloodshed. But I fear that the impending conflict will touch Puteoli, Greece and edge of the map soon enough. When Rome sneezes, the world gets a cold.*

*If things stay the way they seem to be now, I find no joy in the Ides of March...*

*Marcus Phillipus visited yesterday, bringing news that I should expect a second visitor in the near future. The boy has requested to see me. I have of course assented to his request (as tempting as it was to take revenge on Julius through his heir, for how many times did Caesar refuse an audience with Cicero, or childishly keep me waiting?).*

*Phillipus speaks well of the boy - and not just because, apparently, the boy speaks well of me.*

*I am still undecided as to how I should play things in relation to Octavius. At present I have more questions than answers. What are his intentions? Will he join, or oppose, Antony? How much can we direct him? How much has Balbus dug his claws into the fresh meat?*

*... But all this talk of impending civil war has brought on a headache, as well as heartache. Tell me more of the personal, rather than political. How is Caecilia? Please pass on my gratitude for the recipes. You should be justly proud of her. Should she become as admirable a wife as she is a daughter then I envy her prospective husband. She reminds me a little of Tullia, which is both a curse and a blessing. But I weep for Rome now, rather than my daughter."*

*

Cicero averted his attention from the correspondence to the door as it creaked open. His secretary entered, carrying a bowl of porridge, sweetened by a mixture of honey and berries. His complexion was dark, but his expression was bright with intelligence and warmth. Tiro had first entered into service for the famed advocate in his late teens. Cicero, recognising and rewarding the youth's virtues, decided to educate - and then free - his slave. Upon gaining his freedom though Tiro devoted himself even more to his former master, acting as his secretary and political agent. Indeed, next to Cicero himself, no one loved or admired the statesman more that the perpetually boyish-looking secretary.

"Is that a grey hair, Tiro?" Cicero exclaimed in mock horror as Tiro placed the bowl of steaming porridge upon his desk.

"I keep telling myself that it's a trick of the light, even at night, but I believe it is." The philosophical secretary had adopted his master's dry sense of humour, as well as his politics, over the years.

"I'm tempted to add your grey hair to the list of crimes I'm compiling, to be read out in the Senate when the time is right, that Mark Antony is responsible for."

As well as some light lunch for the dyspeptic statesman, prepared according to Caecilia Atticus' recipe, Tiro placed a pile of letters on the desk for the senator's attention.

"Thank you, Tiro. What have our informants got to say for themselves, aside from that of wanting more money for their information?"

"Antony has bought off his co-consul. Although we may not strictly define Dolabella as Antony's ally, he will not now provide any source of opposition towards Antony's legislation and ambitions."

"It's now mathematically impossible for me to think any less of that man," Cicero flatly exclaimed, his face uniquely screwed up in derision. Tiro knew that the mere mention of Dolabella, Tullia's dissipated husband, would stir up unhappiness in his master's heart - but the secretary felt duty bound to report the situation.

"Balbus has been composing various proclamations, written in Octavius' name, and posting them up for the legions to see. I believe however that the boy has also been writing his own propaganda. Either he is conceited, or talented. The young Caesar is vowing vengeance for his father's murder - and rewards for loyalty. From all accounts he has the sympathy and support of Caesar's legions in Apollonia."

"But will they follow him into battle?" Cicero asked, absorbing the information whilst blowing upon his porridge.

"That depends on how much he will, or can, pay them. We should not forget though that every legionary who serves Octavius serves not Antony."

"We will then allow the boy to have his toy soldiers. Meddle not in his recruitment drive. Indeed I might even encourage the youth to recruit an army, especially if we can in turn recruit him to our cause."

"I'll be curious to know what you think of him after his visit. I wonder what Caesar saw in the youth, to name him as his heir?"

"Hopefully it wasn't himself," the statesman replied, wincing slightly at the thought rather than at the taste of his lunch.

22.

A bedraggled line of wagons, traders, immigrants and would-be labourers snaked into the sea-port town of Tarentum. Oppius gave a small bribe to the official at the gate of the walled city and the wine merchants were duly allowed in without any fuss. From Lupiae they had first travelled to Rudiae - and then onto Uria. The Appian Way now brought them to the bustling port of Tarentum. The air reeked of garum, the ubiquitous food stuff of Rome and her dominions. Made from sardines, spiced in all manner of ways, the fish paste lubricated trade in the Mediterranean as much as wine and olive oil. Octavius turned his nose up at the pungent stench, his eyes almost watering, whilst Roscius and Casca breathed in the moreish aroma as if it were a fine bouquet.

The unassuming party of merchants made their way to the nearest tavern, heavy-legged and empty-stomached. Their journey had been incident free, until now. Whilst Oppius and Roscius ventured inside to inquire about lodgings for the night, the rest of the group were suddenly approached by a dozen men, as dubious in character as they were in appearance. The stale smell of wine on their breath even overpowered that of the garum. The self-appointed leader of the band of men addressed Cleanthes.

"You're new to Tarentum my friend, no?"

"Yes, although such is the hospitable atmosphere I'll definitely be visiting again," the tutor answered. Casca rolled his eyes in exasperation at the tutor's ability to misjudge his audience with his sarcasm.

"So you don't know about the toll charge?"

"I am sure that I don't own the monopoly on ignorance in this place, but no."

The rest of the men, out of work dockers, formed a circle around the outnumbered wine merchants. Casca snorted, either in derision or resignation at the prospective brawl. Agrippa's left leg began to switch, either in nervousness or excitement. Octavius edged behind the wagon, forming the intention to race inside of the tavern and hide should a fight break out.

"Are you trying to be funny?"

"Judging from the lack of laughter, I fear I'm failing rather than trying," Cleanthes replied, giving off the appearance of being amused, rather than intimidated, by the careerist thug.

"You'll be laughing on the other side of your face in a minute." Spittle accompanied the reply. Just as much as the money, or amphora of wine, that he intended to extort out of the merchant, the swarthy ringleader wanted now to teach the wiseacre a lesson in respect.

"No, we'll rather be laughing behind your back. Now fuck off before I, rather than the wine, give you a sore head," Oppius commanded upon coming out of the tavern. He had assessed the situation, as well as the odds, immediately. The centurion also subtly and briefly made a fist to indicate to Roscius and Casca that they should refrain from using their swords. Oppius knew that the authorities could turn their backs on a brawl, but they would not turn a blind eye to murder.

Just as the swarthy docker grimaced and his fingers began to move for the chisel tucked into the back of his belt Oppius' fist slammed into his face, crunching upon the cartilage of his nose. Once floored the centurion methodically stamped on his groin and then his head, rendering his opponent unconscious.

Roscius roared as he quickly grabbed an amphora of wine from the wagon and launched it at two oncoming assailants. The roar transformed itself into more of a laugh as the large porcelain missile found its target. "Two birds with one stone," he would go on to boast later that evening to Casca.

A pock-marked youth cut off Octavius' escape route into the tavern and, for a second or so, time stood still as the two adolescents sized each other up. Fear rather than confidence egressed from Octavius however - and the wiry docker sneered at the wine merchant, anticipating victory. He would have done better to anticipate the punch from Agrippa which quite literally wiped the smile off his face. Marcus followed up the blow with two shots to the body, winding his opponent, before an uppercut left the teenage thug slumped upon the ground at the entrance to the inn.

A girlish scream sliced the air - and was abruptly silenced - as Casca violently grabbed a docker by the hair. He then yanked his head back and - at full-speed - punched the whimpering bully in the throat.

The more cowardly, or wiser, of the would-be extortionists here decided that they would like to live to fight another day - abandoning their drinking companions and scampering off down the street. Some dragged themselves away, whilst others groaned on the cobble stones around them.

Agrippa flexed his sore hand. Cleanthes gently shook his head, either in amusement or disapproval. Roscius and Casca grinned to each other, having visibly enjoyed the brawl. Octavius masked his feelings of shame and inadequacy. Oppius scowled, thinking that they had drawn attention to themselves. He would not now get the chance to taste Tarentum's wine - or women. If he smelled fish tonight, it would be because of the garum he sourly joked.

The sun blazed down over the wagon containing the party and several casks of wine - or vinegar as Casca called, or rather condemned, it. Tarentum was behind then, the outskirts of Puteoli before them. The languid heat inspired torpor in the group but Casca finally spoke up and addressed his comrades.

"This silence is deafening. Cleanthes, Gaius tells me that you used to be a poet. Want to keep us awake, or send us to sleep? Do you remember any of your verses?"

"Poems are like old lovers Tiro, some you remember – those with good lines and that were attractive enough to make your friends jealous. But most one remembers to forget," the tutor replied, smiling and squinting in the afternoon sun.

"Why don't you let one of your old lovers come back to haunt you, or us even, now? As long as you don't bore the horses to sleep you can't do any harm," Agrippa asserted whilst using a sharpening stone upon the edge of his gladius.

"There is a poet in all of us so I'd be happy to let others have the floor, but as I've read enough philosophy to know never to argue with someone who is holding a sword, I'll oblige you. Apologies if my memory proves as rusty as my performance but this humble offering is called *Ode to Indifference*.

*"Our summer fruit, massaging ray;*
*Warmth can Indifference display,*
*For Carefree's platitudes*
*A Platonic attitude.*
*He shrugs outside Revenge's fray.*

*Too frothy is the blood at birth,*
*Age its own carelessness unearths.*
*Shine your light upon me*
*Passionate Apathy*

*In youth's hollows; now show your worth.*

*Oh that I may drink from your cup*
*When down desired pick me up.*
*Of Sisyphus they laugh*
*And Tantalus they starve*
*But let us from thy harvest sup,*

*Those who the gods have played jokes on,*
*Those fathers who their sons poison*
*But do not lend the cure.*
*Let me this night procure*
*The punch line, antidote; un-con*

*Life by not falling for its bait*
*Like an animal that can't wait*
*To fall into the pit.*
*Oh Indifference fit*
*Into my soul, despair placate."*

The party clapped and Cleanthes performed a mock bow.

"How was the work received?" Agrippa enquired.

"Ironically, indifferently," was the reply.

"There was a time when poetry would flow out of Caesar," Oppius pensively exclaimed, "a conceit or line would come to him and Balbus would find himself having to transcribe odes and epigrams beneath official legislation. Meetings would be topped or tailed with Caesar and Marcus Brutus trading quotes from Homer. But I look forward now to trading blows with Brutus - and skewering the bastard."

Octavius barely heard Cleanthes or Oppius though as he wistfully surveyed the fertile lines of the landscape and remembered Briseis - and his own attempts at poetry in her honour. He pictured lying next to her in bed, their sweat-glazed limbs entwined. He nuzzled her, their fingers laced together. He whispered the words, like kisses, in her ears,

*"I want to wake up*
*To the dream of you.*
*Your head upon my chest*
*As the sun pours through*

*Our room, warm with love –*

*Sweet from words expressed.*
*Your eyes alight with fun*
*And the thrill of my caress."*


But even before the news of Caesar's death had annulled Octavius of his desire and any commitment he felt he might own towards the serving girl, Octavius had become philosophical, or cynical, in regards to the relationship. Cleanthes was right; it was lust rather than love. He would now be married to his duty, cause. Women would be but a welcome distraction, to be enjoyed like a fine wine or good play. Romantic love was chimerical. Agrippa and Cleanthes were worth a thousand serving girls.

*"It was worth getting up in the morning*
*If the day held her mien -*
*I would wake to a dream.*
*Now, when I am not asleep, I'm yawning.*

*She aroused me and gave my life a point.*
*The clouds would blow away*
*Each time her hips would sway.*
*We belonged, like a ball and socket joint.*

*But what when her peaks have been mounted, pray*
*What when the zenith's seen?*
*We wake up to the dream;*
*'Tis better to chase than to seize the day."*


"How far till we get to the villa?" Agrippa asked, snapping Octavius out of his reverie.

"You'll probably routinely ask that question another two times before we arrive, if that's any indicator. We'll get there when we get there," Oppius replied.

"I just hope that Balbus has been visited by some genuine wine merchants of late. The piss we're drinking is as sour as an aged drab's –"

"Thank you Tiro, for proving my point," Cleanthes chipped in, cutting off the sentence.

"Uh?" the veteran responded, scrunching up his face in slight bewilderment.

"There is indeed a poet in every one of us."

The six friends lazily smirked - and one of the horses whinnied - in the glistering light as the wagon crossed into the verdant pasture of Puteoli, the first step of their long journey almost over.

23.

The varnish of his tan concealed the grain of his years. Various papers littered a large cedar wood desk, inlaid with tortoiseshell. Four ornate bronze lions at the feet of the desk surveyed all. Cornelius Balbus composed letter after letter to loyal and wavering Caesarians (clients, centurions, senators, merchants). At present Balbus was drafting a letter to a particularly god-fearing and superstitious client.

*"...Nature abhorred the unnatural act. After the Ides lightening struck the dockyards. Winds moaned through the capital for days, uprooting trees and houses alike. Dogs could be heard howling throughout the night outside the house of the Pontifex Maximus ... There is still a Caesarian cause. There is still a Caesar..."*

Balbus carried on writing, propaganda oozing from his pen like honey from a hive, but his thoughts also turned to this new Caesar again. The secretary recalled Julius' comments about the boy.

"He is intelligent without being conceited, confident without being arrogant. He's aware that the gods gave him two ears and one mouth - and knows to use the former twice as much as the latter ... he sees how things are and how they should be - and I warrant he'll learn how to bridge the distances between those two peaks ... his tutors speak well of him. It's clear he is more of a Cicero than Scipio but ultimately he should become a statesman, not general. I do not want Octavius to spend his life in the saddle on campaign, replicating the glory-hunting of his great-uncle ... he has but asked one favour of Caesar - and that was to intercede on his friend's behalf to release this Marcus Agrippa's brother ... Should anything happen to me Cornelius, I want you to act as Octavius' secretary - and serve him as loyally and adroitly as you have me old friend."

"You are going to announce him as your heir?"

"Not publicly. But I have altered my will accordingly."

"And your son by Cleopatra?"

"He will be provided for, but his mother is too much like his father to be wholly trusted. She can be Queen of Egypt for as long as her immortality lasts, but she'll not get her claws into Rome."

"And what of Brutus? You once imagined that he would take your place as the First Man of Rome."

"I love Marcus as if he were my own. But he longs for a past that never existed in the first place. I want the future to eclipse the past, not be hampered by it. Octavius is the future."

"Should dame fortune cheat on her favourite paramour - and something happens to Caesar - I promise to serve him faithfully, Julius."

"Thank you, Cornelius. And I will make good on my promise to make you Rome's first foreign-born consul old friend. It'll be worth it just to see the look upon the faces of the old men when the new man is announced."

An attendant knocked and then entered the secretary's study.

"Master, Caesar is here."

For a sublime moment or two Cornelius believed that his old master had returned - after all, hadn't Balbus propagated the idea of Julius' divinity himself in various proclamations? But reason duly took hold.

"Time to embrace the future," the politic secretary remarked to himself, and went out to greet his guests.

*

"Caesar."

Octavius had grown attuned to flattery over the years but still his new name did not chime quite right. The secretary descended the steps of his villa with outstretched arms. Octavius removed his sun hat and courteously bowed to his host.

"Oppius, Roscius. I wish the circumstances were different but it is good to see you both again, nevertheless. Tiro, I have arranged to have you quartered near the wine cellar. You must be Cleanthes? Atticus speaks highly of you. My library is open to you."

"I hope that doesn't preclude me from sharing the wine cellar with Casca, though."

"No, indeed. Well said. And you must be Marcus Agrippa? Oppius tells me you handle both your drink and a bow well."

"But not at the same time, unfortunately."

Balbus remarked how his house was open to all his guests as an army of servants appeared from nowhere and attended to the party's belongings. Cleanthes would later remark to Agrippa whether the secretary employed a servant whose sole task it was to keep his tongue oiled, such were the compliments that dripped from it.

"We have much to discuss my friends, but such things will wait till morning. Tonight you should rest, unless you would like the wine cellar opened up to you this evening, Tiro? The serving girls may well open up to you too, if you ask nicely, Roscius. Caesar, both your mother and step-father are staying with me. Would you like me to send for them?"

"Thank you Cornelius, for everything," Octavius replied, expressing gratitude not just for the hospitality.

\*

The two loyal Caesarians reclined over couches around the fire in Balbus' triclinium. Trophies and curiosities from the four corners of the known world decorated the walls. A sculpture of Odysseus, which for once Atticus was the under bidder on, stood imperiously in the centre of the chamber. A statue of Caesar (which Atticus would have happily been the under bidder on) next to the mantle also naturally attracted one's attention.

"So, Lucius, what do you think of the boy?"

"He growing up and growing on me. But that still may not be enough for what lies ahead."

"I understand that you encouraged him to lead the Apollonian legions to Rome after Julius' murder. Nothing good could have come from that," Balbus remarked, reprovingly.

"I know. I was angry. I just wanted vengeance," Oppius replied, feeling added guilt in that he had also persuaded Agrippa to encourage Octavius to lead the legions to Rome.

"The boy felt the same I warrant, but he did not allow his passions to cloud his judgement. Also, I have spoken to Marcus Phillipus. He implored Gaius not to take the name of Caesar and claim his inheritance. Yet the boy has proved brave and ambitious. So we have intelligence, courage and ambition. If Gaius has inherited some of Julius' blind luck then we may well win back Rome."

\*

"We defy augury," Octavius replied after hearing how his mother had consulted a soothsayer as to her son's future. He predicted dark times.

"Would you not be counselled by your mother, or your step-father, instead of a soothsayer then?" Marcus Phillipus asked.

Balbus had provided the family with the guest property on his estate. Gaius, Atia and Marcus Phillipus greeted each other with warmth and tears. They sat down to eat as if it were dinner time back in Apollonia. But once the meal was finished and Balbus' attendants had disappeared, Marcus Phillipus addressed Octavius' fate.

"Your counsel is always welcome, as long as you are aware that I will keep my own counsel too. I love you both dearly but the times call for your son to become a man. I am aware that Antony will view me as a threat for claiming my inheritance. I am aware that the libertores will view me with suspicion, at best. The Republicans in the Senate will look upon the new Caesar with contempt, or be dismissive of me. The Caesarians may be harder to win over than anyone else. Yet I am spurred on by Caesar's faith in me. You did not question his judgement when he was alive, not once. Yet you question his judgement now?" Octavius exclaimed, staring at his parents with a certain amount of disappointment and chastisement.

"We cannot protect you when you go to Rome," Marcus Phillipus warned.

"When I go to Rome, it should be others who should look to be protected," Octavius calmly replied, the long shadow caused by Caesar's statue darkened the youth's already brooding looks.

"Mark Antony will not give up your inheritance easily."

"I know, but in defying my wishes he will also be defying the wishes of Caesar, which will lose him support with the Caesarians."

Marcus Phillipus smiled, admiring Octavius' politic philosophy. Like Julius, he had considered everything. Like Julius, he would not alter his course once his mind was set.

"At least promise me that you will meet with Cicero before you venture to Rome."

"I give you my word," Octavius solemnly replied.

"Then I will give you my support."

Atia was now as resigned as her husband from dissuading Octavius from his course. Tears welled in her eyes again.

"You will always be my sweet-natured boy with his head in a book, who sometimes needs his mother to nurse him in my eyes."

"I just hope that I can still sometimes see me as such," Octavius uttered as he got up, clasped his mother by the hand and sweetly kissed her on the forehead.

"I love you so much."

"I'm pleased to see that you have as great taste in sons as you do dresses, mother," Octavius replied, eyes glistening too.

Atia let out a laugh-cum-sob and the family continued to enjoy their evening together.

24.

A couple of braziers flanked Marcus Brutus, flames tasting the salty air. He had asked for his desk to be brought out onto the balcony of his coastal villa. The poetic vista consoled him not, though. He dismissed his attendants, desiring solitude. Porcia was asleep. The russet of dusk had bled into the sable evening. Brutus tilted his head back to drain the last of the undiluted wine and as he did so he caught sight of the Northern Star. Julius had once described himself as being as constant as the Northern Star. Perhaps the boast was closer to the truth than a conceit the praetor mused, for without Caesar to guide it Rome was a rudderless ship - in a storm. The Senate steered it not, fractured and scared as it was. The people were divided, too. Some were distrustful of the Senate. Some recognised the growing tyranny of Antony. The legions marched not under one standard. Was the choice a civil war or Antony ruling by the sword? Or how long would it be before the smell of fear and the tremors of division were felt in Gaul - and an heir to Vercingetorix attacked? Have I, in murdering Caesar, brought about that which I strove to prevent? - Tyranny and the downfall of Rome. Did I spare the wrong consul?

Brutus buried his head in his hands, masking a pained expression. He finally picked up his stylus, which seemed to weigh as heavy as a dagger, and commenced to draft a letter to his ally and mentor.

*Dear Cicero,*

*You wisely set down in On the Nature of the Gods that, "If anyone ever tried to improve anything in the natural world, he would either make it worse or else attempt the impossible." Perhaps the same is true for the political world. We either underestimated Julius' auctoritas or overestimated our own. The ghost of Caesar still haunts Rome, whilst I am in exile. How long before Antony usurps enough power to decree me an outlaw? I should now be presiding over legislation in the capital - instead I am bound for Macedonia, to preside over grain storage ...*

*... What option do I have but to exit the stage for now? But I am yours to direct. This race is but half run - and as Julius once argued it is where one is positioned at the end of the course that matters. Both Cassius and I will glean support and funds to build an army. Antony*

*is not Caesar. He neither possesses Julius' abilities, or fortune. The "feckless boy", as Pompey rightly judged him, will fail - fall. Despite my protestations above know my friend that I am still Brutus and my commitment to rid Rome of tyranny remains as stolid. I am as constant as the Northern Star.*

*Your friend and student, Marcus Brutus.*

Brutus put down his stylus and pinched the bridge of his nose. He was unsure whether the wine was causing his headache, or if by partaking of some more he would remedy it. He read over the letter again, ruminating upon whether to tell Cicero how the ghost of Caesar was also haunting his dreams.

*

The encampment was just outside Atina, buried in the woods. A thick canopy of trees blocked out a majestic night sky. Lentil soup and a side of honey-glazed venison sat over a crackling fire. Gravius - and a select band of men from his cohort - were now devoid of any possessions marking them out as legionaries. The centurion downed another measure of sour acetum - thinking that he would be able to afford a fine vintage after this job was complete. Most of his men were now sleeping off their own measures of wine, but Gravius was still awake, holding court around the fire with his lieutenants.

"It was shortly after Alesia. We were on patrol and discovered this Gaulish deserter in a cave. After spending ten minutes with Scylla and Charybdis (Gravius here proudly held up his two scarred fists) I proposed some sport with the surrender monkey. We found a length of rope and a dice. He was told that if he threw a one, two, three, four or a five we would hang him. His eyes near popped out of his head as if he had already been hung upon hearing this. But there was also this one shred of hope lighting his expression as he asked, 'What about if I throw a six?', 'Well, if that happens' I said, whilst putting a reassuring arm around his shoulder, 'you get to throw again.'"

The men cackled in unison with the fire.

"But to business. The plan will be to march to Venatrum. Our quarry is currently cooped up in Puteoli. I will send a scouting party along the Appian Way. Our contractor has also placed some agents close to the estate where the boy is staying. Either way we shall be provided with intelligence of the party's position in advance. I know of a perfect spot for an ambush between Venatrum and Allifae. There are to be no survivors."

"The poor bastard won't know what's hit him," one of the lieutenants remarked, shaking his head in sadness but grinning nevertheless.

"I'll know what has hit him. My axe. But let the gods bless the poor bastard all the same - as he's about to make us all rich bastards," Gravius declared.

Again the band of brothers laughed as Gravius sniffed and spat out the phlegm caught in his throat. No one complained as the green missile landed limpet-like upon the venison, missing its intended target of the fire.

*

Marcus Agrippa yawned and gazed at his bed with a look of desire as if the serving girl from earlier was lying across it - but he continued with the letter to his friend.

*Dear Rufus,*

*The night has been long so you will forgive me if this letter is short. We have arrived safely at Balbus' estate. You'd like it here. There are more staff than dishes on the menu, just about - and the staff are dishes in themselves. I caught the eye of a serving girl tonight. I just hope that's all I caught off her.*

*You ask what Gaius' plans are? I'm not sure if he even knows them. We are like an army marching to battle, not knowing the strength of our enemy. Or enemies. It is a shame that your father would not allow you to join our party. Employ all your arts as a young advocate to change his mind...*

*... I was talking to Oppius and one could almost reduce it down to mathematics - which side will have the most money to purchase the most legions. At present no one contingent - whether it be ours, Antony's or the Senate's - has the necessary force to defeat the other two... Lucius remarked that our greatest strength at present could be our perceived weakness, for the Senate and Antony are unlikely to collude to see off the threat of an eighteen year old ...*

*Your tired friend, Marcus.*

25.

Citrus sunlight poured down over the emerald garden. The felt lawn was bordered by all manner of ornate flowers. Bowls of grapes, olives, cured meats and sweet pastries were placed on a table, which was housed underneath a tent. Balbus stood to attention and invited his guest to sit.

"Please, let me know if there's anything I can get you."

"This water will suffice, thank you," Octavius replied.

Balbus raised a corner of his mouth in a fleeting smile, recalling how Julius would have the same meagre breakfast. With a nod of his head Balbus instructed his attendants to depart.

"Your great-uncle, or father as we should grow accustomed to calling him, was the most accomplished man I have ever known. If you do right by his name then I will do right by you Gaius."

"I have no intention of seeing his name, or accomplishments, dishonoured Cornelius."

"Now, to business. And the business of Rome is business. One of our tasks is to convince people - the merchant and political classes, the mob, and legions - that by investing in Caesar their futures will be more prosperous. We have retained the support of the majority of Caesar's clients - senators who owe their position to Julius, merchants who have profited from his legislation and favours, soldiers who served under his standard. We must persuade these constituencies that they are, by betting on you, betting on the eventual winner."

Octavius listened intently but refrained from comment.

"As soon as you enter the capital as Caesar you will be crossing your own Rubicon. Are you prepared for the consequences? Power can change a man Gaius; turn him into a monster - a serpent feeding upon its own tail. The course of honours is a race that never ends. Even if one becomes the First Man of Rome you'll still be fated to look over your shoulder, worried about who stands behind you - and as such you may take your eyes off where you're going. Knowing such, do you still want to cross the Rubicon?"

"Aut Caesar aur nihil," Octavius calmly replied, gazing out onto the well tended garden.

"What are you prepared to do? What kind of person are you willing to become? Would you slit the throat of your best friend?"

Octavius thought of Agrippa.

"No, but I would slit the throat of the man that asked me to do such a thing," Caesar responded, with a look as steely as a blade.

*

Oppius' arrow thudded into the centre of the target, adding to the tightly grouped bunch. He proceeded to instruct Agrippa.

"Never ask your men to do something you haven't done, or wouldn't do. Fail to prepare, prepare to fail. Do not break a promise over pay. Train hard, so you can fight easy. Promote discipline, but never be cruel for cruelty's sake."

Agrippa nodded his head and then fired his own arrow into the target next to the centurion's. Again the bolt landed outside the inner circle, where but one shot resided. Oppius raised an eyebrow, hoping that Marcus was just having an off session. They all had things on their minds.

"For as long as I can remember I wanted to be a soldier. Yet I have of late thought that I do not want to solely be a soldier for the rest of my life."

"What do you want to be then, Marcus?"

"A general can build an army - but it is usually for the purpose to destroy something."

"Or protect. But your point is taken."

"We, Gaius and I, want to build something else. Something better."

Marcus pulled back his bow and fired off another shot, which again landed outside the inner target.

"And what is it you wish to build?"

"An empire."

"You're certainly aiming high, Marcus. Nearly as high as that last arrow."

"Really? There I was thinking that I was just getting my eye in," Agrippa replied, nodding towards the target and the make-shift face upon it: a lop-sided grin, nose and two eyes, marked out by his arrows.

*

The breeze wafted through the tent. Wood pigeons darted across the pastel blue sky. Balbus was impressed by the speed at which the young Caesar took things in. The clarity and insight with which Octavius expressed himself also reminded the secretary of his former employer.

"Hirtius, our consul-elect and one time secretary to Julius when he was writing his books, passed this way recently. Suffice to say he can replicate Julius' prose style better than his military or political genius."

"Julius once joked to me that he used his stomach more than his head," Octavius replied, recalling the scene of his uncle whispering the comment in his ear.

"Aye, our Hirtius is quite the gourmet, or glutton. One of the arms of the curule chair may have to be removed, just so he can fit on it. It is doubtful whether Hirtius or Pansa will side with Antony, as my agents report that Antony is reluctant to allow them to inherit the consulship. He wishes to remain as dictator, or serve as pro-consul in Gaul - yet Decimus Brutus has a grip on the office there and would rather give up his mother than his legions. Mark Antony has a number of legions loyal to him in Macedonia. But ultimately he is relying upon winning over our Caesarian legions. Partly because he too wishes to win over the Caesarians - and to undermine Antony - Hirtius will not oppose you or your bid to claim your inheritance. And where Hirtius goes Pansa will follow. And he has recently followed him to Cicero's villa."

"We must divide to conquer," Octavius remarked, surveying the map on the table and political situation.

"Exactly. We must play a long game - and you have time on your side to do so. There are other positives, too. Our campaign is well funded. We have at our disposal the war chest that Julius was intending to take to Parthia. Marcus Phillipus pledged his support this morning too. Our clients are not without means and the will to finance you, for their present support, will buy future favours."

"And what future favour will purchase your present support, Cornelius?" Octavius remarked, in a spirit of candour rather than offence.

"I want you to honour a promise that your uncle made to me before he died."

*

Whilst Oppius, Casca and Roscius went off to drill the men whom Balbus was providing to escort Octavius to Rome, Cleanthes and Agrippa, finished off their lunch.

"I have to confess Cleanthes, I've been impressed by the amount of drink you can handle," Agrippa exclaimed, as the tutor drained another cup.

"The harder I practise, the luckier I get," Cleanthes replied, winking at his companion.

"Why do you drink so much, if you do not mind me asking?"

"I drink to forget, Marcus."

"To forget what?"

"I can't remember. But no more on that. I was speaking to Roscius last night. He seems to think that you could make a great general one day."

"Wine truth I warrant," Agrippa self-effacingly replied, inwardly cheered by the comment however.

"Perhaps. But to be successful in this life Marcus you should, even more than a great general, be a good husband and father. Your devotion to Gaius and Rome are admirable but make sure that they do not become the sum of your existence. Tullia brought Cicero greater consolation to his life than his study of philosophy or becoming consul. And would not Caesar have traded all his victories to have his daughter Julia back? Remember Marcus, to win on the battlefield you have to dominate, but to succeed in your personal life sometimes you have to submit, sacrifice ground."

"And how successful have you been in your personal life?"

"I forget," the tutor replied, burying a wistful smile in his wine cup.

*

Octavius and Balbus continued to plot. The secretary advised that Octavius should cut his hair; he should address the legions with a short martial style, not that of a floppy-haired teenager. He suggested the date, time and even gate that Ocatvius should use as to when to enter Rome. In order to sow the seeds of the new Caesar's dignitas and authoritas the secretary would employ his agents and clients to arrange rallies, both for civilians and military constituencies, in towns along the way to Rome. The two men worked on the import and wording of various correspondence and pamphlets. There would be a distinct difference between Caesar's public and private mandate towards avenging Caesar's death. As well as schooling his new master in the sport and stratagems of Roman politics, Balbus shared some stories about Caesar.

"Whilst Crassus used to hide himself away in his treasury counting his money, Julius would be in Crassus' bedroom, counting the times he made love to his wife ... Julius once remarked that though Pompey had more hair, he had more brains ... Sometimes Caesar's clemency was sincere, sometimes cynical ... I remember him quoting Thucydides the evening after returning from Spain and the civil war: *The right way to deal with free people is this - not to inflict tremendous punishments on them after they have revolted, but to take tremendous care of them before this point is reached, to prevent them even contemplating the idea of revolt, and, if we have to use force with them, to hold as few of them as possible responsible.* For all of his charm and brilliance Julius, for me, towards the end, was enmeshed in remorse. He was trying to atone for his past by creating a better future."

Twilight's mellow glow suffused the air. The lines across the map were becoming blurred, Cornelius' hand ached from having written so much. The secretary decided to call time on their day's work. As Balbus did so however one of his attendants strode up and handed him a scroll. He opened and surveyed it immediately.

"It seems that Antony has dispatched Lepidus to Spain in order to recruit to his cause the legions posted there. I warrant his mission is to also sound out Sextus Pompey about his support," the politic adviser remarked, his eyebrow arched in intrigue.

"Should we be worried by this news?"

"The news certainly shows that Antony is worried, if he needs to ask his former enemy for help. We can use such desperation and treachery to our advantage. This news also reminds us how we must get you to Rome sooner rather than later. The stage is set for the young Caesar to enter Rome."

"I have one other stop to make beforehand."

"Cicero? You should keep to our timetable," Balbus warned, partly fearful of Octavius being detained too long, but more so he was worried about the seductive influence the former consul could have upon the studious youth.

"I mean to keep to our schedule, but I also must keep my promise to Marcus Phillipus."

"I count Cicero as a friend - but also a political opponent. Julius admired him greatly. He once remarked that the only things which would endure as much as his deeds would be Cicero's words. Critics of Cicero have called him inconsistent and hypocritical over the years but one could argue that he has always remained constant in his stance - to have a foot in more than one camp. I sense that this new crisis has re-invigorated the old man as well. For many a month he just pined away, mourning for his daughter. For that I can forgive him. Tullia was an accomplished young woman, wise in everything aside from her choice of husband and her blind devotion to the wastrel. I dare say Cicero was also in mourning for past glories and influence. Although Julius admired the former consul - he also often ignored him. Be wary of the wily old man though, Gaius. Marcus Tullius spoke in my defence at a trial in Rome many years ago. Such was his eloquence that even I started to believe that I was innocent," Balbus issued with a twinkle in his deep-set eyes. "If he offers to champion you in Rome, remember that his ultimate champion is Brutus."

"I'll duly trust him as much as he trusts us," Octavius remarked and smiled, concealing however how much he was genuinely looking forward to meeting the revered statesman and writer.

*

The wind rustled the leaves of the cypress trees. Crickets murmured in the background, along with chimes of laughter from the serving girls who attended to Roscius and Casca inside the house. Octavius and Agrippa sat on the porch. The air was still stodgy from the smell of the Trojan Pig, pine nuts and marinated vegetables that had been served at dinner. Stars studded the satin cloth of a clear evening sky.

"How was your day?" Agrippa asked.

"Long, but rewarding. Cornelius can be trusted I think," Octavius replied, going on to recount the latest news and strategy that they had mapped out. "And how was your day?"

"Shorter than yours, it seems. It mostly consisted of a long lunch with Cleanthes. But I intend to have a long night. You must join us. I'll let the First Man of Rome have first choice with the staff."

"I'm not sure. It's late."

"You're Caesar, you can alter the calendar if needs be to make time. Besides, if you're to become a politician you need as much practice as possible at screwing people."

Octavius laughed out loud, the first time he had done so since hearing of Caesar's death.

"What would I do without you, Marcus?" Octavius then expressed, fraternally patting his companion on the back and getting up to join the revelry.

"Not as much is the answer," Agrippa replied, good-humouredly.

26.

Antony woke but remained in bed. Despite it being mid-afternoon the consul instructed his attendants to keep the curtains closed. The light hurt his eyes. A couple of candelabras, on either side of his king-size bed, illuminated the chamber. The scent of wine and perfume stained the air. His mistress Tertia - a mime and actress - had long since departed to attend rehearsals. Antony glanced at Caesar's red leather boots, which sat beside Caesar's throne in the far corner of the room. He stared forlornly at them, remembering his former general and how his feet were the wrong size for the boots, as he attempted to wear them yester night.

An attendant announced Domitius Enobarbus, a little too loudly for the hung over consul's liking, and showed his lieutenant in.

"Morning Domitius," Antony warmly said, "excuse me if I don't get up. How was your evening?"

"So good that I can barely remember it," Enorbarbus replied, looking not a little hung-over himself, having attended the lavish and late party.

"That's the spirit. You deserved a night off – and a night on Lucillia. I take it that's who you left with?"

"Yes."

"Did she?-"

"Yes.

"With the?-"

"Yes."

"Whilst she?-"

"Yes."

"Say no more. The smile on your face was as wide as her legs I warrant. May the gods bless the daughters of fishmongers. But there was no need for you to be up as early as a fisherman, my friend. Or is there anything urgent to report?"

"Nothing of urgency but I thought you might like to know that Hirtius and Pansa are now on the road to Rome, after staying with Cicero."

"I hope the fat bastard ate the sanctimonious prude out of house and home. Hirtius and Pansa are even more determined to take up their Consulship after talking to the old man I suspect. They can have their consulships so long as I can have their legions. Can they be bought off?" Mark Antony asked, seemingly as equally concerned with removing bits of spiced mutton from between his teeth as he was with politics.

"Even if they could I fear that that Cicero, using Atticus' money, could outbid us. They are pro-Senate, partly because they are consuls-elect and will head the Senate. They have little love for Brutus and Cassius, though. If they side with the Senate too much it will only drive the Caesarians towards us I warrant."

"What's the latest on securing the Caesarian legions? They served their General well. Is it not natural that they should want to serve under his lieutenant?"

"I'm afraid that their silence is deafening. Balbus and Octavius have been writing to them, too. Some are zealously loyal to Caesar's name - and Octavius has been self-styling himself as Caesar's avenger, as well as heir. Others are swallowing his promises of increased pay and fulfilling Caesar's land grants."

Mark Antony waved his hand dismissively and replied, "Once the boy has been silenced the legions won't be so deaf to our advances. Have you heard from Gravius?"

"I have kept him apprised of Octavius' movements. He has selected his spot where to unleash his ambush. They will make it look like bandits. Lucius Oppius is accompanying the boy, though," Enobarbus answered, with a hint of caution creeping into his tone.

"Lucius is a good man. Perhaps we should have tried to recruit him from the start. As good a soldier as Oppius is he cannot take on Gravius and his cohort alone, though. Even in a one to one fight with Gravius I'd back our man. Gravius never fails in his missions. His mission is to eliminate the boy. Therefore Gravius will not fail in his mission to eliminate the boy. There, is that not one of your beloved syllogisms? Logic dictates that Octavius is as good as dead. Isn't that right?" Mark Antony pronounced – and then yawned.

"Not quite," his friend whispered in reply, unheard.

27.

*Dear Atticus,*

*Octavius is here with me. Gaius Julius Caesar Octavian. He has more names than pubic hairs. His hair is cut short, centurion style, but one thankfully senses he is not cut out for military life. His build is slight. He smiles, but not too broadly or toothily. His eyes often narrow in reflection, or steeliness, but his reserve never manifests itself into rudeness – although I'm not sure if his calmness is not ultimately borne from coldness.*

*His party, including your friend Cleanthes, arrived this afternoon. Balbus has furnished him with an armed escort – large enough to mark him out as a figure of importance but not so extensive as to provoke the idea that the boy means trouble. Marcus Phillipus introduced us. His followers call him Caesar, but Phillipus does not, so neither do I. I greeted Gaius affably enough but then remarked how I couldn't attend to him immediately as I had some work to complete. I didn't wish to instil in the youth that the world revolves around him (a delusion that his great-uncle suffered from). He showed no offence, which I'm not sure if I was pleased with or not.*

*Lucius Oppius, Marcus Phillipus, Octavius and I had a late supper. Oppius was silent for most of the evening, which speaks volumes. He ate his stuffed quail with satisfaction but he wants to taste blood even more I dare say. Marcus Phillipus sung the praises of both Octavius and yours truly – music for both of our ears. Octavius is respectful and friendly. The youth is engaging in conversation but loves not the sound of his voice over others. We all seemed to be in unspoken agreement not to speak about Caesar or politics. We spoke of literature, history – indeed everything that is of little importance to us of late. Octavius was witty, articulate, charming. He reminds me of a talented actor who has the skill to attune his performance to each individual audience. He reminds me of my younger self – again, I was unsure whether to be pleased about this or not. This conceit resonated all the more when the actor started to deliver my lines – and quote me! Phillipus asked the boy which lesson he most took with him from his reading of philosophy. His reply was thus, "to get on as best we can, with the aid of our own dull wits". Imitation is the sincerest form of flattery – and flattery will get him everywhere.*

*In short the boy has a sense of style and a sense of humour. I only hope that he has a sense of decency too. He doesn't wholly trust me – and why should he? – but I will attempt to gain his trust. The last Caesar all but destroyed the Senate. Perhaps, through my influence, this new one may help to restore its authority.*

*We shall have the day together tomorrow. So I will take leave of you now before sleep blunts my thoughts. Sorry for the brevity of this letter my friend. Let me just say though thank you for the recent loan to finance the restoration of the apartment block I rent out. The structure had become so dangerous that even the rats had abandoned it. Your loans to restore the House of the Senate – and in turn banish any rats there – are similarly appreciated. Finally, but not least of all, thank you for the gift of sending Caecilia to visit. Her company – and culinary skills – have been of great consolation. She was out most of today sketching and did not have the chance to meet our other guests. She has her father's acumen in judging character though and I'll be most interested in what she thinks of Octavius, should there be a chance for them to meet. Is he the heir apparent or heir abhorrent?*

*I shall write again anon dear friend.*

*Cicero.*

*

*Dearest Octavia,*

*Thank you for your letters - and apologies for my tardy reply. Taking on the world is more time consuming than you might expect. We arrived at Cicero's estate this afternoon. There is a simple elegance to the estate, reflecting the character of our host. He is in his sixties but still handsome enough to turn the heads of fifty year old widows. Probing, humorous eyes gleam beneath a pronounced brow. His complexion is a little sallow but when he is animated in conversation, or smiling at a witticism (often his own), his expression enlivens to shave ten years off his age. In this respect Cicero reminds me of Caesar. His dress and diet are austere - yet, unlike Cato, Cicero doesn't make a song and dance of his simple tastes and stoicism.*

*I have just come from dinner. The conversation flowed as easily as the wine. Thankfully we spoke not of politics, although Cicero did drop in one or two barbed comments concerning some of his enemies in Rome. As you yourself explained it has become the fashion in Rome for householders to plant mosaics before their front doors, with a simple welcoming message. Cicero joked how the message outside*

*Fulvia's house should be, "Beware of the dog!" He also described how our "Master of the Horse cannot even control his frisky wife".*

*We also spoke about literature. I complimented him upon his library, to which Cicero sagely replied that: "A home without books is a body without a soul". I helped to make his evening when the discussion turned to philosophy and I quoted our host. He smiled with such a sense of pleasant surprise - and unaffected gratitude - that the moment made my evening too, I warrant.*

*Although Cicero is clearly conducting a long term love affair with himself he is healthily self-deprecating and eager to listen as well as speak. I tried to be neither cloying nor distant. Although I wished to impress him I didn't wish to try too hard. As the evening closed he took me aside and expressed the following: "I am in my old age Gaius – the crown of life, the play's last act. I have of late mused that what I do from here on in will decide whether my life can be judged a comedy or a tragedy. Yet I now see that it is what we might do from here on in which will decide my fate - and that of Rome."*

*Only you - and Cleanthes - can know what his words meant to me, Octavia. I have not taken this path from a sense of destiny, but rather from a sense of duty. To do my duty - to bring harmony to the classes - I must become a synthesis of Caesar and Cicero.*

*My only sorrow was that Julius - and yourself - were not present this evening. I still miss him. The world seems emptier, lesser, without him. I feel like I am conducting a long term and clandestine love affair with my grief - and the feeling of revenge to which my grief is married.*

*I miss your company and consolation, too. But I shall be in Rome by the end of the month. You asked in your letter if I am ready to come to Rome. Should we not rather ask, is Rome ready for me?*

*Gaius.*

28.

Octavius reclined on a chair in Cicero's verdant garden and gazed out over a sumptuous, summery vista. Olive groves, vineyards, and homely stone cottages with wisps of smoke swirling into the air populated the landscape. The smell of freshly-baked bread emanated from the villa. Octavius sat beneath a lime tree. A vermillion sun poured through the branches, sprinkling light across the ground all around him.

"This is one of my favourite views. I come here often. Most people sit here and look back at the villa and admire the architecture. But I prefer to take in nature," Cicero remarked, similarly looking out upon the lush contours of the view. "It's as if the landscape has been sculpted by a god for our enjoyment and admiration. There is an intelligence and order to nature which far eclipses the talent of any mortal architect. I believe that we are in possession of a divine spark, Gaius – and when we witness such a scene as this our spark is inspired to burn brighter."

"All the parts of the world are so made that they could not be better adapted to their use or more beautiful to see," Octavius replied, quoting his host's treatise.

"I should thank Cleanthes for extra book sales. You can quote me better than I can."

"You should rather thank Caesar. Julius furnished me with your works and encouraged me to read them above all others."

"If only Julius would have listened to me, as well as read my books, perhaps we would not be in the state we are in now. I would you listen to me now, though, Gaius. Your uncle, Pompey and I have all made compromises with ourselves and behaved dishonourably. Our divine sparks have burned darkly upon occasions. When most topics were discussed Socrates liked to argue first on one side and then on the other. But on one subject he maintained a consistent point of view: he declared that the human soul is divine. When it leaves the body, it has the power to take the road back up to heaven; and the better and more decently it has behaved in life, the easier this road will be. You still have the chance to save yourself, Octavius. One cannot save one's soul - and Rome."

"You tried."

"I know, but I failed," the elder statesman replied, his face etched with sorrow.

Cicero surprised himself by the candour of his confession - and the affection he was developing for the youth. As much as his counsel had been politically motivated he genuinely did not want Octavius to share Caesar's fate. For once the confident and witty statesman looked sheepish.

"I see so much of myself in you, Octavius. I was far from a robust youth, too. But I thank the gods for my less than perfect constitution, for it encouraged me to remain indoors and exercise my mental faculties. For it is not by muscle, force of speed or dexterity that great things are achieved, but by reflection, force of character and judgement. Despite your adopted name you too, like me, will be considered a new man, as well as a young man, when embarking upon the course of honours. But one does not need to possess a noble name to possess a noble character. Your father, Gaius Octavius, proved that. Gaius was a true servant of the Republic. Even more than Cicero or Caesar you should endeavour to become the man he was becoming, before fate curtailed his destiny. He would have made consul. I would have championed him, as I can you. You do not have to command legions to command respect, Octavius."

Octavius felt an uncommon affection for Cicero for praising his father so. His reposeful expression dissolved into a fond smile. Later that evening he fancied that history may record that, in the same way that Alexander the Great was tutored by Aristotle, Octavius Caesar was tutored by Marcus Tullius Cicero.

The moment between the two figures was broken as an attendant brought Cicero some bread and olive oil. He placed the plate on the small bronze table which sat between Cicero and his guest.

"A meagre lunch I know - and it is not just because Hirtius has visited and my stores have depleted. Did you ever meet Hirtius, when in the company of Caesar? One should eat to live, not live to eat. But your uncle's former secretary is a good man. He will make a good consul. He was devoutly loyal to Caesar, too - and you can trust him with your life, Gaius." Cicero was here tempted to add that Octavius could trust him with his legions also, but that would come in time, the elder statesman hoped. For now, he would just plant certain seeds. In reply Octavius merely gave a nod of his head.

"Certainly you should trust Hirtius above our present consul. Antony looks to the state of his affairs more than the affairs of state. I hear that he's just taken a female mime for a new mistress. She may keep her mouth shut, but the same can't be said for her legs I warrant," Cicero joked.

Octavius smiled, yet again remained enigmatically silent. Cicero would write to Atticus that evening how "*the boy is sphinx-like in his responses. He has perhaps read every word and speech I have composed, yet I cannot even read his intentions for tomorrow.*"

"But underestimate Antony at your peril. You will not be able to best him alone, Gaius. You will need the help of the Senate."

Octavius here recalled how Balbus said that the Senate would need his help to subdue Antony, but mentioned it not to his host.

"Even when - and that 'when' is currently an 'if' - Antony's consulship ends he will be in a strong position."

"Nothing is so strongly fortified that it cannot be taken by money," Octavius calmly replied, again quoting from an essay by his companion, "I will win at the odds."

Cicero was astounded by the youth's knowledge – and also hubris. Perhaps he is the son of Caesar, rather than Octavius, the republican worried.

\*

The bucolic scene strewn before Agrippa on the other side of the estate was equally agreeable. A few woollen clouds ambled across a duck-egg blue sky. The farmland was awash with greens and browns. A goat bleated in the background, in contentment rather than complaint. The sweet scent of dried dates wafted up from the bowl which sat beside him on the bench. But Agrippa noticed not the above as he surveyed the valley beneath him, sketching the scene.

The young woman arched an eyebrow in curiosity, rather than disappointment, at seeing a stranger sitting on the bench she resided upon yesterday as she painted. The girl was dressed in a silk stola, dyed tyrian purple. The colour offset a pair of vivacious blue eyes which could sparkle with both intelligence and humour (a humour which could gently mock others - and herself - but which was never cruel). Her pink full lips were often raised in a smile, which could inspire a similar smile in others. Two blonde curls hung down to frame a sun-kissed face that would be deemed attractive in any age. The rest of her blonde hair was stylishly pinned up on her head. A pair of polished silver earrings, given to her by her father, hung down from her ears but otherwise the girl was unadorned with jewellery or make-up, which was rare considering the fashion of the age. The shimmering dress, which flattered an already enviable figure, reached down to her feet where small, pretty high in-stepped feet wore pretty white silk slippers. She carried her work and utensils herself, having dismissed her over-fussy attendants for the day.

"I am not disturbing you I hope," the girl sweetly remarked. She smiled amiably - yet also in part humorously, as though knowing already that she would be amused by the stranger. She fancied he was a guest of Cicero's, a scion of some patrician family. She knew the type. Haughty perhaps; a trait she was not altogether immune to. Privilege would have bred a vulgar arrogance and sense of entitlement. His education would have been expensive but knowledge would have slipped through his fingers like sand.

Agrippa turned around and smiled when seeing the young woman before him.

"My hope is that you do disturb me," he charmingly replied, friendliness and good humour infused in his tone.

Although retaining her poise she thought him handsome - and unlike most young aristocrats she had encountered. His build was muscular, soldierly. His nose was broad - a fine Roman nose. His hair was short, his tunic plain. Perhaps he wasn't a patrician, she thought. Although he was still a man she judged, interested in one thing in a woman - or two, once he discovered how wealthy her father was.

Caecilia Attica walked over to the bench. Agrippa first politely bowed and then considerately brushed the bench, before the young lady sat down upon it next to him.

"My name is Marcus Vipsanius Agrippa." He continued to grin, almost like a fool, as he spoke. "What's yours?"

"A strange gentleman who asks for a lady's name and gets what he wants may soon ask more from the lady, so I will leave you ignorant for now if I may?" Attica satirically replied.

"You may. I'm no stranger to being ignorant. It's fine."

Attica was amused at the refreshingly self-deprecating reply. The two strangers momentarily gazed at each other with wonderment and something else.

"Now, may I ask something else of you? It's a woman's prerogative to be selfish and demanding, no?"

"I thought such a prerogative belonged to a wife rather than just a woman, but you may."

Her accent and burnished complexion bespoke of a certain foreignness Agrippa thought to himself. Perhaps she was part Greek. Her dress both captured and reflected the saffron light, like her eyes.

"May I see what you are working on?"

"Certainly. Though try not to be as critical as a wife."

His manner seemed uncommonly warm and honest, albeit his wit belied a nobleman's education. She could not recall ever having heard the name Agrippa before – and her father knew everyone who was worth knowing she believed.

Attica raised her eyebrow at seeing the half-finished work. Again this Agrippa confounded any pre-conceptions she had about him. The picture was indeed of the view, although his talent was akin to that of an architect rather than artist. He had captured the form of the landscape, if not its beauty. Yet she was intrigued to see that Agrippa had added to the landscape by inserting an aqueduct and irrigation system onto the plains.

"As informed as your drawing of the aqueduct is, I fear it has ruined the rest of the picture – and will ruin the view before us if constructed."

"The aqueduct is intended to save rather than ruin the valley. The greens will be greener, the browns will be browner. The soil will also be richer, as well as the colours, if irrigated properly. Fresh water will improve the quality of life of the workers, as well as the crops. It should not just be the province of the augurs to look to the future. Aqueducts, sewers and roads should be looked at - as well as the entrails of pigeons and gulls."

Attica scrutinised the stranger, as if he were the work of art that she was unsure of how much to admire or not - both for its accomplishments and originality. She could not quite work him out, both in terms of where he had come from and where he was going.

"So are you a guest of Cicero's, or an architect with a bad sense of direction?"

"I'm a guest in a manner of speaking. I am a companion of Caesar's. And are you too a guest of Cicero's, or a lost wife looking for her husband to nag?"

"I'm the former. If I were a wife I dare say that my husband would be searching for me, not I him. For if I needed to nag him I'd as soon as lose him. But tell me, how close are you to the new Caesar?"

"Close enough to ask you to join us both for dinner this evening. Would you like to?" Agrippa asked, not without a little pride - desiring to impress the sophisticated and beautiful woman with his connection to Octavius. He smiled, with hope gleaming from his aspect. He had only admired such aristocratic women from afar before but here he was, close enough to smell her perfume and hear the rustle of her silk dress.

"No, I would not like to have dinner with Gaius Julius Caesar this evening," the woman exclaimed, shaking her head. Agrippa's smile immediately faltered. He lowered his gaze. "But I would like to have dinner with you, Marcus Vipsanius Agrippa". Immediately the smile returned and he looked the remarkable girl in the eye, his expression as bright as his heart.

\*

After dinner Octavius returned to the garden and sat upon the same chair that he had occupied that afternoon. He was accompanied by Cleanthes rather than Cicero now, though. The sky was mauve, the clouds purple, as night settled in. The air was still balmy and sweet with the fragrance of the lime tree that the companions rested under.

"Cicero said that he bought the estate for the views, rather than the house. I can see why," Octavius idly exclaimed.

"If you have a garden and a library, you have everything you need," Cleanthes replied, quoting their host's remark at dinner. "It would be nice to throw in Balbus' vintner and staff too, however. Are you not tempted to purchase a similar villa, with a library and garden? Lucullus retired to his estate and was content to let Rome be Rome. What is stopping you from leading the good life?"

"My duty, to Caesar," Octavius replied, his brow furrowed, his tone as adamantine as his heart. Had grief now wholly manifested itself into revenge? - Cleanthes worryingly thought.

"And when you have fulfilled your duty, what will you do then? Will you, as when Cincinnatus defeated the Aequi, give up your command and live a quiet life? There are still fields of knowledge for you to plough, Gaius. Or have you set yourself upon this course for your own honour rather than Julius? You may be considered a great man if you achieve your ambition and avenge your father, but perhaps the greater man still is he who can relinquish, rather than retain, power."

Octavius listened to his friend in silence, the shadows concealing his brooding expression. He judged his tutor sententious, patronising. He was going to argue that if *his* father had been murdered – and he was in a position to exact his revenge – would he not do so? So too he was tempted to choke the fine blooms of his tutor's moral philosophy with the weeds of political philosophy – and quote Caesar. "*Sulla was a fool for resigning as dictator when he did.*"

Yet Octavius bested any ire he felt towards his friend and desisted from responding harshly. He knew Cleanthes meant well, but the Gaius of Apollonia was a fond memory. Octavius Caesar was the reality now. Yet it was with the former's vulnerability and admiration that he turned to his tutor, clasped him on the arm, and expressed:

"What will be, will be Cleanthes. Know that I treasure your friendship and wisdom. Please stay with me when we get to Rome. Now more than ever I need someone to remind me that my conscience is more valuable than my fortune. If you wish to retire to your garden again however, I'll understand."

"We used to study history together Octavius. Now we're in a position to help write it - and someone needs to be here to correct your grammar. As to my garden, I'm far more worried about you getting out of control rather than my weeds," Cleanthes cordially replied whilst squeezing his pupil affectionately on the shoulder. "Now where is your other companion, who will also hopefully keep you on the straight and narrow? Agrippa is a fine young man and equally fine friend. Don't think that I don't know how you often talk together in the evening, going over the day's events and planning for the future."

"He said he had something to do, which could rather well mean he has someone to do," Octavius remarked, arching his eyebrow and the corner of his mouth in a knowing smile.

"Such is his proclivity to catch the eye of servant girls that this philosopher will consider it wise to always sit next to him at dinner so as to be served well."

The two companions here added a chorus of laughter to the nightingale's evening song.

*

Agrippa and Attica had conversed on their bench long into the afternoon - about nothing and everything. Attica felt immediately and uncommonly comfortable and content in his company. Agrippa was neither intimidated by her intelligence or sense of humour. Laughter bloomed from her lips as he matched her witticisms with his own. Attica resisted from telling him her name. So many vacuous would-be suitors viewed her as a trophy to be won or conduit to being a client of Atticus' once they discovered who she was. As charming and gregarious as the girl could be she often felt lonely, isolated. With her father and Cicero alone could she discuss art and politics and be part of a serious or satirical conversation. Her friends were her books. Towards the end of their afternoon together she made Agrippa promise that he would not go back to the house and ask who she was. As tempted as he was to discover more about his captivating companion, Agrippa honoured his promise.

"Now I must keep my promise and venture back to prepare dinner. Thank you for today, Marcus."

"What are you thanking me for?" he replied.

"Just for you being you - and for letting me be myself, that self who I like to be."

She then sweetly walked up to Agrippa, squeezed his hand and stood upon tip-toe to kiss him on the cheek. The stunned and smitten Roman cherished the lingering sensation as the beautiful girl - or was she truly a goddess? - darted back onto the track leading through the woods, her heart skipping, akin to her pretty feet.

*

The moon shone with a mellow, erbium-tinged radiance. Stars glistened with pride, like peacocks showing off their plumage. The night air was still warm. The shutters were left open and Agrippa watched sparrows hop from branch to branch on a birch tree outside. Cicero had given Attica use of a guest villa at the southern edge of his estate. Although possessing all manner of staff Attica had cooked and served the meal herself - freshly picked mushrooms in her special sauce followed by spiced lamb. She dismissed all of her attendants for the evening. Not only did she not wish to intimidate Agrippa with her status, but also she didn't wish to be disturbed (or have one of the staff report back to her father about her guest).

Attica had changed her stola, yet the dress was equally elegant and the pale blue dye brought out the brilliance of her eyes in a different way. Contrary to fashion she also removed the ivory pins from her hair and long blonde tresses flowed freely over her shoulders and down her back. The conversation similarly flowed freely. More than once Agrippa gave thanks to Octavius for having encouraged him in his study of literature and philosophy. He was familiar with the authors his mystery woman spoke so admiringly of - and when she mentioned Herodotus he duly quoted him, "*Of all possessions a friend is the most precious.*" Her eyes gleamed with pleasant surprise and the girl shook her head a little, as though the man before her was too good to be true. Agrippa proceeded to talk about his friend a little, recounting a story from their time together in Apollonia.

"For the most part we just went to visit the famed astrologer Theogenes for a joke. Neither of us is superstitious, thank the gods. His study gave off an air of wisdom, with all manner of scientific apparatus and ancient parchments decorating the chamber. The air of the room - or rather the stench of his garb - also suggested that, although devoting his life to foretelling the future, Theogenes was not the best judge of predicting his bowel movements."

Laughter cascaded out of his dinner companion. And her laughter was music to his ears - silvery, sweet, unaffected. Agrippa noticed how her eyes would narrow, yet beam, when he made her laugh or grin - and she would gaze fondly at him as if no one else in the world made her feel like he did or mattered to him like he did (which was indeed the case).

"His voice was as rough as the wine he gave us. First he interviewed me and I gave him the time, date of my birth and so forth. Theogenes then retreated to another room, where he seemed to work his way through a bottle of wine as well as my horoscope. On his return - and I dare say this may have been the drink talking - he professed to have never seen such a favourable fate before. I was destined for greatness, despite my inability to pay him as handsomely as his more affluent clients. Although I had faith in my scepticism, still I couldn't help but be happy with my reading. As happy as Gaius was for me though a gloom came over him when the astrologer turned to commence his reading. Although Gaius jested and appeared indifferent he was worried I think that somehow my fate would eclipse his, or similarly that our paths would diverge. Through a combination of teasing and bullying him he finally agreed to the horoscope. Gaius rarely loses his composure but he did that afternoon as he paced up and down with a fixed look of apprehension across his face."

"And what was the outcome?" Attica asked, leaning towards him over the table.

"Theogenes finally came back. The door seemed to take an age to creak open for Octavius. If the wizened astrologer had been intoxicated whilst conducting my reading his sobriety had returned. He stared at Gaius, his mouth agape. He then fell to his knees and pronounced that Gaius would be "the master of the world". We laughed at the incident afterwards. But then and there, as the old man clasped the hem of Gaius' tunic and made his pronouncement in all sincerity, we somehow felt the hand of fate upon us."

"And will you be a great man, Marcus Vipsanius Agrippa?"

"I'll try."

"In which case you'll succeed. But, tell me, do you have a philosophy by which you will live this great life?"

Agrippa paused before answering, enchanted by the way in which the light of the brazier glowed upon her honey coloured skin.

"Fail to prepare. Prepare to fail," he smiled and exclaimed, remembering Oppius' advice. "And do you have a philosophy by which you live your life?"

Attica gazed at her guest, partly staring into his soul and partly wishing to infuse it.

"Be kind, for everyone you meet is facing a hard battle," she replied, embodying loveliness and wisdom - quoting Plato. She was like no other girl he had met. And Agrippa realised that evening - indeed perhaps at the very moment that she uttered those words - that he loved her like no other girl he had ever met, or would meet.

"Will you be kind now and finally tell me your name?"

She hesitated, but finally spoke.

"Caecilia Attica."

Agrippa's eyes briefly widened in surprise but then everything fell into place - her wealth, knowledge of art, her staying with Cicero. Attica looked down, in fear of witnessing the greed and sense of opportunity in Marcus' eyes that she had observed in others. But as she looked up she bathed in the genuine warmth, good humour, and something else in his aspect. Agrippa had fallen in love with Atticus' daughter, not dowry. And she knew it.

"Will I ever see you again?"

"I'll make sure that the first aqueduct that I construct runs past your house."

Attica but half smiled at the comment, dwelling still on how she might never see him again. He would become a memory, or a dream. Her father had always respected her decision when she did not like the prospective husband who auditioned for her. But would he now respect her choice of someone who he might not consider suitable, both because of Agrippa's class and political affiliations?

"You are to venture to Rome, I back to Athens, shortly," she expressed forlornly. While just before the girl could not take her eyes off her would-be suitor, Attica now averted her glance, for when she looked at him now she saw something, somebody, that might be lost to her. And already it brought her pain.

"Before this evening Caecilia I often dreamed that I would win fame and fortune for myself, or to help Gaius. But now I wish to do so to be good enough in the eyes of your father - and win you."

The girl smiled, but tears began to stream down her cheeks. She sobbed as she spoke and shook her head.

"No, you don't understand. I think I love you. You've already won me. I don't want you to now lose me."

Agrippa tenderly laced his fingers into hers and stood up. Attica too arose and then buried her head into his chest, crying as she did so.

"Fight for me Marcus. Don't give up on me, us."

"I'll wait for you. Should I fall behind, wait for me," he replied, his strong arms cradling her.

"I'll try."

"In which case you'll succeed."

A sob turned itself into a bouquet of laughter. Her face was wet with tears. First Agrippa brushed his thumb over her cheeks. Her slender arms pulled him closer. Their lips met in a sweet, then passionate, then loving kiss.

29.

A persistent greasy drizzle had followed the party throughout the morning, but fortunately the skies cleared by the afternoon. The young Caesar stood upon a rostrum in the market town of Casilinum and addressed the crowd - having come straight from the town's temple, where the young man had displayed sufficient piety. Balbus had pre-arranged some supporters but curiosity and the promise of some Caesar-esque largesse had brought people from their homes to the square. Equites, farmers, soldiers, guild members and civil servants rubbed shoulders alike - along with their wives and children - to see the adopted heir of Julius Caesar. There were already plenty of smiles all round as Balbus had organised for a merchant to lubricate the proceedings with free wine, bread and fresh fruit. Heads bobbed up and down amidst the sea of people to get a better view of the Caesar.

A welcome breeze cooled Octavius' flushed features. The sound of the breeze mingled with the whispers which wended their way through the throng. As a soldier's drills will aid him in the battlefield, Octavius had repeatedly rehearsed his speech to suppress his nerves and narrow any scope for errors. He took a deep breath, like an actor preparing to go on stage, and commenced his address.

"I come not to bury Caesar, but to praise him. I come not to bury Caesar's reforms, but to save them. And I come not to bury Caesar's promises, but to keep them."

Octavius' voice was audible and calm. His lungs and temperament would not allow him to bellow. His tunic was plain, but fresh and white, gleaming in the afternoon sun. Balbus had given Octavius one of Julius' old belts as a talisman.

"My father once told me that Rome and its riches should not be the preserve of just Romans and the rich. Before my father we had but two classes, the taxed and the taxing. But the peace he won and the reforms he promoted purchased prosperity for all. He knew, through living in the Subura all those years and campaigning alongside good legionaries from all across Italy that, as the builders say, the larger stones do not lie well without the lesser."

Balbus' supporters, planted throughout the crowd, began to nudge their neighbours and nod their heads - but they were not the only ones to do so.

"How unfair the fate which ordains that those who have the least should add to the treasury of the rich. But that seems to be the fate that the present authorities have in store for us. Taxes are now due to be raised as high as the colonnades on the villas that they are constructing. The only taxes which are due to be rescinded are those imposed by Caesar upon certain luxury goods I have heard. One should be a friend to business, but not to corruption …We must cleanse the augean stables."

Heads that formerly nodded in agreement now shook their heads in disappointment after hearing such scandalous proposals.

"And certain self-interested factions of the Senate justify their actions by claiming that Caesar acted unlawfully in enacting his reforms, so we must now make them null and void. They are wielding their styluses, as they did their daggers against my father, to attack your freedoms and wealth. They hide behind ancient or brand new laws to defend their actions. But should these self-styled optimates, best men, be standing before me now I would not flinch in telling them that the good of the people is the greatest law."

Clapping and cheers filled the pause that Octavius here artfully allowed. Cleanthes, watching the performance from the side of the rostrum, smirked - thinking about the irony of Octavius quoting Cicero to endorse his Caesarian mandate. The tutor also recognised lines from Terence and Plato. Indeed, Cleanthes mused, the only person who he wasn't quoting was his teacher.

"Now I can only but hope that I have inherited my father's political acumen and fortune in war. And I desperately hope that I have inherited his abilities in regards to his conquests over women."

The crowd erupted with laughter. Octavius smiled and enjoyed the moment too, yet then raised his hand to silence them. Oppius looked on, impressed, as Octavius started to orchestrate the crowd as Julius had once done so commandingly. Balbus had offered to compose the speech but Octavius merely asked him to read over his own composition - which he edited not. Although youthful in appearance Octavius was projecting confidence and maturity. Cleanthes had coached him a little in regards to his delivery - he sawed not the air with his hands, nor strained his voice - but it seemed he was a natural.

"But I have inherited my father's name and the promises he made - both of which I intend to honour. I have inherited my father's debt, as well as his fortune. His debt to the people of Rome - and I shall see to it that his gardens are bequeathed to the public. And I shall see to it that the gift of three hundred sesterces is paid to every good citizen in

Rome, too. And I shall see to it that his promises of land grants to his loyal legions are not revoked." Octavius turned his head to address a section of the crowd consisting of legionaries and centurions and nodded to them in gratitude and respect. "My father craved not a revolution. Nor do I. He believed in the Republic. As do I. He believed in the providence of the gods. As do I. He believed in tradition and the family. As do I. I stand before you now, not just a servant to my father - but consequently a servant to all of you. For who was it who took from the rich to give to the deserving? Caesar! Who was it who gave thanks and worship to the gods, rather than to the senatorial cartel of the Metelli, Claudii and Brutii? Caesar! And who shed his own blood to win our peace and prosperity? Caesar! And who was it they perniciously accused of being a tyrant, but died being our benefactor?"

"Caesar! Caesar! Caesar!" was the reply from the crowd. Fists punched the air. One could not be sure if the throng were cheering for the Caesar past or the one who stood before them. Perhaps the lines had become blurred and it was both.

Though a feeling of anger simmered at the rally for the opponents of Caesar (who if present were wisely quiet), such a mood was eclipsed by a fraternal and celebratory atmosphere. Wine and food continued to be freely distributed. Octavius spent a number of hours listening to the grievances and petitions of a number of his supporters. He took time out to speak to a group of soldiers who had served under Caesar. Cleanthes noted down names and addresses to forward on to Balbus and his clerks - who would write follow-up messages. A widow, not a little charmed by the attractive and well-mannered youth, thanked the young Caesar for his visit to the town. She could not remember the last time that anyone of note had deigned to truly speak and listen to the people. The audience to the scene would later quote Caesar's response, as he warmly clasped the earnest woman by the hands, "my father once told me that the higher we are placed, the more humbly we should walk." Balbus had also arranged for Caesar's heir to have a number of private meetings with key supporters and donors to the Caesarian campaign. For the moderates Octavius trumpeted his new found friendship with Cicero, implying that he would work with the Senate to champion their cause. For the more devout Caesarians however, Octavius expressed himself in more bellicose terms towards the libertores and other enemies.

Oppius and Roscius spent the afternoon in the company of their fellow soldiers, assuring them of Octavius' desire for revenge. Akin to his father, Octavius would reward loyalty, too. Neither Antony nor the Senate would match the wages that the young Caesar could and would pay. Most of the centurions ended the afternoon swearing loyalty to Octavius Caesar, in the name of Julius Caesar, and promised to extract similar oaths from their comrades.

Agrippa and Casca had the far from onerous task of touring the local taverns, both garnering and measuring support for the Caesar. They sometimes just listened to the gossip and wine truth. At other instances they engaged their drinking companions. The responses to the address were favourable. The affluent did not feel that the young Caesar was a populist demagogue, in the vein of a Clodius. He had no intention of stirring the mob to violence, or championing the poor above all other interests. The Senate were living in the past if they thought they could undo all of Caesar's beneficial reforms and re-establish an oligarchy. Like them, Octavius was a progressive conservative at heart. Yet in the less seemly establishments – which Agrippa and Casca were happily thorough enough to visit as well – the people were equally enthusiastic about the young Caesar. Like his father he had the common touch. He possessed a sense of humour and spoke to them rather than down to them. Although educated his air was that of a tribune rather than a haughty patrician.

*

An old friend of Balbus' and an ardent Caesarian, Valerius Macrinus, accommodated Caesar and his retinue that evening at his estate just outside of town. Gaius, Agrippa, Oppius, Casca and Roscius relaxed in the opulent triclinium over several jugs of Macrinus' finest vintage. The day - and drinking session - had been long.

"Today was a great success. To today - and tomorrow!" Agrippa announced, raising his cup and a smile to his friend. He was, like Casca, far more inebriated than his companions, what with them having embraced their duties earlier.

"Julius would have been proud of you today Gaius," Oppius then earnestly expressed, using up his ration of compliments for the year, and looking at Octavius with not a little affection and approval. They fleetingly shared a private moment.

"Thank you."

"But don't let the praise go to your head quicker than the wine," Oppius added, reverting to his disgruntled self - but warmly winking at the boy.

"To Octavius!" Roscius exclaimed, but before he raised his arm to complete the toast, Oppius stopped him.

"No, old friend - to Caesar!"

"To Caesar!" the companions echoed, clinking their cups.

For once Octavius felt a little uncomfortable in his skin. He smiled and was choked with emotion; he blushed too. He was saved from further discomfort however by Cleanthes re-appearing.

"Valerius has informed me that the entertainment has arrived."

"Please don't tell me that they're musicians," Roscius replied, rolling his eyes.

"I wouldn't call them musicians, although you may approve of how they'll play with your instrument."

Valerius Macrinus here entered the room and ushered in a dozen well dressed women of ill-repute.

"For your entertainment, gentlemen. They're as fine as Caesar's speech - and cleaner than your jokes, Roscius," their host jovially exclaimed.

All manner of lissom figures - some wearing little more than a smile - sauntered into the triclinium. The glow of the fire shone upon tanned, roseate and black perfumed skin alike. Some giggled, some simpered or appeared sultry as they draped themselves over sofas or encircled their prey.

Roscius licked his lips at the banquet of flesh sumptuously laid out before him, not knowing which dish to try first. His eyes bulged, as did something else - beneath his tunic - as he thought to himself how much he preferred life on a political campaign as opposed to a military one.

Tiro Casca gulped as twin sisters sat either side of him and ran their hands up and down his legs. Not knowing how to combat such an assault he decided to surrender to it.

A sweet-faced girl with startling turquoise eyes and a similarly arresting figure perched herself upon the arm of Octavius' chair. She wore an elaborate wrap-around silk stola that he quickly figured out was solely held in place by an ivory brooch in between her breasts. The courtesan smiled alluringly as she ran her hand through his short fair hair and stroked his cheek.

Nearby a strikingly tall Nubian woman sided up to a partly aroused, partly intimidated Cleanthes.

"And who are you?" she asked, or perhaps demanded, in a husky foreign accent.

"That's a good question. And one which I can happily debate with you in the bedroom."

The woman at first appeared a little confused by the reply but then shrugged her shoulders and led the stranger off to an adjoining room, nearly pulling Cleanthes' arm out of its socket as she did so.

A lithe Egyptian woman caught Oppius' eye, or vice versa. She reminded him of his long-term lover during Caesar's Alexandrian campaign. He smiled as he recalled how her legs would wrap around him so tight than not even Hercules himself could have escaped her clutches - not that he would want to, Oppius mused. The fond smile and glint of dark desire upon his face was invitation enough for this new dusky-skinned figure to straddle the handsome Roman on the sofa and sensuously kiss him.

Agrippa alone resisted the entreaties. He yawned and excused himself from further revelries by citing tiredness, which was indeed the case - albeit not the reason as to why he absented himself. A part of him perhaps wanted to remain and enjoy his host's hospitality - but yet he was content to retire to his room. Lying upon his bed Agrippa dreamily composed a letter and love poem to Attica, his smile as wide as any of his companions.

30.

Grey clouds, like slats, were tiled across the sky. The rally in Allifae had been, akin to Casilinum, a success. Indeed the number of supporters had been greater as news of Caesar's arrival preceded him and people from the countryside as well as the town came out to see the heir. Word was spreading. Seeds were being sown - and taking root. The Appian Way was again unfurled before them, its flagstones spotted with rain. Dense woodland flanked the road on either side.

Oppius and Roscius set the pace at the head of the party, along with a quartet of soldiers. The rest of Balbus' men, thirty strong in total, marched either side of the road and brought up the rear. Inside the rectangle were the baggage carts. Octavius rode on one of the carts, attempting to catch up on some correspondence. Casca marched by the cart's side, his expression as dour as the weather.

Behind them were Agrippa and Cleanthes. The grey mare pulling one of the wagons spotted the road with something other than rain, and the tutor had to pull his companion out of the way to save him from stepping in the steaming excrement.

"I'm sure, Marcus, that Attica would not want you day-dreaming about her to such an extent where you did not know where you were walking."

"What? How do you know?" Agrippa replied, astounded that Cleanthes could know about Attica and himself. He hadn't even told Octavius - or he hadn't told him especially.

"I may not be Gordianus the Finder but I'm not blind. You've been walking around with a love-struck look on your face ever since the morning we departed from Cicero's estate. And only a blind man, or a man devoted to someone, would have left the party the other night when those sirens turned up. The wax in your ears was the name of Attica, no? And don't think that I haven't noticed you clandestinely reading Catullus."

Agrippa blushed, but smiled also.

"Of course, I also discovered your secret through having visited Attica on the morning we left. I met her through her father some years ago."

Agrippa laughed and shook his head.

"I could live a thousand lifetimes, Cleanthes, and you doubtless would still own the ability to surprise and confound me. But I must ask that my secret becomes your secret, too. I must ask you to keep this from Gaius."

"Hmm, keeping secrets from each other now are we? You two really are indeed as close as a married couple," Cleanthes joked. "But I give you my word that my lips will remain as tightly shut as Crassus' wallet."

"It's just that I do not want Gaius to be tempted to use my friendship with Attica for political means, to get closer to Atticus. Similarly Caecilia does not want to tell her father yet for fear of Atticus or Cicero using her to use me to reveal Gaius' intentions. Or indeed they could just forbid our relationship altogether after discovering my loyalty to Caesar. I adore her Cleanthes. She's smart, funny and beautiful. We are each of us angels with only one wing, and we can only fly by embracing each other," Agrippa exclaimed, as much to himself as his companion, quoting Lucretius.

*At the touch of love everyone becomes a poet*, Cleanthes thought to himself, and smiled fondly. He then remembered *her*, *his* angel.

"For what it's worth you have my blessing, Marcus. Attica is indeed a remarkable and accomplished young woman. As much as I try to forget – and drink aids me in this quest as you know – she reminds me of my first love. My sole love."

Again Agrippa turned to his companion, astounded.

"Can a philosopher fall in love?"

"Oh, I was much happier and wiser than a philosopher then."

"What happened, if you do not mind me asking?"

"We were due to be married. But she passed away," the tutor replied, his wistful expression falling into mournfulness. "Plato once said that one word frees us from all the weight and pain in life. And that word is love. But what he failed to mention was that if one loses that love, then the weight and pain return." Cleanthes was now speaking to himself as much as his companion. Agrippa's countenance couldn't help but mirror his friend's pained one and crease in sympathy.

"When was this?"

"It was a long time ago, although it sometimes feels like yesterday. But I do not wish to speak about it further. I already still think about it too much. Ultimately I'm a bad stoic, Marcus. Or a sad one," the mercurial tutor quietly uttered, rain or tears spotting his cheeks.

Octavius finished composing a letter to Octavia. He smiled to himself on recalling Cicero's words, "And how is your sister? I met her once. She was half her husband's age but twice as clever." Octavius then glanced at the granite-faced Tiro. He had grown fond of the gruff veteran over the past weeks. He was a walking argument as to why Rome bested its enemies.

"Tell me, Tiro. You've fought on all corners of the map. Which armies do you rate?"

Although Casca's expression changed very little upon hearing the question, he was always happy to recount old war stories and be consulted on military matters.

"Well the Gauls were brave whenever they outnumbered us three to one. But they would often also just down swords, like guild members their tools, and surrender. The Greeks seemed more concerned with being well groomed than well trained. Sometimes I think their officers wanted to fuck us rather than kill us, such was their effete manner. I rated the Britons. The gods were right to give those savages their own island, away from everyone else. They can out drink anyone, and out fight most. But by far the greatest, finest army we faced was Pompey's. His legions were well-led, well-equipped and well-disciplined. But Caesar had Bellona for his mistress it seems. Pharsalus was a close run thing. But quality will always best quantity."

"And what of the Egyptians?"

"The Egyptians? They were more likely to poison us with their cuisine than kill us on the battlefield," the veteran exclaimed, laughing at his own joke.

Oppius and Roscius briefly turned their heads back at the audible cackling of their comrade. The centurion then gazed intently ahead once more, furrowing his brow in concern, or scorn, that the two scouts he sent ahead of the party had not reported back as ordered.

*

 Dried blood and tiny blisters of rust stained the blade of Gravius' lieutenant as he held it aloft. Once Gravius gave the word he would swipe his sword downwards, giving the signal for the men hidden in the woods on the opposite side of the road to attack. Their brown and russet tunics camouflaged them well. The overcast sky helped conceal them, too. The gods were on their side, Gravius thought, although he put more stock in himself and his men than any deities.

The orders were clear. Once he had given the signal his men, numbering fifty, would attack the party on both sides simultaneously. A complement of archers and javelin throwers would launch their missiles before joining the rest of the cohort to race down the grass slopes between the trees and road. The priority was to find and assassinate the boy - but no one was to be spared. The mission called for corpses, not prisoners or witnesses. They would bury the bodies in the forest.

Enobarbus' agents had confirmed that Lucius Oppius was leading the party. He looked forward to doing battle with the famed centurion, who had made his name off the coast of Britain all those years ago. He would need more than the Legionaries' Prayer to keep himself safe now, though. Prayers had done little to help the two scouts that Oppius had sent along the Appian Way. They had duly revealed the proximity of the rest of the party, before Gravius slit their throats.

Gravius first heard the tamp of boots and rumble of wagons on the road, before he spied the party. The menacing centurion gripped the handle of his giant double-bladed axe, a trophy won from a warlord in Long-Haired Gaul. His eyes glinted as brightly as the steel in anticipation of the attack and slaughter.

"Archers at the ready," he instructed, grinning.

"We will soon be in Rome, Lucius."

"Where will you head first once there old friend - the baths or brothels? Just make sure that both are clean. You're itching to get back to Rome it seems. I don't want you itching from some pox when departing from it."

"Fear not, I've got more wits and sesterces than when I was last in Rome. And where will you head to?"

"I can tell you who I won't be visiting."

"Who?"

"My ex-wife."

Roscius tossed his head high and roared with laughter. However Oppius' attention was fixed firmly on the road. He noted the dark marks splattered across the flagstones. Blood rather than rain. Fresh blood. Something was wrong. The centurion's keen eyes darted left and then right. The forest had crept even closer towards the road. Something was amiss. They were in the perfect position for an ambush!

"Defensive positions!"

The bellowed order was soon accompanied by the sound of a flurry of arrows whooshing from bows. A number of javelins also skewered the air. Thanks to their commander's constant drilling the reactions were rapid - second nature. Balbus' men crouched behind their large shields. Without a thought for himself Tiro swiftly moved to cover Caesar with his shield - and thankfully so as an arrow thudded into it.

Gravius cursed the gods that his initial salvo had been blunted by Oppius' good, or lucky, judgement. Yet his anger only spurred him on down the slope to his quarry, his giant axe swinging in his hand.

Oppius ordered his men to close ranks around the baggage carts. If they kept their heads then they may just keep their lives, too.

Whilst the rest of the escort manoeuvred themselves to defend - Oppius and Roscius attacked. The hulking legionary charged up the slope to meet a brace of the brigands. Their war cries turned into screams however as Roscius turned his shield horizontally and rammed into them both. All three of the combatants were floored but the legionary recovered the quickest to stab one in the chest and the other in the throat.

Oppius sped to the crucial point of the ambush to help even the odds - whilst shouting orders to his own men. Shields and swords clashed against each other but still his voice could be heard over the melee.

"Agrippa, get into position on top of the cart. Start shooting the bastards. Cleanthes, to me. Roscius, to Caesar."

After delivering his orders, Lucius got in position to outflank the line of attackers outnumbering the defenders. He efficiently unsheathed and unleashed the two daggers he kept upon his belt. Despite his enemies being side-on, both blades bit into the ribs of their targets and felled them.

Even before the order had been issued, Agrippa raced towards the wagon in front of Octavius' to retrieve his bow. He launched himself on the vehicle. Fear and exhilaration coursed through his body but Agrippa quickly centred himself. He found a target and released the arrow, shooting over the heads of his comrades to plant the shaft into the chest of an attacker.

Octavius had drawn his sword but he resisted not when Tiro instructed him to hide himself beneath the cart. The veteran stood by him, gladius and shield at the ready to protect Caesar. And protect Caesar he would have to, for a trio of the attackers made a bee-line for the prize. Tiro flinched not, despite it being three to one. For Casca it was like being on his training ground again as he parried and lunged to fend off the brigands. Yet his opponents were not as ill-trained and fearful as his students back in Apollonia.

"Give it up old man. It's three against one."

"I hope you count as well as you fight," Roscius exclaimed, slightly breathless from his sprint.

Whilst the trio were distracted by Roscius, Tiro threw his gladius into one of them, having dropped his shield down to leave his chest exposed. He then swiftly grabbed Octavius' sword to, along with Roscius, confront the remaining pair. With vicious yet efficient strokes they soon hacked them down.

Gravius stood with a boot on the dead man's chest as he worked his axe out of the shattered collar bone. Blood spotted his face. He licked his lips, enjoying the familiar metallic taste. Despite the screams and commotion around him, Gravius calmly located and walked towards his prey, smirking wolfishly as he did so. The enemy were well disciplined and accomplished fighters, but his cohort would out-match and outnumber them in the end. Although outnumbered himself, Gravius was confident of out-matching the two legionaries guarding the Caesar who cowered beneath the cart.

"You'll flee if you know what's good for you. Just leave the boy to me. It took two dozen daggers to kill the last Caesar. But it'll take just one axe to send this one to the ferryman."

Recognising a seasoned soldier and brute when he saw one - it takes one to know one - Tiro approached the powerfully built opponent with caution. Roscius continued to guard Octavius. The two men traded blows and insults. In another man's hands the axe would have proved too unwieldy to duel with but Gravius handled his weapon as nimbly as Casca did his sword. Such was the force of one of Gravius' blows that his axe splintered his opponent's shield, at which point Casca pulled Gravius close to him and butted his nose. Yet Gravius absorbed the blow and butted the veteran back. With his opponent slightly disorientated Gravius cleverly lengthened the reach of his weapon by holding the end of the shaft and swiped low, beneath Tiro's shield, to slice him deep into his shins. Before Tiro had the chance to recover his opponent buried the axe-head in his chest, cutting through his leather breastplate as if it were papyrus.

Octavius' face dropped at witnessing the veteran fall. Even if Roscius could best the ferocious brigand he sensed that they could not survive the attack.

Eight of Balbus' men faced close to twenty of the enemy in their ever dwindling shield wall. The ratio was similar on the other side of the road. Such was the attackers' numerical superiority that they could surround and out-flank the shield wall. And that was their plan, as the bandits were ordered to back off from the shield wall before one last, decisive, offensive.

But little did the rogue cohort know that one man stood in the way of victory - albeit he stood behind them. During the fight Oppius had ordered Cleanthes to collect up as many stray swords and pilums as he could. The centurion did the same, despatching a couple more of the enemy whilst doing so. The first javelin thudded into an attacker's back - and its gore-tipped point glistened as it poked out of his sternum. Ere the first man fell Oppius clasped another pilum and, standing twenty metres away, he launched it at the enemy standing next to his first victim. The third turned towards the danger, but still not in time. A sword then twirled through the air and could be seen jutting out of the enemy's shoulder. Confusion and fear infected the enemy line as Oppius, as if he were completing a training exercise, struck his targets. Balbus' men responded and moved forward as many of the enemy suddenly turned their backs to them. The tide of the battle turned within a minute. Oppius continued to methodically attack the line from behind, as Cleanthes handed him his missiles. Yet not all of Gravius' men panicked and found themselves sandwiched between the enemies. The man at the far end of the line, possessing a javelin still, peeled away. If he could bring down the centurion then all would not be lost. Oppius was blind-sided to the assassin- but Cleanthes was not. The pilum briefly whistled through the air before spearing into the tutor's stomach, as he moved himself in front of the centurion. Oppius looked to Cleanthes but the tutor, wincing in pain, gently shook his head to communicate that he was finished, or that Lucius shouldn't worry about him. Oppius drew his sword, already slick with blood, and fixed his storm-filled eye towards his would-be assassin.

The axe-head dug into Roscius' shield. Roscius took his chance to strike at the handle of the weapon. The legionary's blow was powerful enough to crack the shaft and render the axe useless. Gravius grunted, gifted his opponent a nod of respect, and drew his gladius.

"Why do you protect this whelp? Because of his name?"

Gravius pointed his sword towards Octavius. Octavius, desiring revenge for Tiro Casca, had grabbed a nearby gladius and shield - but Roscius beckoned him back. The brigand was too fierce an opponent.

"No, because he's my friend," the legionary calmly replied.

Witnessing that the tide had turned upon one front, Agrippa focused on the other. Although the two rows of combatants were hazardously close together, Agrippa bided his time and sent another wretch to the underworld, shooting him in the face. The scream momentarily curdled the air before the clang and curses of battle drowned out the sound again.

Gravius' lieutenant lunged at Oppius but the centurion deftly avoided the thrust and quickly jabbed his sword up into his enemy's neck, tearing his gladius out sideways rather than backwards. The centurion then ordered for the remainder of Balbus' forces to converge on the remaining enemy.

A cheer soon went up as the bolstered shield wall overcame the remnants of the enemy, routing them.

Gravius was dextrous with his axe against Roscius - but deadly with his sword. Too swift. Too savage. Blood poured from cuts upon the legionary's arm, thigh and hip. Drool fell from his mouth as Gravius stood over his enemy and slit Roscius' throat, the curve of the fatal wound mirroring the grin on the rogue centurion's face.

Tears streamed from Octavius' face - and he gripped his sword as if he would attempt to avenge his friend's death - but a firm hand upon his shoulder stayed any rush of blood.

"Gaius, attend to Cleanthes. I'll attend to this," Oppius said.

At witnessing his tutor behind him, dying, Octavius raced to his side.

"Unfortunately for you, I've killed your two best men," Gravius goadingly remarked.

"Unfortunately for you, I'm better. Marcus, if this bastard tries to run away then stick an arrow so far through the back of his head that it comes out the other side."

Agrippa nodded grimly, as he stood in a horseshoe around the two combatants with his other comrades.

As when two wild stags, with their nostrils flared and haunches up, will butt and shatter the silence of the forest - so too did the centurions clash, their swords and shields striking each other like antlers. Balbus' men cheered their commander on. Agrippa nocked an arrow, deciding that he would unleash the bolt if the enemy looked like he was winning, rather than running.

Cleanthes lay upon the grass on his side, his knees tucked up, his eyes half closed as if he were about to drift off to sleep. His body twitched in pain with each breath he took. Petals of blood bloomed ever outwards upon his tunic. Octavius kneeled before him, clasping his limp hand.

"Stay with us," the youth, partly ordering him, partly pleading, exclaimed. Tears soaked his cheeks.

"It's time to cross over. There's someone waiting for me on the other side I hope," the tutor quietly replied, a contented smile suddenly enlivening his ashen features. With what little strength remaining, Cleanthes squeezed his student's hand.

"When you cross over I'll be waiting for you. I just want to be as proud of you then as I am now."

Octavius thought he heard his friend whisper a woman's name. His grip on his hand - and on life itself - then ebbed away. His serene expression remained however, as the words of Socrates came to him: *Death maybe the greatest of all human blessings.*

Gravius attacked more than his opponent. His blows were forceful, the angles of his strokes diverse. Both men tried to foot swipe, head butt and push each other to the ground but both men were experienced and equal to the tactics. Oppius realised that he would need to come up with something different to penetrate his opponent's defences, else the duel would be one of attrition – and his body was already tiring. He decided he would risk it all - not on the throw of a dice, but rather on the throw of something else.

Although Gravius was adroit and experienced enough to look for Oppius throwing his gladius, he wasn't expecting his opponent to throw his shield at him. The large scutum crashed against Gravius' body and momentarily blinded him. Oppius was quick to take advantage of his opponent's disorientation. He grabbed Gravius' wrist on his sword arm with his now free hand and - with a gap opening up between his round shield and body - the centurion swiftly stabbed his enemy in the stomach. The gladius protruded out of Gravius' back. Oppius made sure to look his opponent in the eye as he slowly twisted his sword, feeling the intestines wrap around the blade.

*

The road was littered with corpses, or wounded who would soon be so. Blood browned the yellow grass. Night descended. The wind howled and caused the rain to slant into mournful faces. Prisoners were tortured - and the enemy confessed to being Roman soldiers - but the secret of who was their paymaster had died with their leader. Neither Oppius nor Octavius regretted his death however. The prisoners were then executed. The young Caesar took the time to thank and praise every soldier individually - and he helped them bury their comrades. The only bodies they took with them were Casca, Roscius and Cleanthes.

31.

When the party reached the town of Praeneste, Oppius recruited more men and purchased horses, provisions and equipment. They would now travel in safety - and luxury. Balbus' men were granted a short leave of absence for the evening and following day. Oppius gifted each man a bonus and recommended a couple of establishments at which to spend their bounty.

A joint funeral service was arranged for Roscius, Casca and Cleanthes. They hoped that their three comrades would enter Elysium together - and to jolly them on their way Oppius poured an amphora of Falernian over their bodies. Their companions, after the service, also worked their own way through a measure of the vintage, celebrating and mourning their friends. Oppius spoke for Roscius, Agrippa for Casca, and Caesar for Cleanthes for the funeral orations.

*"... Rome has lost a legionary, I have lost a friend. I never had to check to know you were by my side. And even now I would take your ghost and memory over any other soldier to fight alongside me. In death you kept your oath - and therefore your honour - to defend Caesar. As such you fought for Rome till the end..."*

*"... My cup will be raised as high as my esteem. Actions always spoke louder than words for you but I hope that you can hear me now, Tiro. In treating me like a man I became a man. In disappointing you I believed I was disappointing myself - for somehow you imparted in your teaching a piece of your Roman soul, as well as your military knowledge. I will abide by your lessons in honour of your memory - and to keep me safe. Oppius gave me your letter. I hope to inherit your courage, as well as your sword. I will sharpen the edge at night - and by day sheathe the blade into the enemies of Rome ..."*

*"... I feel like I have lost another father - and from your will it seems I have inherited another estate. Part of me wishes to venture back to Apollonia and tend to your garden. Yet - and you would be all too conscious of the irony - the seeds of virtue that you helped sow into me means that I must abandon your estate for another. I must tend to Caesar's gardens - and ensure that they are gifted to the public ... Yet far more important is what is unseen that I inherited from you - to recognise man's follies but to not always condemn them. To question, yet not always negate. That goodness should be valued over knowledge - and that philosophy cannot and should not bring faith ...*

*Death will not snuff out your flame. Your teachings will not vanish*
*with the closure of your academy ... I pray my tears do not water down*
*the Falernian. After this night there will be no more tears spilled - just*
*the blood of our enemies."*

*

Evening. Puteoli.

Cicero, Tiro and Caecilia Attica sat around the dinner table. Braziers
heated the chamber. The pungent aroma of oysters still filled the air.
Marble busts of Thales and Democritus sat upon the centre of the
table. The servants had departed to leave Tiro and Caecilia to their
venison - and Cicero to his sweetened porridge.

"It was a shame that you did not get to meet our guest last week,
Attica."

"I hear he is honourable," Attica replied with a hint of a question, as
much as an assertion, lining her tone.

"Who told you that, my dear?" Cicero's smiling eyes briefly
narrowed in curiosity, or suspicion.

"Oh, no one," the woman remarked, shaking her head and
dismissing the hearsay - and the "no one" in question.

"What did you think of him, Tiro?" Cicero asked. Having already
questioned the secretary about the young Caesar, the conversation was
more for their dinner guest's benefit.

"He has a modicum of Caesar's wit - but thankfully only a modicum
of Caesar's ambition. But these traits may ripen - or rot - with age. In
some ways he seemed to me more studious than ambitious. For
instance he would perhaps wish to know about our friend Thales here
- and question the sculptor about his methods - rather than just blindly
covet the bust because of its rarity and value. Cleanthes said that he
wanted Octavius to return to his studies and complete his education.
But the tutor owned doubts, as well as hopes, that this would happen."

"And what of his companions? We know all too well of Oppius. All
your father's gold Attica could not buy his allegiance - a trait which
would prove admirable should he serve our cause. But what of his
other lieutenant, this Agrippa?"

The sound of the silver fork falling first clattered on the plate, and
then clanged against the tiled floor. Attica, suddenly flustered, nearly
dropped her knife, too. Thankfully the blonde curls which fell down
the sides of her face concealed her blushes.

"He is steadfastly loyal and has Caesar's ear as much as Balbus I
warrant. We should still spend our time courting Salvidienus, or rather

we should let Salvidienus court us. His son was close to Octavius on Apollonia but the family are staunch Republicans."

"Alright, continue in that vein. But do not encourage too strong an alliance with the self-regarding would-be optimate. That I have to suffer the man's prose is enough. I do not wish to suffer the man's company. Oh, there are so many throws left in this game of dice, not even Euclid could calculate a winner. Yet if the gods would permit me to load the dice I would still favour Brutus. Did I tell you both what he said to Mark Antony at their meeting after the Ides? Antony joked, 'Have you perchance a dagger under your arm even now?' To which Brutus drily replied, 'Yes - and a large one should you desire too, to be a tyrant.' Now there is a man with a sense of humour and sense of fearlessness for doing what's right. I warrant that it'll be a matter of when rather than if that Brutus musters an army and returns to Rome."

Although somewhat sighing at first when beginning his speech, Cicero beamed with paternal pride by its close. The young woman listened with rapt attention, humouring her host (having heard the anecdote before).

"So what do you think the fate of Rome will be?" Attica asked, partly curious and partly indulging the seasoned statesman. Figuring that his master may now wax lyrical for some time, Tiro turned his attention to some notes he had to catch up on. Years of service had weakened the secretary's sight - and he squinted over the parchment to decipher his own shorthand.

"Firstly, the fate of Rome equates to the fate of us all. But to the matter. The wish is father of the thought, but Mark Antony and young Octavius will hopefully tear the Caesarian party apart. A house divided cannot stand. As such Mark Antony will not have the strength to defeat the Senate. And the Republic will be restored. Already some of the legions that Antony was relying on are siding with Octavius, or rather the pay rise he's promising them. Our agents have informed us that Antony is even going to have to leave Rome to win back the mutinous regiments. Although he is married to Fulvia - perhaps it's all just an excuse to get out of the house."

The years fell from his wizened countenance as Cicero smiled at his own remark.

"But in all honesty my dear I am unsure as to the future. At my age even the past becomes unclear. We will see what fate has in store for Rome. The hen is the wisest of all the animal creation, because she never cackles until the egg is laid. But let us not talk of politics any longer. We will depress ourselves. Or, it seems, worse - for we have bored Tiro it seems."

At hearing his name uttered Tiro pricked up his ears and turned to Cicero, as if awaiting instruction.

"Instead of admiring your own shorthand I would you look up and, wide-eyed, admire Attica's latest fresco on the wall behind you. The picture, still glistening with wet paint in the firelight, was that of the view of the valley from her bench. Azures, yellow-greens and textured browns brightened up the previously bare wall. Dominating the centre of the image however was a mysterious male figure, gazing out across the valley also.

"You flatter me by saying, my dear, that the figure in the painting is a young version of me. I neither had the stomach for soldiering in my youth, nor a soldierly build like that. Moreover I owned but my wits, rather than this estate, when I was your protagonist's age. But it really is quite an accomplished work. Thank you. Your father could have saved a small fortune in employing yourself, rather than commissioning overpriced Greek artists, to decorate the walls in his own villa."

But the winsome artist was barely listening to the praise of her host as she stared at her own work, lost in thought - thinking about Agrippa; her friend, world. Attica found herself praying to Octavius, to keep him safe. Later that evening she wrapped her blankets tightly around her, closed her eyes and imagined his muscular arm coil itself around her waist. She recalled how his rough hand tenderly caressed her back - and then scrunched up her buttock and pulled her pliant figure even closer. She smiled, mischievously, remembering the sensation, and placed her hand between her silken thighs as she drifted off to sleep. Her body tingled. Tears - of happiness at finding him and fear of losing him - soaked her pillow. She had never felt like this before, because she had never been in love before.

\*

Moonbeams poured through the open windows. Brutus closed his eyes and breathed in Porcia's scent - honey and roses. She had finally drifted off to sleep. Her husband however could not sleep. Nor did he wish to, for the ghost of Caesar waited for him there. The quack doctor attending to his burgeoning army had brewed all manner of sleeping draughts - as foul as any nightmare - but to no avail. Brutus quietly slipped out of the bedroom and headed to his study. His eyes had become accustomed to the dark. Where before his night-time reading had been Plato and Sophocles - muster books and quartermaster reports now lay open upon his desk. Philosophical problems had given way to calculating rates of interest. He, Rome, was at the mercy of the money lenders. Would all their fates be decided on who could borrow the most money? He read the letter from Cassius again. Octavius had adopted the name "Caesar" – and was on his way to Rome. Brutus smiled, grimly. Would this Caesar now haunt his waking world, as Julius did his dreams?

32.

Morning. A swirling crest of smoke - fuelled by homes, forges and ovens - hung over the sprawling, hilly city in the distance. The white marble of the Palatine still shone through, like coral beneath murky water, however. Indeed a stranger may have mistaken the stately grandeur of Hortensius' villa atop the Palatine as being the estate of a god rather than man, Octavius idly fancied. Hortensius, that famed advocate who proved, for Cleanthes, that "one can be master of the law without serving justice". The party could also discern the Aqua Appia and Aqua Martial wend their way around Rome's towering hills. The Viminal, the Aventine (the people's hill), the Capitoline with ornate temples flowering upon it like a stone garden, the Quirinal, Caelian and the Esquiline - with its senatorial properties lining the crown of the hill and the slums of the Subura littering the bottom, the houses as rickety as the inhabitants' prospects.

The gilded sun was still ascending in a vibrant sky behind Caesar, the sun seemingly appearing like a halo over his head. The evening before bore witness to a comet streaking across the starry firmament, auguring the arrival of good fortune. Aye, Balbus had been astute in choosing his date for Caesar's arrival. Octavius, riding a white gelding akin to his great-uncle's famed steed, trotted at the head of the party. Agrippa rode alongside his friend, pensiveness etched in both of their faces as they took in some of the tombs of Rome's dead lining the Appian Way. A particularly ornate and original design caught Agrippa's eye and he slowed to read the inscription.

*"Stranger, should you stop to admire the beauty of this tomb, know that the woman housed inside was more beautiful still. Helen was her name. We were betrothed, but she passed away before we were married. Although never her husband, I feel like a widower. I will try and live my life as if still inspired by her bright soul, so that in death, I may marry her in the afterlife. And so my sad story may become a happy one."*

Agrippa thought of Cleanthes, then Attica.

"So, what do you hope that someone will say on your tomb?" Octavius asked his friend, with half an eye still on the magnificent villa of the Palatine.

"That I died peacefully in my sleep at a ripe old age. And that I did not owe anyone any money. On second thoughts, that I owe a huge amount of money - and to my bitterest enemy."

"I shall make sure that our bitterest enemies are lying in their tombs before us Marcus," Octavius darkly declared, as he thought of those responsible for the deaths of Caesar and Cleanthes. "They must die," Octavius coldly stated, as if a logician were determining their fate.

*

The sound of the breeze whistling through the pillars and effigies of the tombs was soon eclipsed by the murmuring and hubbub of the crowd, ever-increasing in number, which was spilling out of the city to greet Caesar's heir. Balbus had sent letters ahead to loyal Caesarians to arrange a welcome for Octavius. Water vendors and costermongers had set up stalls. Soldiers, citizens, plebs, woman of rank (and their nubile daughters, dressed in their finest stolas and jewellery), merchants and the political classes populated the crowd alike. A few wore the black toga pulla as a mark of respect and mournfulness. Yet many wore their gayest attire. Children were placed on their parents' shoulders to get a better look at the Caesar. Anticipation and expectation rippled through the throng. Many carried placards, articulating their support for the Caesar.

*"A Rome without a Caesar would be like the Cyclops without his eye."*

*"Caesar, save Rome - from itself!"*

Agrippa whispered into his horse's ear and stroked his neck to sooth the nervous animal, not used to such scenes.

"Look smart men, eyes front - no matter which wench attracts your attention," Oppius ordered in all seriousness, but with a smile also. In response the infanteers tightened their formation and step and puffed out their chests, like sails billowing in the wind.

"At such times it should be my duty to remind Caesar that he is mortal - so what would you like someone to say about you upon your death?" Agrippa asked.

The clip-clop of hooves and caligae across the flagstones was soon muffled out by the congregation, as an increasing number of people spied the party and cheered. Octavius raised his voice to his friend to make himself heard.

"All the world's a stage - and all the men and women merely players. When I come to the end of my life I just hope I can look back and say that if I have played my part well, clap your hands, and dismiss me with applause from the theatre." Irony and sincerity vied for sovereignty in Caesar's expression as he spoke. "But let us talk no more of our end, my friend. We are all but in Rome - and he who is tired of Rome is tired of life. I want to introduce you to Octavia as soon as possible, Marcus. We shall have dinner - and the food will be as fine as her company."

Octavius warmly smiled, thinking about his sister. The idle fancy crept into his thoughts again that he would like to see his best friend and sister betrothed, to formally make his lieutenant part of his family.

Cheers began to mushroom into jubilant roars and salutations. Petals were strewn across the road ahead. Agrippa slowed his pace a little, allowing Caesar to march at the vanguard of his party alone. Agrippa was content to be the second man of Rome. The scene had an air of a military triumph however - and he was tempted to whisper in Caesar's ear, "Remember you are mortal; remember you are mortal."

Octavius was both touched and amused by the crowd's adoration. He waved imperiously, yet also affectionately - Caesar-like - at the people below him. Women gazed up, almost swooning. Men nodded approvingly, remembering Julius Caesar. Priests and augurs pronounced prayers and blessings, perhaps hoping to be spotted and provided with patronage. As the party passed a segment of the crowd who appeared impoverished, Oppius ordered a number of his men to distribute food and alms. Some raised their hands in gratitude to the Caesar, worshipping him like a god.

Not everyone viewed the young Caesar with such adoration and affection, however. From the city walls a trio of optimate senators looked down with disdain at the interloper from Velitrae. The adopted son had inherited his father's arrogance. The mob was displaying certain atavistic tendencies too - servitude and vulgarity.

"How long do you think the boy will last?"

"About as long as the bread he's handing out. Antony will chew him up and spit him out. He's far too wet behind the ears. An aedile has more influence and could politically outwit him. I look forward to his speeches, too. Will there not be pauses in the oration when the boy has to suck his thumb?"

The self-important senators let out a chorus of laughter, albeit the man who stood close to them, overhearing the exchange, merely raised an eyebrow and the corner of his mouth in a half-smile. Domitius Enobarbus thought to himself how Octavius had inherited Caesar's luck. He knew not the details but the party had somehow survived Gravius' attack. An agent from Praeneste had sent word ahead. It was the very last dispatch that Antony had read before the consul had ventured out to Asculum, to quell the disquiet among the Caesarian legion encamped there.

"I shall deal with the whelp when I return. The boy needs to get used to waiting upon my decisions anyway. This will be good practice for him."

The aristocratic senators beside him laughed again at a jibe, yet Domitius shook his head - in disappointment or amusement. If the reports were true - and Octavius had gleaned the support of both Balbus and Cicero - then the Senators may well now possess a shelf life as long as the bread that Caesar's heir was distributing.

Oppius offered a subtle nod to a brace of fellow centurions who stood with their cohorts on either side of the road. As Octavius passed they saluted in unison and then drew their swords in a guard of honour.

"*Caesar, Caesar, Caesar.*"

The chant swelled, rumbled, like magma inside the belly of a volcano, waiting to explode.

"*Caesar, Caesar, Caesar.*" Citizens soon took up the soldiers' cry.

Balbus and Oppius hadn't informed Octavius of this part of the reception. They wanted Caesar's reaction to be genuine, as the authenticity would add to the performance. Cornelius had also expressed to Oppius, whilst planning the young Caesar's arrival into the city, how Octavius needed to be convinced of his greatness as well as the people.

"*Caesar, Caesar, Caesar.*"

Agrippa soaked up the colourful and jubilant atmosphere. He started to compose in his head what he would later write to Salvidienus, who had begged him for more news on what had happened and what was going to happen. He would posit how they would soon all be debating the future of Rome in the Senate, instead of under a shady tree in an Apollonian field. Agrippa thought of Rufus but briefly however - and he started to compose a letter to someone whose mettle was more attractive.

*"In some senses Rome was always more of an idea than place to me - a just, intelligent and magnificent idea. Yet today I witnessed the semi-divine city which housed that idea ... And riding through its gates was Caesar, who embodies the idea of Rome ... But for all its expanse and opulence my mind's eye rested upon a far more just, intelligent and magnificent image ... More than Rome or Caesar I aspire to the idea of you ... I keep your letter by my bedside. I house it in a sealed jar, so as to preserve its perfume ... Every night I drink in your scent*

*and swim in your words ... Oppius asked me if I was drunk the other evening, as he caught me 'grinning like a fool' as I thought of you ... You make me want to be a better man Attica ..."*

"*Caesar, Caesar, Caesar.*"

The words thumped out from hundreds of lungs, in tune with his beating heart. Caesar beamed, as brightly as the midday sun. The light spun his fair hair into gold. He waved, warmly and magnanimously - and shook the occasional hand. The people loved Caesar. He was Caesar. Therefore the people loved him. And he would return their love. He would provide food for their stomachs, a sense of glory and worth to fill their hearts - and spectacles and entertainments for their eyes to feast upon. Caesar should be a servant of the people, as much as their master. His client list would be every Roman citizen, equestrian and farrier alike. Laws, libraries and religion would edify. Odours and ordure - and the cacophony of sound - poured out the gates of the city as Octavius approached its entrance. The people's love - and his sense of destiny - bore him upon a cloud. He would become the First Man of Rome. *If Sulla could, why can't I?* - Gaius asked himself, quoting Pompey. Again, irony and sincerity laced the thought. Octavius smiled, mercurially.

"*Caesar, Caesar, Caesar, Caesar, Caesar, Caesar.*"

He had never felt so close to Julius as now. He sensed Caesar's burden, pride and ecstasy - admiring and pitying his great-uncle more as a result. The cheers chimed in his ears, spurring him onwards. The gates sucked him in too, Charybdis-like. Inside, the walls and buildings bred shadows. Agrippa fell behind as the tide of supporters increased between them.

"*Caesar, Caesar, Caesar.*"

The people swarmed around the heir. Some just wanted to touch his cloak.

## Endnote

Many of the major characters who feature in Augustus: Son of Rome existed. Much of the narrative adheres to historical events. But Augustus: Son of Rome is very much a novel - so I have made stuff up too. Apologies for any historical inaccuracies, whether they are unwitting or not.

Over the years I have had the chance to meet - and work with - a number of authors whose books proved to be a source of inspiration and information for Augustus: Son of Rome. Tom Holland, Adrian Goldsworthy, Conn Iggulden and Simon Scarrow continue to entertain and educate. I am not alone in also owing a debt to Cicero, Shakespeare, Plutarch and Suetonius - whose works are equally entertaining and educational. In regards to further reading about Augustus and his era I can strongly recommend Ronald Syme's The Roman Revolution, Josiah Osgood's Caesar's Legacy and Anthony Everitt's biographies of Cicero and Augustus.

Should you have enjoyed spending time with the characters of Lucius Oppius and Julius Caesar then you may also want to read the novella series, Sword of Rome. The book covers Caesar's invasion of Britain, the Battle of Alesia, the crossing of the Rubicon and the Battle of Pharsalus.

Augustus: Son of Caesar

Richard Foreman

Dedicated to Anthony Foreman

1.

"Three's company, four would have been a crowd. I'm glad Marcellus is away on business," Octavius whispered to his friend, Marcus Agrippa. Octavia – Octavius' sister – had left the room to check that all was running smoothly in the kitchen.

"What's wrong with him?" Agrippa – muscular, good hearted and good humoured – asked whilst mopping up the remainder of his squid in mushroom sauce with a slice of freshly baked bread.

"He loves himself far more than anyone else does in this world – and the next. He over-dresses and underwhelms. Every time he opens his mouth and speaks I find myself wanting to open my mouth too – and yawn. Marcellus –"

Agrippa darted his eyes towards the door behind him and he heard the rustle of his sister's silk stola. Octavius swiftly altered the course of his conversation.

"– is away, inspecting a potential business interest in Perusia."

In truth Marcus Marcellus was inspecting the wife of his potential business partner in Perusia. Although he would be losing sleep this evening, it would be due to courting his new mistress rather than regretting missing the company of his young brother-in-law.

Octavia entered the triclinium carrying a plate with a further slice or two of bread for Agrippa. Even standing apart, as opposed to next to each other as they were now, one could discern a strong resemblance between brother and sister. They shared the same fair complexion and hair, fine features, the same expressive (but also at times unreadable) eyes. Neither possessed an overly gregarious manner yet they were charming and memorable in any company. Agrippa could not help but notice the bond between them. Octavius cherished and respected his sister more than any other woman.

This was their second evening in Rome. It was perhaps the first time Agrippa had seen his friend wholly relax and be himself – after a seemingly non-stop round of visits and visitors – since entering the city. The cheers had been plentiful and people had come out to greet the new Caesar and the pandemonium had continued since.

"You will be pleased to know that Marcellus is often away on business so you may wish to come to dinner again. I am well aware that you would rather stomach my food than the company of my husband." There was as much good humour as censure in the remark. The playfulness in Octavia's expression – and her wit – briefly reminded Agrippa of Caecilia, his intended. They had recently met – and fallen in love – at Cicero's country estate in Puteoli. What with Caecilia being the daughter of the republican-minded Atticus – and Agrippa being the lieutenant of a Caesar – the two lovers were prudently keeping their relationship a secret.

"So, Marcus, what do you think of my sister here?" Octavius remarked whilst fondly and mischievously gazing up at his blushing sibling. "We shared much when we were young. It's only fair that we share a certain amount of awkwardness and embarrassment now."

"She is charming, witty and beautiful – to the point where I have my doubts that she could be related to you."

Octavius laughed in reply whilst shrewdly examining the look that Octavia and Agrippa exchanged. He sensed warmth, but no heat, between the pair. He would ask Agrippa how attracted he was to his sister in private. As Caesar had offered his daughter Julia to Pompey, to strengthen the alliance between them, so too Octavius (ever conscious of his great-uncle's stratagems) could utilise Octavia one day in a similar regard. Also, he wanted to see his sister and best friend happy. A union between them could furnish such happiness.

The trio continued with their meal as servants first entered with a course of spiced turbot on a bed of cucumber and rocket, and then roasted pork in onion gravy. Octavius ate little and watered down his wine more than his friend. But then it was mathematically impossible not to dilute his wine any less than Agrippa, who cordially complimented his hostess on every dish and vintage.

"So tell me Marcus, are you betrothed yet?" Octavia asked, thinking that such was his appetite he needed a woman in the kitchen as much as his bed. As Agrippa was caught with a mouth full of honey-glazed crackling Octavius replied for him: "Marcus is married to my cause."

"In that case you should make sure that you have an affair," Octavia playfully replied.

"Was that a proposal?" Octavius retorted.

"Gaius, you are lucky that Marcellus isn't here," Octavia, with slightly less playfulness infusing her tone, answered back whilst crimsoning, unable to look Agrippa in the eye.

"It could be you who proves to be the lucky one sister," Octavius remarked, suggestively raising his eyebrow, "but I do indeed consider it a piece of good fortune that Marcellus is away."

There was more mirth than malice in his comment but nevertheless Octavia's mask slipped a little and she seemed hurt by her brother's jibe. Akin to her sibling though she recovered her composure quickly.

"You must forgive my brother, Marcus. Ever since he stopped begging me to help him with his homework he feels he can say anything without recourse. But, although he thinks little of my husband, he constantly writes to me and speaks highly of you. And we both know how seldom he speaks highly of anyone."

"If you speak highly of everyone then the compliment is diminished," Octavius somewhat sententiously asserted. There was a pause then as both he and Agrippa remembered Cleanthes, the original author of the saying. Cleanthes, Octavius' satirical and sagacious personal tutor, had died whilst their party was attacked by hired assassins as they ventured along the Appian Way towards Rome. The pair remembered the legionaries Roscius and Tiro Casca who had also perished, protecting Octavius, in the skirmish. The two friends fleetingly shared a look, their faces exhibiting sorrow and attempted consolation. A little confused as to the import of the strange moment between her guests Octavia changed the subject.

"Now, although I can no longer help you with your homework brother, is there anything I can do? What are your plans?"

"I will claim my inheritance," the young Caesar stated, simply and sternly. Witnessing how taken aback his sister was by his reply Octavius smiled and flippantly added, "How else will I be able to afford to keep mother in shoes?"

A short pause ensued, before Octavia responded: "You cannot afford to make too many enemies."

"I can if I befriend the legions. And I will need my inheritance to do so. I heard today how, before Caesar's body was even cold, Antony visited Calpurnia. Taking advantage of her frail state he secured Julius' papers and treasury. But he will not take advantage of me."

Agrippa frowned, recalling his visit to Caesar's house that afternoon. It was not just the lack of a retinue missing from the former dictator's house which had made the property seem empty – even the acoustics made the house seem like a mausoleum. Octavius described Calpurnia as being the shadow of the woman she once was. Her nerves were frayed from grief as well as the stress of Caesar's creditors calling on her. Octavius instructed his aunt to now direct all the money-lenders to him, to answer for the debts.

Aside from his debts the only thing which Octavius had inherited from Caesar that afternoon was a servant. Calpurnia introduced the aged Jew, Joseph, to Octavius. A large head bobbed up and down on a scrawny body. There was more hair sprouting from his ears and nostrils than his scalp. Hopefully his head housed more sense than teeth. When Calpurnia exited Octavius had interviewed the servant, who had served both Julius and his father before him.

"So, Joseph, tell me – why I should take you on?" Octavius had asked whilst sitting on a large chair behind the ornate cedarwood desk of the former dictator. The elderly Jew had squinted and raised his eyes as if looking up to his brain for inspiration on how he should respond. Yet there had also been a humorous glint in his aspect as he answered.

"Well, if my hand doesn't shake too much and cut your throat, I am a skilled barber. I shaved your great-uncle most mornings."

"Our fellow here either has a sense of earnestness, or humour, Marcus, wouldn't you say?"

"Indeed. And do you have anything else to offer?" Agrippa asked, amused and somewhat intrigued by the wizened Jew.

"I can offer you my prayers. Your enemies pray to the same gods as you. As such you may receive equal good fortune from them. Your enemies do not pray to my God however – so I may tip the balance of divine favour."

Octavius laughed.

"Caesar never mentioned your peculiar humour to me Joseph but he did say how you were one of the most honest and loyal men he had ever known."

"I fear I had little competition. Most of the men Caesar knew were politicians."

Agrippa recalled the comment and smiled inwardly. He would report the encounter in his letter to Caecilia later in the evening. He loved sharing his day with her in a letter – and longed to share her bed.

"You still have the option of returning to Apollonia. Mother has enough shoes already. You can return to your studies – live a quiet but contented life," Octavia argued.

Her words echoed those spoken by Cleanthes, shortly before he died. Octavius gently shook his head and grimly replied (quoting a line from an old play that resonated for him): "I am in blood – stepp'd in so far, that, should I wade no more, returning were as tedious as go o'er."

2.

Morning. The camp of the Fourth Legion, just outside of Asculum.

A watery mist poured itself over the rows of tents. The smell of wet grass and steaming porridge hung in the air. Familiar sounds accompanied familiar smells: the clanging of pots and pans and tamp of marching caligae. Antony stood in the principia by the sacellum, the shrine which held the legion's eagle. He was conscious of holding the meeting in the presence of the sacred totem. He would employ any device necessary to help stir loyalty and secure support. He had deliberately left a half-eaten centurion's breakfast, of cooked meats and cheese, on the table. He wished to convey that, at heart, he was still one of them.

Sunlight began to drift into the tent, as did the cadre of senior officers Antony had arranged to meet. He told himself again that he was here to bargain – not beg. He smiled and nodded but would wait for all six men to enter before he spoke.

First was Cephas Pollux. Caesar had once joked that such was his hard-headedness that he need not wear a helmet into battle. Although usually as garrulous as a Spartan it would perhaps be this ardent Caesarian who would speak for the group. His rank and experience merited seniority.

Next came Gratian Bibulus, limping a little from where the damp air was cramping up an old knee injury. There were fewer superstitious men in a devoutly superstitious army. After each battle he would order his cohort to dilute their wine with blood and toast their fallen comrades. He also abstained from sex until he earned the pleasure through the killing of an enemy.

Felix Calvinus followed. His nickname was Paris due to his good looks and way with women. Enobarbus had informed Antony of his taste for gambling, as well as women. Providing the price was right, Calvinus' loyalty could be bought, Antony surmised.

Upon his heels entered Manius Sura. His nickname was Patroclus, such was his way with men. As he grew older his lovers grew younger. Drink appeared to be a vice too. The Etruscan's nose was as red as the clay soil of his homeland.

Aulus Milo's bulkiness nigh on blocked out the light as he entered the tent. A blacksmith's son from Ravenna, his immaculately maintained armour and weapons were a testament to his former mentor. Tiro Casca had taken the recruit under his wing upon first joining the army – and Antony thought how Milo would run him through in a second if he knew that he was behind the attack on Octavius which had led to his Casca's demise.

Matius Varro was last to enter. Like Enobarbus, Varro was as much a scholar as a soldier. His manner and education bespoke of a moneyed and privileged background yet Antony was unaware of his family and Varro's life before the army. Although studious and somewhat introverted Matius was a good officer – and when he had a drink inside him he could be gregarious and entertaining. Many a time had Antony been there when Varro had enthralled half a cohort by reciting Homer around the campfire – or composing satirical epigrams about comrades or politicians. Varro had always intrigued Antony a little – perhaps now more than ever. For just as Matius' past was a blank page Antony could not be rightly sure where his loyalties would lie in the future either. Varro had served under Caesar yet one often found him reading tracts by the likes of Cato or Brutus.

Antony stood with his hand resting on the golden pommel of his long cavalry sword. Tanned, scarred, stubble-dusted faces stared back at him. The figures were a marriage of honour and savagery.

"Gentlemen, welcome. Stand at ease. I may wear a toga more than a uniform nowadays but I am still as much your friend and comrade as I am your consul," Antony warmly expressed, borrowing his opening from a speech which Caesar had once given to potentially mutinous officers. He approached the soldiers, smiling and clasping them heartily by the forearm in a Roman handshake.

"Cephas, how are you? I trust you have had time to visit your wife, or at least your mistress? It has been a long time – too long. Much has changed."

"But not for the better," the centurion gruffly replied, recalling the loss of Caesar.

"No, Caesar's death casts a shadow over us still. You are right," Antony enjoined, whilst inwardly seething at the officer's impudence. He retained his composure and gracious manner, however, to work his way down the line.

"Bibulus, the last time I saw you we were in that brothel in Pisa. It was a shame that snowstorm kept us there an extra night, eh? ... Screwed any of my former mistresses lately, Calvinus? ... Sura, I have with me an amphora of your favourite vintage ... Milo, I was sorry to hear about Tiro Casca. I know you were close. He was an old friend to me too ... Varro, you are looking well. Enobarbus sends his regards."

Antony then beckoned for his attendants to serve some wine and food. Once the servants departed Antony formally opened proceedings.

"You know why I am here. You can either refute these rumours or confirm them – and then what will be will be. It has come to my attention that a number of officers wish to declare their loyalty to Octavius." Sternness displaced warmth in the consul's tone.

As the officers had discussed beforehand, Pollux would speak for them.

"Permission to speak freely, sir."

"Granted."

"It is not our desire to choose between you and Octavius – but rather we wish to serve you both. The legions want you to become allies, not opponents. Only by operating together will we be strong enough to defeat the Senate's forces and avenge Caesar's murder."

"Are you somehow saying that I should treat this boy as my equal, that we should hold joint command?" Antony replied, ire and bewilderment firing his aspect and flaring his nostrils. "He's just a fucking boy, with about as much noble blood as a Gaulish drab. He has spent more time potty training than he has training to be a soldier."

Antony's hands gripped the pommel of his sword even tighter but, despite his rush of blood, the weapon remained in its scabbard. Although brave enough to fight any man, Antony was smart enough to realise he could not defeat every man. In contrast to Antony's fury and bombast the deputation of officers remained calm. Antony increasingly sympathised with the philosophy of Pompey and Caesar, that it was the army, rather than the Senate, who ultimately decided the fate of Rome. He currently needed the legions more than the legions needed him.

"I apologise my friends. But be wary of the boy. He'll fill your ears with promises rather than your purses with gold – whilst I will make good my word and grant every man an additional one hundred denarii who serves under my banner. You will be rewarded accordingly too."

"Octavius has promised five hundred denarii to every man."

"He is but a child, playing with pretend money. Your men can be spending my bonus within a fortnight. They may find it more difficult to cash in mere promises."

"The first payment from Caesar has already arrived, with a letter from Oppius to say that more will follow. And Oppius' word is as good as any bond I warrant," Aulus Milo announced in his rough, rural accent.

The light dimmed outside and Antony could hear the faint splatter of rain against the tent. The offer – and its apparent acceptance – filled his breast with rage and astonishment and he shook his head in disappointment.

"Have you become mercenaries rather than centurions – willing, like some harlot, to be purchased by the highest bidder? Has the rainy season washed away your honour? Does this eagle behind me mean nothing to you? You should be ashamed to look upon it."

All, aside from Pollux, could not look Antony, or the gleaming eagle, in the eye. They lowered their heads in shame though their resolve to side with Octavius (or better still encourage the two Caesarians to join together in a coalition) remained the same.

"If you match the boy's offer then we will reconsider. Know though that our actions are not solely motivated by money. If we declare for you we would also want to defeat Decimus Brutus for being Caesar's assassin, as well as for being your enemy. Cassius Longinus and Marcus Brutus should meet the same fate."

Although a flabby stomach hung over his belt beneath his breastplate Antony still possessed an imposing physique. His bulging biceps tensed, as did his face in a sneer, as he approached the senior officer.

"You seem to have forgotten your basic training Pollux. A general gives orders to his army – the army does not command its general. I came here today to make peace with you all but it seems you wish to declare war."

A pregnant pause ensued. Sweat trickled down Pollux's brow. He could smell the cheese and salted ham on Antony's breath as he stood and snorted in front of him. Pollux and Milo, akin to Antony, gripped their swords. The pair had formed a pact beforehand that they would defend each other if things should turn nasty. Both men were devoted to Caesar and resented Antony for making peace with Caesar's assassins. Finally Sura spoke and eased the tension.

"We should not give the libertores the satisfaction of having us fight among ourselves. We all stood together at Alesia and Pharsalus. We should all stand together now."

"Aye, we should draw breath before we draw any swords," Calvinus enjoined, fraternally placing his hands on the shoulders of Antony and Pollux. "All of us here have carried the legionary's shovel but let us not dig a hole for ourselves by becoming so entrenched in our positions that conflict becomes sovereign over a will to compromise and conciliate."

"Antony, if any legions declare for Octavius then know that being for him does not mean that we are against you. We urge you to return to Rome though and embrace the young Caesar. The gods, as well as the legions, would smile on such a union," Bibulus, raising a hand to the heavens, declaimed.

*Embrace him*? *I'll crush him* – Antony sneeringly thought to himself but nevertheless smiled and eased the confrontational atmosphere.

"Who am I to argue with you, or indeed the gods, Bibulus? Sura, you are as wise as you are valorous. We should not fight amongst ourselves. Come, let us not waste this time together or this fine vintage."

Matius Varro observed the scene in silence, half amused and half worried.

Playing the host again Antony filled his guests' cups. The rain drummed harder on the roof of the principia. A low gurgle of thunder sounded in the background.

"Let us raise a toast, rather than our voices. Let us drink to peace between friends and war upon our enemies," Antony cordially announced whilst inwardly judging which of his former friends might prove to be his future enemy.

3.

*Dear Cicero,*

*Antony returned to Rome today. Agrippa and I watched him enter from the Servian Wall. Such was the size of the army that accompanied him – it must have numbered around five thousand – Agrippa wondered whether Hannibal and Alexander had come back from the dead and allied with the consul. Although it should be noted that Antony pronounced the force to be his "personal bodyguard" rather than an army.*

*Rome seems a living, breathing mosaic (fragmented, but the whole appears cohesive) – a marriage of circadian appetites and divine inspiration. I find myself longing for the quietude of the countryside sometimes, though I know if I was so located I might then yearn for the diversions of Rome. Streets drip with wealth or conversely poverty. I try to remain anonymous but when recognised the populace offer their condolences and support. Coins are thrust into my hands (which I give back) and I receive dinner invitations from strangers, whether walking through the Subura or Forum.*

*Invitations from senators have been conspicuous by their absence though. If you know of anyone who can hold their drink as well as a conversation I would be grateful for an introduction. Unlike Aulus Hirtius I will leave enough food for their breakfast the next day too.*

*Thank you for your previous letter and the copy of Demosthenes which accompanied it. Which, to your mind, is his best speech? I shall take note and read it with added interest.*

*In reply to your letter I share your surprise – and contempt – at the open corruption which made Lepidus Pontifex Maximus. Antony appears to be dishing out favours to all and sundry yet he is far from in credit with everyone – the populares and optimates alike – as a result. At least the Vestal Virgins are likely to want to keep their virtue in his presence. Ironically however Lepidus is the only man whom his wife remains virginal towards.*

*I look forward to you returning to Rome. I would welcome your counsel and company.*

*Gaius Octavius Caesar.*

Cicero sometimes smirked, sometimes grunted and sometimes furrowed his already wrinkled brow at reading and re-reading Octavius' letter. The aged statesman sat at his desk, his back to the open window. Outside pink blossom coloured and scented a well-kept garden. Flowers craned their heads towards a glistering sun, gently fanned by a spring breeze. Bees thrummed and birds performed their trill songs and courtship dances.

Cicero's secretary, Tiro, sat at an adjacent desk and diligently ploughed through a variety of correspondence.

"Tiro, read this. It's from our baby Caesar," Cicero remarked, handing over the letter. "I will de-code his shorthand for you. He first reminds me of Antony's martial intentions and strength – as if I need reminding of such a thing," he uttered and sighed, briefly slumping in his chair a little before regaining his vigour and train of thought. "The sight of five thousand troops attending upon Antony does not blind me to his own recruitment campaign. The Fourth Legion will probably declare for Octavius. Money and promises are also being offered, through Oppius and Balbus, to other Caesarian forces and retired veterans. But our young friend fails to mention this in his gossipy missive. But the truth is we must turn a blind eye to his illegal recruitment of a private army – for every soldier who declares for Octavius will be one less man standing in Antony's ranks.

"Again we find ourselves employing the arts of politicking and rhetoric but ultimately we will need to remember simple arithmetic. We must count up who will command the most legions. Antony commands six in Macedonia, three in Campania. As he commands Lepidus, so too might he command his legions. Antony will look to sequester the legions posted in Gaul but Decimus Brutus will not hand over a single pack mule from his forces there. Hirtius and Pansa will command the forces loyal to the Republic although we need to squeeze more money out of the optimates to maintain their loyalty. Blood from a stone is a phrase that comes to mind though Tiro. Why is it that our best men have so often proved to be the worst men over the years?" Again Cicero sighed but again he mustered himself as he witnessed Tiro's reactions whilst reading the letter. "And how arrogant does our young friend think he is, flaunting his modesty so? He says he has tried to remain anonymous – aye, about as much as Antony has tried to remain celibate. There is not a street corner in Rome where he has not acted out the role of the disinherited orphan who is only trying to do right by his father and the people. Yet, though the mob may have fallen for his act, the political classes are snubbing him – hence his plea for me to grant him some introductions. In order not to snub him myself I shall send a few letters of introduction – but to those

Caesarian senators who he already knows and possesses the support of."

Tiro wryly smiled at the wily statesman's cunning and Cicero permitted himself a chuckle, pleased as he was by his own stratagem.

"This is just like old times Tiro, no? Again we are trying to steer a politic course between Scylla and Charybdis. Again we seem to be stuck in the middle."

"You should judge it as akin to being centre stage," Tiro answered, fondly gazing at his master – and then popping a brackish olive into his mouth.

"You know how to both flatter and ridicule me better than I can myself, old friend. But let us not fool ourselves, Rome is where one sees the action and garners applause. I can but wait in the wings for now. Antony is too powerful at present. I cannot risk him arresting me, or worse. Anything new to report?"

"Despite the enmity in his letter Octavius has requested to meet Antony. Doubtless he will be asking for his inheritance."

"The most he will get from that meeting is an insincere promise of a part payment."

"Agrippa also disclosed in a letter to the young Salvidienus that it is Octavius' intention to approach his cousins for support, Pinarius and Pedius, who were also benefactors in Caesar's will."

"The old Salvidienus has been quite a font of information."

"The likelihood is that he has passed the same information on to Antony. He is hedging his bets."

"Everybody has to stand somewhere though when the fighting begins. In the same way that the father intercepts his son's mail let us try to intercept the father's. We may be able to use Salvidienus to feed Antony false information."

Tiro handed the letter back and echoed Octavius by asking, "Which is, to your mind, Demosthenes' best speech?"

"His longest one. When I was a young advocate someone once asked me which speech by Hortensius I preferred. With my sense of humour overruling my sense of judgement I replied 'the shortest one'. But I miss my old rival. I remember attending a lavish party he once arranged for his fellow advocates at his country villa. After dinner he had his musicians play and – as if by magic – all manner of woodland creatures ventured out from the forest. Of course our host had trained them to do so by having the animals equate the music with being fed. But it was quite a sight.

"Believe it or not I found myself missing Caesar the other day too. Julius may have been a tyrant, thief and butcher but one could never have accused him of being boring. Cluvius, a banker friend, left this property to both Caesar and I. I purchased Julius' share at a more than reasonable price. When he visited he used to lounge in the exact same spot where Octavius decided to sit in the garden. I was going to tell the boy but I did not want to encourage him in any conceit that he is his great-uncle re-cast. Yet he is as impressive as Julius – but in different ways. If I had not met him for myself I would now be saying that the heir is but a puppet of Balbus. But our baby Caesar is his own man, for good or ill. I am told he lives quite modestly, despite his wealth. Perhaps I could be an Aristotle to his Alexander. However, although I may flirt with Octavius know that I am still married to Brutus and his cause Tiro. For all of the olive branches that Octavius offers with one hand I am worried that he clasps a knife in the other. As you know my friend, I am not one for being superstitious – unless there is a full moon," the satirical statesman said with a wink. But his features then dropped, the light vanished from his eyes. "But I had a strong presentiment the other evening that somehow Octavius will be the death of me."

4.

"Don't think, just do," Quintus, the young Roman officer, whispered to himself as he crouched on the mountainside, waiting for the signal to attack the oncoming wagon train (carrying a cache of arms, bound for Antony's forces in Macedonia). Quintus thought how diametrically opposed this new mantra was to that of his father's, "Think before you act," who had often expounded on his theme whilst walking his son to Orbilius' lauded college in Rome. Quintus hoped that the gods would forgive him for choosing the advice of his centurion over his tax-collector father during his first engagement.

A sweaty palm clasped a zealously sharpened gladius. Dusk was a dull red, akin to the colour of his dusty leather breastplate. Despite the drop in temperature his helmet still felt like an oven, with his head the guinea fowl inside it. His hand shook a little as he opened his canteen and took another swig of water. A craggy-faced legionary beside him offered an encouraging wink and smile. Sometimes he thought it was the legionaries who commanded him, rather than he them.

Again he listened intently – more intently than he ever did during his lectures in Athens. It was whilst studying at the Academy that his now general, Marcus Brutus, had recruited him. Initially the auspicious senator, now more renowned for murdering Caesar than for his philosophical writings, had lectured at the institution. But his tenure was a mere cover whilst Brutus recruited the brightest and the best for his cause. Boredom and a yearning for adventure had motivated Quintus more than a belief in the Republican cause. Brutus' noble character had inspired the student, rather than his politics. He felt sure that should Cassius Longinus or Mark Antony have attempted to recruit him then he would be still holding a stylus rather than a sword.

The sound of the distant shushing sea and the wind sighing through the pass was increasingly accompanied by the approaching clang of metal, as well as the carping of gulls. Brutus, remembering his Polybius, had adopted a tactic of Hannibal's. The plan was to attack the enemy with a small mobile force and then withdraw. The enemy would then give chase – and be ambushed. There would be little room for manoeuvre or retreat inside the killing zone.

The general, riding a handsome grey charger, with a brace of arrows protruding from his shield, gave the signal to attack. The hounds were finally let off the leash.

Battle yells curdled the air. An avalanche of men and metal poured down the mountainside. Roman soldiers appeared out from behind trees and boulders, as if from nowhere – like spirits from the underworld. Most of the enemy were Greek and no match for Roman drills and brawn. Pilums and arrows zipped through the air. Horses whinnied. Men screamed. Dust was kicked up from the track and mountain, forming a gritty mist.

Quintus' speed fuelled momentum and surprise as he attacked a youth who appeared little older than himself. Bearing down upon him the pock-marked enemy held up his shield in anticipation of Quintus' sword crashing against it – but at the last moment the Roman officer changed his angle of attack and stabbed rather than slashed. The slim blade slid between the enemy's ribs. Quintus stabbed again – and again. The enemy fell, blood gurgling from his mouth and covering the Roman's sword as if it were sheathed in a red scabbard. Quintus had been swifter than him, more deliberate. He appreciated even more what the quartermaster had said, quoting some veteran legionary called Tiro Casca – "There are the quick and the dead." Adrenaline and a desire to prove himself and not to let his comrades down spurred Quintus on to find his next combatant. Brutus ordered a decurion to take his cavalry troop and prevent any wagons from escaping.

Resistance melted like snow on a bakery chimney. The enemy were swiftly outnumbered and outfought, caught in a murderous vice. It was a slaughter rather than a battle. The tang of blood replaced that of the salt in the air. Although exhilarated, from surviving and proving his mettle, Quintus did not share the blood-lust of his comrades. He killed a couple of the wounded men out of pity, rather than cruelty, and offered up a brief prayer in silence to both of them. Brutus allowed his men to dispossess the enemy of any of their valuables but forbade any acts of torture. Night descended and made the blood appear brown upon the grass.

*

Embers still glowed from the previous night's fires as the chariot of the dawn rode across a soft blue sky. A few veterans still drunkenly caroused and finished off their jugs of acetum but most in the camp were sleeping off the celebrations. The victors had raised their cups to Brutus, Mars, Cassius, the Republic, Fortune, Bacchus – and then Brutus again.

Quintus had excused himself from the celebrations halfway through the evening. Tiredness, rather than triumphalism, had got the better of him. Yet he awoke early and took advantage of the relative quiet of the camp to sit in the shade of a cypress tree and compose a letter to his father. He recounted a little of the skirmish – suggesting that his education was not wholly going to waste, for "*I felt that Euclid and Pythagoras were on my shoulder in the melee, as the gods had once protected the heroes of Homer; their instruction helped me predict the trajectory of the missiles fired at us.*" On finishing the letter Quintus possessed a fancy to compose a poem as he gazed on the encampment – and then stared out across the towering mountains and eternal sea.

"*Dread kings rule over their own,*
*But over those kings is the rule of Jove,*
*Famed for the Giant's defeat,*
*Governing all by the lift of his brow.*"

The young officer pensively closed his eyes and soaked up the birdsong and massaging beams of the sun. Nature accepted him, both as a worshipper and its herald. *The world may be at war but let me be at peace.* Upon opening his eyes after his repose the youth picked up his copy of Pindar and read.

"I wish more of my officers would bury their head in a book rather than in between the legs of Greek slave girls."

Quintus immediately recognised the voice – and swiftly commenced to stand to attention before his general.

"At ease. You have little desire to stand and I have a desire to sit."

Brutus' tone was amiable but weary. The dark circles around his eyes – Quintus fancied that they could serve as archery targets – bespoke of a lack of sleep. The general briefly took in his junior officer before sitting down. He had a pleasant, friendly face and was short of stature. The uniform still didn't quite fit right. Conditioning had shed the youth of his puppy fat though he was still tubbier than the rest of the recruits from the Academy. He owned a wry sense of humour and appreciated logic, although he would not become its slave. His tutors had spoken highly of him and he had won prizes for his verses.

Brutus sat down next to Quintus on the grass.

"Was yesterday your first time in battle?"

"Yes, although I suffered many a beating under Orbillus, if that was any preparation," Quintus drily replied, making reference to the revered tutor.

"Why did he beat you? Were you an unruly pupil?"

"No. He beat myself and others because he enjoyed it, sadly. The lecturers at the Academy, however, desired to bend their charges over their desks for different reasons. My friend Publius preferred the

Greek attitude to discipline, as opposed to the Roman. When in Athens, he used to say."

"It seems little has changed since my days there," Brutus replied, more disapproving than wistful. Julius, whilst Servilia was his mistress, had paid for Brutus to study in Greece. He had proven to be one of the Academy's finest students yet often whilst attending lectures he would daydream and yearn to be riding with Caesar on his latest campaign.

"And did you kill for the first time?"

"Yes," Quintus replied, with more grief than pride in his expression.

Brutus couldn't help but feel an affinity for the virtuous student and placed a hand on his shoulder in consolation.

"I thank you for your service, as does Rome. You fought well and survived. If the gods haven't blessed you already may they do so now. But to die for one's country is also a sweet and glorious thing. Would you die for the cause of the Republic?" the commander asked, his dark eyes boring into the soul of his young officer.

"I would prefer to live for it," Quintus answered, unable to share Brutus' fervour.

"You do not have faith in the Republic?"

"Permission to speak freely, sir?"

"Granted."

"The only thing I have faith in is my scepticism."

Brutus' tanned, leathery face cracked into a crooked smile. He had been similarly intellectually precocious in his youth. Perhaps he would promote the candid young officer to his personal staff.

"But you should have faith. There are more things on heaven and earth than are dreamt of in your philosophy, Horace."

5.

Lucius Oppius sat up in bed, combating his dehydration from the wine the night before by downing a large cup of water. Battle-scars lined his torso like some half-finished map. His body was taut, a catapult waiting to be fired. His expression was stern. Oppius had witnessed too much barbarity to think much of people. Civilization was but a poultice over the wound of man. Yet in the face of such misanthropy he still valued honour, duty and friendship as if they were rocks he could cling to during life's storm – and he considered the army to be a home to those virtues far more than the Forum. He had served as Octavius' bodyguard for over two years now, having been personally ordered to do so by Caesar. At first the centurion had deemed the task to be a dull chore. His desire was to serve under Caesar on his campaigns and earn promotion and booty, not babysit his bookish nephew. But Oppius, over these past few weeks, had started to understand just what Julius had seen in his heir – his steeliness and acumen. And what had once been a chore was now becoming an honour.

The mission of accompanying Octavius on his perilous journey from Apollonia to Rome had also afforded Oppius the opportunity to further mentor Agrippa. The centurion could scarce believe how the youth had managed to possess such an advanced appreciation of tactics and strategy with little formal training. Yet diligence and an attention to detail were alloyed to Agrippa's natural abilities. Whilst attached to the legion in Macedonia Agrippa had been conscious of learning the duties of the quartermaster and engineer, as well as the decurion. Two weeks into serving with the legion Agrippa had spent half a day with a cobbler – and the other half training up a cohort, teaching them how to repair their own boots when on campaign. Old enough to be his father, Oppius would have been proud to call Agrippa his son.

They were remarkable young men taken on their own but together they were greater than the sum of their parts, Oppius judged. Yet even together Antony could prove too powerful and wily for them. If the consul was smart he would grant Octavius at least a portion of his inheritance during their meeting later today – lest he lose sympathy with a number of Caesarians. Oppius hoped that he could somehow facilitate an alliance between Octavius and Antony but he feared that battle was as good as lost.

The officer rose and dressed quietly, careful not to disturb the raven-tressed woman strewn next to him on the bed. Her milky flesh appeared almost translucent in the pale sunlight. He partly did not wish to wake her because she was sleeping so peaceably but mainly he wished to avoid the awkwardness that would arise from him not remembering her name. He knew she was the wife of a libertore though. Oppius smiled, remembering his own crude joke to Agrippa the night before. "I am going to pump her – for information." The joke was worthy of his former comrade and friend, Roscius. Unfortunately she had been bereft of intelligence, though not of passion.

*

Joseph removed the hot towel from around his young master's head and then rubbed an ointment, of his own concoction, into his freshly shaven face. Octavius had been uncommonly quiet this morning, with Joseph rightly judging that his master had things on his mind – namely his imminent meeting with the consul.

"Thank you, Joseph. May I ask, what did Julius say in regards to Mark Antony, when he was sat before you in the chair?"

The old Jew scrunched up his face and closed his eyes as if he were a librarian trying to recall where a certain scroll resided in his stacks. Finally he spoke.

"Caesar believed that Antony was a better lieutenant than he was general. Caesar encouraged Antony to take on more responsibility but then often regretted his decision to do so. He once told me how he felt sorry for Antony – whilst Caesar had Marius as a mentor and influence growing up Antony was too easily led astray by the wastrel Clodius. Antony's dissolute ways had eroded his potential. He opened wine at an age when he should've opened up his books. Such were his self-destructive appetites Caesar worried that, if Antony obtained an appetite for power (or worse obtained power itself), then it would not just be himself he would destroy."

"Your memory is still as sharp as your razor Joseph, thank you."

"You have your appointment with Antony today?"

"I do indeed. I much prefer to sound out the judgement of my barber, than that of the augurs, as to how things will transpire."

"I'm cheaper than an augur too. Alas though, I would not wish to judge either way as to the outcome of the meeting. Ignorance will have to serve for wisdom. Yet I will duly say a prayer for you."

"Do you think that will help?" Octavius remarked, quizzically raising his eyebrow.

"If it doesn't help, it cannot do any harm," Joseph warmly replied. "Next to God we are nothing. But to God we are everything. That's not from my good book, but yours. Cicero."

"I am grateful to you for your prayers and advice. You could well put all the astrologers, quacks and augurs in Rome out of business."

"I hope not. They may consequently take to being a barber – and put me out of business."

*

Domitius Enobarbus scowled and sighed after reading the report, which was tantamount to Antony's intelligent and disciplined lieutenant losing all of his composure. One of his agents had informed him that the wealthy banker Rabirius was now backing Octavius. Enobarbus recalled a maxim of Caesar's: *It matters not how much you're worth – but rather how much you can borrow.*

The steam from the hot bathing chamber poured out into the reception room and increased his irritability as he waited for Antony to get dressed after his morning workout. Since returning from Campania Antony had started to condition his body again. "It's time I started to resemble the statues of me which have been commissioned. If I am to promote myself as a descendant of Hercules then it is best that I don't possess the figure of Hirtius," Antony had joked. Fencing, wrestling and athletics had replaced the lunchtime bouts of drinking and whoring though the evenings were still filled with revelries and entertainment. Yesternight, amongst the various festivities, a dwarf had climbed in and out of an elephant's mouth – and a Persian prostitute had swallowed a snake.

Antony was running late but tardiness was the least of the faults which Enobarbus forgave his commander for. In some ways, unconsciously or not, Enobarbus acted as a counterpoint to Antony. When the consul started to lose himself in his vices his lieutenant would soberly remind him of his duties (or perform those duties for him). Similarly, whenever Antony was in a rage or gloom Enobarbus would remind him of his good fortune and accomplishments.

The consul finally appeared. His short, black hair was glossier for being damp still. Flecks of grey around the temples gave him a distinguished rather than aged air. The sun had varnished an already healthy complexion. His muscular arms, glazed in massage oil, which had cradled more mistresses than even Archimedes could number, could also crush the ribs of a man as if cracking a walnut. His chest was broad, as was the smile that he wore on seeing his friend.

"Morning Domitius. Anything to report? Or should I say any good news to report?" Antony remarked whilst heartily clasping his lieutenant's arm.

"The policy of including former centurions on juries has gone down well with veterans and the officer class, if not some of the old families in the Senate. But you can't please all the people all of the time. Also, Cleopatra pledges her support to your cause. Unfortunately she doesn't pledge any gold."

Antony grinned on hearing the Egyptian queen's name. He was sorry that he had not had the opportunity to say goodbye before she fled the city after Caesar's murder. Rome's loss was Alexandria's gain, he mused.

"On a different note I've unfortunately just received news that Postumus Rabirius is providing financial support for Octavius – and is granting him a substantial line of credit."

"Pah," Antony replied with a dismissive wave of his hand, "Rabirius is doubtless doing so from greed rather than love. And Octavius needs to borrow money, for he'll get none from me. We are due to meet the pretentious stripling now, aren't we? I think we should leave the boy sweating at the gate for an hour or two. With any luck the pup will be without his sunhat and, feeling faint, will want to return home."

*

The muggy humidity sapped Oppius' strength and fired his impatience at the same time. The centurion, Octavius and Agrippa – along with a handful of attendants and bodyguards – stood outside the gates to Pompey's gardens, which Caesar had gifted to Antony after the civil war. Again Oppius ordered one of Antony's men to inform the consul that "Caesar" was waiting.

Octavius was calm, imperious. He drank another cup of water before biting down on a sharp, juicy apple with visible pleasure.

"He is being blatantly disrespectful," Oppius gruffly remarked.

"It is his dignitas that he is tarnishing, not ours. Besides, I have more time on my side than he," Octavius replied.

"And perhaps it's fear, rather than rudeness, which detains him," Agrippa added.

Pink clouds turned to grey and fomented in the sky, like a smack of jellyfish clustering together. A sudden breeze animated the wind chimes in the fruit trees which resided just behind the garden walls. Their silvery sound was briefly drowned out by the clang of the iron gates finally opening.

"The consul will see you now."

It had been agreed beforehand that only Oppius and Agrippa would accompany Caesar and attend the meeting.

Even in the increasingly dull light the vitality and colours of Pompey's gardens shone through. Octavius noticed a small herb garden – laden with mint, thyme, basil and celery seed – that rivalled Cleanthes' back in Apollonia. Octavius' step-father, Marcus Phillipus, might have similarly coveted the small attractive pond in the garden, filled with his beloved koi carp. Light and shadow mottled the marble pathways and manicured lawns as trellis work, garlanded with myrtle and ivy, hung above large sections of the grounds. Flowers erupted out of rich black soil, dazzling and perfuming the air: roses, violets, amaranths. Bees giddily swirled and then dived into the various blooms, rummaging and mining pollen. Numerous statues welcomed visitors with open arms. Agrippa recognised Alexander (commissioned by Pompey), Odysseus (commissioned by Caesar) and Priapus (commissioned by Antony).

The trio were led to the centre of the garden where they encountered an elaborate fountain – and Antony. The consul was accompanied by Domitius Enobarbus and a handful of burly lictors.

"My lad, it's good to see you. Lucius, I thank you for your service to Julius' nephew. We should share news – and a jug of Massic – soon. You must be the young Agrippa."

An effusive Antony warmly greeted his guests. Octavius thrust out his hand before the consul had a chance to embrace him.

"My sincerest apologies for keeping you waiting but I have been engaged in some pressing affairs of state. And I'm sure you will agree that Rome must come first. Allow me to introduce you to my friend and general secretary, Domitius Enobarbus."

Domitius nodded to the party. He surveyed the young Caesar. His demeanour was polite and relaxed but Enobarbus couldn't help noticing how his bright, piercing eyes took everything in – observing, collating and judging. His appearance was smart but not ostentatious. Whilst Domitius assessed Octavius Agrippa noted Antony's secretary. Balbus had instructed Agrippa to do so, arguing that it would perhaps be through his lieutenant that they would either make war, or peace, with Antony. "Better to deal with Enobarbus that Antony's hot-headed and cold-bloodied brother, Lucius. Or his shrill, ambitious wife, Fulvia." The secretary was neither tall nor short, broad nor slim. His features were neither overly handsome nor unpleasant. His dress was neither gaudy nor commonplace. Agrippa deemed that the secretary could have been anyone – and indeed Domitius was often content for people to consider him a no one. It was his brief to know more about others than they knew about him. "He prefers to observe rather than be observed," Balbus had remarked, admiring the modesty and intelligence of Antony's lieutenant, thinking himself lucky that his employer was devoid of such similar subtle virtues.

"You look well. You have even grown a little I think. Julius was forever fretting about your health, knowing how frail you were as a child – which, after all, was not that long ago."

Octavius offered a perfunctory smile before responding in earnest. "I thank you for your thoughts in regards to the state of my health but as we both know this visit is concerned with the state of my finances. It is my understanding that, after Caesar's death, you secured his estate. I thank you for that service but I have come to Rome to collect my inheritance – and subsequently honour the rest of Caesar's bequests in his will."

There was equanimity in his tone, galvanised by an uncommon resoluteness. Antony transformed a grimace into a smile and replied: "I admire your verve and idealism in wishing to honour Caesar's bequests but you are inexperienced in business and the ways of the world. When I took control of Julius' estate, in the name of the Senate, it soon became apparent that one could not easily separate what belonged to Caesar and what belonged to the state. I dare say that not even Julius himself could unpick the Gordian Knot he had created in his finances. I am doing you a favour by absolving you of your responsibilities in honouring Caesar's promises – else both Rome and you would suffer bankruptcy."

Again the young Caesar smiled. His manner was confident and composed. "It may prove difficult but that does not make it impossible to render unto Caesar what's Caesar's – and to render unto the state what belongs to it. What we can surely agree on to begin with is that the treasury does not belong to you."

Antony moved closer to the arrogant adolescent and his mask of charm began to slip. A sneer replaced his smile and he lowered his voice menacingly. He towered over the youth and spoke down to him. "You may well wear Caesar's belt but do not pretend to dress yourself in his authority. You should be grateful that I have even deigned to see you. Believe it or not I mean well towards you for you are Caesar's great-nephew. But do not take my goodwill and generosity for granted, boy."

The statesman's spittle flecked his face and Octavius could smell the wine on his breath but he flinched not and calmly replied, "Again, you are mistaken somewhat. I am Caesar's son. I would have you read the will, as well as Plautus when he writes that 'he means well is useless unless he does well'. The whole of Rome and Caesar's faction knows what I am entitled to. If you will not listen to me, you may then listen to us."

Enobarbus could sense that Antony was losing his composure and the argument – the one being almost inexplicably bound to the other. Things were not going according to plan. Antony had envisioned Octavius leaving their meeting grateful – for some feigned goodwill and promises of assistance. Failing that, he had remarked to his secretary that he may well intimidate the youth into compliancy or work the brat up into such a tantrum that he would exhibit a lack of dignity and authority. Perhaps he would make him beg. Yet it was the young Caesar who was retaining his dignity and authority. Enobarbus observed fonts of perspiration forming on Antony's temples. Antony had grabbed the pommel of his cavalry sword, a sure signal that he was getting frustrated, and angry.

"I *am* Rome, for all intents and purposes," Antony answered back – this time shouting. The pair of finches on the trellis-work above darted away in fear at the booming voice. "How dare you come here and yap at me like some spoiled pup. Do you not know who you're talking to? I am your consul!"

Antony pointed at himself upon expounding this before stabbing his finger into the chest of his callow antagonist. Yet Octavius, just in his cause and confident of outwitting the brutish statesman, stood steadfast and continued to goad his opponent with a wry smile on his face and amiability still lacing his tone, like poison.

"Dignity does not consist in possessing honours, but in deserving them," Octavius drily asserted, quoting Aristotle. Enobarbus couldn't help but be impressed by the young Caesar's wit and courage (although he knew well that stupidity often resided on the reverse of the coin where courage was minted).

"You impudent little bastard. It seems you think you have an answer for everything. Well perhaps *my* answer is to just cut you out of the will," Antony spat out, baring his teeth and clasping his sword even more firmly. Before his blade had a chance to see sunlight though, Oppius was by Octavius' side, his gladius half unsheathed. Antony gazed at the centurion, fury and astonishment animating his countenance.

"You would draw your weapon against me, Lucius? We shared more on one campaign than you will share in a lifetime serving this whelp."

"You have my sympathies Antony, but Caesar has my sword," Oppius dutifully replied.

Enobarbus instructed the lictors to stand down and sheath their weapons. He wished to douse the flames of conflict, not stoke them.

"You have my sympathies too, Lucius, if you are to side with a boy who owes everything to his name," Antony exclaimed, pursing his lips and dismissively shaking his head at the fresh-faced youth.

"You owe everything to that name too. The gift of this arbour is a testament to that," Octavius calmly replied.

"Caesar loved me more than you," Antony said, raising his voice again.

"We could argue that point until these gardens grow into a forest. What you can certainly boast about is that you loved Caesar's murderers more than me, such was your willingness to make peace with them after his death." Again Octavius' tone was measured and his face betrayed a hint of being amused by Antony, rather than fearful of him.

"I'd be even more willing to make peace with the man who slays the upstart before me. You have made an enemy today. Your friends have made an enemy of me too," Antony remarked, glowering at Oppius and Agrippa. "No more talk. Talk is cheap. It's probably all you can afford. The only money you'll get from me is that which I pay to you for the ferryman. This meeting is over."

6.

*Dear Atticus,*

*Good news (how paradoxical it seems to put those two words together, especially of late). The meeting between Antony and Octavius was a wonderful disaster. Aeneas and Dido had a happier ending. The bad blood between them thickened. Octavius' demands to be granted his inheritance fell on deaf ears. Antony's pride, which has helped him rise so high, may prove to be his downfall. I even heard a rumour that swords were drawn – though unfortunately no blood was spilled. But the Caesarian faction has officially split rather than united.*

*Yet Octavius remains undaunted, indeed he seems to have been inspired by the setback and has campaigned even more vigorously. To half the people he encounters he pleads poverty, citing Antony's refusal to hand over Julius' estate. He plays the victim and the dutiful son. Everything he does is done "in the name of Caesar and the people". It's a tedious and fraudulent mandate of course – but it's also effective. There was an incident at the Festival of Ceres. Octavius asked that Caesar's golden chair, which was bestowed upon him by the Senate, be put on display. Antony refused. Yet my agents report that Octavius worked the crowd and turned defeat into victory. Antony came out of the incident looking unfair and petty. It seems that Antony views the boy as a mere gadfly. I believe, however, that he is underestimating Octavius. Let him.*

*To the remaining half of the people he encounters – soldiers, merchants and officials – Octavius promises riches and rewards. He is speculating to accumulate, using money he has borrowed to buy more support. At present Octavius is planning to host a season of gladiatorial games to honour his father (to his credit he is also paying for a number of theatrical productions of Plautus and Sophocles). The Senate is still rightly wary of the boy but the people are taking him to their hearts. As we know though, the mob can be more changeable than the weather, or a woman.*

*Octavius seeks my counsel and claims he is devoted to me. We regularly exchange letters containing both personal and political matters. He has a mind and wit of someone older than his tender years. I can see why Julius chose him as his heir. Yet he still has much to learn. He believes that he is recruiting me to his cause, but I am recruiting him to mine.*

*The bad news is that Antony is actively recruiting too. He is using the resources of the Republic against the Republic. Even taking into account those centurions and legions loyal to our cause – and those who have been bought by Octavius – Antony still holds the upper hand. Decimus Brutus has again written to me, stating that he will not hand over his province of Cisalpine Gaul to a drunk and a tyrant. What Antony will not be able to win through force of character he may be able to win through force of arms, however.*

*I have heard that Antony will soon be travelling to Brundisium, to gain the support of the legions there. During his absence I will return to Rome, in order to try and gain the support of the Senate. Once his tenure as consul is up we must declare Antony an enemy of the state and denude him of his legions, though a peaceful solution seems about as likely as Antony remaining faithful to Fulvia.*

*I will take Caecilia with me to the capital. She has been urging me to do so now for some time. Do not worry my friend, I will duly keep her away from any rakes or fortune hunting suitors.*

*I will write again soon. Although I am confident of investing in Brutus politically, I want to ask your advice in regards to investing in some prospective financial opportunities.*

*Cicero.*

One of the lamps flickered as the midnight oil began to burn out. The young Caesar sat in his study, fighting off a yearning to sleep. He was keen to finish off his correspondence, even if it meant writing in the half-light. Octavius remembered how his uncle had often worked late into the night, a freshly sharpened stylus furiously working its way across wax tablet after wax tablet. "I'll rest enough once I am dead," Caesar had said to his great-nephew. "Deeds and words can live on though … I will also live on through you."

Octavius, for personal and public reasons, wanted to live up to Julius' expectations and reputation. Still the boy wanted his great-uncle – father – to be proud of him. He would only rest once his enemies were dead.

He decided not to water down the wine, hoping that its sour taste might jolt him back into life. His body ached and he could still smell perfume on his skin. *Aemilia.* She had been another wife of another senator. Since coming to Rome a veritable banquet of women had been laid out before him – daughters, courtesans, slave girls and wives. *It would be foolish to eat just one dish.* Octavius enjoyed kissing compliments and poetry into their ears. Seducing them, or letting them seduce him. He pictured again the way Aemilia's red silk dress had fallen from her slender body, as she deftly unclasped the sapphire brooch pinned to her right hip. *A gift which unwrapped itself.* Aemilia had sighed and whispered the name "Caesar" over and over again as he took her, standing up, in the room next to where his guests were having dinner. Women were a wealth of gossip as well as pleasure and Octavius encouraged pillow talk. Julius had seduced women for similar reasons. Women were a source of intelligence (well, some of them were). Aemilia had been predictably indiscreet and Octavius learned of her husband's enmity towards Antony. It was not even beyond the realms of possibility that the ambitious senator had instructed his wife to bed Caesar's heir in order to communicate whose side he was on. His bed would never have to be cold again.

As well as taking various lovers Octavius had also enjoyed, or in some instances endured, a procession of visitors paying their respects. His mother and step-father had recently written to him, pledging their support again. Balbus, his great-uncle's secretary, provided a wealth of advice and contacts. His sister loved him unconditionally, despite knowing most of his faults. Agrippa and Oppius were seldom far away and would give their lives to protect him. Yet Octavius had never felt more alone than he did now. He was a tiny pebble among millions of others on a vast beach, before an even vaster ocean. He missed Caesar and Cleanthes. There was an ache in the pit of his stomach, like a hunger. Was it fear, guilt, grief or ambition? *Why can't I be as indifferent to life as life is towards me?* Cicero would understand him. The young student was in awe of the statesman's wisdom, writing and achievements. He admired his good humour too in the face of an ignorant, or malevolent, world.

Julius had possessed the same good humour. He knew how to balance a sense of pleasure with a sense of duty. Sex had been a means for him to further his political ambitions but sex had also been a means of forgetting about politics. When Octavius made love he wasn't making war. His enemies were as numerous as his lovers although he wryly thought to himself how some of his lovers may well become enemies as he neither returned their messages nor love. *There is no need to unwrap a gift more than once.* Cleanthes, his former philosophy tutor, wouldn't have approved of his behaviour, Octavius mused. He would have advised him to take Aristotle to bed with him, rather than an Aemilia, each night. Just before Cleanthes had been killed he had urged his student to return to Apollonia and complete his studies. "Everyone thinks he will become master of Rome. But everyone becomes its slave." There had been a time when it was the youth's greatest desire to win the approval of his enigmatic teacher. But his greatest desire now was to avenge Cleanthes' – and Caesar's – deaths.

Octavius sighed. There was no turning back now. In crossing the Ionian Sea, as he journeyed to Italy from Apollonia, he had crossed his Rubicon.

Octavius sharpened his stylus and worked on through the night.

7.

The balmy evening air blew through the windows of the tavern, diluting the pungent smells of wine and garum. As late as it was the night was still young for most of the patrons of *The Bunch of Grapes*. Greasy-haired whores draped themselves over wealthy-looking customers and laughed at their jokes, even if they couldn't quite hear what was being said over the general din of inequity. Wine was continually sloshed into cups by overworked serving girls. Various stains mottled the cracked, tiled floor. Cheers and curses erupted in one corner where a group of sailors played dice, with varying degrees of skill and luck. Bronze oil lamps, strewn with cobwebs, hung from the damp-ridden ceiling.

The three centurions sat around the table in the far corner, dressed as civilians. Oppius remained impassive on hearing the news from Pollux that a number of their friends and fellow officers had decided to side with Antony.

"Calvinus said that he owed Antony his loyalty, having shared many an amphora of wine and mistresses with him over the years. But it was more about money. For once Antony paid someone else's gambling debts, as opposed to his own … Bibulus was instructed by an augur to serve Antony. Who could foresee that? Antony made Sura an offer he couldn't refuse – putting him in charge of recruiting young men … Despite repeated offers, financial or otherwise, at least Matius Varro refused Antony's advances. Yet he has also declined ours. He will remain neutral, for now. Matius said that, instead of Antony or Octavius, we should consider that war is our enemy. Perhaps the bookish bastard is right … But the friend of my enemy *is* my enemy. After Caesar's assassination Antony shouldn't have made peace with Cassius and the rest of the murdering dogs. I fought beside Decimus Brutus at Alesia, he even saved my life that day. But I'll now fight against him, without mercy, for killing Caesar."

Aulus Milo nodded his head and occasionally grunted in agreement as he listened to his friend and worked his way through a second plate of pork chops. His face was a picture of concentration, from trying to follow what Oppius and Pollux were saying and from trying to work out how best to extract all the meat from the bones left on his plate.

Oppius was disappointed, more than surprised, at the news that so many Caesarians were deciding to join the ranks of Antony's burgeoning army. The consul was beginning to offer the same amount of gold as Octavius – and Antony was by far the more prudent option. They were betting on the favourite to win the race. The centurion would not consider his former comrades enemies, yet. But should they take up arms against Octavius...

Oppius' brow creased as he remembered the previous civil war, between Caesar and Pompey. Caesar had triumphed but there were few other winners. On the night when Caesar crossed the Rubicon Oppius' friend, Marcus Fabius, had died. He had been murdered by Flavius Laco, Pompey's agent. Oppius in turn killed Laco at the battle of Pharsalus. The civil war between Octavius and Antony – or Antony and the Senate, or Brutus and Octavius – had yet to commence in earnest but already Oppius had lost Roscius and Tiro Casca. Something had died inside of him with their deaths – as something inside of him had died when his lover, Livia, had betrayed him at Alesia. How much fight was left in him? *Too much blood has been spilled.* The soldier had given his word to Julius Caesar, however, that he would protect his great-nephew. Antony had recently written a letter to Oppius, promising him various rewards should he switch over to the consul's side and abandon the young Caesar. Antony was the safer bet but Oppius would keep his word. He recalled something Caesar had once said: *I love the name of honour, more than I fear death.*

The centurion was distracted from his grim thoughts by the arrival of an ageing, but still buxom, whore. She stood before Aulus Milo, showing off her gap-toothed smile. The neckline of her dress revealed her two virtues to the grinning soldier. Her face was caked with make-up. She had been a beauty once – under Sulla's reign – Oppius mused.

"Seems like you've had a good meal there. Ready for your dessert? I'm Diana," the woman said, winking.

"And I'm all yours," Aulus replied.

"Are you a sailor?"

"No, a soldier. But I'm not about to put up a fight if you wish to win my heart."

"It's not your heart that I'm interested in," the woman said, with an even more suggestive expression.

After the whore led Aulus off upstairs to a private room Oppius and Pollux resumed their conversation.

"Antony will be sending out the likes of Sura and Bibulus to recruit veterans and fresh meat alike, both in the towns and countryside. We need to get to these men before our rivals."

"Agreed," Oppius said, thinking how much his old friend Roscius would have been an asset in working the taverns and recruiting men. "I'll need you to take charge of recruitment. Have Aulus and others find us some legionaries. I have a list of potential officers from Balbus we should approach too. They served Julius loyally. Here's hoping that they will serve Octavius."

"He's young. And an unknown quantity," Pollux said, voicing the opinion of thousands of doubters.

"His money is good and so is his character. He's a Caesar."

"Will that be enough?"

"It'll have to be."

"And how are you fixed for men? Do you need me to find anyone to replace Roscius and Tiro Casca, to guard Octavius?"

"I sent a message off to an old friend as soon as I knew we would be coming to Rome. I'm hopeful he'll respond."

"Have you heard anything more about who could have been behind the ambush on the road to Rome? Tiro Casca was like a father to our friend upstairs. Aulus is as keen as anyone to avenge his death."

Oppius shook his head in reply. Unfortunately the name of Caesar attracted as many enemies as allies.

*

Tattoos covered the sailor's brawny arms and bull neck. Carbo Vedius' face was as brown and weathered as an old wine skin. The ups and downs of the rolling seas he sailed upon mirrored his fortunes at the gambling tables. He had nearly lost all of his money towards the beginning of the evening – and had bullied a shipmate into lending him some coins to keep him in the game – but fortune's wheel turned and Vedius won a number of games in a row. He cleaned out a few of his fellow dice players around the table. He often patted the purse which hung on his belt, enjoying the sound of the coins clinking together. Not wishing to waste his run of good luck Vedius worked his way around the tavern in order to find new players to join the game.

Oppius was now sitting on his own. Pollux and Aulus had gone home. The centurion was finishing off his last cup of wine and about to retrieve some money to pay the bill when the sailor approached him.

"Fancy a game of dice, friend? The wine will be on me."

"No thanks. I'm about to leave."

The navvy's disappointment manifested itself into resentment. The bully was not one to take no for an answer.

"Are you army?" Vedius asked, taking in the man's build and short haircut. "I thought that you boys never ran away from a challenge. Do you not fancy your chances? Have you not made your offerings to Fortuna and Victoria today?"

"The only good fortune I'd ask for now is for you to move along," Oppius said flatly. He was in no mood to suffer the drunken sailor's company or sarcastic comments. Although the centurion wasn't superstitious himself he knew many a soldier who offered up prayers to Fortuna and Victoria before they went into battle. Roscius had sometimes done so – and Oppius didn't look kindly on the man standing before him, sneering at his dead friend's religious beliefs.

Vedius didn't look kindly on the soldier in return. From Britain to Brundisium there was, at best, tension between the army and navy. At worst there was an inexplicable but tangible hostility between soldiers and sailors. Each service thought the other looked down on them (which often they did). Many a legionary and sailor traded blows in taverns across the provinces.

"You army think you're so special. You think that you're the guardians of Rome but really you're its scourge. For a few extra coins that Caesar gave out you marched on Italy and the capital. And you're all about to offer your services again to the highest bidder, whether it be Antony, the Senate or Brutus and Cassius. Meanwhile our taxes will continue to go on buying your jugs of acetum and paying for your whores."

As the navvy was finishing his short speech he was joined by two bleary-eyed shipmates. The first man, who stood to Vedius' right, wore a tunic which was as stained as the floor. His face was leathery, his expression permanently pinched. Drink fuelled his emotions, whether he was feeling a sense of triumph or antagonism. The second man, to the left of Vedius, wore a cloak over his tunic – which hid the dagger tucked into his belt. His face was as flat and square as the stern of a ship. Both men were willing and able to back up their friend should any trouble arise – and given their shipmate's volatile temper trouble was often a safe bet.

Oppius calmly stood up and surveyed the three men and his surroundings.

"Are you coming back to join the game Carbo?" the first man asked. He believed that their luck was in for the night.

"Not just yet. I thought I might have some sport with this dumb soldier first. I had come over to teach him a lesson in playing dice but now I think we should teach him a lesson in respect."

Malice gleamed in the dicer's eyes. The centurion noticed the sailor's hand begin to curl itself up into a fist. The second man also slid his hand beneath his cloak and reached for his dagger.

The trio intended to have their fun and then return to the gaming tables. Three against one were good – and familiar – odds.

But their luck was about to run out.

Oppius quickly grabbed his wine cup from the table and threw its contents into Vedius' eyes – which temporarily took the man out of the fight. The soldier, a veteran of various tavern brawls over the years, then smashed the clay cup into the face of the sailor who was reaching for his knife beneath his cloak. Blood gushed out from his broken nose before he fell to the ground. The first sailor's expression became even more pinched with anger as he stepped closer and aimed a punch at Oppius. At the last moment, before connecting, the centurion bent his head down – and his opponent's fist struck the top of his forehead, fracturing a couple of bones in his hand. Oppius made his punch count as his hardened knuckles swung through the air and struck the sailor's chin.

By now half the tavern was scrambling to move away from the fight, fearing that the violence might spread. The rest of the patrons were wide-eyed and sucked in the scene. A couple of spectators even let out a few cheers whilst others winced at the sight of blood and sound of snapping bones.

As Oppius knocked the first sailor out – adding another stain to the floor – Vedius retrieved the long-bladed knife from his prostrate friend. He could still smell the wine on his face – and drip down his chin – but he could see clearly. The navvy stood before the soldier, swishing his weapon in the air; he grin-cum-snarled, believing that the dagger gave him the upper hand.

*I'm going to cut the bastard open. And enjoy it.*

But the smile fell from the sailor's face as soon as Oppius picked up the stool he had been sitting on.

"You should have just moved on," the soldier said.

Vedius' eyes widened in wariness. He was expecting his opponent to swing the wooden stool – and was confident of avoiding the attack – but Oppius quickly jabbed the chair forward catching the sailor squarely in the chest. A winded Vedius stumbled backwards and fell to the ground. Oppius felt a surge of fiery hatred as he stood over his enemy. The thought coursed through him that he should smash the stool down on the sailor's head – not caring if the blow killed him or not. There would be one less bully in the world. One less Flavius Laco.

He needed to be taught a lesson. Oppius' nostrils were flared and his eyes were ablaze as if he was on the battlefield once more. But the moment passed and he breathed out. Vedius flinched as the soldier bent over him but rather than attack the sailor again Oppius merely unhooked his purse from his belt and tossed it to the distraught-looking landlord.

"Here, this should pay for any damage."

The small crowd duly parted as the stone-faced stranger walked out the door and disappeared into the now cold night.

Carbo Vedius remained on the floor and groaned. Defeated. He felt like there was a marble slab on his chest and he was unable to get up. Yet fear was already giving way to malice and he vowed that he would track the soldier down and kill him.

Blood begets blood.

8.

Octavius woke shortly after first light, dressed and retreated into his study. The humid air throbbed through the open shutters. The window looked out across a verdant garden, vibrant with life and colour. Flowers – violets, lilies, oleanders – perfumed the air. The sound of birdsong and a trickling fountain also thrilled through the window. Pristine sunlight gleamed off the white Carrara sculptures which Octavius had recently bought and installed in the garden – statues of Aeneas, Apollo, Caesar, Janus and Nemesis, the god of vengeance. The garden – and the property as a whole – projected a sense of taste rather than ostentatiousness. The house had once belonged to the general Lucullus.

The former philosophy student had already started to buy books – and Calpurnia, Caesar's widow, kindly gifted him several titles from her husband's library that she thought he might want to bequeath to his great-nephew. Volumes of Polybius and Aristotle made the shelves bow. Bronze busts of Caesar and Alexander the Great sat on either side of the large cedar wood desk, angled so as to face where Octavius sat. Various styli and wax tablets rested in front of him, ready for his attention. Maps covered the walls of the room – of Italy, Macedonia and Gaul – and marks, denoting allies and enemies, covered the maps. A wide-brimmed sunhat also hung on the wall by the door which led out to the garden for when Octavius would sometimes sit and eat his lunch outside.

The first ten letters he wrote were to loyal supporters of Caesar – merchants and officers who had made their fortunes under the dictator's rule. "My first duty is to avenge Caesar's death and support those who supported my father." Octavius also reiterated that he would honour his father's promises in regards to government contracts the dictator had signed with the merchants. He then went on to compose a dozen letters to various senators that Balbus said might be sympathetic towards him. "Although they may not be quite for you yet Octavius, they will be most definitely be against Antony." Octavius tried to reassure the senators of his noble intentions. "My first duty, my only concern, is to secure my inheritance and carry out Caesar's bequests to the people of Rome … My loyalty is to Rome and the Senate, as opposed to its current consul."

Octavius surprised himself by how easily the lies came. He smiled hollowly to himself as he thought about how he had spent years – and

Caesar had spent a small fortune – being schooled in ethics and moral philosophy. But Octavius was now schooling himself in the subject of politics in a fraction of the time – and one of the first lessons he had learned was that the dictates of a moral life and a political career were at odds with one another.

Joseph entered. The aged Jew now shuffled more than walked. Joseph had served with Julius Caesar – and his father before him. Caesar had often taken Joseph on campaign with him as a source of wit and wisdom.

"Morning Joseph. No matter how hard I try you always seem to wake before me. You're almost too dutiful," Octavius remarked. He had quickly grown fond of the dry-witted old man and, like Julius before him, Octavius gave Joseph licence to speak his mind behind closed doors (even if he couldn't always tell how much the Jew was being ironic or not).

"Duty has little to do with it, master. I just try to leave the house before my wife stirs." Joseph's wife was a source of regular amusement, or anxiety, in his conversation.

"I'm sure your wife cannot be as burdensome as you sometimes make out. Despite you painting her as a harridan I'm tempted to ask to meet her."

Joseph gently shook his head and puffed out his cheek in a sigh, perishing the thought. "Be careful what you wish for is all I can say. She will either make your life a misery or, worse, you may be impressed by her and take her into your service … And if I see my wife throughout the day, as well as at night, then my life will be made a misery. Or should I say even more of a misery? I couldn't help but note a piece of graffiti the other day: 'Why do Jewish husbands die five years before their wives?' it asked. 'Because they want to!' was the sage reply."

Octavius broke into laughter. His face softened to reveal the nineteen year old behind the marble-like mask.

"Perhaps I should desist from meeting with your wife then. I think I'm more frightened than curious now anyway. What with Antony, half the Senate and Brutus already against me she could prove to be one intimidating opponent too many."

Joseph thought it was a shame that Marcus Brutus was an enemy of his new master. He had encountered the principled aristocrat many times over the years. Julius had treated him like a son, even when his affair with Brutus' mother, the formidable Servilia, had ended. As soon as the battle of Pharsalus had been decided it had been Brutus whom Caesar had sought out. To make sure he was safe. To forgive him. In another life Octavius and Brutus could have been friends, allies. Both were bookish. Both possessed a strain of pride, or rather stubbornness. Caesar had seen something in the pair of them also – ambition married to abilities. But even more than Antony or Cassius Octavius wanted to see the praetor dead. "Brutus drew first blood but I'll spill the last of it."

Agrippa entered the room with a broad smile plastered across his face. Joseph believed the expression was borne from seeing his friend in good humour but Agrippa had just received a message from Caecilia to say that she would soon be accompanying Cicero on a visit to Rome. Although he would hide the news from everyone he couldn't disguise his happiness. Octavius' loyal lieutenant had woken up before the dawn so, by first light, he was practising his archery. There was due to be a tournament during the games Octavius was arranging, in honour of Caesar. The prize was a sapphire-encrusted bow, made out of gold. His intention was to sell the trophy in order to buy Caecilia something special. He wanted to prove himself worthy of her – and her wealthy father. *Money marries money*.

"You seem to have a spring in your step and glow about you this morning Marcus. Did you finally take my advice and visit the actress Valeria? On second thoughts an encounter with her leaves a man bow-legged and exhausted, as opposed to one having a spring in one's step."

"I thought you wanted me to make war, not love," Agrippa replied. The young soldier had fought off the actresses' advances the night before in order to remain faithful to Caecilia.

"I'm not such a tyrant that I will not permit you the odd evening off, to have some fun. But despair not. If you have missed out on the appetiser, or dessert, of Valeria the main course will be served tonight," Octavius said, referring to the party he was due to host. "I've invited every eligible daughter, widow and wife in Rome. For all of their high-born manners we may consider them to be low-hanging fruit. You shall have your pick of them, after me of course."

Instead of looking forward to the party that evening and grinning accordingly Agrippa pictured Caecilia, the contours of her figure and smile. He admired her immensely. She was as much privately, as openly, amused by things. Her sense of humour was playful but never malicious. Agrippa read over and drank in the fragrance of her letters each evening before sleeping, brushing his lips against her words. He longed to feel her body slot next to his, have the light in her eyes shine upon him again.

*She's coming to Rome. I'll see her soon.*

But could they ever be together? She was the daughter of a wealthy aristocrat, he was the son of a humble freedman. He may as well try to pluck a star from the sky as think he could marry someone so high-born. Caecilia had assured Agrippa that she would win her father over or else he would risk losing his daughter. Atticus wanted to see Caecilia married but he also wanted her to be happy with her choice of husband too. Caecilia told Agrippa about the parties she had attended over the past couple of years – and the would-be suitors paraded in front of her that she had to endure. "They were more like peacocks, boars or serpents than men. Rather than a party I sometimes felt like I was visiting a menagerie … No, I will not wait forever for my father, as much as I now believe love to be eternal … Fate is more powerful than ill luck or party politics. I have been re-reading Plautus and Terence of late. Happy endings are not just the province of plays and literature."

"Of course," Agrippa said, in answer to Octavius. "I wouldn't want to come between a host and his guests." He was smiling as much at the thought of Caecilia as at his friend's increasingly priapic ways.

"Caesar must be Caesar," Octavius replied whilst shrugging his shoulders and making a face, jokingly quoting one of his great-uncle's phrases.

\*

Agrippa left to fit in another bout of archery practise, after Octavius told him that Mutilus Bulla would be entering the tournament. Not only was Bulla, a veteran of Pompey's Ninth Legion, considered the finest archer in the army but he was also loyal to the optimate cause. "If he wins then it is likely that Bulla will claim his victory in the name of the Senate or worse dedicate his triumph to Brutus and Cassius. Unfortunately sport is never just sport where politics is involved. Oppius says he has a plan to combat the threat of Bulla but the desired outcome will be to have my lieutenant claim victory, in honour of Caesar."

Octavius sat in his chair, leaned back and closed his eyes as Joseph rubbed a number of oils into the young man's freshly shaven face. Octavius sighed in pleasure. He mused on his new found wealth and influence. He was the son of Caesar.

*Life is good … But is this the good life?*

Octavius told himself that he would trade his new villa, all the nights with the desirable women and all his power to have his great-uncle back with him. Not just for himself but for the good of Rome. Caesar was worth a thousand self-serving, fractious senators. If he were alive now there would be peace.

*And if Caesar were alive now I would doubtless be back in Apollonia, discussing philosophy with Cleanthes. My only worry would be how I could sneak Briseis into my room at night ... I would be taking orders from my mother rather than giving them out to statesmen and centurions alike.*

Octavius had long lost count of the number of times people had described him as "sweet" and "kind" whilst growing up. *But few will now describe me as such – and they will have good reason for judging me cold and ambitious.*

"Tell me Joseph, do you think that Caesar had any regrets? Did he speak of any?"

Joseph briefly paused in his duties before replying. He could have claimed to have known Caesar more than most. But the manservant knew him enough to admit that he barely knew him at all in some respects. His life was too colourful, his traits too numerous, to frame in one simple portrait. Caesar, right up to the very end, still possessed the capacity to surprise Joseph – be it through an act of compassion or cruelty.

"Julius mourned Julia. He once confessed that she was his greatest achievement and that she was the author of her character for the most part, so his achievement could barely be described as such. She was a remarkable woman. She even turned Pompey into a good man. Well, good-*ish*. Her death changed everything for Caesar, personally and politically. But as to regrets? Caesar spent too much of his time looking forward to stare backwards. Cicero once dared to ask him if he regretted causing a civil war. Caesar replied that he didn't, because he had won."

Joseph took in the reaction on the heir's face as he spoke but, even more so than his old master, Octavius was unreadable.

9.

Candlelight gleamed off polished silver hairpins, gold necklaces and decorative brooches. Most of the men wore simple tunics apart from certain traditionalists and senators of rank who wore togas (the woollen material of which proved uncomfortable in the summer heat). The women added colour to the party by wearing expensively dyed dresses, made from imported silk. Scantily-clad young servant boys and girls weaved their way through the esteemed crowd in the large triclinium carrying Samian ware and silver trays of food: oysters on a bed of rocket, sweetened asparagus tips, spiced sausages, cheeses from as many regions as Rome had conquered ... Servants also kept cups filled-up with the finest wines – Caeres, Tiburtinum and Falernian – whilst others provided bowls of perfumed water and towels for guests to use to wipe their hands.

Oily-haired aristocrats puffed out their chests in self-importance and peered over the shoulders of the people they were talking to in hope of spotting someone more interesting and distinguished to make contact with. They feasted their eyes on various female guests on show at the party. Some of the women turned their noses up and looked haughtily in reply at their advances, some gazed back demurely.

Laughter and conversation proliferated around the house, along with the aromas of fine food and wines and the smell of rose petals and musky perfumes. Octavius had opened up his garden and entire house – save for his bedroom and study – for people to occupy and enjoy. Guests greeted each other, smiling widely or formally nodding. Others gave fellow invitees looks like daggers and snubbed political opponents or people they considered below them in rank. As well as political and business ties the room was a web of personal relationships too, involving extra-marital affairs – past and present. Infidelity in Rome was like Chinese silk – always in fashion. And at the centre of the web, nodding with approval in the middle of the triclinium, stood the man who had organised the gathering – Cornelius Balbus.

The Spanish fixer and financier could be as cold as he was charming, depending on the circumstances. He had once served as a secretary and political agent to Pompey, before aligning himself with Caesar. It was more than just rumour that Balbus had been the architect of the triumvirate between Caesar, Pompey and Crassus. Cato reported that Balbus had been "the oil, or poison, which had lubricated the wheels of the nefarious agreement." Despite his greying hair and burgeoning wrinkles there was still a sense of strength and virility in the Spaniard's tanned countenance. His normally hard, hawkish eyes softened and emitted a playful amiability for the party. He warmly welcomed guests and smiled at those the most whom he knew the darkest secrets about.

Cicero had warned Octavius about employing the agent.

"Everyone owes Cornelius Balbus a favour – especially his enemies. He is always in credit with people and always willing to keep them in his debt. Balbus will work for you for as long as it serves his own interests. The financier is as trustworthy as a Carthaginian and as principled as a jackal. Cornelius probably made more money out of Julius than Julius made himself. He knows where all the bodies are buried because, often, he put them in the ground himself."

Yet Cicero failed to dissuade Octavius from forming an alliance with Balbus. Oppius said that he could trust the Spaniard – and that Balbus "only backed winners." In return for his support Balbus asked of Octavius that which he had asked of Julius – that he could one day become Rome's first foreign-born consul. He was also not averse to helping Octavius bring the men who had murdered his friend and former employer to justice. Caesar was worth a thousand libertores and had granted ordinary Romans more freedoms in six months than the aristocracy had given them in six centuries. Balbus recalled a comment he had overheard from Brutus one evening, as he spoke to Caesar: "Tradition must be observed. I would die before seeing a foreigner serve as a consul of Rome."

*I would see you dead, you treacherous and hypocritical bastard, before I'm even nominated.*

After introducing Octavius to several key guests at the party – and securing promises of political and financial support from others – Balbus decided to collect his thoughts and take some air in the garden. He exhaled, sighing with relief. The party was going well. Guests were having a good time. Octavius was being a gracious and entertaining host.

*He's being Caesar-like.*

Balbus' eyes narrowed and sucked in the scene. A line of red mullet sizzled on the grill. A wild boar, stuffed with a suckling pig, turned upon a spit. Merchants and senators were mixing business with pleasure, sharing salacious gossip and state secrets. Balbus smiled to himself as he spotted Senator Piso continually swivelling his head, making sure that his wife and his mistress didn't meet. Balbus also noticed how the predatory Senator Sabinus couldn't take his eyes off one of the fresh-faced serving boys. Balbus would give the youth to the influential statesman as a gift, in return for throwing a dinner party for Octavius and inviting several people who were wavering in their support for Antony. Other familiar faces came into view – young aristocrats keen on borrowing money, and those who were already in his debt, who would ask him for more time and credit in repaying their loans. He would duly give them the money they wanted. *But money always comes at a price.* Yet Balbus also needed to hunt the big beasts at the party who had little need of capital. They were, like him, bankers rather than beggars. Balbus needed to sell the idea to them that Antony was the past and Octavius the future – a future they should invest in. And in return they would one day be granted a praetorship, or consulship. Any donations to Octavius' campaign fund would be paid back tenfold through government subsidies, mining contracts or the power to collect taxes, in the name of the state. Or he would entice them with titles and honours. Yet tonight it was all about the guests enjoying themselves. Balbus had selected this evening for the party as, although absent from the city, Brutus had arranged some games for the next day to try and win back personal and political support. But people would now be too tired or hung-over to support Brutus' event – or, as Oppius' had remarked, they'd be "too fucked" to attend the games tomorrow.

In the background the Spaniard could hear the sound of wooden swords clacking against each other as a number of gladiators put on an exhibition of their skills in the far corner of the garden. Blushing, or lusty-eyed women, would be taking in their oiled torsos. The men would be placing bets on the bouts. Servants continued to fill their cups. A few of the courtesans, who Balbus had shipped over especially from Athens, draped themselves over certain influential senators and laughed at their jokes.

*It'll be a late night for everyone. All is going according to plan.*

"You must be pleased Cornelius. It seems that the best of Roman society is here this evening. You have Senator Aetius over there in the corner, displaying his predilection for oysters. When he gets home he will show his predilection for pre-pubescent girls, no doubt. I see you have invited representatives from some of our great patrician families. You are keeping your friends close and your enemies closer it seems. If you spot them holding their noses up in the air it's not because they're trying to smell the flowers or food – it's because they're looking down on their fellow guests. Ah, and there's Senator Valerius' wife. It wouldn't be a wine-sodden party without her. The woman's let more gladiators in than the gate-keepers at the arena. And is that Flavius Laetus? I can't remember, is he due in court this time for taking a bribe or receiving one? It's difficult to keep up. Yes, you have assembled quite a cast list. You must be proud. You have a full house, which may explain why the best brothels in town are most likely empty tonight," Cicero wryly remarked as he approached the Spaniard. The latter had taken great pleasure over the years in using his position of influence to deny Cicero access to Caesar when he petitioned to see him. In return Cicero called Balbus 'a glorified secretary', among other things, and tried to turn opinion against the outsider and foreigner whenever the opportunity arose. Although the two men were in some ways rivals there existed a mutual respect – and even admiration – between them. Political opposition did not spill over into (too much) personal enmity. Despite their opposition to one another over the years they enjoyed their bouts of verbal sparring. Both men could be sarcastic and cryptic. They left as much unsaid as said. Both knew the extent of each other's influence and intelligence networks. Both knew not to underestimate one another – and both knew that, to combat Antony, they might have to work together.

"Yes. It's also difficult to keep up with how many of them you have defended as an advocate in the past, or will do in the future. But, Marcus, how are you? Thank you for coming. Octavius will be especially pleased too that you could make it. Can I get you a drink?"

"No thank you. I wish to keep a clear head. I also need to wake early tomorrow, in order to attend the games being put on by Brutus. You are probably unaware of them, else you would not have arranged this party for the night before."

Cicero was also keen to return home to work on a series of speeches he was composing, to denigrate Antony and declare him an enemy of the state.

"Indeed. Accidents will happen. I wish Brutus' games every success of course. But as much as you are always up for a fight I didn't think that the spectacle of gladiatorial combat was your thing."

"I thought that I would show my face and support. Similar to my being here tonight. It's always better to make friends than enemies. It seems I am but one dull star in the firmament however. There are more senators present than attended the last vote in the Forum. Perhaps the Senate should look to hire your caterers to improve attendance rates. Although our revered consul is conspicuous by his absence, I see."

"Octavius would have, of course, invited Antony – as you say, one should make friends not enemies – but he's currently out of the capital if you didn't already know. Few will be mourning his absence, however, I suspect. Tonight is about Octavius. People like to worship the rising, more than the setting, sun."

"Nothing can come of your campaign, Cornelius. He's too young. You're playing with fire and I don't want the boy or Rome to be engulfed in the flames," Cicero said, shaking his head in disagreement with Balbus. The playfulness departed from his voice, to be replaced by hardened seriousness – and a sense of dire warning. Rome needed to break its cycle of violence.

Balbus merely raised his eyebrow in response to Cicero's blunt words. The statesman had seldom been so direct with him before and it gave the politic strategist brief pause.

"They also said that Alexander the Great was too young, when he came to power."

"A somewhat ambitious comparison. Have you been drinking?" the dry-witted philosopher replied. Cicero's playful tone returned, as if it had never gone away.

"No. I like to keep a clear head too. It's my job to make sure other peoples' glasses are filled. But perhaps you're right and Alexander is indeed the wrong comparison. Rather Octavius should be mentioned in the same breath as Caesar. As ever I'm grateful for your counsel Marcus."

*

Octavius' arm ached from all the handshaking and he felt like the fixed smile upon his face must be resembling a rictus. He had lost count of the number of fatuous compliments he'd received, most common among which was, "Julius would be proud of you."

Women were presented to him as well as distinguished guests. Mothers introduced their unwed daughters with all the subtlety of tavern bawds. Occasionally he would share a look with Agrippa or Oppius and roll his eyes. Octavius chose to be amused and intrigued by the scene – performances – before him. *Politics is a game*. He recalled a comment by Caesar: *You can be victorious and become the First Man of Rome – or the other way to win is to just not take part.*

"This is a beautiful painting. Did you commission it yourself?" The aristocratic woman's voice was clear and sharp, like glass. Octavius took in a short gasp of breath as the young woman came into view. She wore a silk stola, dyed light purple, which clung to her lithe body. He could see the present beneath the wrapping. She could have been aged between fifteen and twenty. She turned more heads than even the host did but Octavius was willing to forgive her. She held herself like an elegant flower – surrounded by weeds. Her figure was slender – strength intertwined with elegance. Her light brown hair was bound tight and styled in a bun. There didn't seem to be a strand out of place. Gently arching eyebrows and intelligent, almond-shaped eyes sat over high cheekbones and a classically sculptured face. There was a coldness to her beauty, which only fired Octavius' heart – or loins – even more.

"I did," he answered, turning towards the fresco depicting Aeneas' escape from Troy, carrying his father Anchises on his shoulders as the city burned. Two years ago the bookish youth had promised himself that he would one day attempt to write an epic poem, charting Aeneas' odyssey from his homeland to Italy and the founding of Rome.

"Did you do so because of a love of Homer or because you wish to project the idea of yourself as a dutiful son to Caesar?" the enigmatic woman said with a satirical smile on her lips.

"Both," Octavius said, wishing to honour a direct question with an honest answer. "The painting is not just the work of one artist, however. Light is the load where many share the toil," he added, quoting Homer.

The captivating aristocratic woman had approached the host of the party out of curiosity. She had once been introduced to Caesar, after she had read his books and studied his career. She thought his pride and self-belief justified. If Caesar hadn't come along then the gods would have had to invent him. People – whether they be a senatorial elite or unwashed mob – have the habit of creating chaos from order. People need something, or someone, to believe in. Caesar gave people hope, martial glory and prosperity. He should have been made king or at least been called Emperor. But what of his great-nephew? There were some, from fellow patrician families, who were dismissive of Caesar's heir – citing his youth and less than noble lineage. Yet she had also overheard conversations in which senators and soldiers had been impressed by Octavius, he was wise beyond his years. So far she had given him some credit for being well-versed in Homer. But the shallow lust in his eyes failed to thaw her out.

*Does he just want me for that one, predictable thing? Is he just like all the rest? Does he think that I would be flattered to be another cheap conquest? I intend to be a wife, not a mistress. Why do men think that women should either behave like decorative, vestal virgins or role-playing harlots?*

"You have me at a disadvantage. May I ask your name?"

*I like having people at a disadvantage.* "You can ask the question but I'm not sure I should answer. I wouldn't want to one day end up on some proscription list," the woman said, her sense of humour dryer than the paint on the fresco.

Octavius let out a burst of laughter. His aspect softened – he was starting to like the woman and her black wit, rather than just lusting after her.

"I warrant that I would put myself on any list before such beauty," Octavius half-jokingly and half-nobly replied. "I couldn't promise the same for your husband however," he added, noticing the wedding band on the woman's finger.

It was now time for the usually haughty-looking woman to laugh – and the sound was more joyous and musical for Octavius than the flute playing from an adjoining room. Her round, normally pouting mouth bloomed into a smile. In becoming rounder her face also became prettier too, Octavius judged. As much as the imperious beauty could be privately amused by things she so seldom laughed out loud nowadays. Her husband may have had a sense of decency but he lacked a sense of humour.

"Allow me to keep my name a secret for a while longer. If I remain something of a mystery you may then remember me for longer. I dare say you will be introduced to plenty of hopeful – and hopeless – women this evening who will be keen to give you their name and anything else that Caesar's heir asks for." There was now a flirtatious as well as satirical light in the young woman's aspect as she spoke.

"I will remember you. In youth and beauty, wisdom is but rare," Octavius remarked, quoting Homer.

\*

*I'd rather be in a shield wall than line up and be introduced to some of these simpering senators … Politicians are the scum of the earth.*

Lucius Oppius did his best to smile rather than growl. The centurion employed the tactic of trying to drink himself into having a good time – although unfortunately he had developed too great a tolerance to wine over the years. Oppius spotted the wife of Senator Valerius across the room and downed another cup of Falernian. She was his mission for the evening, according to Balbus.

"Sabina has a fondness for soldiers and gladiators. She will open up to you, in more ways than one … Try to gauge from her which side her husband is on, aside from his own."

Oppius made eye contact with her. She smiled, not even coyly, in reply.

*I've accepted worse missions. The best years of her life are behind her. But perhaps mine are too.*

\*

The wind rustled through the leaves of the fruit trees Agrippa and Caecilia were concealed behind and her silk dress rustled against his tunic. Agrippa kissed her, tenderly then hungrily, as he breathed in her perfume. Caecilia sighed. At first her body went limp in his arms but then it grew taut in desire. She ran her hands over his muscular shoulders, back and arms – storing up the sensations for when he would be absent again. She arched her back and stretched out her entire, enthralled body – tilting her head so that he could kiss her upon the neck. Her body had stretched itself out in a similar fashion before, when she woke from dreaming about him.

Agrippa had just finished speaking to Oppius at the party. He had stood alone for a few moments, wistfully thinking about her. The image in his mind's eye was then suddenly, almost miraculously, fleshed out before him as Caecilia appeared through a small group of ogling merchants and priests. She was a vision of loveliness. Her features and soul glowed. She was a young woman in love. His mouth was comically agape. Diamond droplet earrings hung down, along with her golden blonde ringlets, but he was more captivated by her gem-like eyes, sparkling with good humour and devotion.

The two guests had smiled at one another, sharing a private joke. As much as their hearts raced and yearned to unleash themselves, like horses champing at the bit at the beginning of a chariot race, the two seeming strangers  had politely spoken to each other.

"I'm surprised to find you on your own. I thought that a young man like you would be aiming to charm a young woman at such a gathering," Caecilia had remarked, her tone and smile playful. Agrippa noticed how her complexion had become even more sun-kissed since last seeing her. Her dress accentuated her hour-glass figure, which he wanted to wrap his arms around.

"I am just waiting for the right woman to come along."

"So tell me more about this woman. You never know, I may well encounter her at some point and be able to introduce you both."

"She's the kind of woman who would let me take her by the hand and lead her out into the garden. Once there we would hide behind a tree, where she would let me whisper sweet nothings in her ear. I'd tell her how much each line of every letter she wrote meant to me, when I read them at night."

"She sounds almost too good to be true. But the problem might be that she would start kissing you before you had a chance to speak."

"Well that's a risk I'd be willing to take, for the right woman."

Moonbeams poured through the branches above them and danced in the light of her diamond earrings and pleated, sky-blue stola. The couple sat on a bench. Caecilia rested her head on his shoulder, their fingers laced together. A thoughtfulness had now ousted their joy and passion.

"Do you remember when we first met?" Caecilia asked, tucking her legs up beneath her on the bench.

"Of course," Agrippa answered. He had probably thought about the moment every day since their afternoon together at Cicero's villa in Puteoli. Her vivacious blue eyes had shone in the sultry heat. Her pink lips had curled upwards into a smile. White, silk slippers had poked out from a shimmering summer dress. She hadn't worn any make-up because she didn't need too. *She looked beautiful because she is beautiful.* Agrippa had been sketching the valley he was overlooking at the time and inserting the designs of an aqueduct into his drawing.

"I know I teased you at the time but thinking about it on the journey here – and seeing the capital today – Rome needs more fresh water, to drink and cultivate its crops. As a soldier you will be asked to go to war at some point. But you are and can be so much more than just a soldier. Promise me, Marcus, that you will always build more than you destroy. Save more lives than you take. Do more good than ill each day."

"I will," Agrippa promised, kissing her on the brow and squeezing her hand.

"I'm not sure how long I will be able to stay in Rome. My father may summon me back home. I don't want to lose you." Tears glistened in her eyes as she spoke. A mournfulness was about to oust the happiness that had recently sung in her heart.

"You won't. Why would I want to lose someone who has promised to introduce me to the right woman?" Agrippa slyly joked.

Caecilia laughed-cum-sobbed and affectionately rapped him across the arm.

"I love you, so much," she said.

"I know. I love you too. I don't want you worrying about loving and losing me. I remember another promise from when we first met. *I'll wait for you.* And if I fall behind, wait for me. But I am worried that we may have gone missing from the party for too long. Cicero may be looking for you and he wouldn't want to find you in the arms of his prospective enemy. Instead he may want to introduce you to a prospective husband."

Agrippa also felt uneasy about failing in his duty to support Octavius at the party. Balbus had given him a list of names to introduce himself to and win over to their cause.

"It should be fine. He's probably far too busy talking about himself to mention my name. I'm fond of him though. But let us just stay a while longer here. Let Rome be Rome. I want this moment to last," the young woman said.

Agrippa smiled, nodded and wrapped his arm around her, pulling her even closer, as the birdsong in the trees serenaded them.

*

Wine and gossip continued to fuel the party. The smell of spices and roasted pork and guinea fowl wafted into the house and enticed more guests outside. Courtesans sat across laps and nuzzled their patrons before discreetly leading them away for the evening. Balbus had paid good money for them to show certain senators a good time. Various guests concluded that Octavius was a generous host and he would be equally generous towards his supporters if ever he served in office.

Balbus approached Cicero again, carrying a bowl of oats sweetened with honey – after Cicero had mentioned that the food at the party was too rich for his stomach. He placed the bowl on a small bronze table next to the revered statesman.

"I made it myself, would you believe?" Balbus said.

"I would, if it contained poison. But I know that's not your style Cornelius. Your counsel may be poisonous but not your cuisine. Besides, by my calculations, I'm worth more to you alive than dead."

Balbus nodded, smirked and appreciated Caesar's comment about his erstwhile opponent. "Cicero may not share my politics but there are few men who I would rather share a conversation with. His influence may have diminished but his wit is still as sharp and piercing as a ballista bolt."

"I read one of your books the other day. You were your normal, engaging and erudite self but I thought that you were far too forgiving of the gods. For as much as we might argue that the gods made us in their own image I believe that in some ways the opposite is true – and we have made the gods in our image. Which is why I think that the gods can sometimes be too cruel or petty," Balbus said, deftly plucking a fig from a serving girl's tray as she walked by.

"You may well be right but even if my words didn't persuade you of anything you should look to the virtues of reason and your divine spark to light the way forward. I hope – or I may even say that I pray – that you still possess some faith and devotion in regards to the gods."

A short scream and then guffaw sounded out in the garden as a lustful senator squeezed the breasts of one of the courtesans. The distraction was but momentary and was quickly swallowed up by the general revelry. Balbus and Cicero continued their conversation, as did others.

"I'm not altogether sure that I have the time, let alone will, to worship your deities at the moment. My faith and devotion are all invested in turning Octavius into a god. But do not underestimate how much faith and devotion Octavius has in you, Marcus. I sometimes think he considers you a god. If so, what would you ask of him?"

"That he becomes a good man," the philosopher replied.

"I would posit that he is already a good man, certainly in the context of the company presently surrounding him at this party. The question is can he remain so? Especially once this city and its sins get their teeth into him. Politics is a game played by good actors rather than good men, wouldn't you agree? And the most successful are the ones who believe in their act. But you know even more than I do about how Roman politics work – or don't work. Besides, I should be absenting myself from the party soon. I have a long day tomorrow, helping Octavius distribute bread and money to the people."

*No doubt at the same time as when Brutus' games are due to start.* "Perhaps I have underestimated just how much of a good, selfless man you are too, Cornelius," Cicero replied, sarcastically.

"Octavius isn't your enemy. We both know that Antony is the greater threat to Rome and all those things which you hold dear, including your own life. If ever Octavius comes knocking and asks for your help, answer him. Similarly, if you come knocking Octavius will answer your call. I give you my word." Balbus dropped the glibness and irony from his voice, and wore a look of grave sincerity.

*Aye, but unfortunately there are harlots here who I trust the word of more.*

*

Octavius abandoned his guests and took a turn around the torch-lit garden with the woman who had caught his eye and curiosity. Occasionally they were interrupted by people who wanted to introduce themselves to the host. Sometimes the woman felt irritated at having her time with Octavius disturbed, but she also felt twinges of pride and flattery that Caesar's heir was choosing to spend time with her over others – and that senators considered her of importance for accompanying him. He picked a flower for her and put it in her hair and she thought there was still a boyish sweetness beneath his manly arrogance. They spoke a little of poetry and philosophy but more so the woman came alive at having the opportunity to talk about politics. All too often in the past her father and husband had been dismissive of her opinions when she had tried to join the conversation about matters of state and the personalities of leading politicians. They asked her to leave the room. It was "unnatural" for a woman to concern herself with such topics, her mother had told her. So she learned to think for herself and hide the extent of her education (and not just because she disagreed with her husband and family's opposition to Caesar). Yet Octavius seemed genuinely interested in what she had to say and she felt she could, in some ways, be herself with him without putting on an act.

"Cicero's idea of politics and government should be re-classified as history. His ideal of harmonising the classes is out of tune with the world ... Rome needs one strong voice to guide it, instead of a directionless din of squabbling consuls, self-interested factions and a mob which looks to either beg or bully. Caesar's death was a tragedy for us all."

Octavius grew attracted to her intellect as well as her sharply beautiful features.

"When they murdered Caesar they killed part of me, but at the same time they gave birth to something else," Octavius declared, staring at a marble statue of his dictator father as he spoke. *They gave birth to a monster, one which will not be sated until it kills everyone involved in killing you. Blood for blood. Justice.*

The woman gazed at Caesar's heir, captivated by his power and potency. Her husband was, like Cicero, too mired in an old, stagnant world. He had never satisfied her sexually, though that was not why she had married him. But Octavius was different. Forbidden fruit. *If only I had met him a year ago, before Tiberius. But, a year ago, he would not have been a Caesar.*

The woman stood next to Octavius and admired the statue. He breathed in her perfume, took in the lustre of her jewels and her flawless, pearl-like skin in the lambent moonlight. Her demure glance was met by his amorous gaze. He clasped her responsive hand and pulled her even closer.

"What do you want?" he asked, hoping that she would reply "him".

*I want to be the First Woman of Rome.* "I want everyone I love to be happy," she said, trying to cool her ardour. Keep control. She wanted to convey a selfless, virtuous side. Most men found ambition in a woman to be unattractive or unnatural. She wanted him to see her as more than a mistress. She was worth loving as well as bedding. *Be strong. He will want you more if you deny him.*

The same birdsong serenading Agrippa and Caecilia could be heard in the background. The sultry evening air warmed their skin, glazing it with a film of perspiration. Octavius moved closer – his lips were about to brush against hers – but she pulled away.

"No, I'm sorry. I can't. I cannot give you my heart, nor that thing which most men value even more. But I will now give you my name."

"What is it?" Octavius asked, his voice and features imbued with understanding and affection still. He felt disappointed at her not giving herself to him but he wasn't angry or resentful. He would rather keep her as a friend than lose her as a lover. He wanted to see her again.

"Livia."

10.

Brutus dedicated his games to Apollo – but more so they were dedicated to himself. He needed to raise his prestige. If the people wouldn't give their love freely then he would need to buy it, Cassius had argued in a letter to his fellow libertore. Brutus needed his name to be synonymous with duty rather than treachery. One of his agents had arranged for a number of people in the crowd to chant out his name and call for the praetor's return to Rome. Brutus had at first baulked at stooping to such cheap, political tricks but Cassius persuaded him.

"A noble politician is still a politician," Balbus drily remarked after finding out about Brutus' intentions. "It seems that people can still try to stage manage a performance even when their lead actor is absent."

The crowd was under half of what Brutus' representative had hoped for as he announced the commencement of the games. A number of senators and aristocrats who had promised to attend were absent, lying in bed with either sore heads or a high-class prostitute (or "actress", as some called themselves). The master of ceremonies for the event creased his brow and scratched his head, wondering where the mob were. Questions were finally answered when, as paid supporters began to cheer Brutus' name, they were shouted down by a rival mob (arranged by Balbus) which declared the games' patron a murderer and traitor. *All is fair in love and politics*. Fighting broke out between the two partisan groups and the crowd dispersed. The games went ahead but were, in the words of Agrippa, "about as well attended as an orgy involving lepers".

*

The games which Octavius would arrange, in honour of his father, Julius Caesar, would be another story. Much of the funding for the games came from Octavius' step-father, Marcus Phillipus. The money, generated from the sale of various properties, was freely given rather than asked for.

"You're a good investment," Phillipus remarked.

Octavius was temporarily lost for words. There were tears in his eyes as he embraced his step-father and told him that, more than Julius Caesar, he considered Phillipus to be his father.

"You are the most decent and honourable man I've ever known … I'm proud to call myself your son."

"I'm proud of the both of you," Atia then tearfully declared.

"I'd be happy for you to be proud of me less mother, if it meant that I wouldn't have to worry about you dehydrating from crying too much," Octavius fondly joked.

The games would last for ten days. There would be a feast of gladiatorial bouts. Balbus poached the best of the fighters that were due to take part in Brutus' games to fight for Octavius. Oppius called in a favour and the legendary Decimus Baculus agreed to appear in an exhibition bout with the centurion himself – the *Sword of Rome*. Men would battle beasts and beasts would battle beasts too. "The white sand will turn red with blood," an advertisement boasted. Admission would be free. Influential senators and supporters would be given the best seats and Balbus had arranged for some of Rome's finest actresses and dancers to sit with them. In return for their services the actresses and dancers were given parts in the theatrical shows that Octavius also put on.

Despite their busy schedules Octavius, Balbus and Oppius had all found the time to take part in the auditions process.

*

The crowd – filled with soldiers, tradesmen, Jews, hangers-on, merchants, mothers – squinted in the light of the blazing summer sun and shielded their hands over their eyes as they looked up at the platform in the Forum which Octavius stood on. The smell of garum and freshly baked bread hung in the air from food venders. Octavius wore a look of imperious calm on his face, though his heart was racing and he felt his fair skin begin to burn in the stinging heat. Beads of sweat formed on his brow and he willed them not to fall into his eyes. He wore a simple white tunic, similar to that of what many in the crowd were wearing. He wanted to appear to be one of them. He gazed out, taking in the sea of people, as if he were a captain about to address his crew. Men, women and children stared up at him expectantly. Some even had an expression of wonder on their countenances. For a moment Octavius was tempted to laugh at the scene. The gods seemed to be playing a joke on him or Rome, that the populace would place their fate in the hands of a nineteen year old boy. Several months ago he was spending his days reading philosophy, dreading fencing bouts or being coddled by his mother.

*You're a long way from Apollonia now.*

As well as amusement, however, Octavius felt a sense of duty towards the people before him. Like Caesar he wanted to be above them but with them – do right by them and make Rome even greater. Earlier in the day Octavius had unveiled a new statue of Caesar in the

Forum, of Caesar as a young man. Balbus had commissioned the statue, instructing the sculptor to make sure there was a slight resemblance between the youthful Caesar and Octavius.

A trumpet sounded, calling for silence and the audience's attention. Octavius had given a number of pre-arranged and spontaneous speeches in the capital over the past month but never to so large a crowd. Yet he had confidence in himself. He was no longer a day-dreaming philosophy student. *I am a Caesar ... Make him proud.* His voice carried further than it used to. He was learning when to speak plainly and when to colour the air with rhetoric and hyperbole. He was learning how to read an audience as if he were deciphering a poem. He was learning when to be pious, satirical, conservative or radical. "Know how to be all things to all men," Caesar had once counselled him, "but be no man's slave."

Out of the corner of his eye Balbus gave him a nod of encouragement. Octavius took a deep breath and began.

"These games are not in my honour. Should Caesar still be with us he would posit that these games should not honour him either. Rather these games are in your honour. Our wise friend and statesman Cicero would argue that we all carry within us a divine spark, one which can light the way and lead us to wisdom and glory. Equally, I see before me a multitude of good souls each possessing the light of Rome inside them and the divine virtues which this city has the power to inspire in us all: courage, liberty and duty."

Heads bobbed up and down and nodded in agreement in the crowd. Chests swelled with pride.

"To be born Roman is to have won the lottery of life. Caesar knew this and by bequeathing much of his estate to Rome he wanted to share his winnings with you. And I see it as my duty, both as his son and as a fellow Roman, to make good on his promise. His legacy should be fulfilled. The money is no longer Caesar's. Nor is the money mine. And it doesn't belong to our consul. The wealth of Caesar belongs to you. Mark Antony is not the law. The law is the law."

As if on cue a few shouts of support could be heard in the crowd from some of Caesar's veterans who Oppius and Balbus had invited. Soldiers who had once bellowed out orders on the parade ground or in battle could easily make themselves heard in the Forum. A few in the crowd also thrust their hands up in the air as if grabbing invisible coins.

"I am trying to honour my name. At the same time Mark Antony is dishonouring his as he uses your money to fund a personal army –

though I am not sure if he is recruiting an army of soldiers or an army of vintners and actresses."

Laughter succeeded indignation.

*Rome wants bread and comedy.*

"As much as Antony has tried to silence me I still have a voice, attuned to yours. As much as some of you may have already heard me speak I have listened to you twice as much as I have spoken. I have heard your calls to establish a legion of vigils in the city, paid for by rich landlords, to put out fires in the poorer districts of the city... I have seen how some senators own a dozen different litters whilst children are shoeless... I have heard your worries about overcrowding and unemployment. Immigration, rather than curing all our ills (especially those of the rich who enjoy cheap labour), can cause more problems than it solves... Rome for Romans... Jobs should go to the deserving – not just the privileged... I promise to fulfil Caesar's mission and retrieve Rome's lost standards from our enemies in the east... And I promise to build a network of aqueducts across the capital and the empire; as much as we may wish it to be so Rome cannot live on wine alone... And these are not empty or unfunded promises I offer up to you today. To pay for these projects I will petition the tribunes and senate, in Caesar's name and my own, to instigate a "Villa Tax" on our most affluent citizens... I believe in the institutions of the family and marriage ... Rome is great but we can be greater still. More prosperous, freer."

During the night before, as Octavius composed his speech, Balbus had counselled that the less power one has the more one can promise the people. "False promises are food and drink to those who are in opposition. Promise them the world and when you get into power blame your enemies for being unable to keep your promises." Although Octavius had nodded in receipt of the wily agent's advice he had made a vow to himself that he would honour his promises.

*Rome is a city of bricks. I will leave it as one made of marble.*

"As a Caesar it is my intention to be a servant of Rome, not its ruler. My father is doing more for Rome from the grave than his killers are doing whilst they live. Cassius and Brutus have guiltily run away. They are now embezzling taxes and monies meant for Rome in order to recruit an army which, no doubt in the name of freedom, will try to enslave Rome. I hope that my father will approve of these games. As much as Caesar liked to enjoy himself he wanted others to enjoy themselves too. We are both remembering him and saying goodbye to him today."

Octavius looked out in front of him, hoping to see a throng of faces nodding in agreement and devotion. But instead he witnessed eyes widen and jaws drop. The sound of a hundred gasps created one long hissing sound which drowned out the wind. Fingers were raised and pointed up at the sky behind Octavius – at the chariot of fire.

The sight of the comet streaming its way across the serene blue sky burned itself into the eyes – and souls – of everyone in the crowd. Even the pickpockets throughout the square looked up, amazed. And the entire city too, from the Subura to the Palatine, turned its head as one to the once in a lifetime spectacle. People clutched the sleeves of those standing next to them, whether they were friends or strangers, and pointed at the comet and asked, out loud or to themselves, what was the meaning of it all? Octavius was also not immune from a sense of wonder and speculation. He was dumbstruck – but not for long. Augurs would likely interpret that the comet presaged doom. Doom made the augurs money, and made the people hang on their words even more. Octavius had no intention, however, of letting a cloud hang over his games and blacken his moment in the sun. He would set the agenda before others had a chance to.

"And see the sign. Caesar is saying goodbye to us. The gods are calling their own back to them. His soul is ascending upon the wings of our devotion. Caesar and the gods are giving us their blessing…"

Cheers and chants here went up – and not just voiced by those in the crowd who had fought under Caesar or were paid to give their support.

"Caesar… Caesar…"

The sunlight began to warm rather than sting Octavius' skin as he bathed in the crowd's adoration. Balbus would later congratulate Octavius on his speech and improvisation – "It was divine inspiration". Although Octavius laughed at the cynical agent's joke he considered that perhaps the gods were on his side. The odds were too great, impossible, that the comet should appear at that exact moment. *Am I the son of fate as well as Caesar?* A couple of glasses of wine further fuelled his sense of superstition that night.

*The gods may not have even been heralding Caesar – but me.*

By morning a polished bronze star had been placed on the new statue of Caesar in the Forum. Graffiti also sprung up around Rome, proclaiming that Caesar was a god.

"Let the games begin."

11.

Dusk.

The flames devoured Marcus Brutus' letter but they couldn't burn the contents from his thoughts. The news from Rome was dire. Brutus cursed Balbus for ruining his games. *Snake. For just once it would be nice if you had a taste of your own medicine – or poison.* Brutus poured himself another cup of undiluted wine, as sour as his mood, and gulped it down. Sometimes the drink dulled the ache but sometimes it enflamed his misery and ire. He also cursed Caesar, who seemed to haunt his thoughts more now that he was dead than when he had been alive. His intention had been to save the Republic, not be exiled from it.

*Are you punishing me from the afterlife?*

Brutus also cursed Octavius – at the same time as cursing himself for underestimating the boy. Cicero had claimed in a recent letter that he would be able to guide Octavius.

*Cicero probably thought that he guided me too, when I was young. Caesar and Cato probably thought the same as well. But I was my own man. I am guided by principles, not personalities. But how much is this boy now becoming his own man?*

Finally, Brutus cursed his agent underneath his breath. He had suggested the idea of arranging the games and taken his fee – but had failed to deliver. It had all been money which Brutus could ill afford to spend and waste. He would have to ask to borrow funds again. It was unspoken, but explicit, that the merchants and politicians would want favours in return when Brutus won office. He would have to make compromises, his legislature would be mired in corruption from day one. He would not be his own man.

*Caesar was his own man.*

Horace watched his commander as he paced back and forth by the fireplace and muttered under his breath. His once bright eyes were now red-rimmed. His once strong jaw was rounder. He no longer trimmed his beard. Horace took a mouthful of wine. He was several cups behind Brutus but could still hold his own ("No poems can please for long or live that are written by water drinkers," the would-be poet had recently written in his notebook). He knew better to try and keep up with his commander though. He also knew better than to try and disturb him when he was deep in thought.

The villa they were staying in was built in the crevice of a valley and the chamber let in little light. The room was austere. A rickety desk housed some correspondence and maps. A large jug of wine and an uneaten plate of salted pork and cheese sat on another table. A couple of couches flanked the crackling fireplace.

Brutus had recently dismissed his senior staff but had asked Horace to remain behind after the meeting. The commander enjoyed the young soldier's company and allowed him to speak his mind, even if his thoughts were contrary to his. Caesar had been the same with him, many years ago. The former student was well read and witty. They spoke about literature and history. Crucially Horace also knew when not to speak – when Brutus was in a mood to brood in silence. The poet reminded the praetor of himself as a young man – before his world had started to crumble.

In front of his men the commander still projected authority and a sense of purpose. He was the descendent of the legendary Junius Brutus, saviour of the Republic. He embodied Roman virtues whilst Mark Antony embodied Roman vice. His forces were growing and his army was well provisioned. He was in constant communication with Cassius, Cicero and Decimus Brutus. There was a plan and the gods were on their side.

Yet on nights such as these Horace witnessed a fractured rather than forceful soul. Brutus was less than half the man he used to be. He felt betrayed by the people of Rome and the gods. He had had right on his side but the new saviour of the Republic had somehow become an enemy of it – a faithful lover spurned. Horace likened him to a mathematician whose formulae and life's work had been proved wrong. He had miscalculated Mark Antony's ambition and abilities. He had also miscalculated the people's love for Caesar, which had been greater than their love for Brutus' ideals. In public Brutus had murdered a dictator but in private Horace saw a man dealing with the sorrow of having murdered a friend. Where some might have considered Brutus weak for wallowing in such guilt, Horace considered him to be human – and all the nobler for it.

"Rome is a white bull, willingly laying its head upon an altar to be slaughtered. And Mark Antony is holding the knife. The Republic is becoming a memory Horace," Brutus remarked, thinking that, as punishment for rejecting him and embracing Antony, the mob should be damned.

"Rome is populated by people, not gods. Its leaders are flawed as much as its citizens, although on balance the former tend to transgress more than the latter. Elections are bought, votes are sold. What one man may call a hero another can call a tyrant," Horace replied philosophically.

"But the Republic was and can be different. It desires laws, not tyrants."

"Laws can prove just as tyrannical as men."

"You would have Rome become lawless then? Anarchy isn't freedom. Your philosophical mind is proficient at questioning things but what we need right now are answers. What would you do to save Rome?"

"I would lower taxes," Horace said undramatically. Brutus was somewhat stunned into silence and did not know if the youth was joking. "The more a man can make from his labour the more content he'll be – and incentivised to work harder. More money should go to his family than thieving bureaucrats. Or worse, officious bureaucrats. And he will use that money more wisely than any senator, I warrant. The state has proved itself over and over again to be inefficient or iniquitous when it comes to managing its finances. Large states are more likely to go to war. If we reduce the size of the state – and allow people to keep more of their money – then the likes of Sulla, Caesar and Antony might be less inclined to play the dictator as the job will not pay so well. Ironically though, by lowering taxes – and I say lower rather than abolish for the state must still function properly – treasury revenues may increase due the rewards of work and more money being ploughed back into the economy rather than pocketed by the political classes and their cronies. Lower taxes and there would be less money to fund a dole system which, in the name of government generosity, enslaves people and keeps them on the bottom rung of society."

"Telling a politician that he is unable to tax would be like telling a drunk he could no longer have a drink," Brutus said, wryly smiling and thinking about his friend's arguments.

"A drunk cannot drink wine if it's not there. And similarly a politician cannot spend money he doesn't have. He would no longer have cause to exist – and would have to find a proper job. And a world containing fewer politicians would be a better world."

Before Brutus could reply he was distracted by the sound of a door creaking open. He betrayed a flicker of frustration, or something worse, at seeing his wife but quickly forced a polite smile.

"Are you coming to bed?" Porcia asked, sheepishly but also somewhat pleadingly. She forced her own smile on seeing Horace. She didn't like the satirical young officer and resented him for the way her husband now seemed to confide in him more than her. She was the daughter of Cato. He was the son of a commoner.

As with her husband Porcia had changed, physically and otherwise, since leaving Rome. Her eyes seemed more deep set, her face more drawn. Brutus and his wife argued behind closed doors but the walls were thin. Porcia missed her friends, the theatre and her home. She didn't like being in the company of soldiers – they were "coarse and vulgar". She couldn't remember the last time she had bought a new dress. She wanted him to appreciate the sacrifices she had made for him.

"Not yet. I've still got some work to do," Brutus replied. The politician did indeed need to catch up on some correspondence, most notably he needed to reply to a letter from Atticus to ask for a further loan, but that was not the reason he decided not to retire for the night. The husband and wife no longer made love. He always tried to climb into bed after his wife had fallen asleep. The thought remained unvoiced but Brutus couldn't quieten the belief that his wife had partly manipulated him into murdering Caesar. Her motive had been that Caesar had been responsible for the death of her father, Cato. The door to the issue was ajar but Brutus refrained from opening it fully. Things were strained between them at present but not completely broken.

*I still need her. But I just don't want to be with her right now.*

Porcia motioned, as if to respond, but then merely pursed her lips and retreated from the chamber. The sound of the closing door creaking drowned out her sigh. The fire was unable to thaw out the frosty awkwardness in the room.

*Rather than Rome you need to save your marriage*, Horace thought to himself.

12.

"Think of yourself as an actor. You just have to hit a slightly different mark," Octavius had advised Agrippa the day before the archery tournament.

*If I am an actor then there are plenty in the audience who would wish to boo me off stage right now*, Agrippa thought to himself as the jeers and abuse directed at him seemed to reach a crescendo. Beads of sweat threaded their way down his dust-laden body. His throat was as dry as dust too. His arm ached as if he had been continually punched there for the past three hours.

The archery competition was being held in a converted theatre. The well-to-do were sitting on cushions on the stone steps surrounding the stage whilst the lower-classes crowded themselves onto the sand-coated area in front of the stage. A central channel ran through the throng where the competitors could shoot their arrows into the targets, which were positioned on the stage.

The afternoon sun throbbed, sometimes charging and sometimes sapping the competitors' strength. The tournament had started early that morning but the ongoing rounds had separated the wheat from the chaff and now only three competitors remained: Agrippa, Mutilus Bulla and one other, whose name Agrippa failed to hear over the cacophonous crowd.

Bulla was the threat. The people cheered his name not because he was the Senate's champion (and he would dedicate his victory to the Republic if he proved triumphant) but rather because most of them had placed a bet on the favourite. Bulla had not let them down in the past and it was likely that he would not let them down now.

Bulla's tanned body was taut with muscle. He was both tall and broad, bull-necked and square-jawed. He wore a light blue tunic inlaid with gold thread. Agrippa couldn't help but notice the archer's necklace too, strewn with polished teeth and small bones. Trophies from previous kills. Poking out through his tunic were two legs which were as thick and sturdy as pillars or tree trunks. His brawny, tattooed arms were only a little narrower than his legs. There was an intimidating solidity to his figure. A flat, brawler's face only added to his fearsome appearance. His large, yew bow was decorated with ivory and gold.

Bulla spoke to Agrippa in the early rounds, while he was taking his shots.

"Good aim, boy. This is your first competition it seems... Rest that arm, it'll grow tired soon and feel like a piece of lead hanging off you shoulder..."

His voice was low and guttural. Agrippa continued to take his shots. He'd suffered worse distractions and insults from fellow soldiers at the camp he had trained with in Macedonia.

*He's also too big to get inside your head.*

By the third round Bulla was merely grunting, either appreciatively or dismissively, whilst Agrippa fired off his five arrows.

For the final round the distance to the target was extended as fresh wooden boards marked with inner and outer circles were placed at the back of the stage, and the line from which the competitors were asked to shoot from was moved back by ten paces. Bulla grinned as he watched the youth gulp, assessing the new challenge.

"This should now separate the men from the boys, eh?" Bulla declared within earshot of his rivals, coughing up and spitting out phlegm afterwards.

The third man taking part in the final appeared not to hear the cheap taunt. Agrippa looked him over. He was middle-aged, slim but well-conditioned and could often be found wryly smiling at a private joke. His dress neither singled him out as being rich or being poor. His complexion was pale – which led Agrippa to believe that the stranger was visiting from a foreign, colder land, although after overhearing the stranger speak Agrippa couldn't tell his background from his accent. The stranger had been fortunate to be in the final after nearly being knocked out a couple of rounds earlier (save for a brilliant – or lucky – final arrow).

*At the very least I'll come second. But second isn't good enough...*

Agrippa glanced up at Octavius, who was sitting next to Oppius in the crowd. Agrippa was looking thoughtful whereas Oppius was looking at a busty brunette sitting a couple of rows down from him. Agrippa pictured the look of disappointment on their faces should he not prevail. He sank his chin into his chest. He felt nauseous. Yet his spirits lifted as he imagined the look on Caecilia's face should he present her with the gold, sapphire-encrusted trophy. She was in the crowd, having petitioned Cicero to bring her. Agrippa dared not stare up at the woman he cherished for fear of distracting himself or having his expression betray his heart to Cicero or Octavius. She understood and tried to temper her emotions and reactions too, lest Cicero read something in her profile as he sat next to her.

"If I was looking for gold from a suitor then I could have married someone else years ago," Caecilia had said to Agrippa the previous evening, after he explained that he wanted to win the valuable trophy for her.

"I want to give something to you though."

"You already have – twice," the woman replied, lying next to him on the bed, with a minx-like grin on her face and laughter filling the air. The pair had made love for the first time. Agrippa arranged to rent a clean, well furnished apartment close to where Caecilia was staying with Cicero. He bought a fine vintage, decorated the room with flowers and painted her a picture of the valley where they had first met (this time without including the sketch of an aqueduct).

"I want your first time to be special," Agrippa said, coming up for air after they kissed.

"It is. It's with you."

The virginal girl was nervous at first but then willingly surrendered to the experience and pleasure the second time round; she stretched out her singing body and then held him tight, coiling her legs and arms around his sweat-glazed muscular torso. Agrippa was tender and conscious of not wanting to seem too much of a practised lover for fear of Caecilia getting the wrong idea about his past.

She had sighed, breathlessly and beautifully, as she climaxed. She sighed again now as the master of ceremonies announced Agrippa's name in the list of finalists. Her heart raced and she wanted to briefly catch his eye and communicate her love and support – to combat the majority of the spectators who lacked both for him. The crowd undulated, like a serpent, around the theatre. The smell of cheap wine and sweat wafted in the air. Soldiers and officials began to link arms to prevent the spectators from veering too close to the remaining participants.

"Do you have a preference, my dear, as to who you would like see win?" Cicero asked.

"I hope the best man wins, of course," Caecilia answered, fanning herself in the shimmering heat, hoping to cool her crimsoning face.

"Well I'm not sure who the best *man* may be but the best archer, I am told, is Bulla. He was loyal to Pompey rather than Caesar in the civil war and I'm reliably informed that he intends to spoil Octavius' party and dedicate his prospective victory to the Republic. It used to be that myself and the likes of Hortensius and Cato would give speeches and the mob would listen. Now it appears that monosyllabic archers can do so too. But I suppose it's still preferable to listening the voice of the great unwashed mob itself."

Octavius briefly bit his bottom lip and betrayed his nerves. His anxiety was more for his friend than himself. He would be disappointed but not distraught if Bulla walked off with the trophy.

*The crowd cheered when I arrived and they will cheer when I leave. Their chants of "Caesar" were as much for me as Julius, I warrant.*

Octavius again scanned below him, where the aristocrats were sitting in the crowd, to see if she had come. But she hadn't. Livia's husband, who had opposed Julius Caesar, was now wary of being seen to support his heir. Other women had been in his bed since the party but Livia had occupied his thoughts.

Agrippa gulped down a cup of water and then poured a second over his head to take the sting out of his sunburnt skin.

The young archer squinted as he tried to make out the target in the distance. He would have to draw his bowstring back even further and judge a new arc of flight.

A boisterous section of the crowd continued to hurl insults at the fresh-faced archer. Some of them had bet half a week's wages on Bulla. A stream of curses came out of their mouths accompanied by a surprising amount of spittle which spotted the sand. A lazy-eyed, gap-toothed member of the throng, not content with hurling abuse, was also tempted to hurl half an apple at the unsuspecting young soldier. His rumbling stomach thought better of it however.

"Take no notice of them lad. They probably have more to lose than you, in terms of the bets they've placed on the competition," the strange-accented archer amiably remarked. "I've just been called, by one particular cretin, both a 'wanker' and a 'eunuch' within the same sentence."

Agrippa smiled, easing his tension. "There are a few betting on us it seems. But the smart money is on Bulla," he remarked.

"Money's neither smart nor foolish. But people are usually the latter. You'll do fine though, lad. You shoot well. Remember to control your breathing and as a result you'll control your aim more. This final round won't be won or lost on the first two arrows, so don't despair if you get off to a bad start. You might now be asking why I'm helping you. It's because if I don't win I'd like you to pick up the trophy. Bulla is a rogue and a bully, who'll prove neither honourable in victory or defeat."

"My name's Marcus Agrippa. What's yours?" the young archer said, offering his hand to the stranger.

"Well, 'Outsider' and 'Lucky Bastard' are two of the more polite names I've been called today."

The cacophonous noise continued to stretch upwards, as if desiring to alert the gods to the tournament.

Octavius caught the eye of Aulus Hirtius as he scanned across the audience. The consul designate gave the young Caesar a nod. Originally Hirtius had aligned himself with Mark Antony after the assassination but Cicero had persuaded him to side with republicans in the senate. Julius had always spoken well of Hirtius. He was a competent commander and more scholarly than most of Caesar's lieutenants. Caesar had entrusted Hirtius with editing and completing his book on the Gallic Wars. As to Pansa, Hirtius' fellow consul designate, he would follow his friend's lead. Neither Octavius nor Hirtius knew much they could trust the other at present. Or how much they might need each other. They were neither allies nor enemies – yet.

The young Caesar nodded back, respectfully. *Better to build rather than burn bridges.*

"So who do you think will win Lucius? Marcus or Bulla?" Octavius said, finishing off a plate of asparagus tips and turning towards the centurion.

*Neither of them.*

"I hope that Marcus wins," Oppius replied, his mind preoccupied by the thought of what he might spend his winnings on.

The trio drew lots as to which competitor would shoot first. Agrippa silently cursed his luck when he realised he would be starting the round off. But at least he would be getting things over with quickly and he might be able to put pressure on his fellow competitors by setting down a good score. Hitting the small black circle, which was the diameter of the span of a man's hand, was worth ten points whilst any arrow which hit the larger surrounding red circle on the board scored five points.

As Agrippa stepped up to his mark another wave of jeering hit him like a blast of hot air. Faces were contorted in antagonism and drunkenness. Blackened teeth were bared. A win for Bulla could see a number in the crowd swap their rags for the kind of fine tunics worn by those sitting in the stands. And a loss could mean them not eating or, worse, not drinking for a week. Some even appeared to be scuffling their feet along the ground to try and build up a dust cloud and narrow

Bulla's odds on winning. The determined archer allowed the braying crowd to fall into the background though – ignoring the people as wilfully as a politician would.

Sweat soaked his brow and palms. The latter he rubbed against his tunic, to dry them. He tried to control his breathing and slow his quickening heart. Agrippa remembered something Oppius had told him when the tournament was first announced: "Just do the best you can. Winning will be a by-product." To accompany his advice the centurion bought the young archer a new bow and introduced him to the finest fletcher in the capital.

Agrippa breathed out and nocked his first arrow. Such was the expectation in the air that most of the crowd quietened themselves. If only the same could be said for Bulla.

"You've got more chance of hitting puberty than hitting that target boy," the surly archer remarked – and laughed at his own joke. "Remember, there's no pressure. Ha!"

Agrippa's contempt for the oaf fuelled his determination. Pressure had been shooting fire arrows at the pirate ship off the coast of Apollonia. Pressure had been launching arrows into a group of assassins who had ambushed his friends on the road to Rome, killing them before they killed him. He had succeeded then. He could succeed now.

The string cut into his fingers as he drew back the bow, further than he had ever pulled it back. He narrowed his eyes and strangely the target became bigger.

*You can do this.*

To compensate for the extra distance Agrippa aimed slightly higher – as he pictured the shaft arcing downwards into the centre of the target. He breathed out and in a moment of stillness, just before he believed that his arm might start to wobble from the strain, he fired his first arrow.

There was silence – and then more laughter from Bulla. Cheers from those who had bet on the favourite also reverberated in his ears. The arrow had thumped into the wooden board but outside both circles. Agrippa let out a curse. His blood pumping, in frustration rather than excitement, the archer nocked a second arrow and it zipped through the air – before again landing just outside the target. His face was flush from the heat and shame. He sighed.

*You can't do this… You should have let Oppius shoot instead.*

Agrippa dared not stare up at Octavius or Caecilia. He didn't want to witness the disappointment, or understanding, in their expressions.

Yet he pictured Caecilia's face and heard her voice. He gently smiled as he recalled her words from the previous night: "If you win then I know how we should celebrate. But if you somehow lose then I know how to console you too," the woman had said, with a playful light in her eyes.

His smile widened. *You can do this. But if you can't she'll still love you. And Octavius will not think any less of you either.* Instead of cursing Agrippa offered up a couple of prayers to Venus and Pietas – for had he not entered the competition out of a sense of love and duty towards Caecilia and his best friend?

Agrippa filled his lungs with air and determination and nocked his third arrow.

*Love and duty. Love and duty.*

The shaft struck the board, inside the red circle for five points. A small cheer went up. Further cheers filled the air as the remaining brace of arrows scored five and then ten. The crowd appreciated the adolescent archer's pluck in coming back from such a terrible start. Even Bulla was temporarily lost for words. A portion of the crowd chanted Agrippa's name. The air rippled with applause. He turned and waved. As he did so he took in the looks of devotion and friendship from Caecilia and Octavius. They had both risen to their feet and were clapping.

Bulla shook his head as he stepped up to his mark, in condemnation of the fickle crowd. He snorted rather than breathed as he nocked the custom-made arrow for his custom-made bow. His neck and arms bulged with muscles and veins, like a marble statue of Atlas coming to life. His figure exuded strength as every arrow scored: five, five, ten, five and ten. A special cheer went up when the favourite went into the lead and eclipsed Agrippa's score. As he shot his final arrow and the scorer on the stage made a sign to verify the "ten" Bulla raised his arms in triumph as if he had already won. His chin jutted out in pride and victory. He roared and thumped his chest. The crowd chanted his name and he soaked up the adulation, nodding in approval of their admiration for him.

Many in the crowd began to think about what they would spend their winnings on, believing that Bulla's victory was now a foregone conclusion. The third, non-descript competitor had only made it to the final by accident.

"He's no threat. He's lucky to have even reached the final," Bulla remarked to a friend in the crowd, within earshot of his rival archer.

Agrippa offered up another couple of prayers for the stranger to win. The enigmatic bowman gave Agrippa a reassuring – and conspiratorial – wink as he stepped up to his mark. He seemed impervious to Bulla's words and the multitude of sounds around him. Agrippa noticed a steeliness and level of concentration in his features which had been absent in previous rounds. He examined the shaft and flights on his first arrow before nocking it. He waited a few moments for what little breeze existed to subside. His whole body, rather than just his arm, appeared to adjust itself as he smoothly pulled back the bowstring.

The arrow sang, rather than twanged, as it left the bow.

*Ten.*

A superior technique more than compensated for Bulla's brute strength. The theatre let out a collective gasp of surprise. In four fluid movements the stranger struck the inner black circle four more times. A few might have wondered if Apollo had taken possession of the mortal. Bulla's jaw, which had recently jutted itself out with pride, dropped to the ground in bewilderment. The only face in the crowd which appeared immune from astonishment was Lucius Oppius', as the centurion knew what his friend and former comrade was capable of. Unbridled applause rang out, even from those who had lost money on the outcome. Some stood dumb however, transfixed by the scarcely believable grouping of arrows housed at the centre of the target. They had been witness to a masterclass, or a miracle. Tavern goers would recount the episode for days. People would proudly say, "I was there".

"The harder you practise the luckier you get," the stranger remarked to a sour-faced Bulla. The expert archer then turned to Agrippa. "In answer to your question earlier lad, the name's Teucer."

*

The friends drank long into the night, celebrating Teucer's triumph – although Agrippa retired early to write a note to Caecilia. As he was awarded the gleaming trophy Teucer (a native of Briton who had served alongside Oppius under Caesar – and whose real name was Adiminus) gave a short speech: "I spent a good part of my life and career fighting for Caesar, from the beaches of Britain to the plains of Pharsalus. As much as he gained personal glory from his campaigns he always fought for what was best for the people of Rome. I would be equally proud to use my bow in the service of his son, Octavius Caesar, who shares his father's courage and generosity."

On hearing Teucer dedicate his victory to Octavius a number of staunch republican senators got up and walked out of the theatre. Mutilus Bulla also decided not to stand on ceremony and left the arena before his rival was awarded the trophy. Witnessing the fearsome scowl on his face the sea of people duly parted to let the defeated archer through. He muttered to himself as he left, arguing that he would have raised his performance if he had known the true extent of his competition. "I've been cheated. A plague on you all." Octavius noted how Hirtius remained behind and still applauded the winning archer.

Octavius invited Teucer (along with Oppius and Agrippa) back to his villa. Wine, women and a victory banquet were laid out before them. The pleasure-loving archer licked his lips at all of them. On seeing the Briton up close Octavius realised that he had met the soldier before, in Rome, many years ago – as he and a fellow soldier named Marcus Fabius had come to his house to deliver a letter from his great-uncle.

"We've both become a Caesar since our last meeting, in some ways. After Pharsalus I went home to lead my tribe in Britain. The weather may be inhospitable there but thankfully my people welcomed me back. I think I also raised their spirits by the wagon load of wine I brought back with me. I'm here to raise some capital again, to take back with me and provide for my tribe, should you have use for my bow. I also wouldn't mind finding out who was behind the attack on you on the road to Rome. Roscius was a good friend. Just say the word and I'll put an arrow between the eyes of the man who hired his killer."

Before reaching the villa Oppius also took Teucer aside, partly to give him his share of the winnings from the bet he had placed on his friend.

"I'm glad you're here," the centurion said with relief and a certain weariness. "The world may have turned upside down but at least I can rely on your aim and friendship. In murdering Caesar they killed any chance of peace, prosperity and stability. Rome is again a prize that's up for grabs, which men will wade through a river of blood to secure. Antony can't be trusted. If Cassius gains power he will add Octavius' name to a proscription list in the blink of an eye. My name would doubtless follow. Hirtius will side with his new optimate friends rather than with the veterans who he fought alongside – and had his life saved by – during Caesar's campaigns."

"Have we picked the right side? As Antony has said, Octavius is just a boy with a name. From what I can gather his forces are fewer than half that of Antony's or the Republic's. The odds are against him," Teucer replied. Although he had praised his former general for his courage and generosity during his speech the Briton was also aware of Caesar's ambition and cruelty. It was just as likely that Octavius could inherit the dictator's vices as well as virtues.

"As you showed today, the favourite doesn't always finish first. And as Julius once said, it's where you are at the end of the race that counts."

13.

The tiled floor was sticky with wine, at least Enobarbus hoped it was just wine. Dice, broken jugs, oyster shells, strophums, half-eaten trays of food and olive stones also littered the floor. It had been quite a party. Most of the lamps had burned out but dawn was stirring. If only the same could be said for the occupants of the chamber. Enobarbus noted Felix Calvinus snoring in one corner, being propped up by a dockside drab. Manius Sura slept in the opposite corner, a serving boy lay curled up by his feet. Antony scarcely needed to have a reason to throw a party but he was celebrating the coming together of some of his friends and retinue who had journeyed from Rome to Brundisium: the lute-player Anaxenor, the dancer Metrodorus and the flautist Xanthus (who, by the looks of him, had performed his party trick of sucking up wine through his flute a few too many times).

Enobarbus pursed his lips in disappointment as he took in his general, slumped over a couch – his tongue hanging out like a dog. Metrodorus lay slumped over him, her usually beguiling face smeared with make-up. Her dress left little to the imagination (not that the dancer couldn't fire a man's imagination regardless).

*If less is more she's wearing too much.*

Antony's lieutenant didn't regret his decision to pass on the previous night's revelries. He had work to catch up on. Enobarbus had spent the evening writing to various supporters and would-be supporters of the consul. Some he offered bribes to, promising positions of influence or lucrative government contracts should they side with Antony. Some he threatened, in a veiled way or otherwise. After every upheaval there were always proscription lists. Gradations of guilt were often linked to property prices. The greater the estate the greater the punishment. Despite having procured the bulk of the treasury and the bulk of Caesar's estate (although Antony argued that they could be classified as being one and the same) his commander still needed more resources. Antony would at least agree with Cicero that "Endless money forms the sinews of war" – though they were unlikely to agree on anything else, Enobarbus thought.

It was an arms race but Antony was confident he was winning. "We have a force that's three times as strong as our rivals and a commander ten times more experienced," the general had boasted to his lieutenant. But, having recently come from Rome, Enobarbus knew that the consul wasn't winning on all fronts. Octavius' games had been a success. Priests and augurs would have envied the way he played on superstitions in regards to the coming of the comet. Politicians must have admired – as well as resented – his capacity to make contrary promises to different groups of people. As well as securing support from Caesar's veterans Octavius was also becoming the housewife's favourite (especially perhaps with those wives whom he slept with). Where the son of Caesar used to command sympathy he now commanded respect.

And with Octavius' star on the rise Enobarbus recognised Antony's popularity wane in the capital as though the two figures stood either side on the scales. Graffiti was beginning to spring up around the city labelling the consul a thief and a tyrant. Some propaganda even accused Antony of being part of the assassination plot to murder Caesar.

The people no longer seemed to believe in him.

*But the people change their minds more times than a woman buying shoes.*

The most important thing was that Enobarbus still believed in the man who had saved his life at Alesia. The man who had commanded the left wing at the battle of Pharsalus. The First Man of Rome. And his friend.

*History will treat him well. History will judge him on what will happen in the future rather than what is happening now. Caesar slaughtered a million barbarians during his campaigns in Gaul but he was hailed a conquering hero.*

Should any other man have woken him at such an early hour, with such a hangover, they would have experienced a less jovial Antony compared to the one who had held court the previous evening. But the general forgave his lieutenant for disturbing him.

"Morning Domitius," Antony slurred, his bleary eyes cowering from the light. "From the look on your face – and the fact that you've woken me at dawn – I take it it's bad news?"

His voice was rough, his throat dry. His tongue felt furry and fat in his mouth. His brow throbbed. He felt hungry but knew he wouldn't be able to hold down any food. The morning after was always worth paying for the night before though. As Antony untangled himself from Metrodorus, the dancer stirred a little. Her eyes remained closed yet she still smiled dreamily, a reflex action from hearing her patron's voice and smelling his scent.

Antony picked up a large jug of water as if it were no heavier than a cup and gulped down a third of its contents. He put on a silk robe, embroidered with golden thread, which hung upon a throne-like chair. Enobarbus then passed him the letter. It was now Antony's turn to purse his lips as he noticed the seal on the correspondence.

"It's even worse than bad news," the general remarked, as he scanned the message. "She's already on her way."

*Fulvia.* Even when sober Antony's wife – or just the very thought of her – was capable of giving the consul a headache. The sound of her shrewish voice hammered into him like nails going into a crucifix. In order to maintain his marriage Antony had realised, long ago, that he needed to spend as much time away from his wife as possible. Being on campaign and serving Caesar had provided him with genuine reasons to be absent from Rome (although even when living in the capital Antony would much rather spend his evenings with his mistresses than his wife).

"I'm happy to let you off the leash, as long as you come running when I call your name," Fulvia had once remarked to her husband. She was ambitious for herself – which largely meant being ambitious for Antony. She had been proud to marry the charming, attractive lieutenant of Caesar. He had been the Second Man of Rome, then. She believed that other women envied her or, better still, feared her.

Antony had married Fulvia for her money. She had paid his debts and, even now, her network of bankers, merchants, aristocrats and senators helped cement his powerbase. "I feel like I'll be paying off my debt to her for the rest of my life. I would rather owe the moneylenders," Antony had confessed to his lieutenant one evening. Although Antony wasn't his wife's puppet Fulvia still controlled many of the purse strings. There were still traces of beauty in her sharp features but little softness or femininity in her heart. Satirists derided her and called her a "she-wolf". Her greatest desire was to rule a ruler, govern those who governed. She could be ruthless on a political level and cruel on a personal one. On hearing how Cleopatra often punished servants who displeased her by sticking hairpins into their limbs she imitated the Egyptian queen. The terror on her victim's faces amused her.

"Come Domitius, let us talk outside. There are more pleasant sounds to wake to in the morning than that of Felix snoring."

Antony and his lieutenant walked out onto the first floor balcony of the grand villa. At first the consul winced slightly and shielded his eyes from the rising sun and cloudless blue sky. But then he smiled – his tired countenance becoming handsome again – as he took in the picturesque view. The colonnaded balcony looked out across the crescent-shaped bay of Brundisium. The flower-filled garden of the villa framed the foreground. Petals of amber sunlight and tufts of foam decorated the expansive, shimmering sea. Ships, their sails seemingly puffed out with pride, disappeared over the horizon or skirted along the coast. Many of the ships, Antony thought, would be bringing in supplies for his burgeoning army – or silks and perfumes for his cohort of mistresses. The general had instructed his quartermasters to dictate prices to merchants rather than vice-versa. "Order them to comply, for the good of Rome." When some of the merchants complained that really they were being ordered to do so for the good of Antony the quartermasters argued that they were now one and the same thing.

The sea breeze took the sting out of the humid air. Birds silently winged their way across his eye-line. He could thankfully no longer hear the snoring from inside. All seemed peaceful. Yet the smile fell from Antony's face when he remembered that Fulvia would be arriving soon. His brief moment of peace shattered like glass (or like a plate – which Fulvia was fond of smashing when she grew angry). She had been better as a mistress than wife, Antony thought. She had been fun-loving and had tried harder to please him back then. Fulvia had clung to him out of devotion when they had first became lovers. Now she held onto his arm as if he were her possession when they attended parties together. Marriage had worked its magic and dissipated any affection or passion they felt for one another. Over the years, during their lovemaking, she had grown colder, unresponsive, he judged. *Soon it'll be like making love to a corpse.* Enobarbus had recently reported to him that his wife had been spending a large amount of time in the company of his brother, Lucius. "They deserve each other, such is their raw selfishness and ambition," Antony had remarked. "Lucius can even fuck her, for all I care. She's so cold he may well contract frostbite. Aye, let him fuck her until his cock falls off."

"Has Fulvia mentioned how long she will be staying for?" Enobarbus asked, thinking that he would move his plans forward to return to Rome. Partly because of the influence the lieutenant held over her husband Fulvia little disguised her resentment for him.

"Even if it's a brief visit she'll be staying for too long," Antony replied, sighing as well as joking. He took in the landscape again and filled his lungs with the warm sea air. "There are worse views in the world, no? It's like a painting or a perfect moment caught in time. Have you ever dreamed of going back to a perfect moment in your life Domitius?"

"I like to think that my best days are ahead of me."

Having been a soldier for nearly half of his life Enobarbus had little desire to return to a time of war. He had experienced enough violence and death for ten lifetimes. Enobarbus saw it as his job now to facilitate peace, either through diplomacy or by helping Antony to a quick and decisive victory.

"Sometimes I wish I was back in Rome, during my youth. With Curio and Clodius. I once arranged a competition with the former, to see which one of us could sleep with as many cousins from just one family. Curio won but I had a fun time in coming second. We would make a wager on almost anything. We once tossed a coin on whether one of Clodius' slaves should live or die after having been caught stealing. I led a carefree life. I slept during the day and my nights were filled with parties and love affairs. I was a slave to my pleasures, or rather I was a master of them. The only burden of choice I experienced involved deciding who I should sleep with each evening. Am I still not, in part, the Antony of old though? Can I ever wholly bury him or the past? People only can gain bad reputations, they can never lose them. Or was I happiest when in Egypt? I married together a life of pleasure and a life of duty and martial glory. The Egyptians understood and loved me. The army also taught me that there was more to life than just wine, women and song. I owe a duty to Rome and its people. Julius saw something in me and at that moment I saw something in myself. Hercules is always lauded for his strength, never his wisdom. Yet you are also right, my friend, why should I not consider that my best days are ahead of me? Why shouldn't I complete Caesar's reforms and carry out his campaign in the east to retrieve the standards which Crassus lost? Or better still I should come out from his shadow and initiate my own reforms and military campaigns – be a slave and master to my own ambitions."

Antony grasped the air as he spoke, in hope and determination. Sometimes Enobarbus thought that his general was a man who didn't know what he wanted and sometimes he thought that Antony wanted everything. Sometimes he seduced, sometimes he wanted to be seduced – either by a woman or a cause.

"We also need to be mindful of the ambitions of others. Initial reports have been confirmed that Brutus has conducted raids against our forces and supplies in Macedonia. He's recruiting an army although he will not be able to mobilise any significant force soon. Cicero has been writing begging letters on his behalf, I believe, looking to raise capital and political support for his former acolyte.

Sooner or later we will have to deal with Brutus," Enobarbus remarked. *Soldiers rather than diplomats will ultimately decide the outcome.*

"The self-righteous prig. I agree that Brutus won't abandon his cause. For all of his noble posturing he's just a dog with the bone of republicanism between his teeth. Brutus thinks that he's got right on his side but the gods on are the side of those with the biggest and best legions. Let us deal with him sooner rather than later. I cannot spare the time or men to have a small army chase him around Macedonia at the moment. But I want him dead. Brutus is the figurehead, and once he's gone support for Cassius and the other libertores will scatter to the wind."

"I'll take care of it," Antony's agent stated, having already formed the basis of a plan. Instead of employing mercenaries and arranging an ambush, as he had done in the failed attempt to murder Octavius on his way to Rome, Enobarbus would use subtler means to assassinate the praetor. It would even be the case that Brutus would invite his killer into his own home.

After Enobarbus finished his morning report Antony retired to his bedroom. He would wake at midday and summon Metrodorus – and one of her friends – to his chamber. He still had a day or so to enjoy himself before his wife arrived.

14.

*Time passes.*

Leaden skies snuffed out the dusk. Summer was receding too. Cicero sat in his study, in his house on the Palatine. *The darkness always returns and dominates.* Tiro entered, stoked the small fire and placed a blanket around his master's shoulders. When the statesman had first taken his secretary on he had felt a certain paternal affection for the bright-minded and hard-working slave (whom he eventually freed) but now Cicero was more like the child and Tiro was the parent. Tiro felt his old master flinch as a raucous shout sounded out from the street outside. Drunks – be they rowdy aristocrats or plebs – were an unwelcome disturbance. The writer, whether drafting a book, speech or correspondence, needed quietude to concentrate. Cicero momentarily yearned to be back at his villa at Puteoli, couched in the bower of nature. Fields and streams didn't expect anything of him or remind him of failure. Rome did. Atticus had recently implored him to leave the capital, return to his country retreat and write history books. Be free of politics. Be free from danger. *But I still have it within me to make history as opposed to just write about it. All these years I've told myself that I've been above the concerns of the world but really I've just been hiding from them too much.*

"Thank you, Tiro. Although I could well be shivering from the prospect of Antony becoming dictator instead of merely consul. Crime and taxes are up, business confidence is down. The state's funds are devoted to building up his army instead of building roads, baths and theatres. Our young men are lining up outside of taverns to be recruited when they should be planting and harvesting crops. Such is Antony's desperation for men that one of his centurions may well even try to recruit you, my friend," Cicero joked, appreciating the renewed glow and warmth from the fire.

"I am not sure how much use I'd be. The only experience I have with a blade is using a letter knife," the sharp-witted secretary replied. "But these are indeed dark times." *Rome is like a drunk, staggering around on top of a cliff. It is just a matter of time before he meets his end. Civil war is imminent as surely as night follows day or corruption follows winning office.*

"But it's always darkest before the dawn. Where there's life there's hope." Cicero remarked, his voice and body more animated. He clasped the younger man's forearm to bolster the secretary's spirits. The statesman proceeded to open a message from one of his agents, who had infiltrated Antony's army camp at Brundisium.

*

Laughter and the intoxicating smell of perfume swirled around the air. Teucer had just told another joke: "'How do you want your haircut?' said the barber to the customer. 'In silence'."

The party – Oppius, Agrippa, Balbus, Teucer, Pollux and Milo – were returning to Rome from their mission in Brundisium. Balbus had arranged for them to spend the evening at the house of one Septimus Vinicius, an old merchant friend of Caesar's. As per Balbus' instructions, which out of love or fear Vinicius followed to the letter, their host laid on some entertainment.

"Did you like that one lad?" Teucer called out to Agrippa. Since the archery competition the Briton had grown fond of the young Roman. He spent many a morning with him, practising. At first Agrippa felt somewhat frustrated and deficient compared the veteran bowman but Teucer then made his day by saying that Agrippa was a more accomplished archer than the Briton had been when he was nineteen.

Agrippa didn't respond, however, as he had already left the celebrations. Teucer put the boy's behaviour down to tiredness but Oppius, noticing that it wasn't the first time that Agrippa had turned down some entertainment, suspected that the normally red-blooded soldier was saving himself for someone special back in the capital. *The lad's either noble or stupid enough to remain faithful to someone.*

The Briton merely shrugged in the face of his friend's absence and duly turned his attention to the lissom girl – Clara – lying next to him on the sofa. Age – and the rigours of her trade – had yet to despoil her beauty. There was still a natural air of joy and hope in her aspect. The soldier didn't know whether to be attracted to her all the more for her freshness or pity her all the more, for time would despoil her in the end. It had done the same for his wife back home, but then again the archer had shrugged his shoulders in the face of that too. Vinicius had spotted Clara in the local market and made an offer that the carpenter's daughter could not afford to refuse. The merchant had said that Clara "had potential." He also promised that she would be "his special girl" – though few remained special for more than a month. Women were, for the merchant, either assets or liabilities. And their value always depreciated over time. It was always a matter of when, rather than if, Vinicius would sell his special girls on.

Clara popped a couple of grapes in her mouth and then leaned over, crushing her lips against the fun-loving soldier's.

*I wish she tasted of wine instead of grapes.*

"I've never been with a Briton before," Clara said, beaming enthusiastically. There was a disarming mixture of innocence and curiosity in the girl's unaffected voice.

"We are lovers of wine and women. Unfortunately our love for the former can sometimes hinder our ability to please the latter."

Aulus Milo grinned even more widely than the teenage girl as the Nubian courtesan he had picked out straddled him on the sofa opposite to the archer. Her low-cut gown showed the promise of things to come. The girl Teucer was with may have been considered *beautiful* but his whore was *bountiful*. Niobe was a woman of few words, spoken in broken Latin, but that didn't bother the enamoured centurion.

"I love a woman with a huskier voice than me," Milo remarked to Oppius, who was sitting next to him alongside a bronzed, Arab woman entwining her tattooed arms around his neck.

"Aye, but also one who is slimmer and prettier," Oppius replied, as the courtesan proceeded to thrust her tongue into his ear and twist it around for good measure.

"I agree. I should thank you. You promised me gold but you have also given me ebony," Milo declared, running his hands along the Nubian's oiled, strong thighs.

"Shall we go somewhere quiet?" she whispered into his ear, like a kiss.

"Yes, although we may not be quiet for long," the ribald soldier answered and then laughed at his own joke. Niobe led him off to a room upstairs, although he briefly returned to retrieve a jug of wine.

Cephas Pollux also gave thanks to Oppius for convincing him to side with Octavius, given the favourable position he was now in. Pollux sat in a chair in the corner of the room, with a sweet-smelling dancer on his lap, writhing against his groin and flicking her braided hair in his face as she turned her head sideways to the music playing in her mind. A slit in her gauze-like scarlet dress revealed a slender, silken thigh which gleamed in the light of the ornate lamps hanging from the ceiling. As she rhythmically undulated her feline body the dozen or so silver bangles on her arms clinked together. Her jangling reminded Pollux of a dinner bell. *It's time for me to go eat.*

The lust-filled centurion kissed her – hungrily – and then carried her upstairs. She sighed in his arms. She said something in a foreign language which the Roman couldn't understand, yet he knew what she meant. Pollux made sure to pick a room that wasn't situated next to the one that his friend was in. He didn't want to hear Milo through the walls and similarly he didn't want Milo to hear him.

Despite the obvious distraction of the woman's serpentine leg curling its way around his Oppius noticed that Balbus had disappeared for the evening, as well as Agrippa. "It's my job to remain off stage and to just prompt the actors should they forget their lines," the political adviser once confessed to the centurion. "I'm happy to go unnoticed but not unrewarded."

His expression was often as impassive and unreadable as a professional gambler's, Oppius thought. He was forever working out odds, options and outcomes. Perhaps even Balbus was pushing himself too far of late though. His tan couldn't completely mask the rings around his eyes. But the hard work had paid off. Their mission had been a success.

"As much as you might wake up with a sore head in the morning Antony will feel worse," Balbus had remarked to the soldier as they rode back from Brundisium. "Cicero could now be the key to unlocking things. Octavius will meet with him soon, carrying an olive branch in one hand and a sword in the other."

The Arabian courtesan snaked her arm around the centurion and pulled him closer. She flicked out her tongue and teased him with kisses, on all but his lips. The careworn soldier thought of Livia but only briefly. She hummed in pleasure as Oppius slid his hand beneath her finely embroidered dress. The fate of Octavius and Rome soon fell into the background.

"Pleasure is the beginning and end of living happily," Teucer pronounced, quoting Epicurus, after downing another cup of wine (though half dripped down his chin). Clara grinned and nodded in agreement but then stopped his mouth with a kiss. She thought that the Briton talked too much.

\*

*Dear Atticus,*

*I have just received a report from one of my agents at Brundisium. A lightning bolt has struck, cleaving Antony's forces apart (though he still retains more than half unfortunately). A couple of evenings ago Balbus and Lucius Oppius, along with a number of others, infiltrated Antony's camp. It was a bold move but, as Terence wrote, "Fortune favours the brave." Oppius met with a number of officers and by force of argument, or more likely bribery, the Sword of Rome (a crass title if ever I heard one) cut ties between them and Antony. At the same time Balbus and his agents distributed propaganda throughout the camp. They also offered to pay five hundred denari for any man to join up with Octavius and avenge their former general's death. The legions at Brundisium were Caesar's veterans. A dead tyrant meant more to them than a living consul. Tellingly they had never served under Antony ("the appeaser" – as some of the soldiers called him). Some of the senior officers had also met Octavius in Apollonia. Balbus appealed to both their honour and purses. Not even the Senate could rival the amount of money and false promises that were spread around during the night. Soldiers have spent so much time around whores over the years that they become like them – and offer themselves out to the highest bidder.*

*Antony's greatest enemy was himself, however, as he summoned his men before him the next day. Some shouted out for the general to join Octavius' cause. Some demanded that Antony match the bounty that Caesar's heir was offering. At the beginning of the year the legions had expected to be fighting in a glorious – and profitable – campaign in Parthia. But now they believed they were being coerced into fighting a civil war for a fraction of the reward. My agent also noted how, though Antony might be praised as a soldier and officer, he has no track record as an overall commander. I can picture his snarling face and blood-shot eyes. Antony poured oil, rather than water, on the flames of discontent and mutiny. "You will obey orders!" he shrilly cried, his hand clasping his sword. Blank and dispirited faces looked back at him. Antony longs to be Caesar but thankfully he lacks Julius' charm and clemency. His charmless and cruel wife goaded him on (my agent reported that Fulvia was "as angry as the Medusa, with a withering stare to rival her"). Luckily Antony's better half, Enobarbus, was absent and couldn't advise caution. Antony set an example – the wrong one – and executed a number of popular officers and legionaries. Apparently Fulvia spat in the faces of the soldiers just before they were tortured and killed. Also, it was rumoured that during one centurion's execution blood splattered her chin and she licked it off like wine. I will duly turn such rumours into facts. Fulvia enjoyed herself all too much. Politics is vindictive and treacherous enough already without having women getting involved in proceedings as well. For every scream that sounded out across the camp Antony lost more and more men. Yet still he continued to dig his own grave and tried to instil loyalty through fear. Any man can make mistakes but only a fool persists in his folly. The legions he punished the most – the Fourth and Martia – were the ones which marched off to join*

*Octavius. Antony did half of Balbus' job for him. One man's tragedy is another man's happy ending. When the trickle of legionaries deserting Antony turned into a deluge he saw the error of his ways. But he could not turn back the tide despite promising to match Octavius' bounty for each man. It was too little, too late.*

*So where does this leave us my friend? The Second and Thirty-Fifth legions are still due to join-up with Antony soon, along with a contingent of Moorish cavalry, but his army has been significantly diminished. Victory over Decimus Brutus, as Antony looks to take Ciscalpine Gaul, is not a foregone conclusion. Decimus is up for the fight. He wrote to me the other week to say he would be the anvil onto which Antony could strike but that he would hold firm until the forces of the Republic could attack Antony's rear. "Put a real and metaphorical spear between his shoulder blades." Yet at present the army of the Republic would barely defeat a troupe of travelling players. The Senate, as ever, has been big on promises but short on delivery. Such is our war chest that Hirtius and Pansa may end up commanding an army full of eunuchs, greybeards and housewives. Still, it could be worse. At least it won't be an army full of Gauls. The first words they learn in Latin as children are, "I surrender".*

*We will need Octavius' forces to tip the balance in our favour. I can only hope that by championing him I can sway the Senate into forming an alliance. I believe I can control him, train the errant pup. He should be given praise, titles of distinction – and then be disposed of. What Octavius has been doing, in building a private army, is nothing short of villainy but the enemy of our enemy must be our friend. The ends justify the means. Or am I just telling myself what I want to hear? Perhaps this old advocate has told himself and others more lies over the years than the sum of the falsehoods that have come out of the mouths of the clients I have represented. But I must try to save the Republic. I may not be able to command legions but I can mobilise language and send it into battle.*

*It is getting late. Tiro has just stoked the fire but he has slyly taken away my basket of logs, to prompt me into going to bed. Even the stars in the sky seem heavy-lidded. They are seemingly closing their eyes rather than blinking.*

*I hope you are well. You must be missing Caecilia but if it's any consolation your loss has been my gain. She is a great comfort and great company. I was unsure whether she would take to the capital – Rome can prove too real (or unreal) at times – but she has an uncommon glow about her at present and there is a spring in her step.*

*I joked to her yesterday that, if I didn't know any better, I would say that she was in love. She laughed and replied that she most definitely didn't have a suitor in the capital at the moment.*

*In regards to some other news which may be of interest Quintus Caepio died last week. All in all he was a half-decent advocate and half-decent man. He won or lost cases with an enlightened, enviable equanimity. "Just so long as I get paid," Quintus would say. His funeral was attended by Rome's biggest and best fraudsters and embezzlers – ones who he had represented over the years. Some brought their strapping young sons along and made a point of introducing them to the rich widow. I could ask, do they not have any shame? But, alas, we already know the answer to that question. Sentius Taurus, who duly attended the funeral, approached me recently about acting as his advocate in his imminent trial. He has been accused of accounting fraud, again. I turned him down flat. "Euclid would have to re-write the laws of mathematics to clear your name," I remarked. I half expected Sentius to then ask if I could provide him with Euclid's address or furnish an introduction.*

*The only defence I can muster for Sentius is that at least he is a colourful character. Our new breed of politicians/criminals are so dull that they don't even have any traits to satirise. They spend the half their lives working as clerks to senators and the remainder of their existence as senators themselves. It used to be that men went into office because of their wealth but more and more there is a professional class of politician who enter office in order to extort wealth from their position. In their culture of bribes (offering and receiving), cronyism and expense scandals they make Sentius look like an amateur. Yet these men, invariably of middle-class rank, strut around like patricians and possess an elitist contempt for the likes of soldiers, farmers and tradesmen. Too many consider me an irrelevance too, an antique from a bygone age. They joke or snigger when I walk past. When I challenged one of these oily-haired bureaucrats the other day and said that Antony could well turn himself into another Catiline he looked at me blank-faced. Catiline was neither a memory nor lesson from history for the dullard. "To be ignorant of what occurred before you were born is to remain always a child," I stated.*

*I feel like I may be the only thing standing between Antony and another dictatorship – a Roman Cassandra. But I have no desire to compose the Republic's funeral oration. I will not go gently into that good night. But it's late and I do need to get some sleep. I have*

*impersonated Nestor for too long. I will write again soon and I look forward to your reply in regards to the latest turn of events.*
    *Cicero*

15.

Rain pimpled the marble slabs from an earlier shower. The dapple-grey clouds augured further rain or a storm.

Octavius noticed his foot tapping in nervousness and impatience as he sat on a stone bench in his garden, waiting for Cicero. He put a stop to the movement, tucking his leg beneath the bench. He did not wish to display any anxieties to the statesman – or himself.

Octavius had received a message from Cicero a day after returning to the capital, having met with his newly expanded army. Firstly – and most importantly – Octavius had paid his new soldiers. He thanked them for their support as well.

"I will repay loyalty with loyalty just as I will repay blood with blood in terms of those who murdered my father. I am not a revolutionary, nor do I crave a senseless civil war. I just want to make sure that Caesar's reforms and promises are honoured. I must defend myself and Caesar's legacy."

Oppius also used the visit to set in place a training regime for officers and legionaries alike. The army would need to be battle-ready soon, whether it faced Antony or the forces of the Republic.

The statues of Caesar and Alexander the Great, which had previously resided in the corner of the garden, had been replaced by newly acquired sculptures of Cincinnatus and Aristotle. There was a slight chill in the air and Octavia, who had visited her brother that morning, insisted that he wear a red woollen cloak she had bought him, over his tunic. A small, polished bronze table sat in front of the bench with some of Cicero's favourite foods upon it.

Octavius rose to his feet when he heard the approaching footsteps as an attendant escorted the esteemed statesman out into the garden where his master was waiting. The two men, separated by decades, greeted each other warmly. "When you shake his hand do so as an equal," Balbus said, before the meeting. "There is no reason to defer to him. Remember, he requested to see you. Cicero needs you more than you need him. But do not underestimate him. An old fox is still a fox."

Cicero's usually round face seemed drawn. His brow was wrinkled in fatigue and worry. But there was still a stubborn vigour in his demeanour, his bright eyes were still intelligent as well as rheumy. The veteran politician smiled to himself as he noticed the new statues which had been introduced into the garden to make a subtle impression on him. No doubt the book, strategically placed on the bench, was one of his own. Cicero smiled because he had stage-managed such scenes before. Sometimes men can behave like women and flattery can get you everywhere (even when you know you're being flattered).

"Thank you for meeting with me at such short notice," Cicero remarked, after Octavius offered his guest a seat. The young man heard the old man's knees crack as he did so.

"I meant it when I said that I would always have time for you. I should even be thanking you. This meeting gave me a genuine excuse to cancel a lunch with Flaccus Vatinius."

"One is always full after dining with Vatinius. You feel like you don't want to eat for the rest of the day, or listen to his conversation for the rest of the year."

Octavius laughed. There was part of him which could barely believe that he was in the company of Cicero and trading witticisms with him. But he reined any feelings of admiration and deference in. "Where possible let him speak first," Balbus had advised.

"Is that a statue of Cincinnatus? I have a marble bust of him – a present from Atticus – in my study at my country villa. He had a cause – that of preserving the Republic – and the Senate then gave him an army. You are in a slightly different position, however. I will speak plainly. I neither have the time nor the will to deceive or play games. You now have an army, Octavius, but what I want to give you is a cause, akin to that of what Cincinnatus possessed. Save the Republic from the tyranny of Mark Antony. The enemy will soon be at the gates. When I first invited you to my house in Puteoli I remember talking with you privately in the garden. I posited that one cannot save one's soul – and Rome – in regards to choosing a life in politics. Not for the first time in my life, I was wrong. You now have the opportunity to save both at the same time. You would not believe me if I told you that Julius would have wanted you to act this way or that, nor would I expect you to. But I do see something of Caesar in you, Octavius. I also see something of myself in you. Yet even more so I'm hopeful that there is something of the Cincinnatus in your heart. Should you commit your legions to the defence of Rome – and fulfil Caesar's legacy – will you not return to your studies? A man who gains power may be considered great but one who then freely relinquishes that power may be considered greater. The life of a soldier is far less precarious to that of a scholar, as much as certain academics have had their knives out for me over the years," Cicero said, believing that

Octavius would never now give up his pursuit of power. *He's got the taste for it.*

Octavius smiled politely, as though he was being humoured rather than flattered. He offered his guest some wine and food before responding in earnest. Octavius wanted to convey that he wasn't in a rush to commit himself, either way. The young Caesar had time and an army on his side. *I can afford not to appear desperate – and appearances are reality.*

"I've heard the Senate call me a would-be Catiline or Sulla but never Cincinnatus. The majority of the senatorial elite treat me with, at best, indifference but, at worst, contempt. According to them I'm a stripling and the descendent of a commoner. Either because of pride, stupidity or tradition they view me as a threat or a figure to ridicule. Even if I had the will and means to do so how am I supposed to help a group of people that will not accept my help?"

"If the Senate are in the dark as to how perilous the situation is becoming I will soon make them see the light. We both know Antony is venturing north. Should he defeat Decimus Brutus and take command of his legions then his army in the north will hang over Rome like the Sword of Damocles. He could swoop down on the capital and play the tyrant and thief at will. If Antony gets what he wants then you will never get what you want. He will spend your inheritance faster than he will catch the pox and he will use the former to pay for the whores who'll cause the latter. It is not just a question of the Senate needing you. Equally, if not more so, you need the Senate. Antony is a mindless thug. The only virtue he has is that he's not his wife. Similarly the only virtue Fulvia possesses is that she's not her husband..."

"Antony is more the Senate's problem than mine."

"I received a letter from a friend of mine the other day. He has added a young poet of some promise to his retinue. I read one or two of his compositions. A line from one of the pieces sticks out in my mind at this moment and seems apt. *It is your concern when your neighbour's house is on fire.* I may prove to be first on Antony's proscription list but you will be second. Indeed it wouldn't surprise me if Antony was behind the attempt on your life during the ambush on the road to Rome all those months ago."

"You may be right. But it also wouldn't surprise me, given their hostility towards me, if the Senate proved to be behind the attempted assassination."

Octavius remained stone-faced but his inward eye replayed some of the bloody and terrifying scenes of the attack in his mind. He remembered the deaths of Tiro Casca, Roscius and Cleanthes.

Cicero breathed out, in exasperation. The statesman had hoped to flatter Octavius into an alliance. It seems he wouldn't be able to threaten or scare the youth into submitting to his will either. Yet there is more than one way to skin a cat, Cicero thought to himself.

"Shortly before Julius' death I had dinner with him. He joked that, after he was gone, plenty of people would come forward and attribute all sorts of sayings and legislation to him. 'I will doubtless come across as vain and contradictory, as a result,' he remarked. He also added – with a wink – that people may make things up and therefore he might be considered funnier and wiser that he was also. I mention this because I hope that, when I talk about Julius or quote him, you believe I'm being honest," Cicero stated, his brow wrinkled in earnestness. The philosopher had indeed been to dinner with Caesar before his murder but they had spoken about literature and politics.

"I know how fond Julius was of you. Even if you did somehow put words in his mouth he would probably be flattered that you were doing so," Octavius replied, before drinking some water and putting a honey-coated asparagus tip into his mouth.

"Julius may have considered the Senate as being his enemy sometimes but he still believed in its fundamental purpose. When he defeated Pompey at Pharsalus the Senate was treated with clemency rather than condemnation. Antony has no such respect for tradition, or the intelligence to recognise the Senate's central role in government. If you truly care about Caesar's legacy then you must care about the Senate too. If you truly care for the fate of Rome you should care about the Senate. Antony will not be as forgiving as Caesar if he wins a civil war. He will make the Senate disappear as easily as he can a jug of wine."

Cicero grew a little breathless. As an advocate, during a trial, he would pace up and down – fixing his eyes on the jury or defendant. He no longer had the strength to pace but he believed that he could still make – and win – an argument. Yet Octavius appeared unmoved. Usually youth grew agitated and age bred calm but their roles were strangely reversed.

"The Senate isn't Rome. The Senate may judge Antony to be an enemy of the people. But history has shown that the Senate hasn't always been a friend to the people either. Just ask the Gracchi."

"We could debate the virtues – and crimes – of the Senate all day but the fact remains that sooner or later you – and your army – must choose a side."

*I have. My own.*

"The Senate must also decide whether it's on my side. Surely you do not expect me to just loan out my legions as if I were a pimp and they were my whores?"

"A fair point. But surely you do not expect the Senate to believe that, should your soldiers be similar whores, they will remain virginal? A man who buys a thoroughbred does not let it go to waste by keeping it in his stable."

"The Senate needs to understand that it's my thoroughbred though. Why should I allow Hirtius and Pansa to ride it? I must command my own army within any prospective alliance or coalition."

Cicero briefly looked up to the heavens for inspiration. He could not quite decide which would prove the more difficult task – convincing the Senate that Antony was their enemy or that Octavius was its ally.

*But convince them I must.*

\*

An army camp, just outside of Mutina.

Smoke from campfires belched into the air. Ribald jokes were shared over lunches of various quality and freshness. The sound of drill masters, barracking new recruits, could be heard in the background. Talk was of the previous civil war or the impending one.

A group of soldiers formed a horseshoe around their general. The rapid frequency of sword clanging upon sword created one long metallic ring as Decimus Brutus fenced against two centurions. The legionaries applauded their haughty – but competent – commander's ability. The two centurions, who could have easily bested their general in a proper fight, would be given discreet bonuses. Caesar had put on similar exhibitions of military skill during his campaigns in Gaul, Decimus recalled.

*Had he paid his men to lose too? Probably.*

Decimus magnanimously thanked and praised his defeated opponents after the sparring session. He smoothed his oiled hair and called for a jug of water and some cheese and fruit (he would leave it to the likes of Antony to dull his wits with wine at midday – although as a youth he had been a drinking companion of his now enemy). The autumnal wind was bracing but tolerable. Brutus' pinched, aristocratic face appeared even more displeased when he saw rainclouds on the horizon.

After issuing orders to his senior officers – to provision his legions, levy more troops and schedule even more drills for his new recruits – Decimus was approached by a messenger. The rider seemed even more breathless than his mare as he handed over the three letters – which all contained the same central message: Antony was heading north.

*Let him come. I started this. I'll end it.*

Decimus had been the libertore who had persuaded Caesar to attend Pompey's Theatre on the day of his assassination. "Without me history would have been different," he regularly told those who would listen. "I played the great Caesar like a flute on the day. I was also the one who delivered the death blow when we stabbed him," he proudly boasted, correcting those who thought Cassius or his cousin Marcus Brutus had killed the tyrant. Unlike his cousin however, Decimus acted from more of a personal than political grievance. He had sided with Caesar during the civil war and been instrumental in capturing the key port of Massilia from Pompey's forces there. But Decimus felt he was sufficiently un-lauded and under rewarded when the war was over. Caesar had promoted others instead of him and rightly judged that he would bequeath the bulk of his estate to his undeserving great-nephew. He had to die. Justice had been done. And if Decimus could vanquish Caesar he could do the same with Antony.

*I had no crisis of conscience then. I have even less of one now.*

"The message confirms our suspicions. Antony is on his way," Decimus informed his lieutenant, Rufus Attus, who had served with him whilst he was fleet commander for Caesar against the Veneti.

The grizzled, taciturn veteran nodded in reply. "We must prepare for a defensive campaign until Hirtius and Pansa can be bothered to relieve us. We should begin fortifying the town immediately. Send out parties to scour the province for supplies. Our stomachs are more important than theirs. Military thinking dictates that an attacker needs a ratio of three to one to capture a fortified town. Antony will need twice those numbers. I would rather die than yield to that drunken letch. Hopefully Antony's army will catch a pox before it gets here, as doubtless he is taking the route which takes him past as many brothels as possible between Rome and Mutina."

*Aye, let him come.*

\*

Cicero and Octavius talked long into the afternoon and not only because they were conscious of giving the good impression of not solely wishing to talk about politics. Both wished to convince the other that they were friends, or mentor and student, rather than reluctant allies. There were times when they convinced themselves too.

The pair retreated into the house when the rain started. Octavius had one of his slaves rush to the market to fetch a jar of his guest's favourite goat's milk and a fresh loaf of bread. While they were waiting Octavius, like a proud parent showing off his children, gave Cicero a tour of his library. His books were in some ways a reflection of his thoughts. He wanted Cicero to approve of his library – and him. He wanted to be the teacher's favourite pupil.

As much as Cicero judged that the young Caesar was friendly and engaging – ultimately one could never know what he was truly thinking. A wall of ice surrounded a fiery heart – or a wall of fire surrounded an icy heart. Such insularity could breed loneliness. And loneliness could mean vulnerability. Cicero briefly flirted with the idea of setting a honey-trap for Octavius, using Caecilia, but then he dismissed the idea immediately.

"Such is the smile on her face sometimes and her habit of mysteriously disappearing I could deduce that Caecilia is in love. She tells me that she is spending her days learning how to weave silk but she could just be spinning me a yarn," Cicero joked to Octavius as they sat on two couches facing one another in the triclinium. "Thankfully I believe she is far too sensible a girl to fall in love… But what about you? You are now old enough to have fallen in love. Is there a special someone in your heart?" Cicero was all too aware that the young Caesar was as fond of the fairer sex as his namesake and had even placed a mistress or two in his bed to tease out some information or weakness.

"As much as I may be Caesar's heir I am also, to some extent because of that, a penniless orphan. I'm too poor to have anyone fall in love with me," Octavius cynically joked.

*I composed love poetry for Briseis. I told the wife of Blandus Savius that I loved her last week, in order to bed her. But no, I've never been in love. But could I ever fall in love? Maybe. With someone like Livia…*

"Love is rare but it is also real. The same may be said of friendship and also a trustworthy politician."

"A trustworthy politician? I worry that someone has spiked your goat's milk. But I agree. I believe that my mother and Marcus Phillipus are happily married. He is also a trustworthy politician. But tell me, were you not happily married to Tertulla for a time?"

"It would have been a short time, if that. Imagine marriage – or love – as a block of wood. Life is the axe or whittling knife which slowly or rapidly diminishes it. The dawn of a marriage is always its brightest phase. Things are new, fresh and even interesting. But the night will always draw in and it's how you cope with the boredom and battle of wills. How do you keep the bed warm when lust's flame has died out? Petty disagreements, which should mean nothing, add up and come to mean everything. You may feel trapped or, conversely, give yourself the freedom to do anything to anyone. Men prove to be the cause of unhappiness and infidelity in marriage far more than women. As a philosopher I sometimes discuss the make-up of man – how he can be a paragon of virtue and yet there are occasions where he behaves with all the civility of a stray dog. And then I sometimes think upon women and posit that they are the real paragons of virtue. But then I think about Fulvia… Over the course of my career as an advocate I bested among others Hortensius, Catiline, Cato and even Caesar. But I cannot recall, over the course of my marriage, ever winning an argument with my wife."

"Tell me more about Cato and Catiline," Octavius asked, remembering how he used to question Cleanthes about Rome and its leading figures.

"When you thought that Cato was sober he was usually drunk but when you fancied him drunk his judgement was often sober. His hatred for Caesar was only rivalled by the love he had for the sound of his own voice. He was principled to the point of tediousness and few could live up to his high standards. But he sometimes did – which made him admirable. His death was a mixture of vanity and virtue, tied together in a Gordian Knot that not even I can wholly unpick… As for Catiline when he spoke people listened. When he took off his tunic women – and some men – swooned. He was fantastically handsome, charming and abhorrent. When Catiline failed to get what he wanted by legitimate means he then resorted to illegitimate tactics, without blinking an eyelid. He was a spoiled child, a brattish aristocrat claiming an affinity with the people for his own ambitions, who couldn't take no for an answer. The likes of Catiline and Antony have no appreciation or respect for the constitution. The governance of Rome can be compared to an orchestra playing a piece of music. The orchestra is made up of various constituencies or classes: the people, aristocracy, the army, consuls and others. Should just one instrument be absent from the group then the composition will sound like a chaotic din. For most of my life I have endeavoured to act as a kind of conductor to this orchestra, trying to make sure these separate classes act in harmony with one another. I believe that Caesar also attempted to fulfil this role," Cicero said with feeling, and lying. "Or permit me to bore you a little longer with the analogy that the different institutions and classes in Rome are all vital organs within the same body. Antony is stupid, arrogant and violent enough to think that he could remove one of these organs – such as the Senate or tribunate – and the patient will survive. I'm not sure how long I would survive for if someone cut my head off. Hopefully not even I could insult someone so much that they would want to decapitate me though."

Shortly afterwards Cicero excused himself and returned home to continue to compose his Philippics.

16.

Rivulets of piss ran down the cobblestones of the narrow, sloping streets. The sun was beginning to set. A couple of house fires glowed in the distance.

Oppius and Pollux had just left the tavern, *The Silver Trident*. Pollux had wanted his friend to check out a serving girl there. Oppius mentioned that his fellow centurion might want to have a doctor check her out too. From her bow-legs it seemed she spent more time working upstairs than serving drinks, he argued.

"If I don't fuck her, I may not fuck anyone again," Pollux had said, knowing he may well be leaving the capital to go off to war once more.

"If you do fuck her though, you may not be *able* to fuck again. She could be as dirty as one of Teucer's jokes," Oppius replied, thinking how he had almost lost as many men to diseases from brothels as he had from fighting the armies of Gaul. There is only one thing that a soldier unsheathes quicker than his sword ...

The streets were largely deserted. Some had gone home after an afternoon of drinking. Some were getting ready to go out drinking for the night. The shops had closed so there was little reason for women to leave their residences. Oppius and Pollux had only had a couple of drinks and a light meal of ham and cheese before heading home.

Both men walked in silence but thought the same thought: *War is coming, again. A soldier's life can only end one way.*

So many people – Cleanthes, Tiro Casca, Fabius – had said the same thing to Oppius at some point. "You will die in battle." He could ignore one of them but not all of them. Oppius had been tempted to retire before and after Pharsalus. Caesar would have granted him an honourable discharge, albeit reluctantly. The centurion could have died content, knowing that Flavius Laco had been the last man he had killed. But the army had been his home for so long he didn't know anything different. Some men fear a military life but others fear a civilian one. *Soldiering is the only thing I'm good for.* Oppius felt that his life was somehow the payment of a debt to someone or something he was unaware of. To Caesar? To duty? But how had duty repaid him? He'd won plenty of battles but lost too many friends.

Cephas Pollux walked with his head bowed down in thought. The ghosts of fallen comrades buzzed around him too, like flies. He could wave his hand and shoo them away but sooner or later they would come back, as if to feed on his own carcass. The soldier thought about comrades who were still alive as well and what he would do should he encounter them on the battlefield. *Kill or be killed… If I kill Antony will it be the end of the war as well as him?* As to his fellow officers, who had chosen to fight alongside Antony, he would not seek them out. Except for perhaps Felix Calvinus. *He is always quick to buy someone a drink so he can whisper poison into their ears or manipulate them. So they will turn a blind eye to his corruption and depravity. I could never prove it but I swear he used to embezzle funds from the legions to pay his gambling debts. Aye, I'll seek out Calvinus and kill him. Because the self-serving bastard would do the same to you…*

As much as Oppius and Pollux shared the same thoughts they would remain unvoiced, even after a jug or two of wine. Rome could be a lonely place even with its one million inhabitants.

The streets were largely, but not wholly, deserted. A woman could be heard scolding her drunk husband in the background. A stray dog howled and then yelped as a sot launched an old sandal at it. Four men approached the officers as they strolled through a yard which served as a fish market during the day. Oppius also heard the sound of three men walking behind them.

"Remember me?" Carbo Vedius asked, his guttural voice rough with cheap wine and contempt. A gloating smile was cut into his features, like an open wound. Finally the baleful sailor had found – and cornered – his quarry. One of the men whom Oppius had bested in the tavern along with Vedius had spotted the centurion through the door of *The Silver Trident*. Knowing how much his friend was keen to find the soldier he quickly ran to the quayside inn Vedius was drinking in that afternoon. The navvy roused as many men as possible, as quickly as possible, to get his revenge. For too many sleepless nights, since his painful encounter with the centurion, hatred and humiliation had been his bedfellows.

Oppius calmly took in the menacing group of men standing in front of and behind him. Thankfully his attacker wanted to savour his moment. Although the centurion wouldn't want to stand in a shield wall with the sailors Oppius could tell that they were all seasoned brawlers. Vedius stood in the middle, next to another man he recognised from their first encounter. Flanking them were a bald-headed veteran seaman who wore a long earring with a small anchor at its end. On the other side was a squat, compact brute with no discernible neck. He seemed to seethe rather than breathe, like a panting dog – or one which was about to attack. Oppius noticed the knife in his claw-like hand, its blade mottled with rust and blood. The centurion would have backed himself with four against two – Pollux would have fancied those odds too – but the three men behind them, carrying cudgels and knives, gave Oppius pause.

*It only takes one knife in the back.*

"I remember you – although you'd look even more familiar if laid out, whimpering on the floor," Oppius replied, unintimidated.

"You should be the one on the ground, on your knees – begging for your miserable life. I bet you didn't think that your last battlefield would be a stench-filled alcove in Rome. This yard though will now prove to be your graveyard."

Oppius heard a couple of the men behind him snigger. He could also smell wine on their breath. The wine would give them courage and enflame their anger but it also might dull their wits and reflexes.

"You seem as popular as ever Lucius," Pollux drily remarked. His knuckles cracked as he made a fist. His fingertips lightly brushed against the hilt of his sword on his other hand whilst he turned to half-face the trio of potential assailants behind Oppius.

"It could be worse. We could have bumped into my ex-wife," Oppius said.

"You can laugh. But your luck has finally run out."

"I thought that happened long ago, when I was introduced to my first wife. You were gambling with your money when I first met you. But now you're gambling with your life. Walk or, at best, limp away."

The smile fell from the centurion's features. Despite his apparent advantage it was the sailor who suddenly felt intimidated, though he dared not show it in front of his men. Vedius hoped that the soldiers were carrying full purses so he could honour his word and pay his drinking companions for their help.

Titus let out such a loud laugh that Teucer and Marcus Agrippa heard it from the rooftop they were perched on, which overlooked the yard. The training exercise was turning into something more real and interesting. Oppius had instructed Agrippa to shadow him for the day, as if he were a target or enemy agent. Teucer showed the young archer certain tricks of his trade, such as how to maintain line of sight and find the best vantage point to take his shot. The archers would now shoot more than just theoretical arrows however. Agrippa was keen to attack straightaway but Teucer said that they should wait for a signal, though the two men should nock their arrows just in case.

"Aim for the man in the middle, from the group standing behind them. I'll take out the one on the right. When the fighting starts aim for anyone attacking Pollux and I'll cover Oppius."

Agrippa nodded in reply. His mouth was dry. His heart was beating fast, not from the anxiety over taking a life but because he feared he might miss and one of his friends would die as a consequence. He wondered how much of the forthcoming episode he should share with Caecilia. *I want her to think me brave but not violent.*

Teucer received his signal from Vedius, rather than Oppius, as the sailor gave a telling nod to one of the cudgel-wielding men standing behind the centurions. As much as Vedius had thought about delivering the killing blow to the soldier – slipping his knife in between his ribs and twisting the blade as he looked him triumphantly in the eye – he had no wish to attack the dangerous combatant first.

Instead of Vedius hearing the dull thud of a cudgel striking his antagonist's skull the air was filled with a dog-like yelp and howl as an arrow pierced the base of the sailor's spine. Agrippa also felled his man as the missile punctured his lungs through his back. The soon-to-be corpse gasped rather than screamed. Oppius and Pollux moved with more speed and purpose than their opponents, knowing that Teucer and Agrippa were poised to attack. At the same time as drawing his gladius Pollux moved forward and kicked the man nearest to him in the groin. He then stabbed his enemy through the neck. He later joked to Teucer how his opponent didn't scream in agony because he had "kicked the bastard's balls so far upwards they got stuck in his throat".

Oppius drew his sword and in the same sweeping movement sliced off the fingers of the short but muscular sailor coming towards him with a rusty blade. The knife fell to the floor, as did its wielder as Oppius punched the point of his gladius into his navel. Blood and his intestines splashed onto the ground, mingling with the smell of garum and fish guts produced by the market earlier in the day. Oppius dropped his sword, however, as the bald-headed veteran soldier struck him on the forearm with a short club, studded with nails. The centurion let out a curse but rather than retreat or aim to retrieve his gladius he moved forwards and grabbed his attacker's long earring, yanking it downwards. The bottom of his ear landed on the floor, like a large gob of red phlegm. The side of the sailor's head and shoulder was quickly drenched in blood. He howled in pain. Agrippa put him out of his misery with an arrow through the chest. Teucer killed the man next to him, shooting him in the back as he looked to run away. His last thought was a desire to have his day over again and not walk past the tavern and report on seeing the centurion.

Terror and prudence fired Carbo Vedius' retreat. He could not bring his friends back from the dead. Confusion reigned too. His intention had been to ambush his enemy rather than be ambushed himself. Questions would be asked if he went back to the tavern without his shipmates. More questions would be asked when they discovered that his friends had been murdered. A ship was not the best place for a distrusted or despised man.

17.

*The Temple of Concord.*

The breeze blew away what few clouds hung over Rome as if the gods had commanded the four winds to provide a clear view of the Senate. Attendance was higher than usual, partly thanks to the clement weather. Cicero, not usually one to pray, had offered up a smattering of a prayer the night before so that it wouldn't rain.

"More than bribes, election rigging or false accounting of votes the climate has influenced voting and legislature over the years," the veteran statesman had commented to Tiro that morning. "Rain can put such a dampener on democracy."

In order to generate as great an audience as possible for his return to the Senate Cicero and Tiro had also informed certain senators and gossips that he would be giving a daring, historic, speech.

Tiro had laid out a freshly-laundered toga that morning. He had also arranged for Rome's finest barber to trim what little hair his master had left and shave him. He was back where he belonged. *Centre stage.* His name was on people's lips again. The statesman felt more emboldened than anxious that morning as the two men ironed out the final creases in the speech.

"I know I can save the Republic, Tiro, because I have saved it before."

Cicero sat on the stone steps which circled the temple as it began to fill up with senators. He soaked up the atmosphere and appreciated the irony – smiling to himself. *I'm about to declare war in the Temple of Concord… It was also here, all those years ago, when you ordered the state to take up arms against Catiline.*

The aged statesman surveyed his audience, judging who would be for him, who against him and how many he could win over. Many senators had their slaves provide cushions for them when sitting on the cold, hard steps. Few had been part of the Senate all those years ago, when he had denounced Catiline. *You've survived them all: Pompey, Lucullus, Caesar, Crassus, Cato. Your ideals have also survived them. Let us hope that those ideals can survive you.*

Cicero sighed inwardly, however, as he took in some of his fellow statesmen.

*There's Marcellus Faunos. If only his reputation was as spotless as his gold braided tunic… Domitius Gallus has also deigned to show his red-nosed face. His wine merchant must be out of the capital today… And there's our youngest member, Eprius Minatus. Has your brother forgiven you yet for buying votes from the gilds and rigging the election in your favour, consigning him to be an even greater non-entity in history than yourself? Are you still affecting a more plebeian accent in order to align yourself with the people?… And let the gods be praised it's Mucios Sardus, with his chin resting on his hand, projecting an air of thoughtfulness. I wonder, are you thinking about your latest mistress or which lobbyist has paid you the most this month to propose certain legislation? And the Senate wouldn't be the Senate without the Metellii sitting in a row. Even though you're occupying the lower tier you're still managing to look down on everyone… And I mustn't forget you, Rufus Drusus, mumbling beneath your breath – rehearsing a witticism which you'll do your best with to make it seem like it's a spontaneous comment… Ah, and Antonius Blandus has just arrived. Tiro said that you have recently gained a business partner in Tarius Curio, the sword manufacturer. I wonder whether it'll be this month that you propose we award a government contract to your new company. Or you may show some decorum and integrity and bring the subject up next month… Alfenus Petro. I'm about as pleased to see you as a leper, as you are me I imagine. Though you must surely be looking forward to voting against me. Will you be disagreeing with me out of personal animosity or just habit today?… And in the absence of Antony we have the second most respected scoundrel in the Senate, Dolabella. My rapacious, corrupted, corrupting, philandering former son-in-law. I know how disapproving you are of your disapproving father-in-law. But how much are you truly a friend to your co-consul? He purchased your loyalty through paying off your debts but because of that shame and humiliation you may quietly be cheering me on today. Antony will not blame you for what comes out of my mouth … I have a mountain to climb converting such folly into virtue. My hammer may break in work-hardening such mettle, or a lack of. But the greater the difficulty, the greater the glory…*

Dolabella, after various formal announcements, was neutral in his tone as he introduced the venerable proconsul. Cicero stood and paused – waiting for quiet. *Silence is one of the great arts of conversation.* He asked for a cup of water. He puffed out what little chest he had and felt twenty years younger. Purposeful. He scanned around the temple, appearing to look everyone in the eye. Undaunted. Unbowed.

*Liberty or death.*

"I come not to praise Antony but to bury him. And he will be buried in a grave of his own making. And into his grave I intend to dispose of his tyranny and grand larceny. Fear can silence me – us – no longer. Our former Master of the Horse has befouled rather than cleaned the Augean stables. I here declare that Mark Antony is a despot – an enemy of the state. He must be challenged and defeated, else *we* will soon be challenged and defeated. The Senate and Antony cannot co-exist. It must be one or the other. He has more respect for his entourage of whores, clowns and drunkards than he does this august body of men. He poses a greater threat to Rome than Sulla or Caesar ever did. Should Antony vanquish the forces of Decimus Brutus then he will use his army of the north to garrison and enslave the capital. Even our noblest families will not be free from his ire and avarice. I offer up a simple syllogism. The Clodii and Metelli represent our finest traditions and virtues. Antony has no respect for tradition and virtue. Therefore Antony will have no respect for the Clodii and Metelli. You may well argue with me but you cannot argue with logic. Antony will only remember and admire your names when it comes to him drafting his proscription lists, as he remembers and admires your villas and farmlands."

Cicero deliberately paused and let his grim words hang in the air. *If they will not be moved by duty then let them be moved by fear – a survival instinct.*

"As the Senate once reverberated with the words of Cato the Elder – 'Carthage must be destroyed' – so too must we now exclaim, 'Antony must be destroyed'. For in his actions, if not words, has Antony not pronounced a death sentence on us? Some will argue that the price of war is too high but I say that the prices of despotism, subjugation and poverty are too high. Antony once sent a group of his slaves to my house to vandalise my property and humiliate me because I had dared to criticise him. I would you now send out an army to humiliate him.

"But 'ah, Cicero,' you might declaim, 'are your words and actions not borne from a personal grievance? Should we go to war over someone slandering you?' But – and some of you might disbelieve your ears when I say this – you should ignore me. I do not matter. Antony has dishonoured this institution far more than he has slighted me. The public grievance far outweighs any personal one I might feel. The sot and villain has made a mockery of our sacred constitution and due process. He makes up laws like one of his actress-mistresses would make-up a line when forgetting the words to a play. If one of his friends has gambling debts then he proclaims all debts to be null and void. The idea of the rule of law will soon be considered a myth.

"Antony expropriates land for himself from greed or, worse, seemingly on a whim. He moved into Pompey the Great's villa like a squatter. In this once great man's house there are now brothels in place of bedrooms, cheap eateries in place of dining rooms. In the past few months he has been more a minter of coins than consul. Someone should inform him that there is a wide gap between gain and glory, however. I hear that his accountants no longer count his money but merely weigh it. Money has ever been despised by great men. Antony seems to gorge on it. Was ever Charybdis so ravenous? Power and wine have gone to his head. Our consul possesses henchmen rather than attendants, the wickedest of all is his wife. As we have seen from her behaviour at Brundisium the dog's bite is worse than her bark. Antony's philosophy appears to be that of a villain in a play, 'Let them hate me so long as they fear me'. Should the uncultured, uncouth dolt be bothered not to fall asleep when attending the theatre he would realise that such villains get their comeuppance and meet nasty – but justified – ends."

Cicero inserted another strategic pause. Over the rim of his cup of water he was pleased to see senators nodding their heads in agreement with him. They were becoming more animated – and angry. Someone was finally giving voice to Antony's crimes.

"Recently though Antony has given speeches and instigated insidious and cowardly whispering campaigns against myself – positing that I am a villain who should meet a nasty end. He accuses me of being an enemy of the state?! Perhaps he is a figure from comedy rather than tragedy after all! He accuses me of instigating the civil war, pouring poison into Pompey's ear to break with Caesar. I cannot allow such poison from Antony to infect the truth. When I sensed that a malign war was threatening our native land I never ceased to advocate peace. You all know what I said to my late friend: 'Gnaeus Pompey, if only you had never gone into partnership with Julius Caesar – or never dissolved it! The first course would have befitted you as a man of principle, the second as a man of prudence.'

"Our deluded consul has also recently implied that I was somehow behind the plot to murder Caesar, despite a lack of evidence and witnesses to substantiate such a ludicrous claim. Such is my dedication to fairness and truth that I will not pettily give credence to the rumours that you yourself were involved in the conspiracy. Perhaps people are implicating you because, when trying to find the culprit of a crime, an advocate would ask, 'Who benefits?' And have not you benefitted the most since your friend's death, grasping power and using Caesar's estate to pay off your debts? But I will exonerate you. No one would ever believe that you could be party to such a noble action of freeing Rome from a tyrant. Service to the Republic isn't quite your style. I posit that you secretly celebrated Caesar's death but that you were not one of the authors of it. Yet I cannot exonerate you from the charge of instigating the civil war. It was you, who in stirring up trouble as a tribune, gave Caesar his pretext for crossing the Rubicon. You were supposed to be an envoy of peace but, either through wickedness or ineptitude, you unsheathed the civil war. You were the cause of the Senate having to desert Rome. The blood of Roman citizens and soldiers is on your hands. We still mourn our losses from that disastrous conflict which sometimes pitted brother against brother. Lives were lost. Antony took them. The authority of this institution was shattered. Antony shattered it. Indeed all the calamities we have seen since the start of the civil war – and what calamity have we not witnessed? – we can ascribe to one man, Mark Antony. As Helen was to the Trojans, so this wretched man is to the Republic – the cause of its ruin."

As if on cue a few close supporters of Cicero cheered their mentor on and damned Antony. The mood was becoming more heated. In the space of a few moments a senator could laugh at a witticism but then grow indignant at Antony's transgressions.

"The enemy will soon near the gates of Mutina. If he is not stopped he will then stand at the gates of Rome. We may be waiting for the First of January for Hirtius and Pansa's tenure in office to validate our course of action but this date holds no significance to Antony. The noble Decimus Brutus has decided to stand up to the tyrant. He vows to keep his province in the hands of the Senate and the people of Rome. Brutus is a true servant of the Republic, conscious of his namesake, following in the footsteps of his celebrated ancestor who vanquished Tarquin the Proud. He has given us the lead. Let us follow him in order that we can continue to lead ourselves. He cannot and should not stand alone. I have vowed to protect the Republic too. I defended it when I was young and now I am old I will not abandon it. We must all be libertores now. Will men put up with you, Antony, when they did not put up with Caesar? In your lust for despotic power I can compare you with him but in all other respects there is no comparison. You are not fit to either wear or wash his toga. Antony must not be allowed to return to the capital unfettered. What some appeasers might call peace with honour I call servitude. Do you want the Senate enslaved to a drunk and letch?"

*

Brutus' sandals slapped against the flagstones on the veranda and distracted Horace from his quietude and enjoyment of the view. The valley was marbled with rock and littered with thorny shrubs and skeletal trees but there was still an air of warmth and beauty to the scene, the would-be poet fancied. Horace had never known his commander to pace about so much or project a mood of fretfulness. He likened him to a husband outside his wife's chamber, expecting the delivery of their first child. Brutus was ruminating on the delivery of Cicero's speech in the Senate. Today was the day. Brutus was not just invested in his friend's key address because he had a hand in naming the series of speeches Cicero was intending to give (it had been Brutus who had named them the Philippics, after Demosthenes' attacks on Philip of Macedon). Cicero's speech could well decide the fate of Rome and whether the Republic defied or submitted to Antony's monarchical reign.

*Remember your own advice to me about oratory, all those years ago. "Rhetoric is one great art composed of five divisions: invention, arrangement, style, memory and delivery." Do not just go for the cheap laugh. There's too much at stake. Do not make it all about yourself either.*

His noble brow was furrowed, his beard was streaked with grey. Horace noticed that a jug of wine was seldom further than an arm's length from his general at night, yet to his credit Brutus was never drunk in front of his soldiers. He was seldom sober in front of his wife, however. Brutus glanced at the sundial again, judging that Cicero would still be addressing the Senate back in Rome. He wished he could be back there too.

"How do you think Cicero's speech will be received?" Brutus had shown the young officer a letter from Cicero, outlining his line of attack.

"Caesar filled the Senate with lots of new blood before his demise. They will not have loyalty to Antony, nor he them I imagine. Antony has made little attempt to court the patrician families of Rome either, who still possess a bedrock of wealth and influence. But Antony may be wiser than we think. He has concentrated on building an army rather than building factional support in the capital. Who needs a hundred senators on your side when you have ten thousand soldiers? Curule chairs are won by money and swords," Horace argued.

*But who knows what will happen? Time will bring to light whatever is hidden and will cover up and conceal whatever is now shining in splendour.*

Brutus was about to disagree and laud the ideals of the Republic – and cite the golden age of Athenian democracy – but he remembered that he would only be able to return to Rome and win back his honour with an army at his back. Horace continued: "But if we consider that the Senate has now been cornered by Antony – cornered animals will often fight back. Cicero may shame or frighten the Senate into action."

Brutus remained inexpressive. The Senate and people of Rome had disappointed him too much for him to put his faith in them. Should Cicero succeed though it would mean that generals, as opposed to politicians, would decide the fate of Rome. Decimus needed to hold out for reinforcements. Antony could defeat his enemies' armies separately but not as a whole.

An attendant disturbed both men's thoughts as he came out into the garden and handed his master a message. At first Horace thought it was a letter from Cassius. Brutus was in regular correspondence with his co-conspirator and, although their characters and motives might be diametrically opposed, their fates were inexplicably linked to one another. It appeared that it was good news as a hint of a smile fractured his general's stoical features.

"It seems that we will soon be having a visitor Quintus. An old friend, Matius Varro, will be coming to the province. I will invite him to stay with us. Like yourself he is an officer that prefers the library to the parade ground."

Brutus was about to add that Matius was one of the few soldiers Porcia enjoyed the company of, but he thought better of it. Not only might it highlight that she did not enjoy the company of Horace but the general was in no mood to talk about his wife or even mention her name.

\*

Cicero allowed an increasing number of pauses during his speech, for fellow senators to applaud and agree with his arguments. They also cursed their unrighteous consul and offered up further examples of his heinous crimes against themselves personally or the state. Cicero did not yield the floor too much though. The rest of the Senate were his chorus. He remained the conductor. Feeling that he had done enough to damn Antony as a public enemy the statesman turned his attention to casting Octavius in the role of a potential saviour.

"But there is another noble Roman who feels the same as I do – who would lay down his life for the Republic. Octavius Caesar has, in effect, already saved Rome once. While his forces were posted close by to us Antony was unable to attack and occupy the city, as I believe he still intends to. Octavius desires to enter public life in order to strengthen it instead of, like Antony, usurp it. I have spoken with Octavius on numerous occasions. He is well read – and not just because his shelves are filled with volumes of books by yours truly! At the centre of his garden stands, pride of place, a statue of Cincinnatus. Many of you have met Octavius. Is there a greater example of a traditional, conservative, morality in our younger generation? Antony may try to scorn him as being low-born but his natural father would have been elected consul had he lived. Octavius only wishes to enter the course of honours early whilst Antony wishes to do away with the authority of the Senate and course of honours altogether. We should allow this noble young man to have his wish; it is nothing compared to everything that is at stake. Octavius wants to bend the law, compared to Antony who habitually breaks it. We must give a formal command to the young Caesar. The people and soldiers will rally to his standard yet Octavius will serve under our command and, like Cincinnatus, become a citizen once more when he is no longer needed as a general. Any personal vendetta he harbours will be put aside for the good of Rome. He values the Republic, respects nothing more than the authority of the Senate and desires the fall of Antony over his own elevation.

"I give you my guarantee, my vow, my pledge, that Octavius will always be the man that he is today. Oh what is there in Antony save lust, wickedness, crapulence and ambition! He has plundered our treasury and private lands, taxed us into poverty. He turned Caesar's funeral into a riot, created legislation for personal gain or to punish his enemies. At Brundisium he slaughtered centurions and legionaries, heroes of the Republic. And now, along with his equally despicable brother Lucius, he leads his army north towards Mutina. Reports are already coming in that he is emptying barns and slaughtering cattle as he burns his way through our countryside. Soldiers feast while citizens starve. Fathers and sons are being conscripted into his army. Mothers and daughters are being taken too – may the gods protect them. Despite his vices and treason there may be some among you tempted to send envoys of peace to our second Catiline. The name of peace is sweet, the reality even sweeter; but there is a world of difference between peace and subjugation. Antony desires the latter. Although I can understand such a will to try to find a diplomatic solution it will ultimately prove to be a waste of time – and perhaps a waste of life in regards to those who are sent. Do you believe Antony is marching north with his army because he enjoys the mountain air or the aesthetics of the scenery? Sending envoys will be tantamount to sending two blind men to put out a forest fire or sending a surgeon to revive a corpse. Antony is intent on war. He is intent on our destruction.

"Yet where there is life there is hope. As Octavius' army defends Rome Decimus Brutus defends Gaul. To the military might already at our disposal we will soon be able to add armies commanded by Hirtius and Pansa. Both consuls are familiar with the heat of battle and fruits of victory. They will lead – and Octavius will follow them. The time is ripe. With one voice we must declare Antony an enemy of the state. The people stand with us too. You have seen the crowds in the Forum, crying out for a return of liberty and prosperity. They know what we in our hearts know. Nothing is more abominable than shame, nothing is uglier than servitude. Romans are born for honour and freedom; let us either retain those birth rights or die with dignity. Let us defeat tyranny and Antony together, for they are one and the same."

The cheers for Cicero reached a crescendo and sang out into the air surrounding the temple. Jeers too sounded out, for their despotic consul. Old men rose to their feet (or some merely stamped them) and applauded the great orator who had given voice to opinions whispered in dark corners, among trusted friends. Even Alfenus Petro applauded the man he had labelled "a relic" that morning. The statesman's words had started a fire upon which many wanted to sacrifice Mark Antony. Those who were not persuaded by Cicero's rhetoric and passion nevertheless appreciated his appeals to logic and necessity. Antony needed to be deposed else they would be. To achieve their aim they would need Octavius' legions.

There was a fire burning inside Cicero too. His heart thumped with pride and triumph. He felt thirty years younger, free from ailment or fear. History would record that he saved the Republic, twice – he gloried. Three generations of Romans rallied around him and clapped the proconsul on the shoulder, lauding his words and virtues. He had even converted some politicians he had judged as being beyond redemption. Cicero reacted with due modesty and quiet dignity to all, however. More than any compliment, or suggestion of a reward to be conferred upon him, Cicero took to heart the brief smile and nod of approval Tiro offered him after his speech.

The vermillion sun shone, illuminating and warming the great temple, as if also approving of the historic moment, Cicero thought. He wondered what Octavius would think of his speech. Cicero had advised Balbus to forewarn the boy that he would occasionally be critical of Julius. Cicero explained to Balbus that he did not want to seem too much on the Caesarian party's side, in the eyes of the Senate. In truth he had meant every word of his condemnation of the dictator. History would be his judge, not Octavius.

The die was cast.

18.

The hour was late. It had been a long day for the recently installed propraetor. Octavius had woken to Lucius Oppius standing outside his door. The no-nonsense centurion had worked him hard that morning, helping to strengthen and condition his body for the campaign ahead. He couldn't be seen to be frail. Oppius also gave the young Caesar refresher lessons in swordsmanship. Although Octavius would never be a great soldier he still needed to be proficient in defending himself, both on foot and on horseback. During the afternoon Octavius had a meeting with several senior senators as well as Hirtius and Pansa. They informed him that Dolabella had left the city during the previous night. Cicero remarked that he was as much "fearing the expropriation of his stolen wealth as he was losing his tawdry life". They also spoke about the imminent conflict. Afterwards Octavius visited his mother and Marcus Phillipus. For the rest of the afternoon he had locked himself away to catch up on various correspondence. Work even took precedence over seeing his latest mistress, Valeria. His ardour was cooling for her regardless. "She talks too much – about herself. I'm not sure which she complains about the most, her aged husband or the cost of Chinese silk for her dresses. Thankfully she has duties to perform in bed which prevent her from talking too much. I dare say Valeria has been the cause of her husband's decline and ageing though. She's slowly boring him to death," Octavius half-jokingly reported to his friends.

Octavius sat by the fire with Agrippa. They had, along with Oppius and Balbus, just finished having a light supper. The centurion and political agent had retired to go home. It was a custom of the two young friends to talk late into the night, for at least one evening a week, to catch up on events and share their thoughts. Octavius noticed how Agrippa had shaved off his burgeoning beard. Had he done so out of sympathy for him? Octavius had tried and failed to grow a beard. He had hoped that it would make him look older and more distinguished. Agrippa had shaved off his beard however because Caecilia had said she preferred him without one. It scratched her face when she kissed him.

"They do not trust me, which is apt because I do not trust them," Octavius remarked, in reference to his meeting that afternoon. "The supposed good and the great of Rome spoke to me as if I were an unwelcome smell today. They hinted as much as they could, without being direct, that I was too young and low-born to have earned my new-found position. Ateius Metellus paused and sneered when he said that, 'This is not Velitrae, but Rome'. Although I am the one coming to their aid they acted like I was the one who should be eternally grateful. I bit my tongue so much during the lecture that I thought it was lunchtime. I suffered the glorified bunch of thugs and they suffered me. They have the airs of princes but morals of snakes. Cicero was present and did his best to grease the wheels but the atmosphere was strained. Cicero apologised for the behaviour of some afterwards but I dare say he then went back into the chamber and argued that they had nothing to apologise for. Hirtius and Pansa seemed genuinely gracious though. They skirted over my lack of experience and talked to me as an equal. They both spoke fondly of Julius and we even discussed literature and history – although Hirtius spoke more about the history of certain types of food... But I showed due deference to all. Balbus is right. If I appear to submit to their authority then they may grant me more freedom, believing that they'll be able to rein me in at any moment. I will even allow Hirtius to take temporary command of one of my legions when we march north. I will be sure to remain its paymaster however."

Agrippa nodded his head in agreement but was more distracted by his thoughts concerning his own encounter that day with Caecilia. They had lunched together, as usual. They went to their "love nest" as they called it. Their love making lacked their usual passion and consideration though. Both had been thinking about what was being left unsaid.

Finally, after getting dressed, Caecilia had broached the subject of Agrippa leaving to go to war.

"I have to say it. I owe it to me and to you, Marcus. I do not want you to leave. I would rather you were an architect than soldier," she had said. Her hands had begun to shake a little as she fastened her silver pin into her hair.

"Can't I be both? You fell in love with both. Octavius needs me," Agrippa had replied, trying to be reasonable.

"I need you too. We could leave, together, today. Run away. I have money. I could get more from my father." Her voice faltered with emotion. She was upset with Agrippa for leaving her but also because he appeared to be so reasonable and calm. Love should defy reason.

"I want to change the world – not run away from it."

"The world will change as it sees fit to do without us. But *our* worlds will change if you go. I can't sleep, I can't eat properly, thinking that I might never see you again."

"We will see each other again, I give you my word."

"But how can you make that promise?"

"Because I'm a better soldier than I am an architect. And you've given me something to live for."

Caecilia returned not his conciliatory smile.

"Even if Octavius comes back, having been victorious, he will lose in the end. He has too many enemies. Even Cicero remarked to my father in a letter the other day that Octavius should be praised, used and then disposed of. It's folly, rather than heroic, to fight for a lost cause."

From the beginning they had promised each other that the world of Roman politics would not intrude upon their relationship. They would be on the same side even if Octavius and her father were not. Caecilia had broken that promise and something had shattered as a result. Both wished that she could take back what had just been said.

The smile had fallen from Agrippa's face as though a little piece of him had died. Dejection had stabbed at his heart as he realised she did not believe in him and his cause. He also knew he would have to keep what Caecilia had said from Octavius in case his friend enquired where the intelligence had come from. Octavius would then ask him to forsake her or, worse, use her to extract more information about their enemies. Yet at the same time Agrippa needed to warn Octavius of Cicero and the Senate's intentions – although he told himself that things could wait. Octavius was already aware that he could, or would, be betrayed by the Senate. He didn't want to burden his already overburdened friend.

Caecilia had seen that she had hurt him but didn't apologise. Her pretty features, flushed with anger, had grown pale with sorrow. Yet her pride still overruled her love.

But love had overruled Agrippa's pride. He didn't want to argue. He wanted to remain hopeful – for both of them.

"The war may be over with one decisive battle. Once we can mobilise all our forces we will outnumber Antony."

"You cannot believe that. Even if you defeat Antony then the armies of the Republic will turn on you. And if, somehow, Octavius survives that encounter then Brutus and Cassius' armies will return to give battle. I just do not want to see you shackled to Octavius when he eventually falls. Stay here, with me. If Octavius truly respects you as much as he says then he will respect your decision to choose a different path. You should not think that the name of Caesar is synonymous with glory. Consider the beaches of Britannia, the forests of Gaul, the plains of Pharsalus and his own death. The name of Caesar is synonymous with blood," Caecilia had argued, quoting her father, trying to scare or shame Agrippa into staying. "Why do you have to go?"

"Because I'm a soldier," Agrippa replied – quoting Lucius Oppius, when he overheard someone ask him the same question. Agrippa had answered with a sense of duty in his voice but he recalled how Oppius had spoken with remorse or resignation. For months, since meeting the centurion, the young soldier had wanted to be like him – but not at that moment. The grief on Oppius' face as he spoke had given Agrippa pause.

A silence had swollen up between them. Caecilia had been ready to leave – but couldn't. She wanted to say a thousand things – both words that she had rehearsed in her head and ones that would come at the spur of the moment. In her nightmares and waking dreams she pictured him falling in battle. Tears moistened her eyes as if she were already mourning him.

Agrippa had gazed out of the window. He could see the grand, gleaming properties in the plutocratic district of the *Keels*, named after certain extravagant houses there designed in the shape of a keel.

*She comes from that world. A different world. From old money. She comes from those same patrician families who scorn and wish to destroy Octavius. Who wish to undo Julius Caesar's land reforms and the opportunities he provided for the poor to better themselves. They want to return to a Rome found in the history books. But it's a fiction. She may be from the past but I want her to be part of my future.*

Agrippa didn't doubt that Caecilia loved him but he did doubt that her father would ever consent to his daughter marrying him.

*Unless, shackled to Octavius, my star can burn bright enough.*

They had each made a promise to write to one other every day. They kissed each other, one last time. They embraced, one last time. The room had immediately felt colder and emptier when she left, Agrippa thought to himself. He had noticed that the plants she had bought, when he had originally rented the apartment, were dying. Love nests sometimes only last a season.

The flames continued to flick upwards in the fireplace. Octavius continued to talk and Agrippa continued to vaguely listen.

"I said my goodbyes to my mother and Marcus Phillipus this afternoon. More tears burst forth from her eyes than water gushed from the statue-fountain of Salacia in the garden."

"Have you said goodbye to Octavia also?"

Octavius paused before answering, transfixed by the dancing flames. "I will write to her."

Octavia understood her brother's need to go to war but that did not mean she approved of it. Octavius furrowed his brow as he briefly thought of her husband. He had just discovered that Marcellus was having an affair and, despite his own infidelities with married women, felt no contradiction in condemning his brother-in-law's behaviour. The propraetor would arrange for them to divorce when he returned to Rome. As much as Octavius believed that his sister was too good for most men he wanted to marry Octavia off in order to cement a political alliance. He needed supporters amongst the populares and optimates alike. Lepidus was a candidate. Despite or because of Rome's great families looking down on him he needed to form alliances with them too. Though the Clodii and Metellii claimed to be principled – and would only breed with certain bloodlines – they were pragmatic too. If Octavius proved victorious in the north one of the families could decide to form an alliance with him. Octavius needed to increase his powerbase. Like Caesar he had no desire to disband the Senate but ultimately it needed to be directed and overruled occasionally.

"Sometimes saying goodbye in person can be too awkward or painful," Octavius added.

Agrippa nodded and stared philosophically into the fire.

19.

*Dear Atticus,*

*As you may have heard I have continued to deliver my Philippics. Some of my more dove-like colleagues have complained about my scathing tone but I would argue that I have not been scathing enough where Antony is concerned. I caught wind of a rumour that, after hearing about my speeches, he put me on a proscription list featuring just my own name. Antony thinks he can take everything from me – little realising that at my age I have nothing to lose. He will be sorely disappointed that I have converted my wine cellar into a library for Tiro and there are no suitable outfits in my closet that he can pass onto his harem. I've little doubt that the wretch will take pleasure in burning my books though, in order for one of his bestial orgies to run on longer into the night.*

*Unfortunately, despite my vigorous efforts, Antony still has supporters in the Senate. Someone raised a proposal yesterday. Instead of declaring that we were in a state of war he wanted us to say that we were merely experiencing "a public emergency". This is what happens when we allow advocates to become politicians. Statecraft becomes a matter of semantics.*

*Pansa has just marched north with his recently levied army. With both of Rome's consuls now absent it has been suggested that I be declared a temporary dictator. I have refused the honour – although if anyone else wishes to fill the dreaded role I will challenge them and accept the position. My aim in politics, as you know, has always been to strengthen the constitution rather than strengthen my own personal political power. My crowning glory is to make sure no one wears a crown. And that includes Octavius. He is devoted to me and has even taken to calling me "father" in his letters. I have indulged and obliged him by sometimes calling him "Caesar" in return. I hope that the boy will not feel too betrayed if I have to betray him.*

*More than a chink of light begins to shine over Rome – and that light comes from Macedonia. Brutus has ousted Antony's other deplorable brother – Gaius – from the province. Brutus has won battles on the ground and in hearts and minds. He has defeated soldiers and won them over to our cause at the same time. The tide is definitely turning.*

*Cassius too has plunged another dagger into the heart of tyranny. Antony's partner in crime, Dolabella, mustered an army and travelled to Smyrna. Under the banner of friendship he entered the city but then promptly tortured and murdered its governor, Gaius Trebonius. Cassius was in the area however and not without men and a cause. He hunted the dog down. I was glad when I no longer called Dolabella my son-in-law. I am even gladder to pronounce him dead. Despite Cassius' noble act however the Senate has been slow, cowardly or inept in not awarding him greater powers and resources. They have blocked my proposal to grant Cassius an official command in Asia. Suffice to say I have written to our friend to encourage him to take command unofficially. Brutus may be the better statesman but Cassius is the better general. They complement each other. Hirtius and Pansa are merely keeping the seats of the curule chairs warm for them.*

*In short, Antony no longer has forces to call upon in Macedonia and Syria. The noose is slowly tightening around his neck. Let us leave space however for his shrewish wife's head. Fulvia either applauds his crimes or instigates them. Some women should be seen and not heard. But she should be neither seen nor heard.*

*In terms of a woman I am pleased to see and hear more from, Caecilia has been spending an increasing amount of time at the house. Perhaps she has grown tired of Rome and shopping. She certainly seems distracted or listless. I asked her if she would prefer to go back to my country villa – or to venture home to you – but she answered that she would like to stay in the capital. She has taken a surprisingly strange interest in events in the north – asking me for daily updates about the military and political situation. There is little change day to day but winter is turning into spring and as soon as the final snows melt in the north blood will seep into the ground. Decimus continues to defy Antony at Mutina. Antony has surrounded the town but Decimus' resolve and his defences remain strong. Shortly before Antony's army arrived Decimus slaughtered his baggage animals and salted the meat, in preparation for the siege. Antony will not be able to starve him out. Perhaps we should have taken note of Decimus more when he carped on about how he should have been given more credit for Caesar's victories. Despite his heroism however he will be glad of reinforcements and sharing in the glory of defeating our pernicious enemy. The veteran legions, commanded by Hirtius and Octavius, should be within striking distance soon. Once Pansa's army arrives they will be able to surround Antony and the besieger will become the besieged... I do so hope that Antony decides to fight to the death.*

*Cicero.*

20.

Dusk glowed, brazier-like, on the horizon. Wisps of cloud encircled the jagged mountaintops in the distance. The heat of battle, or rather a skirmish, filled the air. Oppius stood in the rear line in order to assess the progression of the attack. Also no one in the front line would dare try to retreat past him. Other skirmishes had broken out over recent days between the two armies, camped close to one another. Some had been due to accidental manoeuvres or over-zealous junior commanders attempting to prove their mettle. Some were planned offensives in order to probe the enemy and gain intelligence about the strength and morale of the opposition.

The fighting was more chaotic than coordinated as the two cohorts clashed within a forest, which bordered a river. On the far side of the river stood the fortified town of Mutina. The woods had been eerily quiet an hour ago, save for the plaintive sound of birdsong and the wind blowing through the vernal trees. Blood now began to splatter against bark, ferns and the mulched-up ground. The unnatural roars and high-pitched screams were depressingly familiar to the veteran centurion. A faint smell of sulphur filled his nostrils from the gaseous nearby marshes. Oppius had his sword and shield at the ready and gave nods of encouragement to the young legionaries around him. Armour glinted through trees in the fading light. Too many of the new recruits would wear as much armour as they could, thinking that it would make them invulnerable, Oppius thought. But every armour has its weak point. Every army has its weak point too. Many thought that his own side's weak point would be Octavius, who would act rashly or naively – sending soldiers to their death in the name of glory. But the young Caesar seldom suffered a rush of blood. Oppius was impressed by the way he listened, deferred to the more experienced Hirtius and (prompted by himself and Agrippa) was concerned with logistics and his legions being equipped and provisioned correctly.

The screams grew louder as did the clanging of arms. The advance line had orders to fall back if they met too much resistance. The fresh, rear line could then counter-attack. Due to the terrain there was little method to the enemy's advance and similarly there was little method to the cohort's retreat. Yet over the sound of everything else Oppius could still hear the reassuring voices of Pollux and Milo issuing commands and holding the line.

*The retreat shouldn't turn into a rout.*

*

Enobarbus had been out on a routine inspection of sentries and the camp's defences when the enemy had attacked. He gave orders for the focal point of the offensive to be reinforced by legionaries further up the river bank. They would neither be broken here nor break through to the enemy. Enobarbus observed the fighting from a watchtower in the vicinity. Night was drawing in. Neither side would want to fight in the darkness nor commit too many men to the pointless clash, Enobarbus thought to himself. Neither side wanted a war of attrition. He was pleased, however, that the legion, filled with new recruits and veterans alike, was pushing the enemy back. He would instruct the quartermaster to give the combatants an extra ration of wine for the night.

*

Pollux' arms ached. His voice was hoarse. His bearded face was smeared with grime and gore. His men were starting to be overrun. He suddenly punched his shield forward, knocking his hare-lipped opponent back into a tree. At the same time he stabbed his gladius forward, piercing the leather breastplate of another enemy. The centurion quickly withdrew his blade and turned around, attempting to parry a spear thrust from a feral looking legionary. But the spearhead wasn't deflected totally and it sliced through his thigh. Blood gushed from the artery and Pollux fell to one knee. By now the enemy that had been knocked into the tree had recovered. He too, his sword at the ready, stood over the formidable – but wounded – centurion. The prospective victors grinned, savouring the moment. They were hyenas, bringing down a lion. Pollux pursed his lips in resignation. Both men were about to deliver killing blows. He could try to parry one but he could not avoid both. The centurion didn't think that he would die in such a way but every soldier who dies on the battlefield probably thinks that.

A shield flew through the air and crashed into the feral-looking infantryman's chest. Oppius slashed his sword downwards, cutting open the hare-lipped legionary's neck and chest.

The tide of Antony's forces crashed against the advancing second line of Oppius' cohort and was buffeted back. Fresh screams and battle cries curdled the air. There was a stand-off, however, among some combatants as they stood, weapons drawn, refraining from engaging with their enemy. Some were too fatigued or too cowardly to fight. Some remembered their conversations over campfires that "Romans shouldn't fight Romans" and that Caesar's veterans shouldn't fight each other either.

Oppius gave the order and had his junior offices pass it along the line that they should retrieve any wounded and form an orderly withdrawal. Enobarbus passed on an order that the second line should be ready to beat back any enemy advance but that it was not to move forward itself. Enough blood had been spilled – wasted.

*

Night descended. Agrippa and Teucer stealthily crept through the forest, wearing dark brown tunics. Their faces were blackened. The line of enemy sentries downstream had thinned as reinforcements had been called in to deal with Oppius' attack. Six men had now become two standing on the riverbank next to a beacon, which was due to be lit if any enemies were spotted.

The heavy rain in the morning had softened the ground, muffling their footsteps. The archers reached the treeline. Their mission was to eliminate the sentries and swim across to the town in order to deliver a message to Decimus Brutus. Hirtius had lit his own fires in the camp over the past week to indicate to Brutus that reinforcements had arrived but neither army could be sure if it was aware of one another. Oppius had come up with the plan of creating a diversion and having the messengers swim across the river. Teucer volunteered for the mission. Decimus would recognise and trust the archer – and Octavius offered him a healthy bonus. After hearing the Briton had signed up Agrippa decided to join his friend on the near suicide mission. "I'm your second best archer and one of the strongest swimmers in the legion," Agrippa had argued, after Octavius had tried to dissuade his friend from taking part.

As Teucer whispered instructions as to which sentry Agrippa should target the young officer began to doubt whether he should have volunteered for the dangerous mission. He could be killed whilst trying to take out the sentries. The current could be too strong and he could drown in his attempt to swim across the river. Decimus' men might mistake him for a spy or enemy combatant and fire upon him. And should he succeed in delivering his message to the general then he could well perish during the swim back.

Teucer, observing the doubt and anxiety in his friend's face, offered some words of encouragement.

"Don't worry lad, we'll be alright. I'm not fated to die tonight. I intend to die an old man, in bed, lying next to my wife – or better still a mistress half my age."

Arrows thudded into the sternums of the sentries. The two nimble archers quickly rushed out from the treeline and, using their small, freshly sharpened daggers, slit the throats of their enemy. Agrippa briefly wondered if either of the two dead men had a wife or intended waiting for them back home. After his debriefing about his mission Agrippa had written a letter, which he gave to Oppius for safekeeping and asked him to open and deliver should he not come back. Agrippa had had tears in his eyes when writing the heartfelt missive.

*…I never knew what I was capable of until I met you. I never knew what, or who, I wanted until I met you. I never made love to anyone until I met you… I should have married you but I hope that in the eyes of the gods – and in your heart – we are married… But if you are reading this then I am gone and I want you to consider yourself free to marry. Love again… As much as time seemed to beautifully stand still when we were in our apartment together, as if we were two figures captured in a painting, I do not want you to live in the past and mourn me too much. You've got too much to give the world… Please do not let the memory of when we were last together be the abiding memory you have of me…*

The cold water suddenly concentrated Agrippa's mind back onto his mission. But rather than thinking of the woman he loved as a distraction Caecilia was his goal – the reason why the soldier would be able to swim across and reach the other side of the river.

*

Octavius appeared thoughtful on the outside but worried about his friend. *Should I have ordered him not to volunteer for the mission? All this will be for nothing if I gain wealth and power and have no one to share them with. Talent and loyalty should be rewarded. Marcus, Oppius, Octavia. They're more important – real – than trinkets and honours.*

Octavius sat around a rectangular dining table in a large tent, accompanied by Hirtius and Oppius. His small plate of ham, cheese and asparagus tips was half eaten. He had barely touched his wine either. His co-commander shared not his austere appetite. He sat with various full – and empty – plates in front of him. Aulus Hirtius was a general, statesman, scholar and gourmet. A crop of black hair, streaked with grey, sat upon a round, plump face. Buried in his soft, pink features was a flat nose, thick lips and a small set of hazel eyes which shone with intelligence and amiableness. Despite his girth Hirtius still managed to ride and fight as well as the next man. He had also consciously trained harder over the past six months, knowing that he would likely have to resume military service. The folds of his tunic hung over his low hanging belt. Although Octavius did not entirely trust the consul, whose first loyalty was to the Senate (or himself), he enjoyed his company. "Hirtius is as well read as he is well fed," the propraetor had reported to Cicero in a letter. Octavius and Hirtius had, on more than one occasion, spoken long into the night with one another over dinner. He praised the consul on his ability to mimic Caesar's writing style when finishing off his commentaries. He listened, enraptured, as if he were a boy again, as Hirtius spoke of his time on campaign with Caesar. "I can remember the start of one battle. Julius was worried that, due to our superior numbers, some of the mounted officers might retreat at the first sign of difficulties. So he duly ordered that all officers should relinquish their horses and fight side by side with their men. Suffice to say Julius was the first one to hand the reins of his charger over, to be sent away... Julius was a man of extraordinary abilities. He strengthened the Republic." Suffice to say, when in the company of Cicero and other leading senators, Hirtius had argued that Caesar had weakened the Republic.

Although Hirtius was not entirely pleased or comfortable with being saddled with the youth as a co-commander the experienced soldier never patronised or criticised his junior. Hirtius was also genuinely impressed with the mature manner and sharp intellect of Caesar's heir.

The consul smiled and licked his lips as an attendant brought out a large oval plate, filled with lamprey and red mullet swimming in a mushroom sauce. The general had instructed his scouts and messengers to bring back his favourite foods whenever they could. In order to preserve his produce it was often heavily salted, which led Hirtius to drink even more wine than he was accustomed to. No matter how much food or wine Hirtius consumed, however, he never appeared satiated or drunk. Such was the amount of food and drink at one end of the table, compared to the other, Oppius fancied that it might collapse.

"They will have made it across by now," the centurion remarked, sensing that Octavius was thinking about the mission and his friend. "Decimus will have given instructions to his men to capture rather than execute anyone they find."

"And do you believe that he will remember your archer from his days campaigning in Gaul?" Hirtius asked, seemingly more interested in removing his fish from its bone than he was concerned with a key military operation.

"Teucer is thankfully far too an annoying character to forget. Also, Decimus would have sat in on various archery tournaments over the years amongst the legions which Teucer would have won. He will know and trust him."

"They are also laden with official, sealed letters from me," the consul replied, trying to reassure himself as much as others.

"Not only will we be swimming with the weight of expectation on our back but we'll now be crossing the river with a lead pipe strapped to us," Teucer had half-jokingly complained, when he heard about the messages he would be carrying.

Oppius had commented, before they marched north, that Decimus was a more than competent general – which was high praise indeed from the centurion. His flaws included arrogance and self-regard, however. He believed himself Caesar's equal – and superior to everyone else. Decimus judged that he was entitled to a consulship; Caesar owed him the honour due to his martial achievements and family name. "Without Caesar I cannot be consul but without me Caesar could never have become a dictator," the general had commented, when Mark Antony was promoted over him.

As well as being a slave to his pride Octavius condemned Brutus as a traitor. As well as breaking his oath, having sworn to protect Caesar, Decimus had been the one who had manipulated his friend into attending the Senate meeting on the morning of his assassination. Octavius even caught wind of a rumour that the libertore had boasted about "outwitting the wily general and statesman."

During his meeting with Agrippa, just before he left for his mission, Octavius had been tempted to alter his lieutenant's brief and order him to kill Brutus when he reached Mutina. But circumstances dictated Octavius needed to rescue his enemy rather than damn him for now. Caesar had even given instructions in his will for Decimus to act as Octavius' guardian. *Yet I must come to his rescue. Life has a black sense of humour. Principles have to be sacrificed for pragmatism. Life has thrown up the irony too that Gaius Trebonius has been slain by the ally of my enemy. I'm glad he's dead but I feel deficient for not having held the dagger or given the order myself...*

Octavius' soul burned – certainly his stomach turned and he was unable to eat – when he thought about how he was not honouring the promise he made to himself and his supporters: that he would avenge Caesar's death. *They must die.* "A man who forsakes a vow forsakes his honour," Julius had told his great-nephew many years ago. He had taken Octavius aside after his grandmother's funeral; the boy had

325

impressed his great-uncle in composing and delivering the funeral oration. "You have brought honour to your family today, Octavius. More than martial glory, material gain or political success – family and friends matter. Compassion is as great a virtue as courage. The power of a stylus is greater than that of a dagger. Read Cicero as well as the latest dispatches about my campaigns..."

*Caesar and his legacy matter. Decimus, Mark Antony, Cassius, Brutus. I must destroy them all else they'll destroy me and Caesar's legacy.*

"We should attack as soon as Pansa arrives. The latest communication has him arriving at midday, the day after tomorrow. Antony still seems to be obsessed with capturing the city, perhaps out of pride. Or he wants Mutina as a base of operations. But he will not be able to starve them out or assault the walls within the next few days. We can and will attack Antony from three sides. We have him right where we want him," Hirtius said, staring with delight at a spiced radish on his fork and popping it into his mouth.

*Or Antony has us where he wants*, Lucius Oppius thought to himself.

21.

Insects buzzed around oil lamps hanging from the ceiling of the tent. Four wine cups, with varying amounts of Massic left in them, pinned down the map which was spread across the table. Antony gazed at the plan of the nearby town, Forum Gallorum. He thoughtfully stroked his beard and nodded in satisfaction. The general could not think of a better location in the surrounding area, or province even, in which to set his trap.

Antony was joined in his command tent by his brother Lucius, Domitius Enobarbus and his highest ranking centurions – Gratian Bibulus, Felix Calvinus and Marius Sura. Although the latter trio of officers looked pensive as they stared at the large map of the battlefield for tomorrow, their minds were on other things. Bibulus mulled over which gods he should make offerings to tonight. Manius Sura at the smooth-faced serving boy who he had just ordered to top up his wine cup (having not volunteered it to help flatten out the map). Felix Calvinus' mind turned back to the game of dice he had been playing before being summoned to Antony's war council. He hoped that the break from the table wouldn't ruin his run of good luck.

Enobarbus looked at the three centurions. Each face told a story – a war story. *They may all have their vices but they possess the right virtues as soldiers.*

"Domitius, can you update us on how our ruse is progressing?" Antony asked, his tone more business-like than usual.

"Our messenger, carrying intelligence that we mean to continue to besiege Mutina, has been captured. The message is in code but our enemy will be able to decipher it. As for the plans this evening the men have been instructed to leave their tents up and let their campfires continue to burn as if they were still sitting around them. Should a scout from Hirtius' army reconnoitre the camp he will conclude that the bulk of our forces are still present. We will march out under the cover of darkness. The men have been told to carry only their weapons and a day's rations."

"Excellent. Thankfully Hirtius will believe that I am arrogant enough to remain in one place and have my enemies come to me … Bibulus, you will take your cohorts and conceal yourselves in these woods on the right flank. I can also provide you with cavalry and archers. When you appear from out of the treeline march your forces double time towards the enemy but there will be no need to break formation or have the men charge and sap their strength and momentum on the soft ground. Manius, you too will conceal yourself just over this reverse slope here."

Antony was tempted to make a joke that the centurion would enjoy lying with his men, but desisted.

"Enobarbus, Calvinus and I will hide the majority of our forces within the town itself. Lucius, you will be our lure. You will be accompanied by nearly a full legion. We will need to make the prize tempting enough for Pansa to give chase and have him pursue you into our ambush. I have little doubt that he will take the bait. Despite Pansa's close friendship with Hirtius he will be eager to cover himself in glory over that of his co-commander. But Pansa is not his friend's equal on the battlefield. I have campaigned with both soldiers over the years. Pansa's victories often came as a result of his veterans carrying him rather than from Pansa leading them. Once he has taken the bait, Lucius, you will lead him here." Antony pointed to a space on the map just south-east of Forum Gallorum. "The area is partly marshland. Pansa will be trapped like a fly in honey. Once his forces are bogged down you will turn on your pursuer. At the same time we will attack. The enemy will either rout or perish. You may well have thought, as I have done, that there is a chance that you will face former comrades in battle tomorrow. They will be thinking the same sad thought – but not when their swords are unsheathed. I will be willing to show clemency to our friends after the battle but not during it. Should the opportunity arise to cut off the head of the opposing army then do not hesitate to take it. The body of men around it will soon falter without its direction. The quicker we gain victory the more men we will inherit from the defeated army. Many will swap sides and believe our cause is just once they see that our money is good. If we can just subsume a third of Pansa's army then we should obtain a numerical superiority over Hirtius' and the whelp's forces. As to the latter I will pay a substantial bounty for anyone who can capture or kill him. Let his first battle be his last. I know the boy. He will run away at the first sign of trouble or not even turn up to fight, feigning illness." Antony thought to himself that, no matter what may occur, he would spread the rumour that Octavius hid in his tent while his army went off to fight. *He's no Caesar.*

Antony ordered his attendant to bring out another jug of Massic. They would drink to each other and the battle ahead. Morale had returned in the camp. His army was well paid and well provisioned for. The memory of Brundisium was just that, a memory. After leaving Fulvia behind Antony had spent more time with his officers and legionaries alike. He shared jokes and old war stories with them over jugs of wine around the campfire. Fulvia had encouraged a culture of harsh discipline (often doing so behind her husband's back) but Antony – like Caesar before him – believed in rewarding soldiers and treating them like men as opposed to children.

Antony went through the plan once more and then dismissed his senior officers. They had to ready their legions and also attend to their vices. The general asked his lieutenant to remain a little while longer, however.

"Do we know if Decimus is aware that his allies are close by and ready to relieve him?" the general asked, conscious that, out of all the opposing commanders he would face, Decimus was the most experienced and dangerous.

"I'm afraid that we cannot be sure either way. But if our ruse works and we defeat Pansa's army quickly then there will be little that Decimus will be able to do. Both he and Hirtius will fail to come to Pansa's aid in time."

Again Antony stroked his beard and nodded in satisfaction. His strategy of dividing and conquering would work.

"And what of events in Macedonia? Is our agent in place? It's poetic justice that Marcus Brutus should die by an assassin's blade, don't you think?" Antony said, permitting himself a sly smile.

"He is in place."

22.

*There are two sides to him.*

Horace had spent the day in the company of Matius Varro. The centurion had arrived the evening before and, after having dinner with the lady of the house (Porcia had made a point not to invite Horace), had retired to his room before the young officer could meet him. Brutus was absent, attending to the imprisonment of Gaius Antony. He spent the following morning in town, sitting for a sculpture which some of his supporters in Athens had commissioned and intended to display alongside statues of Greek heroes who had fought for liberty. The irony wasn't lost on Horace that Brutus was spending the night arranging for the illegal detainment of an official, and the morning being honoured as a champion of political freedom.

Brutus had asked his adjutant to look after his friend while he was away. Horace had heard a number of rumours before meeting the enigmatic centurion. From his dusky features – thin lips, narrow eyes and slender face – some thought Varro was Spanish, Sicilian or Greek. More questions were raised, rather than answered, about his origins when people found out the soldier could speak five different languages fluently. When asked about his homeland Varro would often reply, "Well where do you think I'm from? If that's what you think then that's where I'm from…" Varro looked good for his forty plus years, handsome despite the rigours of military service and well-conditioned because of them. During his career the accomplished officer had fought under both Pompey and Caesar and, as well as commanding troops, had served as an envoy to the Senate. Indeed some judged Varro to be a spy as opposed to a soldier. Such was his rapid rise through the ranks at a young age it was rumoured that Varro must have had some form of a patron looking out for him, and at various points of his career it was whispered that he was the bastard son of Pompey, Lucullus or Sulla.

Varro was as well read as any student at the Academy and he would often put his education to use by drafting wills for his men or helping them find the words to write to loved ones. Such was his knowledge of literature and philosophy Horace was unsure whether to admire or resent his fellow scholar. When Varro was caught in a private moment he would appear thoughtful or brooding, but no one would ever be able to guess what the soldier was thinking or brooding about. "He is a closed book, but one worth reading," Brutus had told Horace.

Varro was well liked and possessed plenty of friends – but no close friends. If Horace had to classify the two sides of the centurion he would cite the Varro who was sober (who, even more than thoughtful, seemed troubled) and the Varro who liked to drink. Suffice to say everyone preferred the latter – including Varro himself, Horace sensed. The young poet judged that there were different types of drinkers, or drunks, in the world. Ones who were angry, ones who were sad and ones who were dull. Matius Varro was rare, however. He was a happy drunk. He neither became garrulous or excitable – just contented. "Drink lubricates the soul," the centurion had confessed during the afternoon, wearing a wry, satisfied smile on his face. But he wasn't a slave to wine like other soldiers – and men in general – Horace had encountered over the years. *Subdue your passion or it will subdue you.*

The two men spent the day walking along the valley. They wore plain tunics, rather than their uniforms, but still carried their swords and daggers. The weather was pleasant, as was the scenery. Pinkish clouds, which had clumped themselves together like frightened sheep, began to separate and shafts of amber sunlight shot through the gaps as if the gods were firing arrows made of gold. Craggy trees had started to blossom again. Moss and flowers softened and brightened up the rocky terrain.

Sometimes the men discussed philosophy and literature, but they also knew the virtue of silence and enjoying their own thoughts. As they set off that morning Horace was keen to hear about the latest news from Rome and the civil war.

"Has the fighting commenced in earnest yet? Has the civil war started?" Horace asked. If Antony was defeated then he could think about returning to his studies and poetry.

"In some regards the civil war started as soon as Caesar was assassinated. Or you could say it never ended. We are still fighting the same fight which Marius and Sulla fought and Pompey and Caesar continued. Rome is in a permanent state of war. Periods of peace are like brief intermissions between acts in a play – a tragedy rather than a comedy."

"War may be in Rome's make-up. You may drive out nature with a pitchfork but she'll constantly come running back," Horace replied.

Varro was impressed by the young soldier. *Brutus is right to speak well of him.*

"How do I know that we are in a state of war? Because the Senate has asked me to travel to Athens in order to assure its politicians and populace that we are not at war. Brutus tells me that you wish to be a poet, not a soldier. Maybe the latter will furnish you with the material to be the former after this is all over. A battlefield can be a crucible of extremes but it's the job of a poet – or perhaps more so a philosopher – to chart the extremes of the soul, so that he can steer his readers through a middle course. Homer sailed between Charybdis and Scylla so others didn't have to, though, ironically, he inspired many to do so. But cultivate the golden mean and you will avoid the poverty of a hovel and the envy of a palace," Varro said. Drink had already started to lubricate his soul.

"You could have been a poet yourself it seems."

"Unfortunately I would have been, at best, a second-rate poet. Which would, of course, have made me a first-rate songwriter."

Horace laughed. *There are two sides to him. I like one. I'm just not sure if I trust the other.*

*

Brutus returned that evening in uncommonly good spirits. He announced that he would be throwing a party the following day, which would include a troupe of actors performing a play in the evening. He hoped that Varro could stay another night to attend.

A burden had been lifted. After months of ambushes, skirmishes and political manoeuvring Brutus had subdued the province. Cassius held similar sovereignty in the east. As their armies grew so did their influence. Balbus had recently composed some propaganda stating that the two republicans were now "living like kings".

Matius Varro sat at his host's marble dining table. The room dripped with expensive mosaics, ornaments, paintings and sculptures alike. Porcia had spared little expense buying rich silk curtains, Persian rugs and couches worthy of Cleopatra. Although Brutus did not give his wife much of his time he did give her plenty of pin money in compensation. Shopping took her mind off things. Winter had passed but there was still a hoarfrost between husband and wife.

Whereas Brutus and Cassius would argue that they were receiving "donations" for their cause Matius knew that, in some cases, they were being financed through extortion money. Brutus had also returned to his former enterprise of charging extortionate rates of interests on loans he gave out.

"A toast, gentleman. To good friends and good conversation," Brutus exclaimed, holding his cup of Falernian aloft, smiling at his companions, Varro and Horace. "We may also be inadvertently drinking to victory at Mutina tonight if the battle is over and justice has prevailed. I received a letter from Cicero to say that Lepidus, who is encamped with his legions on the other side of the mountains in Long-Haired Gaul, has refused to declare for Antony. I should also say that the snake has failed to commit his legions to the army of the Republic. He will doubtless be the first to congratulate and pledge allegiance to the victor however."

"Like his wife, he'll get into bed with anyone," Matius joked.

Brutus let out a burst of laughter, not knowing the last time he had done so.

The wine and conversation continued to flow throughout the evening. A fire was lit. Laughter and wit crackled along with the burning logs. After dessert Brutus retrieved his bound copy of Homer and the three men played a game of Homeric lots, where each man took a turn to open the book at random and read a line. The line was supposed to represent the fate of its reader, either defining his character or prophesising his future.

Horace volunteered to go first. Many a time had the boy-poet snuck into his father's study and played the game on his own. Such was his intimacy of Homer he need only be given a first line to then quote the rest of the passage from heart. Horace had forgotten the amount of times his mother had called him into the room to perform his party trick in front of her friends. Horace, to dramatically heighten his submission to fate, solemnly closed his eyes as he opened the book. When he opened them the intoxicating phrases were like silk to the aspiring poet. Horace read out his line, smiling a little both before and afterwards. He would heed the words and he hoped that Brutus would take the poet's wisdom to heart too.

"Curb thou the high spirit in thy breast, for gentle ways are best, and keep aloof from sharp contentions."

Matius nodded in sympathy. Brutus' expression remained unchanged. Horace passed the book back to his host who, after draining his cup and nodding to a slave to re-fill it, turned his attention to divining his fate. Brutus had always preferred philosophy to poetry – and Roman authors to Greek – during his youth but he was familiar with Homer, if not as enamoured with him as his companions. Brutus didn't appreciate the constant interventions of the gods in the story, believing that man forged his own path in the world and was responsible for his actions. But his hands were still clammy and his heart beat that little bit faster. It was just a game, he told himself. The general opened the book. He read over the lines first in his head, from a passage which he had put a mark next to previously: *There is nothing nobler or more admirable than when two people who see eye to eye keep house as man and wife, confounding their enemies and delighting their friends.*

Either because of the lump in his throat or the awkwardness he would feel in saying the words Brutus recalled another line from Homer and offered it up to his friends, hoping that they would not see through his act.

"Without a sign the brave man draws his sword and asks no omen but his country's cause."

Brutus puffed out his chest as he spoke but Matius wasn't convinced by his performance. Horace's eyes blazed as brightly as the fire, believing in his commander, Homer and the fact that he may well be taking part in a moment of history. Drink was lubricating his soul.

Brutus took another swig of barely watered down wine and passed the book along, relieved to be rid of it.

Like Horace, Matius Varro had grown up with Homer. He could still vividly recall being seven years old and hearing a grey-bearded actor in the market perform *The Iliad*. Each day he would recite a different book and each day Matius would place a small coin in his hat, along with others, as payment. He read *The Odyssey* a week afterwards, devouring yet savouring each line. Every word was a jewel – precious, eternal. Homer fired a spark and other authors fuelled the flame. The boy worshipped Socrates, Aristotle, Thucydides and Plautus more than any god. Literature represented another world – a better world – to escape to. And philosophy helped pull back the veil covering the sometimes noble – sometimes ugly – face of the real world.

The centurion cradled the tome in his hands as if it were a holy book. A breeze whistled through some shutters on the other side of the room. The book creaked open and Varro sucked in the words on the page – compelled and condemned to read the line which most thrummed upon his soul. The soldier's voice was clear, calm and yet sorrowful: "Hateful to me as the gates of Hades is that man who hides one thing in his heart and speaks another."

23.

Rain freckled Lucius Antony's face and armour. Sweat glazed his forehead and also streaked the flanks of his coal-black mare. He harried his commanders to harry his men – riding at the front, rear and alongside his forces at differing points. He hoped that some of his soldiers would take note of his courage and leadership and praise him over their campfires at night. The ground shook from Pansa's pursuing army. He had used his cavalry and archers to slow the enemy's advance, but he didn't want to slow them too much. The plan was working and the trap would soon be sprung.

Lucius Antony had gritted his teeth during his brother's war council. Lucius believed that he should have been allowed to command a wing of the army, rather than just acting as a lure. Had he not proven himself? Had he not been behind the procurement parties who had raided the north in order to feed his brother's army? Did the legions not look upon him as someone above the rank of centurion? He refrained from speaking out though, knowing that his brother would use the incident as an excuse to belittle him. Lucius felt like he had lived in the shadow of his older brother all his life. People had befriended him, both in his youth and now, in order to get closer to his brother. People smirked whenever Lucius mentioned being a descendent of Hercules. One could see the family resemblance when the two men stood side by side but Lucius' features were leaner – more hawkish. No one had ever deemed Lucius to be as handsome as his brother. No woman ever chose him over his brother, indeed the older brother often slept with the younger brother's mistresses (one of which Lucius had been genuinely fond of and thought he might marry). But one woman might choose him over his brother soon.

*Fulvia… She pretends she doesn't care about his infidelities with younger women. But she does. She is only human after all as much as some might call her inhuman for her coldness and cruelty… She has already given me the eye… I could have had her already. But the time isn't right. It will be. Revenge will be sweet for both of us. Sleeping with Fulvia will more than make up for him sleeping with a dozen of my former mistresses… Her beauty may have faded but her powerbase hasn't. She has the political and financial connections I will need. But I have the name – and support of the army – that she needs… No matter what the outcome here today I will advance my cause. If my brother proves victorious then he will give me a province to govern, where I can grow my own war chest and army, or I will be the First Man of Rome and Italy whilst he attends to Brutus and Cassius in the east. But should he be defeated the faction will still need a leader. I will be able to challenge the boy Octavius and win over Caesarian support from his faction too. But let's just take one battle at a time.*

*

*The gods are on our side.*

Gaius Vibius Pansa did not hesitate when the breathless scouting party returned and reported that they had located a sizeable enemy force travelling towards them on the Via Aemilia.

The commander galloped at the head of his army. His freshly dyed cloak billowed in the wind. His polished armour and helmet gleamed in the midday sun. Pansa was of average build. Cicero described the consul as being "a modest man, with a lot to be modest about." He had spent his career being proficient at carrying out orders given by other people. But now he had a chance to lead instead of follow.

*We must engage the enemy before they reach the town.*

Pansa heard cheers behind him as his men sensed that they could swallow up the inferior force with ease. He also heard them jeer, taunting the retreating soldiers. The general grinned, wolfishly, at the cavalry officer next to him.

*Lambs to the slaughter.*

Pansa knew that, behind his back, senators and senior officers judged that he was not his co-consul's equal in military prowess. But he would prove them wrong. The general issued orders for his cavalry to outflank and encircle the fleeing enemy, curving around them like the horns of a bull. It was a manoeuvre worthy of Hannibal, Pansa thought to himself. Perhaps he would be able to persuade Hirtius to write up the commentary for the battle as he had for many of Caesar's campaigns.

The enemy seemed to be suicidally heading towards the open ground instead of the relative sanctuary of the forest or town. Their retreat would be slowing due to the soft, boggy soil, Pansa judged. The general watched with satisfaction as his cavalry commenced to draw their swords – the blades freshly sharpened from the night before.

The noise was not that of the wind moving through the trees, but men. Soldiers. Thousands of them. The town became a hive of activity but Pansa realised quickly that the men he could see advancing towards him were not townsfolk. The sunlight bouncing off helmets, from legionaries marching over the ridge, also caught the stunned general's eye. Two wings of enemy cavalry poured out from the woods and Forum Gallorum. Their intention was to outflank and encircle Pansa's forces. The Republic's army would be gouged upon the horns of the bull. Antony ordered his cavalry to ride around the rear of his enemy in order to prevent it retreating. The blood drained from Pansa's face and he felt like a hand had gripped his heart. His throat became dry and he croaked out an order for his legions to form up in defensive formation.

Antony grinned. All was going according to plan. Not even Caesar could have planned and executed things more effectively. Thankfully his men had retained their discipline whilst occupying the town, despite the temptation to loot and rape. Lucius had done well. The general would take his brother aside afterwards and personally thank and praise him. Although he would not laud Lucius in public and feed his vanity and ambition, Mark Antony thought to himself.

*You can either surrender or die, Gaius. I will be fair and present the same offer to Hirtius, when I encounter him. Lambs to the slaughter…*

\*

The weight of evidence was against Antony splitting his army and attacking Pansa, Hirtius argued that morning. Oppius replied that most of the evidence could have been supplied by Antony. Caesar had employed similar ruses and false intelligence before too.

"I am not asking you to trust me, but to trust Oppius," Octavius added, not wishing to force the consul into thinking that he was ordering him to do anything.

"If I am wrong then the only harm done will be that of a few sore feet. But if I am right and Antony is planning to intercept Pansa on the Via Aemilia then we will need to converge our armies immediately," Oppius calmly, but firmly, stated.

Hirtius at first appeared unmoved but then he breathed out. *What harm could it do?* Caesar had trusted Oppius in military matters, all those years ago. And Hirtius trusted Caesar, when it came to his military judgement. The general had provided the centurion with two cavalry squadrons and two infantry cohorts. Hirtius also allowed Octavius to grant Oppius the use of the propraetor's personal.

"Will today be the day?" Octavius asked the veteran officer shortly afterwards, when they were alone. The anxious look on the youth's face made him appear ten years older.

"Hope for the best, plan for the worst," Oppius answered, unsure if he was putting the boy at ease.

"Should I ride out with you or remain here?"

The centurion believed that Octavius wanted him to answer the latter. He remembered the ambush on the road to Rome a year ago. Octavius had hid beneath a wagon as two of their friends were slain trying to protect him. Physical courage is a strange animal though, Oppius mused. He had seen some soldiers fight like lions in one battle only to whimper and run when next lining up in a shield wall.

*Fear can be as great a spur for heroic actions as bravery. The heat of battle enflames hearts in different ways.*

Octavius pictured the wild, contorted expressions on the faces of men who fought. He recalled the barbaric battle cries. He believed he was unable to lose control in such a way – become inhuman. *Or perhaps a man fighting for his life is the true face of humanity. But what will the men think of me if I choose not to stand with them and share their fate? History says that, to succeed in politics, one must garner martial glory too. History doesn't have to always repeat itself though. Wars are not just won on the battlefield.* Octavius also remembered something Caesar had once said to him: "The successful commander is sometimes the one who doesn't have to fight." Octavius didn't want to be labelled a coward but he also didn't want fail on the battlefield and let people see behind the mask. The propraetor tried to show that he was torn and disappointed when Oppius recommended that he remain at the camp. Octavius wanted to say to the soldier that he wanted Oppius to be proud of him – but didn't. Oppius wanted to say to Octavius how proud he was of him and that Caesar would be proud of him as well – but didn't. The two men merely gave each other a cursory nod.

Although he felt it prudent to leave Octavius behind at the camp Oppius elected to recruit Agrippa to his small force, who had successfully returned to the camp from his mission to Mutina. He asked Pollux and Teucer to accompany him too.

The quartet sat on their horses next to each other on the ridge of a hilltop which looked down over Forum Gallorum, the Via Amelia and the battle. Flat grey clouds marked the gloomy sky, like lesions. Oppius cursed Antony beneath his breath but he also begrudgingly gave him credit. He had skilfully deceived Hirtius and manoeuvred most of his army during the dead of night. Similarly his army was now moving with method and purpose as it converged around Pansa's legions. *Should I leave Pansa to his fate?*

Oppius' cavalry squadrons and cohorts wouldn't be able to tip the balance in Pansa's favour but they may just be able to help the defenders hang on long enough until Hirtius' army could arrive. The centurion knew that he would be sending countless soldiers to the deaths if they joined the battle – but more men would eventually die if he did nothing.

Agrippa observed the officer's face in profile. Worry and age coloured his expression. Somehow the veteran soldier could look both careworn and determined at the same time.

"Teucer, Agrippa – head back to camp and inform Hirtius of the situation. He needs to mobilise as many legions as possible, as quickly as possible. Tell him if Antony wins here today – either defeating or recruiting Pansa's army – then all will be lost for the rest of us."

A part of the Briton wanted to try and talk his old friend out of his decision to stay and fight but he knew Oppius well enough to know that his mind was made up. A brief nod and forced smile from the centurion said enough. A month beforehand Oppius had handed the archer several letters and briefed him on his affairs. The letters were to go to Octavius, Agrippa and Livia – should Teucer ever be able to locate her.

A lump rose up in Agrippa's throat. He wanted to say something to the centurion – to thank him, praise him – but couldn't. Agrippa felt a presentiment, churning in his stomach like hunger, that he would never see his friend and mentor again. Oppius, witnessing the anxiety on the young soldier's face, did his best to put him at ease (despite feeling ill at ease himself).

"Don't worry lad. I know it may seem like a suicide mission but I've been through worse. Sometimes it's not about advancing or retreating, sometimes you've just got to hold the line."

## 24.

The afternoon sun gave an extra sheen to the marble colonnades the slaves had polished that morning. Local dignitaries, merchants and scholars all paid court to Brutus as if he were royalty. Perfume, the smell of shellfish and bouquets of wine infused the air. Musicians played in the background. For the entertainment, later on in the evening, Brutus had organised for a troupe of players to perform a comedy.

The host and his wife smiled in unison as they greeted their guests. Brutus' arm ached from shaking hands. He received endless compliments as well as pledges of political and – more importantly – financial support. Porcia lied as much as she smiled, telling people how much she preferred Athens to Rome. She gazed at her husband, with affection and admiration, and duly charmed their attentive audience.

"I knew your father. He was unique – a keeper of the flame of the soul of Rome," Voluscius Caepio remarked to Porcia, in reference to Cato. Brutus took in the portentous local administrator. His hair and skin were as oily as his manner. He bowed to Brutus that little bit lower when he shook his hand, but the host was also aware of his guest's reputation for haughtiness and cruelty towards his slaves. Brutus wryly smiled to himself as he recalled how Voluscius had uttered the same words about Cato to him, many years ago, when talking about Caesar.

Brutus had smiled little that morning, however, as he read through a letter from his mother, Servilia. He had thought that, by putting distance between them, she might prove less overbearing. But he was wrong. As usual the letter was a litany of complaints and demands.

"Cicero believes he is solely responsible for galvanising the Republic – although that may be true in that everybody is now bored with his speeches and self-aggrandisement... Remember to think of Decimus and Cassius as rivals as well as allies. If they were willing to stab Julius in the back they will not balk at doing the same to you. Make sure you have more funds and legions at your disposal than them. Bleed Athens dry if you have to, in order to save Rome."

Servilia apportioned most of her letter though, either subtly or overtly, towards Porcia. The two women had never been fond of each other despite their family connection through Cato. Cicero had once quipped to Caesar over dinner that the two women were dogs, fighting over the bone of Brutus' spare time. Servilia deemed Porcia too prim, proud and obsessed with her dead father. Porcia judged her mother-in-law in return to be licentious, manipulative and obsessed with Caesar. From her knowing about the recent discord between husband and wife Brutus realised Servilia had planted at least one spy within his household.

"I have heard gossips in Rome argue that you were motivated to murder Caesar out of a devotion to your wife – and her devotion to Cato and will to avenge his death. You must be seen to be motivated from principle and a love of Rome. A wife must stand by her husband no matter what. And she must realise that she is the wife of a general, not just a praetor, now. Porcia's sensitive character is not suited to the climate or the challenging times ahead. You must save the Republic, even at the expense of saving your marriage. You will need to forge an alliance with one of the Metellii or Claudii to strengthen your influence in the Senate. Many women in their clans are coming of age. As much as I loved Cato dearly he is of no use to our cause now. I know that you will do the right thing. Porcia herself, if she still loves you, will understand…"

Brutus tossed the letter into the fire after reading it. As much as he had inwardly criticised his wife of late he resented anyone else openly speaking out against her. They didn't understand or appreciate her in the way he did. *I still love her. I think.* Brutus was all too aware of the friction between his mother and wife. Servilia had neither liked nor approved of Porcia from the start. She wasn't good enough for her son – but perhaps no one was. Servilia grew jealous of Porcia's influence over Brutus, little realising that, by her desire to direct and hold her son close, she had driven him away.

The hurt of losing her son to Porcia was compounded by the hurt of losing Caesar to an array of mistresses – although Caesar's love affair with himself held an even greater sway over his actions. As much as Caesar had gifted to Servilia a giant black pearl, worth more than all the jewels he had given other women combined, it was not enough for her. Julius had once told Servilia, with seeming genuine affection, that she would always have a place in his heart, but he could not give her all his heart. She tried to take a more active role in politics, to be of greater value to Caesar so he would spend more time with her. She even offered her daughter, Tertia, to the dictator as a mistress so she could spend more time with him – try to influence him – that way. But Caesar was his own man and she realised she could never be Calpurnia or Cleopatra (who had given the dictator that which Servilia had wanted so desperately to give him over the years – a son). Some days she woke up and would try to devote herself to Caesar and win him back and other days she would brief against him and curse his name. She took other lovers but life proved a shadow of what it once had been after being Caesar's favoured mistress. And eventually age withered her. Servilia no longer turned the heads of those in power. Other – younger – women captured their eye. She increasingly drank to dull the ache and emptiness in her heart. She sometimes behaved inappropriately in a bid to be the centre of attention again, like she had been in the glory of her youth. She often wore more make-up to appear younger but, as Cicero cruelly joked, "she is unable to paint over all the cracks."

Sometimes Brutus was ashamed of his mother. Sometimes he resented her. But he also felt sorry for her. Rightly or wrongly she blamed Caesar for her unhappiness. Did Brutus blame him too?

Although she had not plunged a dagger into him Servilia had been an integral part of the conspiracy to assassinate Caesar. She had encouraged her son to meet with Cassius. The conspirators had also met at her house to plan the deed.

*For all of your criticisms of Porcia did you not act from personal rather than political motives in wanting Caesar dead? But in my pride, jealousy and out of revenge for hurting you did I not kill him for selfish reasons too?*

Brutus glared long into the fire that morning, hoping to find answers. But he just found more questions and sorrow.

\*

Horace began to feel exhausted from all the pleasantries and small talk. He told himself that the party was good practise for when he would have to seek a patron as a poet. He laughed at terrible jokes and agreed with ill thought out comments as if playing a game with himself.

The adjutant had spent the morning double checking the latest accounts for his general. The numbers for income and outgoings had become dizzying compared to just a few months previous. Soon Brutus and Cassius' forces would eclipse those of the Republic's. Brutus had recently arranged a recruitment drive for men and capital. He and his agents had travelled to various towns and instructed them to pay a donation so that the army could defend them against Antony and his tyranny. Brutus called it "protection money".

Horace allowed one of the slaves to fill up his cup again, although he was conscious of diluting his wine more than usual. The party would go on into the evening and he wanted to have a reasonably clear head when watching the play, considering that he been allowed to compose a few extra lines and scenes for the production. Brutus had kindly put the suggestion to Ovidius Cinna, the lead actor and manager of the group of players. Cinna was aged around forty though he seemed to have the energy of a twenty year old. When Brutus had heard that Cinna was in the area he invited the troupe to perform at the party.

"Our host tells me that you are a budding writer, Horace. My advice would be don't give up the day job though – and I'm not saying that because I do not want any rivals. I remember when I started out as a poet, many years ago. I would wake up in poverty one day and, in the next, merely be more debt-ridden," Cinna exclaimed, laughing at his own joke and warmly clasping the young officer on the shoulder. "Less is more. Never write two or three words when you can write just one. Although you will need to win over the husband for a patron it is often the case than his wife will control the purse strings. So win over her as well. Have a wealth of compliments to draw from when conversing. Employ different ones for different ages. Different vintages have different tastes. Similarly your patron may want you to do more than just sing for your supper. Shut your eyes and tell yourself it's all for the art or, if it proves to be of greater consolation, think of the money."

Horace attempted to dip his toe in the waters of complimenting wives of possible patrons during the party but his shyness – and ineptitude – caused him to fail. The women thought him of too lowly a rank or not handsome enough.

*If they only knew that I was a poet, that I could immortalise them in verse. Poetry can be as lasting as marble or rust like iron. I could fill their ears with music. There's certainly plenty of space between the ears of most of them. Most of the women here seem fit for satire and epigrams as opposed to love poetry though ... Some of the dresses are so tight that I may need to call on the army surgeon to cut them out of their clothing, although in some cases I suspect that there will be plenty of civilian volunteers who'll be up for the task. At some point I will need to play my part and attract a patron or a patron's wife. But as much money as it takes to enter society I need to one day be wealthy enough to be free of it. Live the quiet life in the country. This is what I pray for. A plot of land – not so very large, with a garden and, near the house, a spring that never fails and a bit of woodland to round it all off. Aye, we all must play our part to get what we wish for. Just look at the performance being played out between Brutus and Porcia. But am I not already playing a part in telling myself that I'm destined to become a great poet. Cinna may be the only honest man here, for at least he admits that he's an actor.*

Horace wended his way through the ever increasing throng and headed out to the garden at the back of the house. The breeze immediately cooled his flushed face and refreshed his thoughts. A few other guests had commenced to congregate outside and could be seen whispering – and canoodling – in corners. The lone figure, standing at the foot of the garden, attracted his attention. Although it seemed that Matius Varro was desiring privacy Horace approached the centurion. He was still a slight riddle, which the poet had still to unravel the meaning of.

Matius gazed, or glowered, out across the valley rather than back at the house. Campfires dotted the plains and reminded the soldier of Pharsalus, the days before the battle. *So many died then and for what? Caesar, Pompey, Antony, Brutus and Cassius. All charming, brilliant and mad. Perhaps Caesar was different though. He knew his life was being played out on a stage and that life is a joke played on man. The best thing you can do is just laugh along with it.* Matius appeared to be in no laughing mood, however. As much as he stared off into the distance the centurion appeared to have something at the forefront of his mind.

"I hope that I'm not disturbing you, Matius."

"No, it's fine. I needed a break from the party. I was just collecting what few thoughts I have left rattling around inside my mind," he replied. A smile lightened the darker expression which had previously shaped his features. There had been a storm on his brow – murder on his mind. The centurion sighed, gently, relieved at being freed from his reverie.

"I hear that you will be leaving us later, after the play. You are packed and ready to go."

"Duty calls," Matius replied, unconsciously clasping his sword as he spoke.

"Brutus will be sad to see you leave, not least because he has yet to try and recruit you to his cause."

"Brutus is doing a more than adequate job of creating and training a grand army without my help. The question is, Horace, which you are wise enough to have asked yourself, will Marcus be as equally adept

344

at disbanding his army when the war is over? I hope that, in his cause to become a great man, our friend does not forget how to be a good one. It may prove to be the death of him."

"He may, like Caesar, become a god," Horace half-joked. But Varro still wasn't in a laughing mood. He looked grim. The centurion's voice was mournful, prophetic, as he shook his head and replied: "Nobody lives forever."

25.

*The gods are on our side.*

Antony surveyed the battlefield. Pansa's army was all but surrounded, he surmised. The enemy had yet to rout or surrender – with the veterans bravely fighting on and propping up the new recruits – but the day would be his. A few cavalry skirmishes around the main fight had proved inconclusive but the general couldn't help but notice the bodies – of men and horses alike – littering the ground, stuck in the mud, like macabre statues. The marshland had aided Antony in deterring the enemy from making a quick retreat but it also now hampered his forces from attacking as efficiently as they could.

As usual the battle would be won by the infantry. Cohorts formed up in their shield walls and crashed against each other, butting like rams. Swords stabbed outwards between interlocked shields and soldiers fought each other furiously for a quarter of an hour before the second rank replaced the first, to carry on the fight. They were like two boxers, standing toe to toe. Antony judged he would win because he had greater reserves to call on.

Unlike other battlefields which Antony had fought on there were pockets of open land spread over the plains where the ground was too soft to occupy. Despite the discipline of some of the officers and cohorts the fighting broke up and became chaotic in places, where small clusters of men – or individuals – fought one another.

Pansa, it seemed, was trying to lead from the front, Antony observed.

*He's either brave, mad or foolish. At least he's showing some character for once though.*

Antony gave orders for Calvinus and his cohort to engage Pansa and the men surrounding him – to break through and kill the consul. If their commander fell there would be little motivation for his legions to fight on. Antony preferred to spill as little Roman blood as possible. The more lives spared today, the greater force he would have to attack Hirtius, Decimus and Octavius within the coming days. Antony dreamed of being able to face the latter in single combat. He would embarrass the stripling and then kill him, skewer him on his long cavalry sword like a piece of meat.

*I'll swat him like a gadfly.*

\*

Their horses churned and spat up mud as Agrippa and Teucer galloped back towards their camp. The tamp of their hooves seemed calm compared to the beating of Agrippa's heart. The fate of Rome was potentially in his hands. If he couldn't deliver his message then Hirtius would not reinforce Pansa. If Pansa wasn't reinforced then Antony would defeat him and possess the momentum and men to defeat Octavius.

They were being pursued by half a dozen enemy cavalry. The patrol had spotted the two archers and were closing quickly. Their mounts were stronger, swifter and fresher.

"Ride on, I'll deal with these bastards behind us," Teucer breathlessly remarked to his comrade.

Agrippa was going to argue that they should stick together but he knew that one of them needed to deliver their crucial message. Teucer was the better aim and Agrippa was the better horseman. The young soldier merely gave a nod of acknowledgment and appreciation.

"Go on, fuck off. If I get misty eyed it'll ruin my aim. And don't look back," Teucer added.

Agrippa kicked his heels into the flanks of his mount and, despite the temptation to do so, didn't look back.

The field they were riding through was on a slight slope. Once Teucer reached the top he slowed his horse and wheeled it around to face the oncoming enemy. Sweat trickled down his back. He took two deep breaths and then nocked his first arrow. For the first time in his life Teucer recited the Legionary's Prayer: "Jupiter, Greatest and Best, protect this legion, soldiers every one. May my act bring good fortune to us all."

It brought the soldier comfort that he had left instructions for Oppius to send his money back to his tribe in Britannia – should he die.

*If Oppius perishes too than Octavius will honour his promise to look after my people. The future of Rome is in good hands. The lad and Agrippa have got something about them. I've drunk enough, whored enough and killed enough. It's time to let the next generation make the same mistakes as the old – and come up with some new ones too.*

The first arrow sang through the air and thudded into the chest of the lead decurion, knocking him back off his newly purchased black colt. The impressive shot didn't deter the rest of the patrol however, indeed it seemed to spur them on to cut down the archer before he could fire on anyone else. They barked orders into the ears of their mounts and the horses snorted and rode on harder in reply. Javelins were readied. Teucer and the enemy knew that there would not be time to fire on all six before they reached the top of the slope. It was a suicide mission. The Briton could and would still try to defeat them all though. Teucer was able to fire off three more arrows – and kill three more of the enemy – before the horsemen were in range of their target. Even the thought of his imminent death didn't distract the archer from his aim. The thought of attempting to retreat was similarly dismissed. *I won't show my back to the bastards.*

Teucer was able to fire off one last arrow – and fell his enemy – just before the spear punctured his lung. He prayed that Agrippa would now be safe. Teucer's last thoughts were that he hoped he would soon see Roscius and Fabius again, in the afterlife, and share a drink with them. The Briton slumped forward on his horse and died. His death, however, did not prevent the remaining enemy combatant from stabbing the archer several times with his javelin out of a frenzied sense of revenge for murdering his comrades. The cavalryman, once he had regained his composure, thought twice about pursuing the second archer – just in case he was as remotely accomplished a shot as the first.

*

Squelching sounds could increasingly be heard across the battlefield as rain filled the air and the glutinous ground grew even softer. Mud and blood smeared the armour and faces of all. The first wave of men to die began to add a fetid stench to the proceedings.

The veteran legionaries surrounding their consul recognised the prospective threat and duly closed ranks and reinforced their numbers. Bibulus had ordered his cohort into a wedge formation. They had moved through their own lines and then broken part of the first rank of the enemy's shield wall. The officer had arranged for his best spearman to be at the vanguard of his force and once in range of their target he gave the order for them to launch their volley. The superstitious centurion offered up all manner of prayers, to all manner of gods, that he would succeed in his task.

The consul, who had fought valiantly throughout the day, saw the swarm of spears arc towards him. But it was too late. His eyes were stapled wide in surprise as a javelin pierced the side of Pansa's armour and ribs. His eyes only half-closed as he fell to the ground, however. Their commander was still alive and the senior officers around him bellowed out orders to continue to fight. A member of the consul's bodyguard, Libo, cradled Pansa in his arms. The commander tried to speak but a trickle of blood issued forth from his mouth, as opposed to words. A legionary, with tears in his eyes for his commander, cut the spearhead from its shaft so they could move him. The plan was to now get their general to a physician. The army of the Republic would fight on and await for his return and orders. Libo gave the order for a squadron of cavalry to accompany him. Thankfully Antony's forces hadn't entirely surrounded them. They rode free from the battlefield towards Bononia, where a surgeon could attend to the general.

*

Their lines were thinning. Determination alone cannot win battles. When some of the Republic's soldiers were not fighting for their lives they had time and space to think about surrendering. The tang of blood was in the air, as was the prospect of defeat – or a massacre. Too many corpses were already sticking out of the ground. Curses, grunting and an incessant metallic clash of arms rattled the air.

Mark Antony had at first been jubilant at hearing the news that Pansa had been seriously wounded and conveyed from the field of battle. But then he gloomily thought how one man could no longer give the order to surrender.

*And if he dies I will not have the opportunity to humiliate him and the Republic. Pansa has swapped sides once. He could do so again.*

Antony admired and pitied the great mass of men, knee deep in mud and gore, fighting a losing battle. A survival extinct or savagery compelled them to struggle on, he judged. Years of training or a devotion to a cause motivated others. Experience had taught the general that most men would be fighting for the friends alongside them too. But many of their comrades had fallen. There would soon be no one to fight on for.

*They must now surely be questioning whether they should continue to fight...*

Arms ached. Armour was knocked out of shape. Sweat soaked the felt lining of their helmets. Skin and chips of bone flecked the muddy ground. Some must have questioned whether they would last the day. Others questioned whether they would get paid. Antony noticed that there were plenty of soldiers with their heads now hanging down, bowing to defeat.

But then, as if the sun had come out from behind the clouds, heads rose back up. A small relief force had arrived, marching northwards along the Via Aemilia. Oppius gave command of one of the cavalry squadrons and cohorts to Pollux while he took command of the remaining units, including the force of praetorian guards. A vague hope spread throughout the ranks of Pansa's forces. Hirtius' army was on the way. Some also recognised Oppius, believing that the *Sword of Rome* was worth another two cohorts.

Calvinus and Sura gave orders for half their soldiers to disengage and manoeuvre themselves to face the oncoming enemy.

Pollux's wounded leg began to throb but he was itching to fight still. His old friend, Aulus Milo, rode next to him.

"How's the leg?"

"Hurts like a bastard. Thankfully I won't lack for enemies to take my frustration out on," Pollux replied, thinking the thought that his friend now voiced.

"Do you think they made it back to the camp?" Milo remarked, in reference to Teucer and Agrippa being able to pass on Oppius' message to Hirtius.

"I checked the map. There were no taverns or brothels on the way for Teucer to stop off in. So yes."

The grizzled veterans laughed, hoping that it wouldn't be the last time they would do so. The two centurions soon after dismounted, drew their swords and marched alongside their men.

Mark Antony briefly coloured the air with curses. All was not now going according to plan. Although but a dot in the distance he was sure that Oppius was leading the small force which was about to attack him. Antony still felt a shard of betrayal when he thought about his old friend.

*You can't win today, Oppius. All you can do is die trying. You picked the wrong side. Should you somehow survive then your name will be one of the first I'll put on a proscription list, even though you've probably not got a pot to piss in or any property to speak of.*

Antony summoned a messenger. He instructed the rider to give orders to Bibulus that Oppius was a priority target.

Oppius took personal command of the praetorian guards. Many faces before him were familiar, veterans from Gaul and Pharsalus. None of them, whether from professional pride or habit, would show their back to the enemy. He could hear a mass of soldiers behind him as Antony's cohorts marched towards them. But the centurion was happy for the enemy to sap their strength, trudging through the mud. His sweaty palms tightened around the ox-hide straps of his shield. His head felt like an oven within his helmet but Oppius, like the stone-faced praetorians before him, didn't display any discomfort.

Pansa's army had fought well to survive this long, the centurion judged.

*We just need to do the same. Hold out until Hirtius arrives. The longer we can endure the more hope they'll be. And where there's hope there's life.*

Before an unnerving silence could take root the centurion addressed his troops: "The walls protecting Rome begin here. We are its first and last line of defence. I could say do Caesar proud today. Many of you fought for him as he fought for you. But more so do yourself proud today. Be all you can be. There's iron in your hands and iron in your hearts. And they'll be gold in our purses if we see out the day. Reinforcements are on the way but let's not give them too much work to do, eh?"

Laughter broke out and the tension in the air – and in the soldier's expressions – was eased.

"We have but one task to do today: hold the line. Rome expects that every man will do his duty."

The centurion had to nigh on bellow this last order lest his words be drowned out by the roar of the enemy as they attacked Pollux and his men across the way.

The attack was diminished, although not defeated, as a volley of javelins scythed down the front ranks of the advancing legionaries. Men behind them lost their momentum and formation as they stumbled over their fallen comrades.

Oppius and Pollux had deliberately positioned their forces on the firmest ground they could find. They also bolstered the ranks of new recruits by inserting veterans to fight alongside them. They would hold the line against the first offensive. The question was though, how many subsequent offensives could they endure?

\*

Antony gripped the hilt of his sword, making a fist. He was tempted to enter the fighting himself in order to take his mind off things and feel like he was making a difference. He still possessed the greater reserves although they were unfortunately positioned on the wrong side of the battlefield, unable to wipe Oppius and his cohorts off the map. Antony's forces also still surrounded the bulk of Pansa's army. The mass of his legions still remained on the battlefield, like a giant block of ice. But his forces were chipping away at it and it was melting from the heat of battle. But the general had expected to be triumphant by now. Antony was tempted to use some of his forces to fortify his position but then he dismissed the idea, believing that he was on the cusp of a complete victory. Would his ruse still last? Or would Hirtius and his army arrive in time? Should he send a message to Enobarbus, back at the camp near Mutina, to order the remainder of his forces to join the battle? Antony began to have more questions than he had answers to.

*

The fighting continued on numerous fronts. Endless wars had created veterans and veterans prolonged battles. Whilst some shield walls held their ground others broke and the fighting became more frayed and disparate. Despite Antony's numerical superiority, of infantry and cavalry alike, he was still unable to outflank and rout his enemy. At the beginning of the day the general had been willing to offer Pansa's army clemency and the opportunity to be recruited to his cause. But now he was willing to put them all to the sword. They were an obstacle, which he still annoyingly needed to remove.

The corpses and wounded began to pile up on both sides. The chilling high-pitched screams of the injured and traumatised could be heard over rasping battle-cries. Mud caked upon armour and could be found in hair, ears and mouths. Sometimes the ground was more red than brown, however, with pools and rivulets of blood.

*

Lucius Antony's cavalry attack, which he had ordered so as to break through the enemy cohort's flank, proved ineffective. The veterans kept their shape and Pollux called upon his own cavalry – and a smattering of archers – to drive the horsemen away.

Pollux continued to growl and bark orders at the newer recruits. He felt a trickle of blood wend its way down his leg from where one of the sutures in his wound had broken. He seethed in both anger and pain. His gladius was awash with blood and sinew as he relentlessly stabbed at the enemy shield wall and pushed it back.

Where the cavalry had failed Calvinus hoped that his infantry would succeed. Calvinus wanted to kill Pollux out of personal spite and for strategic reasons. The tough, veteran officer was the keystone. If he could remove him from the formation then the whole edifice might collapse around him. Both centurions had never seen eye to eye. Calvinus resented Pollux for being promoted before him and Pollux believed Calvinus had accepted bribes over the years and, through working with the quartermasters, embezzled funds from the legion.

Calvinus wanted his enemy to come out from behind the shield wall, so he could isolate him. He soon got his wish when Pollux saw him in the opposing ranks. Pollux went for him, like a red rag to a bull, ducking his head behind his scutum and charging forward. The handsome yet battle-hardened officer was startled by his enemy but not afraid of him.

"Calvinus," Pollux exclaimed, pointing his sword at the opposing centurion. "We know how treacherous you are. But at least try not to be spineless." The former drill master's voice out-sounded everything going on around him, to the point that the two shield walls ceased fighting.

With his blood also now up – and not wanting to lose face in front of his men – Calvinus moved forward. His sword crashed against Pollux's shield. Such was the force of the attack that Pollux's wounded leg nearly buckled. The two centurions traded blows and curses. Hatred fuelled their reserves of strength. Pollux suddenly forced his opponent back. The lines of Calvinus' shield wall opened to allow the combatants to fight on but then closed again, swallowing them up.

Calvinus snarled-cum-grinned. He was confident that he could defeat his wounded enemy but he now didn't want to leave the result to chance.

"I never liked you Pollux," the centurion breathlessly remarked. "Someone do me a favour and kill this bastard."

The more honourable veterans in the circle of soldiers around Pollux didn't move but a number of the more bloodthirsty new recruits looked to impress their officer. Pollux killed one legionary and wounded another but, like Caesar trying to fight off his assassins, he was outnumbered. They stabbed him like a piece of meat. Pollux' blood freckled Calvinus' face as he stood over the centurion's butchered corpse. He sniffed, drew some phlegm up into his mouth and then spat on his fallen opponent. The vain-glorious officer was about to add some derogatory remarks but, rather than words sticking in his throat, Aulus Milo's javelin did. The hulking centurion had led a few veterans into the belly of the beast of the enemy's ranks. Milo slaughtered a number of the legionaries who had murdered his friend, his sword slashing open necks and faces. There were tears in his eyes as he realised he couldn't save his fellow centurion yet Milo and his comrades fought courageously and retrieved the body of his friend so he could be buried with full honours.

*

Despite the stamina, bravery and skill of the praetorian guards their lines were thinning. Oppius found himself plugging the gaps with fresh-faced youths who were more used to handling a hoe and shovel than sword and shield. The centurion took a rare rest to catch his breath before he would again return to the front rank. His body ached and felt like one giant bruise. His armour had been battered out of shape.

*Either the fighting's got harder or I've got older… At least we've given all given Antony more than just a bloody nose. He might now not have the numbers to overwhelm Hirtius.*

Oppius offered up a prayer that Octavius and Agrippa would live through the coming week. He thought it would be too much to ask the gods that he could do so too. The veteran stared down at the sword in his calloused hand. The hilt had been worn down. The blade was chipped.

*You haven't lived a bad life. I would have liked to have had a son or daughter though. I would have liked to have seen Livia again too.*

Lucius Oppius sighed. The old soldier soughed like the wind, expelling any last regrets or sorrows and walked towards where the fighting was at its most intense.

"Just hold the line," he wearily uttered, unsure this time if he possessed the strength or luck to do so.

\*

One side seemed to collectively gasp in relief and the other in horror. Death had ploughed through their ranks but many now in Pansa's army believed the gods were on their side. Prayers of salvation turned to ones of thanks.

Despite the need for haste Hirtius gave some consideration to his offensive. Like Antony he ordered his legions to attack at different points – from over the sloping plain and through the woods and town. Trumpets sounded, alerting Pansa's forces that reinforcements had arrived. Endless polished helmets gleamed in the late afternoon sun. An ocean of men descended upon the battlefield, come to wash away their enemies. Their mail armour rhythmically clinked as cohort upon cohort came into view. The sky even seemed to brighten for the almost defeated soldiers. As with Pansa's hardened troops many of Antony's veterans decided to fight on instead of surrender. They were either too proud or too fatigued to move off the ground they had gained. Death still had some furrows to plough.

Antony's horse became skittish but the general tried to remain calm. He gave orders for his legions to form up in defensive formation. If they had not already been fighting all day Antony's forces may have had a chance. If Antony had fortified his position they may have survived.

\*

"Hold the line," Agrippa called out, with authority, from his sweat-strewn mount. "Reinforcements have arrived."

His words, which rang out across the line, boosted the spirits of the defenders and diminished those of the attackers. Agrippa rode at the vanguard of a squadron of cavalry which had skirted the woodlands and come out on the southern end of the Via Aemilia. The legions, which were marching behind him, kicked up a cloud of dust behind the trees.

The line had held not across the way, however, as part of the shield wall collapsed. Even Aulus Milo could not hold back the tide. A fair part of the cohort began to rout. Neither side were aware of the imminent reinforcements. Manius Sura led the attackers and his eyes soon became fixed on the prize of an enemy standard. The centurion picked up a stray javelin from the ground and skewered the retreating aquilifer.

*I'll cover myself in glory today even if everyone else doesn't.*

As Sura bent down to clasp the standard he felt the ground ominously shake beneath him. Several enemy horses galloped in a row. The centurion raised his hands, in surrender, but Octavius' cavalry blade was already moving through the air.

Octavius, along with Agrippa, volunteered to lead the first party of soldiers off towards the battlefield. Hirtius sketched out a plan of attack. He addressed his senior officers, warning them of the situation: "By the time we reach Forum Gallorum Pansa's army may have already been defeated. It may be the case that we are outnumbered."

As co-commander Octavius also addressed the men: "I would not have a single man more than I do; for these I have here with me are Rome's finest. The chefs alone can remain back at this camp, in order to prepare our victory feast…"

Octavius would share the fate of his army. He would also do all that he could to come to the aid of his friend, Oppius, who was willing to sacrifice his life for his commander's cause. More than one centurion commentated that Octavius' speech was "Caesar-like".

*

Antony's granite-hard veterans fought on bravely. Few of them had ever surrendered before and they had no desire to experience defeat now. But Hirtius' influx of fresh troops tipped the balance. The weight of numbers told and the dam eventually burst. The bulk of Antony's forces scattered. Some put down their arms and asked for clemency. Some retreated into the woods. Some collapsed and drowned in the marshes. Antony made his escape too just after hearing the news that

Decimus Brutus had broken the siege and attacked his camp, outside Mutina. Like Pompey, after Pharsalus, Antony blamed everyone but himself for the defeat. He prayed that he would be able to evade capture and that Enobarbus would survive the day too, giving little thought for his brother as he did so. The plan, if defeated, was to rendezvous at the foot of a pass leading into the Alps.

*

Carbo Vedius was half-buried in the mud but still very much alive. Unable to return to his ship he ventured north and signed on with Antony's army. He winced when he first put on the uniform of a legionary but the food and money compensated the sailor for his unease. Vedius had at first pretended to be dead in order to live but he continued his ruse and lay like a snake in the grass upon seeing the centurion come ever closer towards him. Every dog has its day.

The centurion had haunted his dreams and plagued his waking thoughts ever since their last encounter in Rome. Vedius vowed to kill Oppius to avenge his friends – as well as satisfy his own animus. He had imagined encountering the soldier again but never thought it possible.

*It's fate… The gods are on my side…*

Vedius planned to wait for his enemy to pass by him. He would then stab him in the back. As tempted as he was to want to look the centurion in the eye when he died, he did not want to give his dangerous opponent an opportunity to defend himself.

Oppius, whether out of habit or a conscious choice to continue to lead his men, was one of the men furthest forward as Antony's army routed. His forearm, as well as his blade, was covered in blood and sinew. He felt light-headed. His throat was dry. He needed a drink, water or wine.

Vedius slowly rose up from out of the mud, a creature more than man. His eyes narrowed. His mouth widened too, into a vicious grin. He could almost taste a sense of vengeance.

*It will only take just one knife in the back.*

Oppius shook his head at the all too familiar scene of carnage and a waste of life before him. Too many fathers would be among the dead, leaving their children orphaned. And conversely too many fathers would soon be mourning sons who had fallen. Flies began to dance around and settle on bloodied, contorted bodies. A clash of arms still rang in the background.

*The war won't end here. But this will be my last battle…*

The sharpened iron point entered and punctured a lung. A soldier's life can only end one way. There was an agonising stabbing pain and a sense of shock. But then there was nothing.

## 26.

The guests departed. Most of the staff had gone to bed, their limbs aching as much as the party goers' heads. Some of the audience had enjoyed the production of Terence more than others. Horace was gripped from the start, enjoying everything for differing reasons. He leaned forward on his seat throughout and mouthed the words to the lines he had contributed to the text.

*Pale Death knocks equally upon the poor man's gate as at the palaces of kings... The greatest lesson in life is to know that even fools are right sometimes... It is of no consequence of what parents a man is born to, so long as he is a man of merit...*

In contrast Matius Varro politely applauded at the end but for the most part sat with his chin buried in his chest. Again it seemed as if the weight of the world was on his shoulders. He was a man staring into the abyss with his reflection looking mournfully back. Others in the audience bowed their heads during the production because they had fallen asleep. Porcia thought that the calibre of acting did not equal that to be found in Rome.

*His accent is from no place in the known world. They think they are all being profound but really they're pretentious. He gesticulates more than a Jew. If he saws the air with his hand any more he may get a splinter...*

Before taking his leave Cinna asked Brutus if he could introduce a couple of his stagehands to his host.

"They admire you greatly."

Although somewhat fatigued from a long day Brutus mustered the energy to accept a few more compliments before he retired to bed. He said that Cinna should fetch the men and he would see them all in his study shortly. The general entered his study, looking forward to having a few moments alone where he could breathe out and collect his thoughts. But Brutus was not alone. Matius Varro was waiting for him.

The once austere study was now opulent. Expensive paintings and statues decorated the room. A small bust of Diogenes sat on a table next to a bust of Cato the Elder. Silk inlaid drapes covered the door leading out onto the balcony. The room shone with polished bronze and gold fixtures and fittings. The floor had been recently re-tiled and gleamed beneath the ornate oil lamps which hung from the ceiling. A newly enlarged hearth also housed a recently stoked fire.

The centurion stood sentry-like next to Brutus' desk in the half light. He had changed into his uniform and his sword hung from his hip too. The general was at first startled – but then pleased to see his friend.

"Have you re-considered and are staying the night? I had hoped that you could stay with us even longer, Matius. Porcia will be sad to see you go, as will I."

"As late as it is I should really leave tonight. Duty calls," the soldier replied, creasing his brow either apologetically or in resignation. *I must kill him.*

"Well I must insist that you come and visit us again when your mission is over. We may know by then the outcome of the impending battle between Hirtius and Antony. Should Antony prove victorious I will endeavour to recruit you, Matius. I have the funds to pay you well and I also have scope to grant you a senior position. Although my army has recently expanded I am in need of experienced officers to command the legions."

"And what if Hirtius proves victorious? Would you then disband your army?" the centurion asked. He raised his black eyebrow in scepticism as if already doubting the honesty of Brutus' prospective reply.

"I would, providing I was confident Rome was secure and protected."

*And who is going to protect Rome from you?* "I'm unsure at the moment as to when I'll be coming back this way."

"Rome needs you, Matius. You served under Antony did you not? You also served with his lieutenant, Domitius Enobarbus. You are familiar with the enemy's strengths and weaknesses. Although I warrant that Antony's weaknesses can be summed up in two words – wine and women."

"Antony might argue that they are the source of his strength and motivation," Matius replied. Brutus was unsure if the dry-witted soldier was joking or not.

"I have a brief meeting to attend to, any moment now. But please let me say goodbye in earnest to you afterwards."

The centurion looked a little uncomfortable, as if he had his own business to attend to but couldn't reveal what it was, but nevertheless nodded. Matius decided to wait outside, on the balcony, before saying goodbye to his friend.

Clouds blotted out the stars. A chill wind numbed his features but the soldier had suffered far harsher weather over the years. A wistfulness shaped his heart and expression as Matius gazed out across the void. The darkness consumed all.

*He's changed. But do we not all change? He's proved that there is a little Caesar in us all in terms of pride, ambition and conceit… Unfortunately the blood on your hands from Julius' death was just the start. You're ankle deep in it now. Soon you will be knee deep in it. And eventually you'll be covered in blood, head to toe, like Coriolanus – a hero and villain in equal measure, like Caesar.*

Cinna entered the room with a wide smile on his still made-up face. Brutus wondered whether the grin stemmed from his natural disposition or from the fact that he was about to be paid. He was flanked by two of his stagehands. They didn't necessarily have the air of men who were lovers of the theatre or Brutus' cause. They were rough-hewn. Stubble dusted the faces of both men. Both had flat, broken noses. Both possessed pot-bellies but were still powerfully built. They looked more like soldiers than stagehands. The man on Cinna's left, Strabo, had a star-shaped scar on his cheek. He closed the door behind him. The man to his right, Menas, smiled amiably, revealing a set of chipped front teeth as he approached his host.

"I suppose you will want paying, Cinna," Brutus remarked, half hoping that the actor would be happy with the reward of having performed for him.

Cinna continued to smile and then nodded to Menas, who stood next to the general. The brawny ex-soldier moved quickly for his size, positioning himself behind Brutus and restraining him.

"This is villainy."

Confusion and indignation fuelled Brutus' tone before he was silenced by Menas placing his large hand over his mouth. His eyes were stapled wide in terror and hatred.

Cinna possessed an air of calm and authority about him. His smile widened, reptilian-like. The stagehand standing beside him similarly smirked. There was malice in his eyes and an ivory-handled dagger in his palm. Strabo had killed before and was looking forward to killing again.

"You will be paying a price today, Brutus, but not in gold. You will be paying for your treachery in murdering Caesar," Cinna announced, with a sneer, as he walked over towards the general's desk and picked up the dagger which Brutus had used to assassinate Caesar. His host had proudly shown him the weapon whilst on a tour of the house earlier.

Whilst a young actor and playwright Caesar had recruited Cinna as an agent in Rome. Cinna had seduced patrons and their wives – and pillow talk bred indiscretion. Knowledge is power. Due to his loyalty to Caesar – and the handsome fees he paid – Cinna also occasionally served as an assassin. When Enobarbus offered the actor the opportunity to avenge Caesar – and to be paid for the deed – Cinna accepted.

"Enobarbus said that you would be keen to invite me to your house when you heard that I would be in the area. Your wife is a great lover of the theatre, although not so great an actress that she couldn't disguise her haughty disdain for us during parts of the performance. It seems you have kept this blade polished and sharpened as though you knew it would be used again at some point. I am a playwright, I am used to dealing with irony and poetic justice. Is it not ironic and just that you should be murdered with the same weapon with which you killed your enemy and friend?"

The smell of acetum on Menas' breath and the cheese on his hand made Brutus feel nauseated. What sickened him more though was the playwright's villainy and duplicity – and the fact that he had been so completely fooled. Brutus struggled in vain to free himself from his captor.

"You thought you were freeing Rome by murdering Caesar but really you were damning it. Antony will now bring order back to the capital. I may well receive the greatest applause of my career when people find out that I avenged Julius' death – and that the people will no longer have to suffer one of your long, pious speeches." Cinna laughed a little at his own joke. An actor wouldn't be an actor unless he enjoyed the sound of his own voice. "I may leave it to fate as to whether your wife survives the night or not. I have promised my men that they can take her jewellery. Should they be in her room when she wakes up then her fate will be sealed. Maybe I should allow them the use of this dagger on her, to cut open her dress first and then her heart. I could also instruct Strabo here to pluck out her eyes. At least then she will be unable to look down on everyone."

Again Cinna sniggered at his own witticism and again Brutus struggled to release himself from the stagehand's clutches. He was more worried for his wife than himself. He loved her. Brutus cursed the playwright but the words merely sounded like muffled moans. He also wanted to beg the assassin to punish him but not his wife. She should not suffer for his sins. He would give up all his wealth to save her. But Brutus recognised the look in his enemy's eyes; the agent would honour his promise to Enobarbus and Antony.

Cinna walked across the room purposefully. He looked his victim up and down, wondering upon which part of his body to plunge the dagger into. He was tempted to strike his enemy twenty-three times so as to match the number of stab wounds Caesar had endured. But the agent wanted a clean kill. The staff would find their master's corpse in the morning, by which time he would have made his escape.

Cinna had nothing more to say. But Matius Varro did.

"Not content with murdering a play by Terence, you now want to murder your host. Even a dog, or a Gaul, has better manners than that," the centurion remarked as he came in from outside.

Alarm struck Cinna's face at seeing the soldier, but then he relaxed once he realised the centurion was alone. His men had easily bested legionaries – and centurions – before.

"There are heroes in drama my friend but in the real world there are only villains."

Cinna nodded his head at Strabo. The stagehand sheathed his dagger and then drew out a sword strapped to his thigh, concealed beneath his long-skirted grey tunic. Matius Varro drew his gladius in reply. Strabo was confident that he could best his opponent. In his experience most senior officers in the army knew plenty about fencing but little about real combat. But for all of the centurion's reading of philosophy and literature Tiro Casca, the veteran legionary, had tutored him in fighting – and winning – ugly.

Matius scooped up the marble bust of Diogenes from the table and launched it at the advancing assailant. Strabo lifted his hand to defend his head and the bust struck his forearm. The bone cracked. The stagehand let out a howl. Strabo lost his momentum and it was the soldier's turn to attack. The stagehand swung his sword wildly to try and drive the centurion back. Matius ducked under the blade but rather than retreating the officer stabbed his gladius downwards and impaled it into his opponent's foot. The howl was this time cut short from the centurion slicing the tip of his blade across his enemy's throat.

Menas slightly lessened his grip on Brutus, distracted as he was by the fate of his friend. Brutus used the distraction to his advantage. He lowered and then whipped his head back quickly, smashing it into the stagehand's face. His nose broke (again) and the blow knocked out one of the assassin's chipped front teeth. Brutus broke free. His anger eclipsed the pain he felt on the back of his head. Menas also shook off the impact of the attack. He roared and raised his dagger but as he did so the general grabbed the nearest weapon to hand – a bronze poker – and stabbed his opponent through the stomach.

Horace had been reading in the library, along the corridor from his general's study, when he first heard Strabo scream in pain. The adjutant instinctively put down the scroll he was reading, drew his dagger and ran towards the sound.

Cinna seethed at the turn of events. His instinct was to flee rather than fight. But the pale-faced adjutant stood in his way by the door. Ironically Horace had been the one person in the household the assassin had been willing to spare that night, when planning his attack. But not now. Horace appeared stunned, with either fear or confusion, as he faced the dagger-wielding playwright. Cinna was less indecisive however. He thrust his arm forward. The urbane actor bared his teeth in a savage snarl as he did so. Horace was unable to parry the attack – but fortunately he didn't have to. Matius, recognising the peril his young friend was in, threw his sword across the room and brought down the agent. No matter how many times the actor had been killed on stage it seemed to come as a shock to Cinna that he could die in real life.

## Epilogue

It was as if he had been stabbed. Agrippa told Octavius that Cicero had said he would use and then dispose of him. The two men spoke in the garden of a house in Mutina, the day after the battle. The garden – with its manicured lawn, dazzling flowerbeds and murmuring fountain – was a world away from the charnel house of the previous day's fighting. Exhaustion and grief had tempered any sense of triumph. The surgeon, Glyco, had endeavoured to save Pansa but to no avail. Hirtius had also died during the fighting. The general had wanted to prove that he was as courageous as Caesar. Octavius immediately gave due praise to his co-commanders, although he mentioned in private that both men had died before they had a chance to turn on him.

Despite Octavius' fortitude Agrippa knew more than anyone how much the news concerning Cicero would hurt his friend. But Agrippa felt he had a duty to tell him – as much as he asked that he be allowed to keep his source for the information secret.

"I wish I could say that I'm surprised. But Caesar must be Caesar, and Cicero must be Cicero," Octavius remarked, his expression half shaded beneath his sunhat. His tone remained wilfully neutral but resentment and remorse churned his stomach. He felt sick. Octavius' faith was shaken in himself as well as in the philosopher. There was a hole in his soul where Cicero, or virtue, once resided.

*If my mentor is willing to betray me then my enemies will doubtless do so as well. But standing armies have more power than sitting senators.*

"The Senate will order you to hand over command of the legions to Decimus Brutus. Reports have been confirmed that Decimus is pursuing Antony across the Alps. I suspect that Antony intends to join up with Lepidus in Hispania."

"The Senate will have more chance of ordering me to hand over the Golden Fleece. I will use and then dispose of them. When will they learn that Rome was not created for the good of the Senate but that the Senate was created for the good of Rome? Let Decimus pursue Antony. We shall neither aid nor hinder him. Our priority should be to further bind the legions to us. We must honour the dead, tend to the wounded and pay any bonuses. With just a handful of legions I was able to demand the rank of praetor. With the eight I now command I can be consul."

During the afternoon Octavius visited the legions. Many banged their shields and called out his name, "Caesar, Caesar..." This time Octavius knew that they were honouring him as opposed to his great-uncle. He smiled, thanked the soldiers for their service and waved his hand. An outward show of gratitude and triumph masked a deeper sorrow however.

*Caesar would be proud of me. But Cleanthes wouldn't.*

He had won a great battle and saved the Republic. On a personal level he had proven his mettle too. Yet in the cold light of day Octavius realised how reckless he had been, riding into the fray with little thought for his own security. He experienced a rush of blood either to save or avenge Oppius. But he would have ice in his veins from now on. He had little desire to see a field of battle again and witness the aftermath of a sea of corpses. His bath had taken twice as long the previous night as his servants looked to wash all the grime and blood from his body. Others could fight his battles for him. It was safer and they were more qualified to do so.

*There is little glory and honour in being struck down by a stray arrow or being trampled to death by a horse.*

When Octavius had a window of time later that evening he began to write a series of letters to a number of families of the fallen. Not only was it the honourable thing to do but it was an effective way of maintaining support. Caesar had composed similar letters of condolence out of both sympathy and self-interest. Octavius also wrote letters to his mother and sister. He was tempted to write a letter to Livia too. He closed his eyes and pictured her smile, heard her laugh and breathed in her expensive perfume. They had stolen glances through crowded rooms. Despite or because of the number of lovers he took Octavius couldn't stop thinking about her.

*Does she think about me too?*

*

Brutus slept surprisingly well after the attempt on his life. He slept in the arms of his wife. He told Porcia that he loved her. He apologised for his behaviour towards her and Porcia even apologised to him in return. The general realised his wife was a source of strength to him, not weakness.

The following day Brutus tried one last time to petition Matius Varro to stay. They spoke in the general's study. The servants had just finished scrubbing the blood from the walls and tiled floor.

"Can your mission not wait?"

"It has waited too long already in some respects. Every day which passes, having not done my duty, is a day wasted – one that gnaws at my soul. I have not altogether been honest with you, Marcus. I am travelling east not in the name of Rome but for my own selfish purpose. Many years ago my father, who served as a diplomat, was sent to Egypt to gauge the character and intentions of Ptolemy XIII. The civil war was still in the balance then, before Caesar tipped the scales in Cleopatra's favour. Both my mother and father were murdered, however, before they reached Alexandria. But I have recently found out who killed them. A man named Apollodorus, a Sicilian. He now serves as a bodyguard to the Egyptian queen. I must kill him. It's the only way I will find peace and lift the burden," the determined centurion declared, although he felt the burden lift slightly for having told his friend the truth.

"Your intentions are noble, Matius. But let me now make an argument for my selfish purpose as well as for Rome. As much as you have a cause, how much of a plan do you have to see your cause through? How will you get close to the queen and Apollodorus? How can you be assured of success, especially as you will be acting alone? A sense of duty and vengeance have not clouded your judgement so much that you will disregard logic, I hope. To travel so far and come so close – and then to fail – will further the tragedy of the death of your parents. I owe you my life, Matius, and I am in no position to ask anything of you. But grant me two years of service and your cause will become my cause. Cleopatra herself will not be able to deny you your revenge."

Matius Varro stared ahead of him, a picture of solemnity – seemingly unmoved either way after having heard Brutus' offer. He noticed the bust of Diogenes – its nose and cheek chipped from being thrown across the room the previous night. The scholarly officer thought about Alexander the Great's encounter with the philosopher. Alexander had granted Diogenes any wish. Diogenes, lying in the sun at the time, merely asked Alexander if he could get out of his light. Matius thought how, if Alexander could have granted him any wish, he would have asked for the opportunity to kill Apollodorus. In some ways Brutus was now granting him his wish. The fires of revenge can consume all, stripping away everything else from a man's existence. His father would have wanted him to avenge his death but not at the expense of his entire life.

*I must kill him – in two years from now.*

Brutus promised the centurion a senior rank and enough gold for Matius to buy his own army to defeat Apollodorus.

"If nothing else Horace will be pleased that you'll be on staff. He will need a drinking companion now that I've promised Porcia I'm giving up the late nights," Brutus said to his friend.

Matius smiled to himself. *People can change*.

*

Tiro had woken his master despite the late hour. The news was important. The messenger had ridden non-stop, changing horses several times, so that Cicero could be one of the first to know about the outcome of the battle. Knowledge is power. The secretary had entered the statesman's bedroom. Wax tablets littered the bed. Tiro wasn't quite sure if the musty smell filling his nostrils emanated from the room or the man. He lit a brace of oil lamps and woke the proconsul.

Cicero sat up in bed. His joints ached in other seasons as well as winter now. He squinted as his eyes adjusted to the light. He then squinted in disbelief as he took in the words of the message. Some of the news was good, some of it unwelcome and some of it unexpected.

The wax tablet felt as heavy in his hands as a tombstone. Hirtius and Pansa were dead. *Where there is life there is despair*. His agent mentioned that Glyco, Pansa's physician, was being detained on suspicion of poisoning the consul. Octavius was the prime candidate for ordering the physician to assassinate Pansa. But Cicero knew the character of Glyco and he would prove innocent in being involved in any conspiracy. Would he let an innocent man be executed though, if it meant Octavius could be found guilty – and eliminated?

Cicero handed the tablet to Tiro, who read over the message with speed and care.

Antony had thankfully been defeated. The Republic was saved. Decimus Brutus was pursuing the enemy of the state over the Alps. "Hopefully Decimus knows to bring Antony back in a coffin rather than chains," Cicero commented. But victory had come at a price. The young Caesar was now in sole command of a great army.

"I must write to Octavius immediately. We should praise and honour him – whilst at the same time relieving him of his rank and legions. Give with one hand and take with the other. We must act quickly before he gets any ideas into his head – or Balbus puts them there. Octavius will listen to me. He will not want to disappoint me. And I am doing this, believe it or not, to save his soul as well as the Republic. I still have a part to play, before I leave the stage, Tiro."

The secretary nodded in agreement whilst believing that Octavius was now the lead actor in the drama being played out. The youth had accumulated more power within just one year than others had accumulated over a lifetime. *It seems that Octavius has inherited Caesar's divine luck as well as his name.*

Tiro instructed a servant to provide Cicero with a cup of barley water and some cereal with honey. He then left the statesman to his stratagems and correspondence. Tiro was tempted to wake Caecilia and tell her the latest news from the north. She had taken an uncommon interest in military matters of late.

*

The terrain was as unwelcome as some of the grim expressions on the retreating soldiers' faces. Although huddled around campfires men still shivered, some in terror, at reliving the gruesome battle. The remnants of Antony's army had, with leaden steps, trudged through the snow and mountain passes. There were equally as many upwards and downwards slopes but their legs felt like they had to endure more of the former. Some died from their wounds. Some died from fatigue. Progress was slow but steady. Food was hard to come by but no one would thankfully starve to death – yet. But no matter what they ate the bitter taste of defeat spoiled their appetites.

Most of the men remained loyal to their commander and only complained beneath their foggy breath. Antony had led by example after the battle and offered his horses to the wounded – ordering his cavalry officers to do so too.

The first time the general had smiled, since the defeat, had been when he had seen his lieutenant at the rendezvous point. Enobarbus was wounded but alive, having escaped from the camp before Decimus' forces could overrun it.

The two old friends had sat around a fire. Logs crackled and cinders, like petals, swirled upwards into the night. Antony had donated the remainder of his vintages to his men. He had drunk acetum before and he would doubtless do so again.

"It was a near run thing, Domitius," Antony ruefully remarked, staring into his half-empty wine cup, dwelling upon again how close he had come to securing a great victory.

Enobarbus wryly smiled to himself, recalling how he had overheard a legionary say the same thing but in relation to how close he had believed Antony's forces had come to being completely wiped out. The lieutenant, despite private criticisms of his leadership, still had faith in his commander.

"Have you sent a message ahead to Lepidus, so he can prepare for our arrival?"

"Aye," Antony replied, still undecided as to whether he should beg or bully the general into furnishing him with the legions under his command.

"And what about Fulvia? Have you been able send off a message to her too?"

"I dare not tell her where I'll be just in case the harpy decides to join me," Antony said.

Enobarbus looked at his general by the light of the writhing fire. His beard was no longer trimmed. His once chiselled features appeared sunken. His armour was battered and besmirched. Antony had not so long ago looked like a marble statue of a demigod. But cracks were now appearing in the stone.

"Maybe it wouldn't be so bad if the harpy did join us. In befouling our food she may improve the flavour."

Both soldiers let out a small laugh. Enobarbus winced in pain slightly as he did so, from the wound in his leg.

"How's the injury?"

"I've suffered worse. Thankfully the cold is helping to numb the pain."

"You will recover, my friend, as we will recover. I will rebuild our army, as much as for those brave souls out there as for myself. All is not lost," Antony declared and gripped his sword.

"Let us hope that Cinna has succeeded in his mission."

"Aye. It is a shame that Cassius isn't a lover of the theatre, as much as the snake is inclined to put on an act for people. Cinna could have ensnared him also. But sooner or later we will see the heads of Brutus and Cassius liberated from their necks. The whelp too shall suffer. His luck will run out, as will his money. There's still everything to play for. We may have lost the battle, Domitius, but we have not lost the war."

*

The dead of night.

More than he had ever craved a drink, more than he wanted to win the archery tournament or even have sex – Agrippa just wanted to see Caecilia's smiling face again. He pictured how her silken hair hung down and framed her elated features as she straddled him whilst making love. He wanted to hear her voice as she hummed in pleasure whilst kissing him or recited passages of Thucydides. He gazed up at the clear night sky. Cleopatra, Fulvia and Servilia combined did not possess the diamonds equal to the celestial scene above as stars beamed upon an expansive sea of black silk. He wondered if Caecilia was staring up at the same sight. *I'll wait for you and I hope if I fall behind you will wait for me.*

Agrippa was exhausted yet still unable to sleep. He sat out on the balcony, flanked by two glowing braziers. Plumes of smoke spiralled upwards across the city. Bakeries and taverns were open once more. He heard the sound of distant celebrations as the recently besieged town enjoyed the taste of freedom and wine. The inhabitants gave thanks to Caesar as much as to Decimus Brutus.

It was as much a time of grief as triumphalism though for the young soldier. He felt little pride in inheriting the title of the best archer in the legion.

Already he missed the Briton.

"Teucer would have regretted not being here, now that the brothels are open again," Aulus Milo had mentioned to Agrippa. "We had a bet. I said that he wouldn't be able to bed all the women in one whorehouse between dusk and dawn. Teucer replied that it was a bet he would happily accept – win, lose or draw."

Agrippa was distracted by the sound of footsteps behind him. Octavius had been unable to fall asleep either. He thought about the savagery of the battle and the vomit inducing smell of corpses. But more than anything else thoughts of Cicero – and his betrayal – disturbed Octavius' peace. There are some wounds and scars which remain unseen. *I thought you were different, better, than the rest. You tried to raise the Senate up but ultimately it dragged you down to its level.* His friend had become another enemy. In cutting Cicero out of his life, a little piece of him had died.

*But enough blood has been spilled. Cicero will lose my ear. I do not want him to lose his life. But I will not put my faith in him – or anyone else – again. I will also never give away my heart. But how can you give away something which doesn't exist?*

Ice – and bitterness – ran through his veins. His soul was as bright and cold as a diamond or a star in the sky.

"Evening. I will soon be saying 'Good morning' I imagine," Octavius said, as he grabbed a chair and sat next to his friend. "Remember when we used to stay up late into the night and talk about the future? Neither of us came close to guessing what would occur."

"I blame the copious amounts of wine we drunk. It dulled our wits and imaginations. I also remember how Salvidienus used to join us occasionally. He would gabber on about becoming an aedile. I must make sure to write and tell him how you're about to become a consul," Agrippa replied, thinking how he would write another letter to Caecilia first.

"A lot has happened in the past year, since those days in Apollonia. As far as we've come though, Marcus, we still have far to travel. But I couldn't ask for a better travelling companion. You've learned your trade as a soldier it seems. I now need you to learn your trade as a general. It's you and me against the rest of the world."

"I can live with those odds. But let's take on the rest of the world in the morning. Tonight we should toast fallen comrades."

"Aye," Lucius Oppius said, appearing out of nowhere like a ghost. Grief and determination infused his heart. The centurion came out onto the balcony carrying a large jug of Massic and three cups. He gave the first to Agrippa, the man whose sharpened iron arrowhead had punctured the lung of Vedius, just before the navvy-turned-legionary had tried to stab the veteran soldier.

Although Octavius duly honoured Teucer and Cephas Pollux there was a streak of selfishness in him, or pragmatism as he called it, which meant that half his thoughts were focused on his own concerns. He recalled a scene from the previous morning, whilst Joseph shaved him. Octavius asked what Caesar had done, after winning a great battle.

The aged Jew lowered his razor. There had been a fleeting moment of indecision in his expression as he toyed with lying to his new master. But his shoulders dropped, he sighed and told the truth.

"He started planning for the next one."

As Octavius raised his cup to his fallen friends he looked up at the glittering night sky. Had Caesar's soul ascended to the heavens and been marked by a star?

*My star will burn brighter.*

End Note

*Augustus: Son of Caesar* is a work of fiction. Although inspired and informed by history I have, in many instances, made stuff up. The keen historians among you will have noticed how I conflated Cicero's *Philippics* into just one key speech. Similarly, I merged the two battles which decided the outcome at Mutina into one. I will leave it to the reader to unpick and separate the rest of the fact from the fiction.

I recommended a number of books and authors in the end note of *Augustus: Son of Rome*, should you be interested in reading more on the period and its leading figures. Since the publication of that book a couple of notable titles have also been released, Adrian Goldsworthy's biography of Augustus (which is the best biography I have read in regards to the second half of his life) and Lindsay Powell's biography of Marcus Agrippa.

Thank you for all your support and emails. They're much appreciated. Please do get in touch if you have enjoyed *Augustus: Son of Caesar* (as well as the *Sword of Rome* and *Sword of Empire* books). My latest series is Spies of Rome, featuring Augustus and Marcus Agrippa. I can be reached on twitter @rforemanauthor and via richardforemanauthor.com

Octavius and Agrippa will return.

Richard Foreman.


For submissions to Sharpe Books please contact Richard Foreman
richard@sharpebooks.com

Also by Richard Foreman

Warsaw

A Hero of Our Time

*Sword of Rome Series*
Sword of Rome: Standard Bearer
Sword of Rome: Alesia
Sword of Rome: Gladiator

Sword of Rome: Rubicon
Sword of Rome: Pharsalus
Sword of Rome: The Complete Campaigns
Swords of Rome: Omnibus of the Historical Series Books 1-3

*Sword of Empire Series*
Sword of Empire: Praetorian
Sword of Empire: Centurion
Sword of Empire: The Complete Campaigns
Sword of Empire: Omnibus

*Raffles Series*
Raffles: The Gentleman Thief
Raffles: Bowled Over
Raffles: A Perfect Wicket
Raffles: Caught Out
Raffles: Stumped
Raffles: Playing On
Raffles: Omnibus of Books 1 - 3
Raffles: The Complete Innings
Raffles: Complete Innings Boxset

*Band of Brothers Series*
Band of Brothers: The Complete Campaigns
Band of Brothers: Agincourt
Band of Brothers: The Game's Afoot
Band of Brothers: Omnibus
Band of Brothers: Harfleur

*Augustus Series*
Augustus: Son of Rome
Augustus: Son of Caesar

*Pat Hobby Series*
Pat Hobby's Last Shot
The Complete Pat Hobby
The Great Pat Hobby
The Return of Pat Hobby

Printed in Great Britain
by Amazon